Swallow the Shadows

Praise for the works of C. Jean Downer

Trailhead

This romantic thriller excelled in the beautiful, lush images of nature and life in a small town set in the Northern Cascades, Washington. Downer's love for the outdoors shines through on every page.

-Sapphic Books Kitchen

Under the Cold Moon

Seeped in fantastical elements and witchcraft, Downer gives readers a meticulously crafted tale of intrigue, mystery, and suspense. By defining a story world with logical, consistent parameters, readers are taken on a compelling ride of suspended disbelief. *Under the Cold Moon* is immersive, entertaining and should not be missed.

-Women Using Words

The writing is smooth and compelling, the (magical) world-building is well done.

-Henrietta B., *NetGalley*

Lies are Forever

Lies Are Forever is very well done. Downer provides readers with an engaging, cohesive storyline that's overflowing with rich, fluid language. The characters are well drawn and work together to weave a compelling and surprising plot. This is fresh, unique storytelling, and it deserves top marks. If you like well-written, suspenseful supernatural fiction, then you won't want to miss this one.

-Women Using Words

Lies are Forever is an enjoyably well written novel with plenty of twists and turns to keep the pages turning. Downer does well in creating a magical world...that we see revealed through Sloane's eyes. Mixing the magical with a whodunnit is ingenious resulting in an intriguing story.

-Della B., *NetGalley*

I absolutely loved this book! I can't wait for the next one! The characters were so much fun, and I loved how they interacted with each other. The paranormal aspect just added the right amount to the story! I definitely recommend this book to anyone who likes this genre.

-Natalie A., *NetGalley*

A great read and an amazing plot.

-Bonnie K., *NetGalley*

Other Bella Books by C. Jean Downer

Lies are Forever
Under the Cold Moon
Trailhead

About the Author

C. Jean Downer attributes her inspiration and creative process to living in a temperate rain forest near the eternal Pacific Ocean with her wife of twenty-plus years, their two fabulous teenage daughters, two lazy dogs, and three chill cats. When she is not writing, she and the love of her life are traveling to new destinations and checking them off their bucket list (okay, even when traveling she's writing but mostly in her head). For more information about her novels and poetry, visit her website at cjeandowner.com. You can also connect with her on Instagram and Facebook @cjeandowner and Bluesky @cjeandowner.bsky.social.

Swallow the Shadows

C. JEAN DOWNER

BELLA
BOOKS

Bella Books, Inc.
P.O. Box 10543
Tallahassee, FL 32302

First Edition - 2026

Editor: Cath Walker
Cover Designer: SJ Hardy
Author photo credit: Adrienne Thiessen, Gemini Photography

ISBN: 978-1-64247-704-7

Acknowledgments

I want to give my heartfelt thanks to Jessica and Linda Hill, superb editor Cath Walker, and all the incredible people at Bella Books, who, during these dark times of book bans and attacks on the LGBTQIA+ communities, continue to stand for inclusivity and publish books that mirror our lives and loves. You are courageous and steadfast, and I'm proud to be a part of your author family.

A very special thanks to our readers. Your continued support of LGBTQIA+ authors and books, your emails, reviews, and comments on social media make the solitary work of writing a place of deep connection.

Dedication

To Theresa, Hayden, and Hadley, always.
Without you, there is no light in the shadows.

PROLOGUE

Denwick, Vancouver Island, 1988

The crypt was cooler than the night air aboveground, and faint amber candlelight flickered from three wall sconces onto Jane West's cloak. She trailed her fingers over individual family niches as she slowly walked past the cinerarium wall for what she feared could be the last time.

"Keanes, Ilieves, Tindalls, Reeds, Emleys, Smalldons…" She whispered each name of the seaside village's original families. Most had long since moved away, but the Keanes and Reeds still lived in Denwick. Her ancestors had also been in the town from the time the Gildey family established it.

She stopped at her family's niches. Her spot was the last alcove in their row. Touching the chiseled letters of her name left her with a deep sadness. Her death date might never be written there. She laid her hands over her lower abdomen, and a more profound sorrow filled her. Her baby might never receive a niche.

"No more sentimental thoughts," she said sternly. The Wests' ashes weren't even in those urns. It was all for show. All for the non-magicals' sake. All because they lived in the nogical world defending the very humans who vilified them. She turned from the wall. Her moment of sentimentality and frustration only masked her actual fear—the real possibility that their child wouldn't be allowed to rest with their family in the magical world, either.

The pendants under her soft linen cloak warmed, drawing her attention to the back wall that beckoned her. The granite's veins branched into the same Tree of Life symbol as the necklaces. The stone wall was her family's portal to the city of Tagridore on the magical plane, where supernatural species returned to live after the nogical world became inhospitable, millennia ago.

She pulled her cloak tight and walked to the wall. Protectors and guardians like her family were the only Magicals to remain here. They were Defenders of each magical species and against Malevolents, the evil supernaturals of the Nether realm, the Abyss, and their human progeny, the Half-Malevolents, which Nogicals named Demons and Cambions.

She approached the beckoning tree and smoothed her hand over the giant stone slab. "I'm not here for passage, but thank you for asking," she told the luminescent mineral deposits. She was there at this late hour for an answer. One that could change her life forever.

A few minutes later, Jane felt her boyfriend's presence in the stairwell before he stepped into the light. Sensing was a new power for her. She was a gifted telepath, but when she became pregnant with their child, she developed the ability to sense. "What did your father say?" she asked. He wrapped her up in a strong embrace and hesitated, tightening his hold on her, and in those two actions, Jane had her answer. "So, he won't help us," she murmured into his chest, crushed with disappointment.

"It's not that he won't. He can't. Not here anyway. Once our child is born, the others will know. They will figure out who you and your coven are…and when they do, they'll destroy us. All of us." He leaned back and held her gaze, wiping away her tears with his thumbs. "I'm sorry for causing you so much pain, for upending your life." He bent close and lightly kissed her lips. "Please forgive me."

She ached to say his name, any of his family's names, but it was forbidden. She had to place a binding spell on herself to keep from the simple utterance that would expose them to danger if overheard by prying ears. "You don't need my forgiveness. I can live with the consequences of my choices. You and our baby were my decisions. And I would make them all over again." She nestled her head into his shoulder. "I had hoped your father could think of a way for us to stay together…here."

"Me, too. But we'll still be together." He stroked her long black hair, held her dark-brown eyes with his. "He'll help me keep you and the baby safe. And he and I have a plan to make sure the others can never hurt us. But we need time."

Jane nodded, blinking away her tears. That was it then. As long as the others remained free to hunt them, she had to leave Denwick. She had planned for the possibility, but nothing would make the pain of disappearing from her life without saying goodbye any easier. Nothing would make living without her parents and grandparents, her familiar, Elvina, and her cousin Dorathea, a choice she would make if not forced to. She released him and wiped her face with the sleeve of her dark-blue cloak.

"I have something for you." His voice was low and gentle, and the candlelight danced in his intense eyes. He reached into his pocket, pulling out a small black box and opening it. "This is my promise of eternal love. Will you give me yours by wearing it?"

The diamond pendant's scintillation mesmerized her. "Yes, of course."

He clasped the necklace around her neck, kissing her shoulder softly, and a warm, tranquil wave moved through her.

She held the icy fire between her fingers. "It's stunning, but I didn't need this. I have freely given you my commitment." She unfastened one of her necklaces. "You aren't the only one bearing gifts. This belonged to my great-grandmother. I found it at my great-aunt's house and placed a charm on it. The key opens our portal to Tagridore for you now."

He dangled the Tree of Life pendant from its chain, and his face became concerned. "A key to your world? Is it safe for me to have?"

"No one will know you have it unless you tell them. And I've secured a place in Tagridore where we can meet if you can't come to New York." Her voice caught. She hadn't said the city's name aloud before, the place where she would live a new life, passing as a Nogical and hiding with their child.

The sconce's candles flickered, a draft from the stairwell nearly blowing them out. They looked up. Someone was in the mausoleum. "It could be them," he whispered. "We need to go. Are you ready to leave Denwick?"

"Not yet. I have a few things to do." She stretched on the tips of her toes and kissed him goodbye. "I'll call for you when I'm ready."

A moment later, Jane appeared in her bedroom at Mallow Cottage, the West family home. Her parents and grandparents had retired to their rooms before she left for the crypt. Their bedrooms were on the same floor, down a wide hall, but the house was large enough that they wouldn't hear her final preparations to leave.

With the flick of her wrist, she floated her bed above the hardwood floor. Her familiar remained curled in a tight furry ball on the plush lavender duvet without twitching a whisker. Jane's pulse quickened as she quietly removed several wooden floorboards, revealing a hidden compartment. She gathered a handful of books scattered around the room and shoved them inside the nook. The evidence she had compiled against the insurgents needed to be safe until she could return.

She had no alternative but to hide the books and run. Their Grand Coven, the three most important *Wiccan*, the governors of the magical world's Northwest Quadrant, was already suspicious of her, and for good reasons. Her research had discovered that one of the three was part of a conspiracy, a dangerous allegiance between corrupt Magicals and Half-Malevolents. And she was close to discovering who the traitor was.

With shaking hands hovering an inch above the loosened floorboards, she whispered, *belúcan*. A white light emanated from her fingertips to the floor, sealing the books and the truth under a potent spell. She marveled at how the light enhanced her magic.

The intoxicating power, like sensing, had only come to be with the baby growing inside her. But it also scared her, often feeling like a wicked indulgence that one day she would need to control.

She got to her feet and, with a wave of her hand, silently lowered the bed. Elvina purred without opening her eyes, and Jane stroked the familiar's silky, dark-gray fur.

Do I even want to ask what you're doing? Elvina communicated telepathically.

I am securing the future. Jane hesitated. *And I'm sorry, El, but I can't take you with me.*

Dramatic words for a vacation, dear. And I'm not upset in the least. Who wants to visit New York City, well, besides you? Why not Madrid, Sydney, Paris?

Because I knew you wouldn't want to go, and I was right. Clever, huh?

Elvina's velvet laughter filled Jane's head, and she bit her lip, trying to stop the sting of tears. What would she do without her best friend? She no longer needed Elvina's magical assistance, but she did need her companionship.

Jane glanced around her room one last time, vanquishing the selfish thought. No one was safe with her and the child here in Denwick, not even her familiar. It was impossible to know how long she and her baby would have to hide. She would have faith that the time would be short and that her parents would forgive her when she returned.

Yesterday, her parents had thrown a graduation and bon voyage party for her. It was part of her plan if she had to escape Denwick. She asked to take a week's trip to New York City. The Nogicals were shocked that her parents allowed her to travel alone at eighteen. But they had no idea that her kind are wiser than their years. She stared at the gift bags with brightly colored bows on her desktop and hoped they would donate the presents.

All of her parents' friends from Old Denwick, and her friends, Ken Keane, Charlie Huxham, even Lore Reed, showed up that afternoon. She would miss them, but she could survive leaving them. But lying to and never seeing her family again, well, that might destroy her, but she had to.

She turned away from Elvina and told herself it was best this way. No goodbyes. A clean break. The words closed her throat, and she gave in to the tears that had been threatening.

Has your secret boyfriend broken your heart, dear? Elvina asked.

No, I'm fine. It's just been a long day.

You don't sound fine. Are you worried about your trip?

She shook her head.

Well if you don't want to talk about it, I've also had a long day and would like to sleep. Are you coming to bed or not?

Not yet. I have a few more things to do before I leave in the morning. She wiped her face and kissed the top of Elvina's head. *Go to sleep. I won't disturb you.*

She steeled her nerves. It was time to see Freya, Elvina's mother, but she couldn't use the enchanted Degas her parents gave her for her sixteenth birthday, her portal to Tagridore. It hung above the mantle downstairs, and the ballerinas in the painting were much too judgmental. They had only been in her life for two years and hadn't warmed to her, so she knew they wouldn't help her sneak away this late. She needed to use her cousin's portal. Dorathea, the coven's High Priestess, lived next door in a hobbit-looking house. Her basement was their covenstead, an enchanted room twice the size of the floor above, where they practiced magic.

All Jane needed was her cousin's house spirit, Alfred, to let her inside. An old spirit with a heavy English accent and an impish side, he had a soft spot for her. She opened a telepathic link to message him. *Alfred, is Dorathea at Freya's tonight?*

Cheers, young West. Surprisingly, they're not together. Your cousin has an early meeting tomorrow, and Freya has a large order of scones due in the morning. They've decided to stay in their own homes this evening.

Jane had planned to meet Freya on a night her cousin wasn't with her girlfriend, but sometimes Dorathea was unpredictable, so she had to double-check. *Will you let me use the covenstead without Dorathea knowing, please? I need her portal.*

He replied at once. *The High Priestess is asleep. Come if you wish but do be quiet. And if you would allow me to say again, you must show those dancers that you control the portal.*

Thank you, Alfred. I'll try to be more assertive.

A moment later, Jane appeared in the covenstead's library. Alfred had lit a few floating candelabras for her, but the candlelight was dim. She peered into the rest of the room, wanting to see the place where she was trained to become a powerful witch, to smell Dorathea's scent of cloves and black pepper, and hear the burbles of viscous liquids brewing. Instead, she swallowed the longing and moved quickly to the back of the library.

Sloane was lying on a sofa. The black Labrador lifted her head and greeted Jane with several tail thumps against the cushion. "Hi, Slo." She petted the dog's back and kissed her muzzle. "I'm going to miss you so much. I might even risk sneaking back just to see you." She wrapped her arms around Sloane's neck and held onto her before straightening and standing before the enormous Lavinia Fontana painting on the opposite wall.

Whenever she wanted to sneak away to Tagridore, she used her cousin's portal because the two women in Fontana's painting gladly agreed to keep her secrets and encouraged her to forge a path of her own making. She lifted her arms and whispered, "*Onpenne.*" Smiling, they welcomed her to enter their room. Of course, the man in the painting never looked at her. She figured he was too afraid to avert his eyes from the woman guarding him with a butcher's knife.

The other woman ushered her to a back door. Jane stepped through and onto a cobblestone path on the other side. Dorathea's portal took her straight to Freya's home and café, a whitewashed building with a lavender canopy in their magical city. Elvina's mother met her at the front of the shop and led her to the back room. "Oh, my dear one," she said, embracing her, and Jane relaxed into the woman's nurturing aura. "Sit, sit. I've made your favorite orange and cranberry scones. I insist you eat with me before taking this journey."

"All right. As long as you don't try to change my mind. I can't bear that right now."

"I promised not to dissuade you or pry." She poured them tea and placed a scone on Jane's plate.

"Good, because you can't know the truth, trust me, it would be the end of us all." She stared into Freya's dark-brown eyes, fear gaining hold of her.

"Calm down, I believe you. How could I not? The gravity of your situation saturates your energy. I want you to tell me everything, but I understand you cannot. I will assist you and the child until you can." Freya placed her cup on its saucer. "When everyone said goodbye to you yesterday afternoon and wished you well on your holiday, they were unaware it could be forever. My assistance will cause great strife. You're asking me to keep a secret that will devastate your family and cause irreparable damage between Dorathea and me. Living without you will be as agonizing as grieving your death. It is not a choice I make without hesitation."

"Don't you think I know that? I'm trying to keep them safe." Jane's voice was sharper than she wanted, and she stared into her tea, fighting against the shame washing over her.

"Have you considered that your family has not asked for a martyr? They are Protectors. They fight. Don't you think they would defend you and your child regardless of who the father is?"

Jane breathed deeply, calming herself. "We are powerful, I know that. But, please, Freya, right now we're not strong enough to fight what's coming. And I don't know who we can trust. A Half-Malevolent is here in Denwick. And it's hungry for more power. It has seduced some Magicals into helping it, and it's only a matter of time before it finds out who we are. The only way to stop them is if I disappear."

"How can this be?" Freya looked at her, incredulously. "Your great-grandfather banished the evil supernatural bound to this land. The coven would have known if it had left any offspring."

"We've been wrong, Freya. Seven Malevolents escaped the Abyss. Five have been returned there. But our covens banished them a millennium ago. Not a hundred and some years ago. But not before they bred with humans." Jane hesitated when Freya looked skeptical. "Half-Malevolents have roamed among us for centuries. My great-grandfather exiled the Malevolent's half-human child to the Nether."

She considered Jane's assertion, tapping her long fingers on the tabletop. "Your coven and I would sense if a Half-Malevolent remained on the land, dear one."

"Not if it became strong enough to hide from us as well as we have hidden from it." Jane trembled, and Freya grasped her hand.

"And you're sure your going into hiding will keep the coven safe?"

Jane nodded.

"Very well. Until you can return I will help you. But I have one request that will make this situation bearable. You will allow Elvina to live with you. She will guard you and help train the child."

"No, it's too dangerous. Elvina could disclose something to you."

"She might be my daughter, but she's your familiar and as such, she cannot tell me anything you wouldn't allow."

Jane knew what Freya said was true, but she had never forced Elvina to obey her and wasn't sure she ever could. "Fine. But only if she wants to come and knows I might need to disallow her things."

"Very well." Freya stared at Jane's chest. "Did he give you that?"

Jane followed her gaze to the diamond pendant. "Yes, tonight. It's beautiful, isn't it?" She beamed with pride over the gift and what it symbolized.

"You are sure there is no other way? Your coven is extraordinary. It would take little to change his parents' minds about you and the child."

"There's no other way." Jane bit into the warm scone, and childhood memories of Freya's pastries and tea overwhelmed her.

"Oh, my dear one. I regret that love has forced you to make such a severe decision. But I trust it will sustain you while you are away."

"It will, I promise." Jane got to her feet, striking a pose of confidence. "I have to go now. Are you ready?"

Freya scooted back in her chair and stood. She gathered Jane's long black hair, sweeping it to the side and exposing the young woman's neck. The Sensor moved within an inch of Jane's skin and breathed in. "Your lover's concealment spell is ancient—"

Jane jerked back. "You promised not to pry."

"I was only figuring out the best way to complement its magic." She ran her hands over Jane's arms, her body, and held her wrists. Then she looked into Jane's eyes and whispered, "*Scield*." Her eyes filled with tears. "Even I will be unable to sense you now."

"Please, Freya." Jane's voice was somber. "You promised to be strong."

CHAPTER ONE

Christmas Day, Kirkcudbright, Scotland, 2023

Sloane West stood in a sprawling covenstead with Elspeth Gòrdan's panicked voice sounding in her head. *They're going to die! Please help us!*

Only minutes before, the child's grandfather, Alisdair Gòrdan, had sent her through a portal to Mallow Cottage, seeking the West Coven's help against The Order's attack. Sloane and the coven teleported to the Gòrdans at once, but they were too late. The smell of death lingered in the frenetic air.

The olfactory memory brought to the forefront of Sloane's mind every loss she had ever experienced. Since she was a little girl, she could smell the loss of life and feel when souls untethered from their bodies. For her, death left behind a malodorous, sulfur scent of decay, not days after the corporeal body begins to putrefy, but at the exact time life's energy was released and added to the universe's constant chaos.

Crime victims, her NYPD lieutenant, and her mother, Jane, had each created their own measure of turmoil in her life. She had only shared how she experienced death once after her mother died. Her ex-girlfriend, Jess, listened quietly but couldn't find the words to reply. Finally, she told Sloane that she was only grieving, and she'd feel better soon. Her ex's words cut deeply. She knew time didn't grant people peace with mortality because death breaks those still living, wounds their hearts and spirits, and plants them firmly in the chaos, forever changed. Death scarred everything. She vowed never again to speak about her relationship with it.

"What are you doing, pet? Check for survivors," Dorathea Denham shouted at Sloane and brought her attention back to the Gòrdans' covenstead. Her second cousin twice removed was a composed woman, never a gray hair out of place, but now she hurried through the room in her dark-sapphire cloak, her long, wavy hair tousled, and waved her hands, switching on lamps of varied sizes.

Sloane's eyes slowly adjusted to the light, and she scanned the scene. It looked like a war zone with tables upended, shelves toppled, and shattered wood and glass covering the floor. Charred strikes marred the walls, and furnishings smoldered. There was no doubt. The Order had once again attempted to destroy a Protector Coven, seeking to release more evil from the Abyss, and this time they had breached a coven's sacred space.

Sloane ran toward the death stench in the air and saw them, a woman with her arm draped across a man's waist. Her other second cousin, Jack Denham, knelt beside the couple and moved his hands along the lengths of their bodies while Sloane pressed her fingers to their necks. No pulse. But no visible signs of injuries.

The girl's parents were dead.

"We can do nothing more for them, lovey." Jack laid his hand on Sloane's shoulder and gently pulled her back. He was a handsome and charming, if immodest, *wiċċa*. After The Order killed her mother and grandparents, he was recruited and trained by the Northwest Quadrant's Grand Coven to maintain the West Coven's power of three. He was also a Sensor like her mother, and it wasn't the first time he had soothed her escalating emotions.

Dorathea was shouting Alisdair's name, her normally stoic voice frantic. The High Priestess was looking through the wreckage for him, and Sloane called to her, "If he's in here, he's alive." She didn't smell any more death in the room.

They continued to call his name, and after a few minutes, Dorathea saw a pile of books move. Elvina and she ran to the ransacked area of the Gòrdans' library. With their palms outstretched, they righted several bookcases, casting volumes from the pile back to their shelves. After a few moments, they uncovered Alisdair's body.

"Do not move," a stony voice yelled at them. Within seconds, a group of people wearing long ecru tunics with jewel-colored wraps had surrounded them. Their hands were outstretched in a defensive posture. How they encircled them, and their brusque speech, reminded Sloane of the *Weardas*, the magical guards that enforced the Grand Coven's rules in their quadrant.

"Lower your hands at once," Dorathea snapped as she continued to examine Alisdair. "We are the West Protection Coven from the Northwest Quadrant." Her polished, English accent was poised again. "High Priest Alisdair Gòrdan invited us to his covenstead, and we discovered they had been attacked when we arrived." She rose and moved within an inch of the commanding officer's face. "I dare say, the *Freiceadan*, guards of the Northeast Quadrant, are indeed late to this horrifying crime."

As Sloane watched the man struggle to keep his confidence under the commanding gaze of her High Priestess, a question came to her. If Alisdair sent Elspeth to Mallow Cottage instead of alerting their Grand Coven about the attack, how did their police know it occurred?

The officer stepped back and cleared his throat. "This is our incident now. You must remove yourselves."

"Or what? Are you prepared to back up your threat?" Dorathea asked, closing the space between them again.

"We'll detain you with whatever force necessary and bring you before our Grand Coven."

Dorathea hesitated before breaking into derisive laughter. "Well then, your punishment saves us a trip, dear. But first, you must secure medical attention for Alisdair. Take him to *Miadarbaile* at once and provide him with protection. Whoever is responsible for the deadly assault did not intend to leave him alive."

The officer grunted in frustration, and Sloane thought they might wear different uniforms than the Weardas' black cloaks, but their shitty attitudes were the same. She watched as two guardians laid hands on Alisdair, and they all disappeared. Three more officers clutched the couple's lifeless bodies and vanished. In a matter of seconds, all the guards had gone except for two. They positioned themselves at the top of an imperial staircase, watching.

"The Freiceadan are as pleasant as ever," Elvina hissed under her breath.

Sloane turned to the familiar sound that reminded her of Bear. She still felt the shock of learning that her dark-gray, long-haired cat she had called Bear was actually her feline familiar, Elvina. She carried the guilt for being the reason The Order took the last of Elvina's nine lives. Now she had to adjust to Elvina in her final human form, a striking woman with hooded, soft brown eyes, velvety, ash-colored skin, and thick, dark grayish-brown hair.

"So they're like our Weardas?" Sloane asked, and Elvina nodded.

"Yes indeed. Thank you for minding your temper," Dorathea told her. "They are without humor."

"She's right about that. I've spent some quality time with a few Freiceadan. They never lighten up, even when things get heavy." Jack pulled a face, and Dorathea tutted at him. "What? I'm only speaking the truth. They are very intense—"

"Where's Calen?" Sloane interrupted, looking around the vast basement. It had just dawned on her that Alisdair's son and Jack's friend wasn't there, dead or alive.

Jack suddenly looked concerned. "I met him in Glasgow at a Nogical's gallery yesterday when I picked up your Christmas gift. He told me he was staying home for the holidays."

"But you're not sure he did?" Sloane asked. She held her cousin's gaze. He looked confused and afraid.

Pointing a finger at her, he said, "No. Absolutely not. He isn't responsible for this violence. I swear on my life. There is no evil in that kind man. And he holds family, his family, above all else. He has proven that to me."

"We can determine his role in this when we find him," Dorathea said. "For now, we must consider he needs our help. The Order will try to finish what they have started." She turned to the Freiceadan. "You, there. We require you to step outside this sacred space. It is time for us to perform a cleansing ritual before the surviving coven members return."

The two men crossed their arms over their chests and stayed in place.

Dorathea pulled her wire-framed spectacles to the tip of her nose and glared at them. "According to the third article of the Protector Coven clause in the Interquadrant Wiċċan Charter, we are bound to perform the ritual within sixty minutes of death, and all non-Protector Wiċċans are forbidden from witnessing."

They mumbled a response like scolded teenagers and left the room.

"We have to perform a ritual?" Sloane asked.

"We do not indeed. I made that gobbledygook up to gain us a few minutes of privacy. Only a Malevolent or its spawn could have broken into this covenstead against Mòrag's wishes."

"Bella and Lachlan were killed by a Sensor, a powerful one," Jack added. "And evil. I would never use my power to drain a brain like that."

Dorathea looked into the room. "Mòrag? It has been a long spell since we last visited, and for that, I apologize. You are safe, come out now, but we only have a few minutes to talk before the Freiceadan return."

The air in the covenstead became heavy, pressing on their chests, and Sloane took a deep breath, fighting against the tightness.

"Can you tell me what happened?" Dorathea fell silent, listening to a voice only she could hear. After a few minutes, she replied, "I understand. We are deeply sorry for your loss. I promise we will keep Alisdair, Calen, and Elspeth safe until they can return to you."

"Their house spirit?" Sloane asked, and Dorathea nodded. "Well, what did it say?"

"Nothing yet. The Order's strike has deeply wounded Mòrag."

"Can I ask it some questions? I'll be delicate," Sloane said, and Jack covered a laugh with his hand.

"House spirits choose with whom they will speak. If you do not hear Mòrag, she has not chosen you," Dorathea told her.

"Fine. At least find out if it knows how many people attacked the Gòrdans. We need something to go on."

A loud howling came from the chimney flue, and the air around them turned thicker.

"*She* will tell us what she knows when the Freiceadan leave and it is safe to speak freely," Dorathea said.

Jack leaned closer to Sloane. "She's a she. I suspect calling her an 'it' upsets her."

"Jesus, are they all temperamental?" Sloane thought about Alfred, Dorathea's house spirit. She and the grumpy old Englishman had had a rough beginning. She looked up and said, "I apologize for offending you. The right thing to do was to ask your preferred pronouns."

The lights flickered, and the weight on their chests eased. Jack elbowed Sloane and whispered, "Nicely done. Are you in therapy?"

"Shut up, Jack."

"Enough. We have no time for such bantering. We must stand before their Grand Coven. Alisdair did not report his fears to his GC as would be usual. He chose not to trust them for a reason. We must find out why."

"Or we could go to the hospital and ask him when he wakes up. If he wakes up...My gut tells me he figured out one or more of their GC members is in The Order. If we show up and start asking their GC a bunch of questions, we'll arouse their suspicion."

Dorathea grinned at Sloane. "Then we will ask only two questions."

"Ooh, how exciting. I haven't seen this group in ages," Elvina purred. "I love seeing how time treats us when others aren't looking."

"This isn't a social call," Sloane said, shaking her head at her roommate. "You know there's a good chance we're offering ourselves up to Magicals who want us dead, right? The Order has positioned itself in magical governments. And this is their endgame. Now they have the power to conduct a final assault. It started with my mother, and they're not going to stop until all our Protector Covens are dead." She turned her attention to her cousin. "We need a plan, Denham."

"We will devise one indeed. Until we do, Elvina, you must go to Alisdair," replied Dorathea, and Elvina sulked. "Watch over him and alert us if anyone visits him. We will question their Grand Coven." She looked at Sloane. "You may be correct, but they will not risk raising a hand against us at their headquarters."

The door to the covenstead opened, slamming against the wall, and the two Freiceadan guards rushed down the stairs toward them. The one Dorathea had dressed down stood face-to-face with her. "If you haven't finished your *ritual*, you have now. Your time's up. Our Grand Coven requests your presence."

"Oh, we are quite done here." Dorathea held out her arm to him. "Take us and make haste. I look forward to chatting with my old friends."

CHAPTER TWO

The Gòrdan covenstead's floor evaporated, plunging Sloane into swirling darkness until an explosive light forced her eyes open. She had teleported, or as Elvina would correct her, "*bestealcedoned*," several times now, but this time, the Wiċċan mode of travel had caused a searing pain in her head. She attempted to alleviate it by pressing her fingers against her temples.

"Are you all right?" Jack asked.

She nodded and looked around. They stood with the Freiceadan at the edge of a forest glade with a mountain looming ahead. Streams of magical creatures flowed around them as if her coven and the guards were a stone outcrop in the middle of a river.

The busy hum of voices reminded Sloane of the 42nd and Times Square subway station in NYC, but this was no concrete transit station. The air was crisp with the scent of pine, and in the distance, you could hear the whoosh of a waterfall. Sloane bent her head back. The winter sky was now springtime blue with wisps of clouds floating past. It was a ceiling. "Jesus, where are we?"

"Try to keep the colorful language to a minimum, please," Dorathea said and followed the two Freiceadan into the meadow.

"This is *Prìomh-oifis*, a government building like Tagridore's *Héahreced*. The Wiċċan in the Northeast Quadrant call themselves the *Cailleach*, and they're rooted to nature. You know how the veil identifies us and approves our entry into headquarters at home?" Jack asked. Sloane nodded, recalling last March when she had passed through the warm, gel-like barrier without getting sticky or wet. "Well, the Prìomh-oifis uses more nature-based means to screen visitors. They've created quite the journey."

He wrapped his arm around Sloane's, pulling her into the meadow of primrose and buttercup. "If you haven't figured it out yet, we use Old English for our magic, and the Northeast Quadrant uses ancient Scottish Gaelic."

"Of course they do," Sloane mumbled, and a bright light caught her attention. A woman who looked more like a hologram, with long, silver hair flowing around her body, seemed to float by, even though Sloane saw that her feet were touching the ground.

"Stop gaping, lovey. A Wiċċan of your stature has a part to play," Jack whispered. Then he smiled widely and nodded at an ethereal man with the same silver hair but shorter and tucked behind his ears, which drew to a point. "I understand your fascination, though. I forgot how much I loved the *Daoine Sìth*. Looking at them, anyway. They can be quite fickle. Not really relationship material."

"Who?" Sloane watched the man glide past.

Jack drew her closer. "The descendants of the *Tuatha Dé Danann*, a fae race once believed to be the gods of this land. They are experts in illusion and can be very seductive and dangerous."

As they neared the edge of the meadow, the mountain and waterfall came into view. Sloane looked around. Some Magicals had stopped to smell the wildflowers while others formed lines to pass through the cascading water. "So where are their offices?"

"We'll only see the Grand Coven's auditorium after we walk the Meadow of Reflection, pass through the Waterfall of Intention, and open our Path of Purpose," Jack said. "I told you it's an interesting voyage."

"Wait." Sloane stopped. "Are we supposed to be reflecting on something? Because I'm not."

"Only if the flowers feel we need to. They'll stop us if our purpose for being here is unclear."

"Right. Of course, they will. That's completely reasonable."

They neared the rushing water, and Jack loosened his grip on Sloane's arm. The two guards on either side of Dorathea stopped and waited for them to catch up. Her cousin disappeared into the waterfall first, and when Sloane hesitated, Jack shoved her in.

It only took two steps to pass through, and on the other side, Sloane emerged, still dry. Physically, she had passed through the water quickly, but her mind had taken a longer journey. The water cleared her thoughts like debris off a path. And now she was acutely focused on determining which of the Grand Coven members were in The Order.

"Jesus Christ. That was an amazing hit of clarity," Sloane said finally.

Dorathea nodded. "It is indeed. You can imagine how many poor souls have tried to bottle it."

They stood on a trail musty with forest litter and lit by wisps of light that led them more deeply into the woods. "God, these trees are unbelievable," Sloane said.

"It is the ancient Caledonian Forest. The Cailleach safeguarded it from the Nogicals' destruction millennia ago."

"Seems to be a theme between the two worlds." Sloane stared down the path that became increasingly dark. "Still not seeing any meeting rooms."

"We are nearly there," Dorathea said. "The Grand Coven is at the edge of the woods. We must complete the Trail of Integrity. Should any duplicity make it this far, the *Spunkie* is allowed to lead the deceiver away."

"What the hell's a Spunkie?"

"The whisps of light we're following. You probably know them by the name, will-o'-the-wisp," Jack said.

Sloane looked at him. "Is every quadrant full of creatures I've never heard of or ones I thought were make-believe?"

"And more," he said. "Remember your mother's book of magical creatures? It would be wise to study it."

She thought about her mother. Would she have been able to complete the Trail of Integrity? She kept so many secrets and told so many lies about her past. Their past. Why? Did she do it because she knew over thirty years ago that a movement to end the Protector Covens had started? But that didn't make sense. Why wouldn't she just tell her family about her suspicions so they could banish them, instead of running away?

As they approached the end of the path, bright light spilled into the dark forest. Once they exited the trees, they entered a lobby with walls and a floor of forest-green marble and dark wood columns. Strong vibrations shook Sloane. Wiċċans robed in colorful cloaks filled the grand room. They walked toward the banks of elevators along the three walls.

Dorathea stopped in front of a pair of golden doors set apart from the others. "Give us a moment," she told the guards, and they stepped back. She lowered her voice and said, "I have known the sitting Coven much longer than I care to admit. They will expect that you know who they are and will not introduce themselves. Ginerva Byrne, a Sensor, sits in the center, Davina Glas, a Shapeshifter, sits to her right, and on her left is Raonaid MacRìgh, a Diviner." She lowered her voice even more. "I know these women but that does not mean I trust them. They have been in power too long and are unwilling to relinquish their positions. They may not wield absolute power, but as we know, entrenched power corrupts absolutely."

Dorathea motioned to the guards, and the two men opened the golden doors. The Freiceadan bowed out at this point, and when the doors closed, Sloane released a nervous laugh. "Jesus, I thought I couldn't experience anything else that would blow my mind. But here we are." She leaned against the elevator car's back wall. "This place makes the upside-down, bizarre escalators at our headquarters seem reasonable."

"You think the Prìomh-oifis is unusual? Wait until you visit the Southwestern Quadrant's government building. The *Yachay Wasikuna*." Jack shook his head. "It's brilliant. I don't want to give too much away, but you only enter 'the house of knowledge' if a dragon allows." He laughed and had a slight shiver.

"Yes, the Wasikuna is a sight to behold," Dorathea agreed. She pressed the hold button, and the car stopped. "When the doors open, follow me to the rostrum. And do not speak unless acknowledged and spoken to. Provide short answers. Do not elaborate." She looked at Jack. "Do not banter or blather. These three Wiċċan lost their humor decades ago, if they ever possessed it, which I do not recall any of them ever did." She faced forward, straightened, and pressed the start button.

The auditorium gave Sloane instant déjà vu. It looked and felt the same as their Grand Coven's room. Wood-paneled walls. A half-moon stadium of seats. Portraits of past Grand Coven members covered the wall behind three women sitting at a long wooden table on a small stage.

Sloane followed her cousin and stood beside her at a podium. Dorathea grabbed the sides of the lectern. "*Uachdaran*, I am Dorathea Denham, the High Priestess of the West Protector Coven. I stand before you with Wiċċa Jack Denham and Wiċċe Sloane West. Our attendant Elvina has also traveled with us to Miadarbaile. However she is not present. Nevertheless we are pleased to appear before you, although the circumstances that have compelled our visit trouble us."

"We are also deeply concerned, High Priestess Denham. We have summoned you here because our top priority is to find those responsible for this deadly violence against our Protector Coven." Ginerva, the woman in the middle, spoke first. She had sharp cheekbones and a shock of red hair on one side of her long, gray tresses. Her appearance was what Sloane had always thought a witch would look like, a severe face with a hooked nose, long hair, and a black tunic. But then she learned better.

Sloane looked at her cousin and waited for her to respond to Ginerva with what was obvious. The Order had killed Elspeth's parents just like they had killed her mother and grandparents, but Dorathea only nodded slightly and remained silent.

Davina, the wiċċe on the right, leaned her ample chest against the table. "The Freiceadan informed us that they discovered you in the Gòrdans' covenstead when they arrived. Is that true?" Her Scots Gaelic accent was so thick that Sloane had trouble understanding her.

"Yes, Uachdaran, that is true."

Raonaid, sitting on the left of Ginerva, tapped her long, bony fingers on the table for an extended moment and asked, "What were your plans for this visit?"

The question was calculated, and Dorathea's hesitation in answering was slight, but it was there, hinting she was unsure of what to say. "Alisdair invited us," she said. "As it was his affair, we had no plans other than arriving on time."

The GC stared at Dorathea for a long moment. Her cousin's words weren't untrue, but Sloane knew what she said wasn't the whole story either. Alisdair's invitation had been a frantic plea for help against The Order's attack. The three wiċċe at the table narrowed their eyes.

"Well, did you arrive *on time*?" Davina asked.

Another loaded question that didn't faze Dorathea, but Sloane balled her fists. She could feel anger crawling up her neck.

"If I may," Ginerva spoke, giving Davina a harsh look. "We do not wish you to feel like you're being accused of wrongdoing, High Priestess Denham. I believe Uachdaran Glas meant to ask what time Alisdair invited your coven to visit. Your answer will help us establish a timeline for this alarming assault."

Sloane noticed the corners of Davina's mouth twitch. It seemed she didn't appreciate others speaking for her. The old witch peered over the top of her spectacles at Dorathea, waiting for an answer, and Ginerva's interference had given Dorathea more time to formulate one.

"Regrettably, we arrived late. I believe only minutes after the attack," the High Priestess said.

"That's quite a coincidence, isn't it?" Davina commented immediately.

Dorathea frowned. "Quite the contrary. It is a devastating fact. Had we been on time, we could have saved our friends."

"But you weren't." Davina sat back in her tall wooden chair.

Ginerva stared straight ahead, and Sloane got the impression there was no love lost between the two. She looked at Raonaid. The wiċċe with the round onyx eyes and hair the color of crow's feathers seemed to enjoy the tension between the other two.

"We were in time to ensure High Priest Gòrdan survived the assault," Dorathea said calmly.

"True, and we are grateful he benefited from your expertise in healing. He is recovering and will provide us with details of this tragic event soon," Ginerva said.

Davina resented the show of gratitude and snapped, "Wiċċa Denham, approach."

"Me?" Jack squeaked. Dorathea moved to the side, and he anxiously stepped onto the rostrum.

"The Freiceadan inform us that you have visited the nogical city, Kirkcudbright, several times over the last year. Is this true?" Davina asked.

Jack's cheeks reddened. "Well...yes."

"Tell us why you have spent so much time here?" Raonaid asked.

"For business, of course." He smiled nervously. "The West Gallery is showing a fabulous Scottish painter, and I was securing her work...we're proud of the talent we bring to Denwick...and our gallery is really something...you should visit sometime." Jack stopped talking when Dorathea cleared her throat.

"What is Wiċċa Calen Gòrdan's role in your business?" Raonaid asked, lacing her skeletal fingers together.

"Well, he didn't have a role per se. He helped me secure a few pieces of art."

"Another extraordinary coincidence," Davina interjected. "Here you have spent so much time with a member of our Protector Coven in the days leading up to this violence." She glared at him. "Tell us, is that all Calen does for you?"

Jack glanced apprehensively at Dorathea. "Um, no, I've known him for many years. This year isn't the first time I've visited him in Kirkcudbright or Miadarbaile, and he's visited me in Tagridore and the nogical village of Denwick after it became my home. We were friends…I have lots of friends…everyone likes me…I'm a likable person." He flashed another uneasy smile.

"Were?" Davina asked, and Sloane winced. "Do you know something about our Protector wiċċa that we don't?"

"Yes, do tell, Wiċċa Denham. According to the Freiceadan, Calen was not among the dead at the covenstead," Raonaid said.

"No, no," Jack stammered. "I know nothing. It was a simple grammatical mistake. Calen and I *are* friends." He steadied himself on the lectern. "Protector Covens are not forbidden from seeing each other. Calen and I have spent a lot of personal time together, but I haven't seen him since—"

"We are not here to interrogate your personal life, Wiċċa Denham," Ginerva said. "I apologize for this line of questioning. I think Uachdaran Glas and MacRìgh have misplaced their suspicion. It is obvious to me The Order has attacked the Gòrdan Coven, and we are wasting time questioning you. The Freiceadan confirmed Wiċċa Elspeth and Wiċċa Calen were not at the covenstead. Our priority now must be to find and safeguard them. I ask you to use your power to help us in this endeavor."

Davina and Raonaid's distrustful gazes turned to Ginerva. Sloane could feel their growing anger. Whatever their game was, Ginerva had undermined it, and that move didn't go over well. She considered the wiċċe sitting in the middle. Either Ginerva was a talented actor and an expert at misdirection, or she was just as suspicious of Davina and Raonaid as she was.

"Thank you for your opinion, Uachdaran Byrne. But you alone do not speak for the Grand Coven," Raonaid said. "Davina and I know The Order has attacked two other Protector Covens, including yours, High Priestess Denham. However, we have no proof they are in our quadrant. To blame this attack on them without evidence is premature."

"What the hell do you think they do? Send notices?" Sloane blurted out.

"Order," Ginerva shouted. She looked at Dorathea. "You will control your *Oileanach* at once."

"In a moment, please. I wish to speak with Wiċċe West." Davina adjusted the spectacles on her nose, lifting her chin to peer through them, scrutinizing Sloane from head to toe. "Aye. I've heard a lot about you. The child Jane West hid from the magical world and hid the magical world from her. I knew your mother when she was young. But I don't remember, did she have the same piercing icy-gray eyes?" She continued without waiting for an answer. "I find it interesting that even though The Order killed your mother before you knew about your heredity, you still found your way to us." She looked back and forth between Sloane and Dorathea. "Isn't it another incredible coincidence?"

"Yes, incredible," Raonaid said. "I think the three of you and your Attendant are either extremely lucky, or you are privy to knowledge about The Order that none of us are."

Ginerva and Davina stared at Raonaid in surprise, and Sloane shoved Jack to the side.

"Lucky? Are you kidding me?" she shouted, grabbing the sides of the lectern. "They killed my mother. The grandparents I never met. Innocent friends. Tried to kill me, and you think we're involved with them? How fucking stupid can you be?"

The Uachdaran stared at her for several minutes before whispering among themselves.

Sloane was losing control. She could feel the intensity of rage cloud her mind. A cooling hand touched the middle of her back. It was Jack. She felt his hand draw the heat from her body, and her anger faded away. He slipped his arm around Sloane's waist and gently pulled her down from the lectern as Dorathea stepped up.

"Uachdaran, we will no longer stand before you and entertain your accusations. You will bring whatever concerns you have to the Northwestern Grand Coven. For now, we will locate and guard the surviving members of the Gòrdan Coven, and you would be wise not to get in our way," Dorathea said, her voice even but unyielding.

Raonaid's lips curled up. "Do not worry, High Priestess Denham. We'll inform your Grand Coven. That's a promise."

CHAPTER THREE

Although entering the Northeast Quadrant's headquarters had been a journey, exiting had been as simple as passing through a nondescript, wooden door. Sloane tightly wrapped her coat around her. Inside the Prìomh-oifis, the season was perpetual spring with wildflowers and warm breezes, but outside, the air in the gray winter sky was biting, and the ground was covered in snow.

"Quickly, follow me," Dorathea said and strode down a narrow cobblestone street.

As they hurried down the lane, Sloane glanced at the row of buildings. They reminded her of the Shambles, a famous street in York. They were the same medieval-style row of timber-framed buildings with overhanging second floors where meat sellers suspended their products in the shade to sell before rot set in.

Sloane read a few of the storefront signs. *Goat's Heid Pub. Bhur Tartan Shop. Cailleach Supplies.* "So this is Miadarbaile?" she asked Jack. "A lot more charm than Tagridore."

"Oh, yes. It's centuries older. Tends to add to the appeal." He linked their arms and hurried after Dorathea. The High Priestess had slipped into an alleyway.

"Mòrag informed me the Freiceadan returned to the covenstead while the Grand Coven was questioning us. But they have now left." Dorathea looked at Sloane. "Ask Elvina if there has been any change in Alisdair's condition. If not, we will return to their covenstead and search for any evidence the Freiceadan overlooked."

"All right." Sloane opened her third eye and spoke to Elvina. *We're finished being questioned by the GC. Any unwelcomed guests there? Alisdair awake?*

Hello, dear. Elvina's velvety voice soothed Sloane like a weighted blanket. *The poor dear is still unconscious. No visitors, only his Mender has been in the room with us. How were the old hags?*

Sloane chuckled. *Jesus, they almost make me appreciate our GC. Well, I wouldn't go that far. But they are all loathsome.*

We're heading back to the Gòrdans'. Let us know when he wakes.

Of course, dear. Stay safe.

"Elvina says he's still unconscious. And he hasn't had any visitors," Sloane told Dorathea.

"Very good." Dorathea clasped Jack's hand, and he held Sloane's. A moment later, they stood at the top of the Gòrdan covenstead's grand double staircase.

"Jesus, I need to take something for the pain," Sloane said, the crack of light reverberating in her head.

Dorathea looked at her curiously. "Jack can make you an elixir."

"Oh, I don't think that's a good idea. *Wrendyks* aren't my forte, remember?" Jack said.

Sloane chuckled. How could she forget? Both times she had witnessed her cousin making potions, he had struggled. The first was a failed attempt to teach her how to make an antidote for a werewolf infection, and the second was for an elixir to sober her up. "Elvina can make me one later. I'll find something cold to drink in the kitchen. It'll help. If we could thin the air out a little in here, that'd help, too."

She opened the door behind them onto a long, dark hallway. The hardwood floors creaked under her weight, announcing each step to the darkness. The air wasn't any lighter upstairs. It was heavy like the house spirit's mood. She sensed Mòrag following her, and when multicolored lights began blinking at the end of the hall, it confirmed her suspicion.

A yule log burned in the living room fireplace, and the room was adorned with red-berried holly and ivy. The brightly lit Christmas tree was decorated with thistle ornaments and tartan baubles that were black with yellow stripes.

"I love the decorations," she said aloud, feeling Mòrag drawing closer. "I bet you had a hand in making the room look so festive." She kneeled beside the tree, searching through the wrapped gifts. Elspeth would never forget this holiday and would bear the wound for life. She read the gift labels until she found one for the child, picked it up, and headed back to the covenstead, no longer wanting a drink or feeling the pain in her head.

She thought of the gift she had for Rose back home. She needed to call her and let her know everything was okay. The coven had interrupted them a few hours ago when she was in Denwick, calling her home from Rose's apartment. It had been right when they had surrendered to the desire growing between them over the past year.

"What's that?" Jack asked as she joined them.

"It's one of Elspeth's presents. I thought I'd take a gift for her to open today." Suddenly, the room felt like a sunbeam hugging her, and then the warmth just as quickly vanished.

Dorathea smiled at Sloane. "Mòrag also approves of your gesture."

"Yes, great idea. It will surely make her feel better," Jack said.

Sloane frowned and put the package in her tote. "Hardly, Jack. A toy isn't going to make the kid feel better."

"I know, lovey. I'm only saying it's a kind gesture," Jack said, slightly wounded.

Dorathea walked to the spot where Elspeth's parents were killed. She kneeled and held her hands above the floor. After a few minutes, she stood. "The Freiceadan have neutralized the scene. I am unable to detect what happened to Lachlan and Bella."

"Let me try where we found Alisdair." Jack touched the floor where the High Priest had been saved under a cover of books. After a long moment, he got to his feet. "You're right, deary. There is no trace of crime here either."

"What the hell does that mean?" Sloane asked, looking around the room. The Freiceadan had also fixed the damage the covenstead had sustained. The room looked as though the fight had never happened. "Is this normal, or were those guards involved in The Order's plan somehow?"

"Their duties do include removing all visible signs of magic from the nogical world, most importantly when a crime has been committed. At some point, Alisdair will have to explain the death of his daughter and son-in-law to the Scottish authorities." Dorathea moved to the far side of the room and sat on a deep-brown leather sofa. "The Freiceadan worked quickly indeed."

"Yeah, and it means we have no evidence," Sloane said, sitting on a green leather love seat across from her cousin. "It wouldn't surprise me if Alisdair was suspicious of their entire GC. What a trio of assholes."

"They *are* precious," Jack said, sitting beside her.

"The Uachdaran were in rare form." Dorathea waved her hand, and a pot of tea with steam trickling from its spout appeared on the coffee table between them.

"My gut tells me Raonaid is the one hiding something," Sloane said.

"I thought Davina was too eager to blame us. The first one to cast aspersion is usually the guilty one. Isn't that what you always say?" Jack asked Dorathea.

"Only in fiction, dear."

He shrugged. "Art imitates life, life imitates art. I rather agree with Oscar Wilde on the matter."

Dorathea filled their teacups and said, "Mòrag, join us, please. You are no longer in danger. We have added our spell to yours. No one will enter your home without permission again."

Sloane breathed deeply. "Jesus, I know she's grieving, but could you ask her to hold it together? It feels like there's a knee in my chest."

"However indelicate Sloane sounds, she is correct, my friend. You have suffered a great loss, but I ask you to be strong until we find those responsible. I am quite sure you would like Alisdair, Calen, and Elspeth to return home to you, yes?"

There was no change in the air pressure.

"Hey, Mòrag," Sloane said, bending her head back. "Everybody's hurting here, but now's not the time to blame ourselves. You couldn't have stopped The Order. None of this is your fault." The lamps flashed erratically. "That's right. Get angry. Angry at them. Focus on defending the family you have left. They need you, especially Elspeth." She paused. "You can start by telling us how many people attacked your family."

Dorathea listened, slowly raising an eyebrow.

"What is she saying?" Sloane asked.

"Two Magicals strong enough to break through her defenses were responsible."

"Ask her if she or Alisdair knew them." The flames in the fireplace soared up the chimney, and Sloane stared at the ceiling. "I'll take that as a yes. Did he let them in?"

The room dimmed.

"Mòrag says they disguised themselves in a shadow and entered the covenstead uninvited," Dorathea said.

"All right, so they broke in." Sloane looked up again. "But that wasn't your fault. The Order is a formidable group, and if one of them was a Cambion—"

"Half-Malevolent, pet," Dorathea corrected.

"Right, whatever. It'll take me a while to adjust to their actual name, Denham. Since I didn't even believe Demons and Cambions existed until this year." Sloane stared at the ceiling and softened her voice. "You didn't have a chance at stopping them." A low whine sounded through the room, becoming louder. Sloane looked at Dorathea again. "Ask her if Alisdair keeps any notes or records hidden away, somewhere the Freiceadan couldn't find them?" Her cousin was quiet for a moment. "Well, what is she saying?"

Dorathea shook her head. "She's not responding."

"Maybe she just needs some time," Jack said.

Sloane tensed. Why the hell did everyone say that? Time wouldn't make Mòrag feel better. Mòrag would make Mòrag feel better. Just when Sloane decided to try a different approach with the house spirit, a loud commotion sounded in the library.

They hurried to the other side of the covenstead and found an entire row of books tossed on the floor. The back panel of the empty shelf was opened, revealing a hidden cabinet.

"Thank you for trusting us, Mòrag," Dorathea said.

Sloane removed photos and a stack of books from the compartment. She handed the pictures to Dorathea and half the volumes to Jack. They sat on the library's repaired furniture.

A look of concern on Dorathea's face deepened as she scanned the photographs. "These are pictures of the four quadrants' Grand Covens. All taken while they were in session. Why would Alisdair have these?"

Jack looked tensely at her. "Does he think all four Grand Covens have been compromised? My God, that would be disastrous."

"Quite right."

"Don't assume," Sloane told them. "We don't know why Alisdair took the photos, if he did." She paged through the books and held one up. "These are similar to the books Jane hid in her bedroom over thirty years ago." She picked up the last one, a leather tome with a triquetra in the center of the cover. She opened the book, and an envelope fell out. "Look at this. It doesn't have a seal flap. Just a blob of wax on this side." Sloane held up the envelope for them to see.

"Please." Dorathea held out her hand. She took the envelope and inspected it. "This is Alisdair's mark." She looked into the room. "Mòrag, do you know why he sealed this with a *teaghlachail* incantation?"

"A what?" Sloane asked.

"A family spell, dear." Jack leaned over the coffee table, inspecting the seal. "I haven't seen one in ages. Only you or a member of your family you've designated can open it. We call it a *hiwcup* spell in our quadrant. You should have Elvina teach it to you."

Dorathea ran her long nail over the wax seal. "Unfortunately, Mòrag has no idea what Alisdair hid inside."

"Then we need to go to the hospital, wake him up, and ask him," Sloane said.

"It could be days before he wakes." Dorathea replied, tucking the envelope into the pocket of her cloak.

"Then we can ask Elspeth to open it. I'm betting if Alisdair sent her through the Morisot sketch to safety, he made her a trusted opener," Jack said.

Sloane stood. "He could have. But whatever is in there might be as cryptic as the GC photos. And she might not know what it means. What about Calen?"

"He would probably know more." Jack's voice sounded worried. "We need to make finding him our priority, regardless. It's not right that he wasn't here when the attack happened, or that he hasn't returned." He paused. "It could mean something unrelated has happened to him."

"Jesus, Jack. What's that supposed to mean? Were you and Calen involved in something that put him in danger?" Sloane looked him in the eyes, but he stared at the floor, pinching the bridge of his nose.

Dorathea gave him an uncharacteristically angry look. "We must first try to wake Alisdair for answers. Then we will search for Calen. And we had better find him *alive*."

CHAPTER FOUR

"Oh, thank God you're here," Elvina said as Dorathea, Sloane, and Jack entered Alisdair's hospital room. "He's been struggling to open his eyes."

"A good sign indeed." Dorathea laid her hand on the High Priest's forehead and moved her other hand inches above his upper body.

Sloane glanced around. This was unlike any hospital room she'd been in. The cramped, windowless space had only a bed, a small table, and a chair. There were no machines with tubes and wires, emitting intermittent beeps, or computers for doctors and nurses to take notes.

A few minutes after they arrived, the elderly man with long silver hair and a round, pleasant face inhaled sharply as if everything that had just happened slammed into his consciousness like a waking nightmare. "Dorathea. Elspeth made it to you. Thank God." His voice was weak and low. "Lachlan and Bella?"

Dorathea eased herself into the chair next to his bed and shook her head.

Alisdair closed his eyes tightly, and a single tear from the corner of his eye rolled over his cheekbone, disappearing into his hair.

"I am so sorry, dear. We did not arrive in time to save them." She waved her hand and surrounded them under shimmery energy. "We can speak freely. If The Order is watching and listening to you, they cannot hear us now."

Worry flashed on Alisdair's anguished face, and he whispered, "Calen and Elspeth?"

Dorathea patted his hand. "We are unaware of Calen's whereabouts, but Elspeth is safe at our covenstead. Alfred is caring for her."

"And Mòrag?" he asked.

"She is understandably shaken. But when the Freiceadan left your home, I was able to coax her out."

"The guards were there?" he asked.

"They were indeed. They appeared directly after we arrived."

His eyes widened, and Sloane could tell he considered the Freiceadan's appearance as suspicious as they did.

"Mòrag was able to show us where you hid books and photos in the covenstead," Dorathea continued. "And this." She pulled the sealed envelope from her cloak's pocket. "Is it evidence of The Order?"

"Aye. You found…" Alisdair's mouth continued to form words, but his voice had disappeared. His eyes widened, and he tried to speak again. "*Och no!* What have they done?" He snatched the envelope from Dorathea and traced his fingers over the wax seal. Nothing.

"What the hell's going on? Why's his voice going in and out?" Sloane asked.

"It's a curse," Jack whispered. "Nasty thing."

"Has he had visitors?" Dorathea asked Elvina.

"None. Only the Mender has entered since we arrived."

"Did you watch her carefully? Could she have performed the curse when healing him?"

"*He*, dear. And no, he cast nothing in my presence," Elvina told her.

"Then The Order placed a *gestillan* curse on you when they breached your covenstead," Dorathea said.

Alisdair dropped the envelope on his chest and closed his eyes again.

"What's a gestillan curse? Why are you making such a big deal about it?"

"It is a binding curse," Elvina told Sloane. "They have bound Alisdair from speaking about any aspect of The Order's attack, or possibly anything he might know about them."

"Fine. Summon some paper and a pen. He can write what he remembers."

"It restricts all forms of communication," Jack said.

"So how do we reverse it?"

Dorathea frowned. "It is a complicated process. One that requires us to know the Wiċċan who cast it."

"All right. The Order's first mistake. Now we know for certain one of the attackers is a Wiċċan who is powerful enough to break into their covenstead, silence them, and send the Freiceadan to clean up their mess."

Voices sounded in the hallway.

"Hurry. Take it to Elspeth." Alisdair thrust the envelope into Dorathea's chest. "I trust you've added a protective spell to my covenstead?"

Dorathea nodded, and the voices in the hall became louder.

"You need to leave at once," Alisdair said. "Don't worry about me. I'm not staying here, and Mòrag can help me..." His voice vanished again.

"I must insist you stay at our covenstead, Alisdair. You are not safe in Kirkcudbright or Miadarbaile," Dorathea said.

"None of us is safe, my friend," he whispered. "Now go before they find you."

* * *

Although it was late afternoon on Christmas Day in Scotland, the sun was only rising at the hobbit house when Sloane and the others returned. Alfred had filled their sacred space with the scent of calming lavender and the warmth of a roaring fire.

Elspeth Gòrdan was curled up on a velvet sofa in the library. She sat up as they entered, watching, waiting, tears forming in her big green eyes after no one else appeared behind Jack. "Are my da and mam coming?" she asked in a little voice.

Elvina sat beside her and stroked her long, golden locks. "We were unable to save everyone, dear. The Order has killed your parents, but your grandfather is alive, and we are looking for your uncle."

The child's face went blank for a moment, and then, as if the words had suddenly struck her like a fist, she wailed at the news, burying her face in Elvina's side. The sound of her grief tore through Sloane, and she bristled and snapped at her former familiar, "If you're going to be so direct, you need to calm her."

Elvina gathered the child in her arms and gently rocked her back and forth. "She must know the truth and grieve. Not facing our tragedies only causes us more pain."

Her words felt like an admonishment, and warmth rose to Sloane's cheeks. She had much to mourn in her life, so she pushed away the constant grief to the edges of her mind, but not because she thought she couldn't survive facing sorrow. She was terrified because she feared she'd lose control and join the chaos death left in its wake.

Jack placed his hand on Sloane's back and led her to an armchair. A carafe and a plate of cookies appeared on the coffee table. "Ooh, what do we have here? Could it be Christmas morning hot chocolate and cookies?" He smiled at Elspeth, but she kept her face hidden in Elvina's side. "Are these from Freya's?"

Elvina nodded and looked at Dorathea. "My mother has stayed with Elspeth since we left last night. She said the child has refused to eat. I told her we were returning, and she thought it best to leave before our arrival."

"You are not responsible for explaining your mother's actions to me. I had already asked Freya to depart," Dorathea said, and Elvina looked away. The High Priestess sat on the other side of

Elvina and the child. She flicked her wrist. The carafe lifted and poured five mugs of milky chocolate.

Sloane reflected on the promise Freya made to Jane to keep her new life in New York City secret. Had she considered the consequences of helping her? Did she consider how their lies and secrets, like death, would change their family forever? Sloane looked at Dorathea. Her cousin's face was stoic, but her eyes were teary. She hadn't been able to talk about Freya since she found out. Helping Jane had caused a deep rift between Freya and her long-term partner, and Sloane wondered if the love they shared would be enough to bridge it.

Sloane dropped her tote against her chair and realized Elspeth's gift was still inside. She retrieved it and placed the present on the coffee table. It wasn't the time to call her attention to it, but it would be there when she was ready. They sat together in silence, only the sounds of the young girl's crying, the bored books in the library zipping through the air like hummingbirds, and the crackling fire filling the room.

After a while, the child's sobs waned. "She's asleep," Elvina whispered and tucked a fuzzy blanket around Elspeth.

"We should rest while the child sleeps." Dorathea snapped her fingers, and throw blankets appeared on everyone's lap.

"I'm good for at least thirty-six hours," Sloane said, draping the chenille cover over her chair. "But you can sleep. I'm going to find Calen. He's out there alone, and we don't even know who's hunting him."

"Let your mind and body reset, pet. Even thirty minutes will help your thinking," Dorathea told her.

"She's right. A few winks will do you good," Jack said as Alfred piped soft cello music into the covenstead.

"Fine," Sloane mumbled and closed her eyes. The rush of being in danger that had kept her awake began to fade, but her rapid-fire thoughts continued. The Order was a dangerous insurgent group. Delusions of grandeur. Violence. More like fascists, they seduced angry, fearful, and disillusioned Magicals. Promised them unity and prosperity and provided a path to restore their rightful place in the world.

The Order had made the Protector Covens, like the Wests and the Gòrdans, their scapegoats. But every usurper group had fatal flaws in its reliance on the cults of personality, division, or suppression. Sloane thought about which flaw her coven could exploit to weaken the rebellion. Her gut told her they needed to strike at the top, find out who was leading The Order, and destroy them.

A few hours later, Elspeth lifted her head and stared, wide-eyed, at her surroundings. They had been waiting for the child to wake, hoping sleep would help calm her. Elvina kissed her lightly on the forehead. "My mother has made us a Christmas breakfast. Would you like to eat? You must be hungry."

Elvina helped her sit up, and Elspeth glanced at the spread of food on the coffee table, her gaze trained on the Scotch pie morning rolls. "Good choice. I happen to know she made those just for you." Elvina plated two rolls filled with mutton pie, smothered in brown gravy, and handed them to her.

"Would you like to open a present from home?" Sloane picked up the package, and the young girl shook her head, retreating into Elvina's arms. "All right. It'll be right here if you change your mind."

They waited for the child to feel comfortable enough to sit away from Elvina's embrace. When she did, Dorathea said, "Elspeth, I imagine you have many questions. And we will answer them all. We are a Protector Coven just like yours. But we are in the Northwest Quadrant. Your grandfather has asked us to keep you safe. I am unaware of how much your grandfather has told you about The Order's threat to our covens. Do you know they wish to harm us?"

Elspeth nodded timidly.

"We believe your gifted grandfather may have discovered the identities of some Order members and hidden their names in this." Dorathea held up the sealed envelope. "And you can help us by opening it, dear."

Elspeth looked at Elvina. "You're safe. Your grandfather asked that you open it for him."

The young girl held out her hand, and Dorathea handed her the letter. When Elspeth's fingers touched the wax seal, the white paper lifted into the air and unfolded, dropping a single photograph into her lap. "I heard two women in our covenstead," she cried and thrust the photo at Dorathea, burying her face in Elvina's side.

Dorathea looked at the picture as if it were something she couldn't understand.

"What is it?" Sloane asked.

"It would seem Alisdair believes the two women in this picture are in The Order. One of them is the GC's Ginerva Byrne. I am unfamiliar with the other woman." She handed the photo to Sloane. "I am less sure if he knew who he had captured sitting at the table behind them."

"Jesus Christ." Sloane flipped the photo over and looked at the back. "He dated it. He took this last week."

"Who is it?" Jack craned toward her, and she handed the photo to him. "Well, I did *not* have him on my bingo card."

"Who?" Elvina whispered, covering Elspeth's ears.

"Andrew Gildey, deary. Sitting right behind them, plain as day." Jack held the photo out to her.

Andrew came from one of the oldest, wealthiest European families in Canada. Sloane thought it made sense that the heir to the Gildey fortune would be sitting with alleged criminals. The first time she saw him, masked behind dark glasses, she had suspected he had something to hide. A loud ring made the others jump. "Jesus, it's just my phone." Sloane grabbed her tote and retrieved it. "Sharma?"

"Yeah, it's me. Are you home?" The lieutenant's voice sounded serious.

"Am I home? Are you home or still in the hospital?" Sloane asked. It had only been a few days since they had stopped a killer and saved a boy's life. She had avoided a bullet meant for her when magic intervened, but Veena hadn't been so lucky. Her best friend had taken two shots to the chest. Thankfully, her RCMP body armor took the hit.

"They released me this morning. The bullets didn't even break skin. But I'm sore. Got one hell of a bruise but otherwise fine."

"Not going to lie, Sharma, I was scared there for a minute." Sloane had known Veena since last March, when she met everyone else in Denwick. She and the RCMP detective had investigated two crimes together and had become close friends.

"You and me both." Sharma paused. "Listen, the caretaker at Denwick Cemetery found another body in the crypt this morning. We suspect it's a homicide."

"You're back at work? What the hell is wrong with Nichol? He's such a son of a bitch—"

"Calm down. I didn't want any time off. Really. I'm not about to let the inspector hand off my homicide case because of a bruise." She hesitated. "I'd understand if you didn't want to relive any memories of what happened last March, but I could use your help. I'm at the Gildey Mausoleum right now, and there are some things...some similarities to your case...when you were held in the crypt...you know...and you defended yourself. I think you might be able to help me make sense of them."

"What do you mean by similarities?"

"I'd rather show you," Veena said.

Sloane rubbed the back of her neck. Didn't the Weardas wipe everything Veena saw that day in the crypt from her memory? How could she know about any similarities? "All right. I'll be there in a few minutes." She ended the call and looked at the others.

"What is it?" Dorathea asked.

"They found a body in the crypt."

CHAPTER FIVE

Veena's unmarked cruiser and a plain white van were the only vehicles in the Old Denwick Cemetery lot. Sloane parked Pearl, the once-enchanted white convertible MG she inherited from her grandparents, a few spots away.

She stayed in the car, preparing the lies she would have to tell Veena, the apricity easing her guilt. After a few minutes, she walked to an ornate wrought iron gate with evergreen ivy twined over its forged surfaces. Dorathea had told her the first time they visited the cemetery that the gate was the original entry to the Old Denwick Church, the small building on the hill where the seaside villagers first congregated. That was before the Gildey family, in a flagrant display of wealth, built a fancier church at the bottom of the hill, converting the original chapel into their personal mausoleum.

The gate was usually chained, but today it was unlocked and ajar. She pushed it open. Its hinges screeched, and a mob of crows flew from the trees, cawing at the disruption. The groundskeeper had cleared the snow from the stone pathway running through the cemetery. She glanced at two headstones as she walked past. Harold and Charlie Huxham, victims of The Order. They were Nogicals, but that didn't matter. The Order killed them anyway because the uncle and nephew dared to obstruct their mission.

The groundskeeper didn't bother shoveling the dirt path to the mausoleum, but the RCMP foot traffic to and from the murder scene had packed the snow enough for Sloane to trek up the hill in her trainers with little trouble.

Sloane stopped at the mausoleum entrance and looked at the Gildey name chiseled prominently above the door. She thought about the picture Alisdair had secured with a family spell. Why the hell was Andrew Gildey in a photo with one known Magical and a supposed other? What did it mean?

Crime scene tape cordoned off the opulent white marble room full of the wealthy family's ashes. She ducked under and walked to a small, wooden door at the back of the Gildey columbarium. The RCMP had left the door open, and she called down from the threshold of a dark, narrow stairwell. "Hey, Sharma. Can I come down?"

Veena's head appeared in a second doorway at the bottom of the stairs. The lieutenant looked like the girl next door. Her long black hair was held back in a large clip with two strands strategically left loose to frame her face, but she was anything but ordinary. She held out shoe covers. "Come down. But put these on."

"Down there?"

"Yeah. We've already processed the stairs."

Sloane descended, and the air became mustier. Halfway down, the fetid stench of death and the feel of disturbed energy met her. She slipped the covers over her shoes and followed Veena into the crypt. Her friend appeared put together in a crisp white shirt and a blazer. But Sloane had worked with NYPD officers injured in the line of duty, and she knew the physical wounds paled in comparison to the mental ones.

A man from Forensic Identification Services was shooting photos of the dirt ground under a wall of funerary niches. Sloane looked at the row of her family's nooks, from her mother's at the bottom to her great-great-grandparents' at the top, except she knew their ashes weren't really there. Dorathea had explained that the urns were used to pacify Nogicals. It was a ruse to keep them unaware Magicals existed.

Veena stood beside one of the four sarcophagi in the center of the crypt and spread her arms. "Merry Christmas. Hope I didn't ruin your day."

"It's going a lot better than your victim's day." Sloane draped her peacoat over the stone coffin next to Veena's puffy coat and took a pair of nitro gloves from her friend. "I have a gift for you at the cottage. We wanted to invite you for a visit when you feel better."

"I'd like that and not because of the gift. Don't worry about me, West. I'm doing okay. But it's good to know I have your ear if I need it."

"Anytime," Sloane said, and Veena flashed her the kind of smile that crinkled the corners of her eyes, but then she looked troubled.

"Listen, if Inspector Nicol knew I asked you down here, he'd demote me," she said, and Sloane lifted her chin at the man from Ident. "He won't say anything to Nicol. Follow me. I need to run some observations by you."

The lieutenant led her to the gray granite wall at the back of the crypt. Its white crystallized veins pulsed into a visible Tree of Life that only Sloane could see. Two cracks spread from what looked like sledgehammer strikes, marring several branches of the tree, darkening them. Her Tree of Life pendant burned against her chest. The key to opening the Northwest Protector Coven's portal to Tagridore was angry about the damage.

"I questioned the caretaker earlier. He told me Mrs. Gildey pays him to clean the stairs once a week so dirt from the crypt isn't tracked into the mausoleum. That's why he was here this morning." She paused and stubbed the toe of her boot into the ground. "But Ident and I only saw one set of prints on those stairs. *His.*"

Sloane stared at her for what was a beat too long. "All right. That's strange. But there has to be a simple explanation."

"Yeah, well, I haven't even told you the strangest part. The same thing happened last March."

"What do you mean?" Dread settled in the pit of Sloane's stomach.

"When we found you down here, Dorathea was ahead of Detective Quinn and me. I looked at the stairs. There was only one set of prints before she added hers. We processed the scene. Excluded elimination prints...James Reed's, Dorathea's, Rose's, ours." She looked at Sloane as if she needed to decide whether to continue. "But you and your abductor's footprints weren't on the stairs."

"What? How can that be?" *Shit. Shit. Shit.* Sloane fought hard to maintain a neutral face. Why did Veena remember? The Weardas always repaired the damage done by magical crime and extracted any memories of the crime from Nogicals' minds, replacing them with versions that didn't include any evidence of the magical world. Sloane stared at Veena and mentally corrected herself. At least they were supposed to.

"Okay, now you'll think I'm losing my mind. The official report says both of your prints *were* there. But I know they weren't. At first Ident said they didn't find your prints, but then they appeared in the evidence, and everyone acted as if the prints had always been there. But I never saw them." Veena's face showed her mental anguish.

"I don't understand." Sloane immediately felt self-loathing for lying, for adding to Veena's confusion, and gaslighting her friend when she needed the truth.

"I know it sounds crazy, and I can't explain it, but, West, neither of your prints was on those stairs or in the original photos." She looked at Sloane, confounded. "Which means we have a bigger problem. How did you and your abductor, or the dead man we just found and his killers, get down here without using the stairs?"

"Hey, take a breath, Sharma. There's got to be an explanation." Sloane had to convince the lieutenant of something, even though all she wanted to do was tell her the truth. But how would that work with someone already questioning her sanity? *Oh, I can explain, Sharma. We teleported.* "Maybe a secret passage," she said. "A tunnel from the outside. We can look."

The crypt was lit with floodlights that cast shadows of the arched niches across the dirt floor and heated the space unnaturally. The coroner had removed the body, but proof of a fight remained. A chunk of stone was blown from the side of one of the sarcophagi, and burn marks were etched in the walls. It was obvious to Sloane that The Order had caused the damage, which meant the victim was also a Magical, and in her gut, she knew who it was.

"What do you think happened down here?" Sloane asked.

"We're not sure yet. The victim was male, fifty-two years of age. Cause of death is unknown. No gunshot or stab wounds. Only what looked to be a minor wound to the forehead." Veena stared at the spot where they found him. "That's another similarity to the incident last March." Her voice was impassive but seemed unintentionally so. Sloane could tell the lieutenant wavered between feelings of uncertainty and confidence that something was happening in Denwick, something she couldn't explain. "There's one more thing," she said, reaching into her pocket.

Sloane braced herself as the lieutenant pulled out a plastic evidence bag.

"You know I shouldn't be showing you this." This time, she made sure her back was to the man from Ident. "We found it clenched in the victim's hand." She lifted the baggie, and Sloane's breath caught. "Yeah, that's how I thought you'd respond. Tell me this isn't the same necklace we found down here when you were abducted. Your necklace."

"It isn't mine," Sloane said and pulled her pendant from under her T-shirt. "But it is the same as mine."

"Well, that's a relief. Not that I doubted you. But the bigger question is, why is jewelry like yours in the crypt with another dead body? And please don't say you don't know. We can both appreciate that this is too much of a coincidence."

Sloane stared at the Tree of Life pendant in Veena's hand. Its troubled energy called to her. "I could probably help you if I knew who the victim was."

Veena pocketed the evidence and followed her to the sarcophagi. "Okay," she whispered. "I'm only showing you this because I think these incidents are related, and I think you can help me." Sloane nodded while Veena opened the photos on her phone. Then the lieutenant showed her the screen. "This is a picture of the only footprint lifted off the stairs. See…only one set. And this is the abrasion to the victim's forehead. Minor. Not even blood splatter. And this is his UK driver's license."

Sloane recognized the picture and name at once—Calen Gòrdan.

CHAPTER SIX

Sloane should have driven back to the hobbit house and informed the others of Calen's murder. Now the Gòrdan Coven had only two surviving members. Not enough to fight The Order with the power of three, but enough to keep the Demons and Cambions their coven had banished to the Abyss locked away for eternity, if her coven could keep Alisdair and Elspeth alive.

She drove Pearl the long way back from the Old Denwick Cemetery, down Second Avenue. Her coven also needed to know about Veena, how the Weardas had failed to wipe her friend's memories.

Second Avenue ran behind Denwick's historic pedestrian block of Main Street. Sloane stopped on the side of the road and stared across a parking lot at the Keane family's Spotted Owl Inn and Pub, one of the original businesses of Old Main. Like the West family, the Keanes were Magical, living in the nogical world to defend their kind. She had learned upon her arrival that Ken, the funny Scotsman, and Fiona, his elegant Jamaican wife, as well as their two adult kids, Rose and Oscar, were vampires. Technically,

Fiona was a vampire. The others were a hybrid species of human beings and vampires called Dhampyres, or, as Rose called herself, Daywalkers. Their human blood allowed them to walk in the sunlight and find sustenance in food rather than only blood.

Rose lived in an apartment above their family establishment and had taken over the business when her parents retired to Miadarbaile this past summer. Sloane looked at the apartment door, remembering the night before on the sofa, when the beautiful Daywalker was pressed against her. She could feel the softness of Rose's golden-brown skin, smell her woodsy scent, and taste the sweetness of her breath.

She sat with the sensual memory. Before the coven interrupted them and called her home, they had finally shared their feelings for each other. Embraced the bond they'd spent the past year creating and denying. A change had happened for Sloane when she had returned to NYC, a realization that overwhelmed her. She no longer wanted to date Rose. She wanted a life with her.

Sloane glanced at her watch. Rose would already be downstairs with Chef, preparing for the lunch and dinner rush. It would start in a few hours, even on Christmas Day, because Rose wanted the pub to be open to people who had nowhere else to be.

Sloane retrieved her cell phone from her tote and texted. *Hey, Keane. So sorry about last night.*

Rose's text was immediate. *You're sorry? I'm not ;)*

Sloane grinned. *We're back. I'd like to see you for lunch if you'll have me.*

I tried to have you last night. Sloane's face warmed, and another text quickly followed. *jk. Is everything okay? What happened?*

Lots to tell you. How about noonish? I'll fill you in.

K. See you then.

A few minutes later, Sloane climbed the front steps of the low sloping-roofed hobbit house. The front door creaked open before she could knock. "Thanks, Alfred." She nodded at the ceiling, and wisps of light like backyard fireflies in summer guided her down a dark hallway. Once in the covenstead, Dorathea's scent of cloves and black pepper enveloped her. The usual sounds of spells brewing and books entertaining themselves were absent, and she glanced at the sofa in the library. The child was no longer there, and only the wrapping on her present remained on the coffee table.

"Elspeth's asleep upstairs, dear," Elvina said. "She opened the gift, a stuffed unicorn from her grandfather. Very sweet. She's napping with it."

"Poor kid." Sloane dropped her tote on the rug and her body in the chair.

"You look like you need a drink, lovey." Jack waved his hand, and a crystal bottle with a smoky black label appeared with four rocks glasses. *Fulsmécte*. A whiskey from Tagridore. Her favorite.

"For goodness' sake. It is still morning," Dorathea said. She sounded like a frustrated mother with a hint of concern in her voice.

"I have to agree. A bit early for the hard stuff," Sloane said, even though she liked the thought of knocking back a few shots to ease telling them her news.

"I'll warm up the tea, unless you would prefer coffee?" Dorathea asked her.

"Tea's good." Sloane waited, rehearsing her next words. After Dorathea handed her a steaming cup of Lady Earl Grey, she faced Jack. Her stomach tightened, and she said, "I'm sorry. Calen is dead."

He gasped. "That can't be. He had to have been somewhere safe…" His voice cracked.

"He was in the crypt. It looks like he was trying to enter Tagridore," Sloane said sympathetically. Jack hadn't revealed anything about his relationship with Calen, but she could tell they had been more than business acquaintances.

"Are you sure it was him?" Dorathea asked.

"Yeah, Veena showed me his ID."

"Wait. You didn't see his body?" Jack's voice sounded hopeful.

"I've asked my mother if the Weardas are aware of the death of a Magical in Denwick." Elvina sat motionless, waiting for Freya's answer. A moment passed, and she frowned. "There was a death early this morning. I've asked her to confirm who the victim was and how they died."

"That's a waste of time. It was him," Sloane said, irritated. "Veena would have verified that the ID belonged to the victim. She might be a Nogical in your eyes, but I guarantee she's better at her job than the damn Weardas."

They sat in silence waiting for Freya's response, and Sloane watched as a marathon of emotions ran across Jack's face. Worry. Sorrow. She was surprised when a flash of guilt appeared. Her cousin poured three fingers of whiskey into a glass and gulped it down and then poured another.

After several tense minutes, Elvina spoke, "Freya has just confirmed it was Calen." She looked at Jack. "I'm so very sorry you have lost a friend and that poor child upstairs has lost an uncle. She has only Alisdair now."

"How did he die?" Jack asked. His body visibly tensed as if in preparation for a punch to the gut.

"She hasn't heard yet, dear," Elvina said softly.

"This is shocking news. Only Alisdair and Elspeth remain," said Dorathea. "We must guard them above all else."

"And figure out who the hell killed him," Sloane added.

Dorathea looked sympathetically at Jack. "I am sorry for sounding impersonal, dear. We will take time to grieve his loss before anything else."

"You don't have to worry about me. He was a good friend, but I've lost better and kept it together," he said, pouring another whiskey neat, and Sloane was sure she saw a look of relief in his eyes.

"Jesus, Jack. That's heartless," she said.

His eyes welled with tears, and he rubbed the sadness away with the back of his hand. "You're right, lovey. But I can't think about it. Not now. Not if I'm going to stay useful."

A lavender pastry box materialized on the coffee table. Dorathea stared at it, her lips pressed together. "Freya wanted to send your favorite," Elvina said to Dorathea, but the High Priestess did not respond.

Sloane opened Freya's gift and took a bite of a meat tart. "Jack's right. We need to focus on finding The Order right now. It's only a matter of time before they succeed in ending one of our covens. We need to know who is in control. Go on the offensive and destroy them from top down. Unless we do, we're stuck defending ourselves, and we aren't doing a good job at that."

"Shall I summon Lucky Baby?" Elvina asked.

"Not this time," Sloane said. Back in their NYC days, when she knew Elvina as her cat, Bear, they had used various whiteboards for Sloane's private-investigator cases. Elvina had named them all Lucky Baby. But this time, Sloane had a gut feeling they needed to limit any written communication. "Whoever is behind the attacks was able to breach the Gòrdan's covenstead, which means they can access ours. We can't document anything we don't want found."

A stiff wind swept through the room, sending flames up the flue. Dorathea spoke matter-of-factly. "Mòrag thought she was invulnerable, too, Alfred. She was not." The fire settled, and the air became heavy. "Refrain from pouting, dear. It is not the time." Dorathea waved her hand over her head in an arc, surrounding them with the same protective shimmering energy she had used in Alisdair's hospital room. "Sloane is correct. We must be careful when and where we speak."

"There's another thing we need to discuss," Sloane said. "Veena found our Tree of Life pendant in Calen's hand."

Jack took in a sharp breath. "I gave it to him so he could meet me in Tagridore without registering at the Héahreced."

"You know we are forbidden from sharing access through our portal." Dorathea tutted, and Jack lowered his head.

When The Order had abducted Sloane and taken her to the crypt, they wanted two things: to kill her and to gain passage into Tagridore. She wondered if Calen was trying to enter the city when they found him, and if he died defending the key. He must have disguised it somehow. Or The Order would have taken it. "Who else can unlock the Tree of Life?" she asked.

"Only our coven possesses keys to the portal. As High Priestess, I make the pendants, and I assure you, I do not make extras. And neither did my ancestors." Dorathea glared at Jack over her spectacles.

"That's not exactly true, dear. You made one for my mother," Elvina said.

"That was an approved exception," Dorathea said dryly, but Sloane could hear her cousin's heartbreak in her words.

Sloane felt bad for Freya, but she also understood Dorathea's pain, the sting, the leveling agony you feel when someone you love has lied to you for such a long time. She was an unwitting participant in the deception that had upended her cousin's relationship, but even so, she felt guilty.

"Whose pendant did you give him?" Dorathea asked crossly.

He grimaced. "The original West Protector. Your great-uncle's. Mother did a terrible job keeping them for the family. She had them on display like Nogicals do with trophies." He shook his head. "The family shouldn't have given her the honor. She also lost your great-aunt's pendant. It's been gone for thirty years."

Dorathea lifted an eyebrow. "That is troubling. We will have to find her key before it falls into the wrong hands."

"Yeah, well, it'll have to wait at the bottom of a growing list of things we have to do," Sloane said. "My great-great grandparents' keys to Tagridore missing is bad, but Veena remembering she saw the same pendant in March is worse."

The others stared at her.

"You must be mistaken," Elvina finally said.

"I thought so, too. But she also recognized the damage the curses caused in the crypt. And the lack of visible injuries on the victims. Either the Weardas didn't do their job, or their spells didn't work on her. She knows something she can't explain has happened again. And I don't think we should continue lying to her. She could help us."

"Absolutely not. We cannot tell a Nogical that we are Magical. It is too risky," Dorathea told her.

"Jesus, Denham. Don't act like a dictator and shut me down. Be reasonable. We can at least explore the idea."

"There is nothing to discuss. Our kind left the nogical world millennia ago. Their memory of us exists in myths and legends. You are suggesting we tell them that all their history is mistaken. That we decide for *all* magical creatures that the Nogicals should know of us. Does that sound reasonable to you?"

Dorathea tapped her long, slender finger against the rim of her teacup, and for the first time, Sloane thought that her desire for Magicals to come out of hiding might be a little naïve.

"I do find it peculiar the Weardas would make such an egregious mistake with Veena," said Dorathea. "Perhaps their supposed oversight with the lieutenant means something more sinister."

Sloane considered Dorathea's suggestion. It made sense. If The Order wanted to control the nogical world, a proven way would be to create fear and uncertainty and then provide scapegoats.

They sat quietly until Jack sighed in exasperation. "My God, let's battle one nefarious scheme at a time, shall we?"

"It's all connected, Jack," Sloane said. "If Alisdair is right, and our GC or theirs or even both has a traitor. We can bet they've turned at least a few of the Weardas and the Freiceadan under their command." She thought for a moment. "Alisdair's photograph has three persons of interest. Ginerva Byrne could be the corrupt GC in the Northeast Quadrant. I'm willing to bet the bent member of our GC is Polydora Nenge and that she spends time with Isobel and Andrew Gildey. Now we need to prove it."

"How? The Grand Coven is made up of the most influential Wiċċan in our quadrant," Jack said. "And they're already suspicious of us."

"Oh, please. Both of you say Dorathea is the most formidable wiċċe in the quadrant." Sloane looked at Elvina. "And your mother is probably the second most, am I right?"

Her former familiar simpered, "Oh, yes. I would agree."

"Who is most capable is not important," Dorathea said. "The Grand Coven's influence reaches everywhere. It will be difficult for us to investigate them without them knowing."

"I disagree," Elvina countered. "You being more powerful than them does make a difference. Polydora's been ruthlessly jealous of you since the elders chose to elect you to the Grand Coven, even though you declined and recommended she take your place. You gave her the control she now holds over us. And she uses it to harass our coven and my mother when she should be grateful."

"I am afraid you're wrong, dear. I do not need Polydora Nenge's gratitude. My history with her is more complicated than bitterness over an abdicated seat. And my superior abilities won't change that." Dorathea set her cup on its saucer and gave Sloane a stern look. "For now, leave Polydora to me, please."

The tone of her cousin's voice told Sloane that the subject of the GC wiċċe was off-limits. "All right. She's yours to investigate. But I'm going after the women in Alisdair's photograph."

"Then we must decide how you will detain them when you capture them," Dorathea said.

"Sounds good. I'll visit Andrew Gildey in the morning and ask him to explain how he knows the women in the picture."

"Alone? We have no idea if Andrew is even Magical, and if he is, how potent he might be," Dorathea said.

"She's right. Maybe I should go with you," Jack said.

Elvina grinned. "That's a good idea. We don't want Andrew to end up dead."

"Ha ha." Sloane glared at her. Over the past year, they had had three chances to interrogate a possible member of The Order, but she had killed each suspect before they could because she couldn't control her anger or strength, or both. She stood and pulled her tote strap over her head. "You'd just be in the way, Jack. No offense."

"None taken, lovey."

"Where are you going now?" Dorathea asked.

"I promised Rose I'd have lunch at the pub. I left her a bit abruptly last night. And I figured our Christmas plans are on hold, right?"

"I suppose they are," Dorathea said. "But please return promptly. We will train tonight. You need to prepare for your meeting with Andrew. And I know just the lesson you must learn."

CHAPTER SEVEN

A thick gray cloud cover had crept over the mountain, muting the bright winter sun. Pearl's heater blew cool air that didn't warm until Sloane was on Second Avenue and parked in the lot behind the Spotted Owl Inn and Pub. She grabbed a small gift box off the passenger's seat and shoved it into her cardigan pocket.

The street-level stairwell leading to the pub below was dimly lit. The amber light from two old brass wall sconces spread vainly into the darkness. The scent of burning wood and Chef's food wafted up to meet Sloane, and her stomach growled. Except for Freya's meat tart, she hadn't stepped away from the chaos to eat in over a day.

Rose was at the end of the bar and quickly turned her gaze to Sloane. Her stomach fluttered when the striking Dhampyre knew she had arrived before she had even appeared. Rose had stopped working the busy crowd to look at her as if she were the only one in the pub, making her legs weak.

"Hey, you. Right on time. What would you like to drink?" Rose asked, meeting her at the end barstool.

"Hi, yourself. Whiskey neat would be great. Thank you."
Sloane stretched over the bar and softly kissed her cheek. Rose
turned to the shelves of liquor. Her tightly curled auburn hair
was swept up in a loose bun, and errant strands had escaped a
headband of her family's tartan. She blew one to the side each
time it moved close to her eye. Watching her caused an urgency in
Sloane that differed from desire, although Rose's button-fly jeans
and black sweater worn close to her curves did light that fire.

Sloane climbed onto the stool and looked around. Rose and
Oscar had decorated the Keane's quaint family pub in traditional
Scottish trimmings, and Gaelic melodies played above the
conversational din.

Rose returned with Sloane's drink and squeezed her hand. "I
was so scared for you after you left."

Her touch was electric, sending the same intensity through
Sloane that it had the night before. "Believe me. Scaring you was
the last thing I wanted to do."

Rose grinned and leaned over the bar. "I have the power to
make you stay if your coven keeps messing with us. I'm very
skilled at mind compulsion. I could *make* you do anything I want."

Sloane got closer. "You wouldn't have to *make* me do anything."

Rose bit her lower lip, her eyes filling with desire. Then she
glanced at the counter flap at the other end of the bar. Oscar stood
there, holding an order up and shaking it at her. "Ugh. Gotta go.
One Chef's Christmas dinner for you, on the house. I'll be back
in a few minutes."

Sloane sipped her drink while the flood of adrenaline that
Rose had caused moved through her. She looked around the
dining room and bar again, recognizing several faces among the
patrons. The couples and families, as well as the singles at the bar,
all seemed happy enough. This wasn't a morose, nothing-to-do-
for-Christmas crowd. She wasn't surprised. Chef's cooking was
better than anyone here could do at their finest hour. And in her
experience, the holidays were seldom anybody's finest hour.

Her gaze settled on a family at a table beside a large stone
fireplace. A young boy was busy playing with a car, no doubt from
Santa Claus. The boy drove it over the table and up the side of the

chimney. He looked happy, without fear, safe in his family's care. Sloane hated that the Nogicals were unaware of the danger they were in. They had no idea The Order would have no problem killing them. Ignorant they were a means to an end.

Her drink was almost gone when Rose returned. "Traditional Christmas dinner, like being at home. Turkey and all the trimmings." She set the plate in front of Sloane.

"Home for some people. My mother didn't do conventional. We usually had takeout from a Chinese place on 73rd Street." Sloane breathed in the aromas. "My mouth's already watering."

"Your mom definitely had quirky culinary tastes," Rose said, and the smile she gave Sloane was both heartwarming and sympathetic. Then she grinned. "Wait until you have dessert. And I don't mean Chef's."

The scent of sandalwood and Rose's flirting muddled Sloane's thoughts, and she sat there speechless.

"I love this side of you, West. All flushed and bothered."

"You keep looking at me that way. You might have to get used to it," Sloane said when she found her words.

"Can you tell me what's happening?" Rose's voice was serious.

Sloane hesitated. Then she told herself not to lie. Not anymore. "The Order has escalated its plans," she said in a low voice. "They assaulted a Protector Coven, the Gòrdans, in the Northeast Quadrant. Which is why I was called away from you last night. Elspeth, their youngest member, escaped through a portal to the cottage. She told us her coven needed our help. When we arrived, her grandfather, Alisdair, was the only survivor. Her parents were dead."

"Oh, my God. The poor girl."

"There's more. The Order killed her uncle in our crypt."

"Here? They're here again?"

Sloane nodded. "I don't think they ever left. Alisdair had been gathering information about them. We found the evidence in his library. He had a photo of three people we suspect are members. One woman we identified as a member of the Northeast Quadrant's GC. We don't know who the other woman is." She lowered her voice. "The man sitting behind the two women is Andrew Gildey."

A tray clattered against the floor, and they turned to the noise. Oscar picked it up, staring at them. Sloane thought she had shared the information quietly, even for the Dhampyre's supernatural hearing, but he had obviously understood every word. And the news had evidently shocked him.

"Oh my God, you must be right. The Blodaeters Assembly voted to join the Grand Covens against The Order. My da and mam attended the meeting with their quadrant's GC earlier today. The GC said nothing about the Gòrdans. If they had, my father would have told us."

"That doesn't surprise me." Sloane smeared a piece of turkey breast through cranberry relish, trying not to react to Rose's news. If the Blodaeters were entering the battle, Rose might put herself in danger. Her pulse quickened at the thought.

"Well, you know what doesn't surprise me? That the Gildeys are involved. How else does a family amass that much wealth?"

Sloane swallowed a bite of mashed sweet potatoes. "Not all rich people are evil, Keane."

"Right, but I'm talking about the super-wealthy. Somewhere, at some point in history, someone in their family made a deal, fixing their moral compass toward greed. Why else would anyone live with outrageous amounts of money while even one person in this world sleeps on the streets and dies from malnutrition?"

"I agree." Sloane frowned. "I also think us Magicals could be doing more. Starting with telling the Nogicals they're in danger."

"Ooh, not a good idea," Rose said, lowering her voice even more. "Their ability to live peacefully with those different from them ended thousands of years ago. Your kind were the last Magicals to live openly among them. And by that time, they feared each other as much as they feared us." She poured Sloane a glass of water from the bar gun. "Just consider the sickening things they do to each other because of slight differences in appearance and lifestyle. Could you imagine what they'd do to us?" The air around Rose sizzled with energy, and she took a deep breath. "Sorry, their atrocities make me so angry."

"Trust me, I understand." Sloane could not only feel Rose's rage, but she saw it dance like fire in the Daywalker's green eyes. "I know what Nogicals are capable of. But evil doesn't corrupt all of them."

"But it can."

"True. And it can corrupt Magicals, too. We know of several who have already joined The Order. And last March, Lore told me there were more. But that doesn't mean we are all joining."

Rose hesitated. "Okay, that's true. Still, revealing ourselves to them is too big a risk."

"Unless the benefits outweigh the costs."

"Except in this situation, history tells us what the consequences would be. It's impossible to change their behavior now."

Sloane shook her head. "After what I've learned in the last year, Keane, I no longer believe in the impossible."

At that, Rose laughed. Quick and loud and full-throated. She glanced at Sloane's plate. "Are you finished?"

Sloane nodded, and while Rose placed the dinnerware in a dish tub under the bar, she removed the small gift box from her pocket and scooted it across the bar.

Rose noticed the gift right away and straightened. "Is this for me?"

"Yes. Open it." The excitement in Rose's voice went right to Sloane's heart, melting it. She caught Oscar out of the corner of her eye. He had stopped in the middle of the dining room and was frowning at her. She figured he still didn't trust her not to break his sister's heart again, but he was wrong. Sloane had left Denwick last March to settle the life she'd had in New York City. It had taken her almost six months to sort out her apartment, grieve her failed marriage, her mother, and begin the process of healing. She had avoided all communication from the Island, including Rose's calls. Yes, she hurt her, but she had made her amends. Now she was staying in Denwick, staying with Rose, if Rose would have her.

Slowly sliding her slender fingers along the seam of the paper, Rose unwrapped the present. She opened the black velvet jewelry box, and her eyes widened. "Oh, wow."

"Do you like it?"

She looked up, her expression soft. "I love it."

"Here, let me." Sloane took the necklace, unhooking it, and Rose turned around, craning backwards so Sloane could slide the silver chain around her neck and close the clasp. When Rose faced her again, she was looking down and holding the mottled jade pendant between her fingers. "I thought it would set off your eyes," Sloane said. "I was right."

"It's beautiful." Rose's visible skin erupted in gooseflesh. "I need you to come with me."

Sloane met her at the kitchen door, and Rose took her hand. She had never been in the pub's kitchen or back rooms, had never met the famous Chef. As they passed through the stainless steel prep area, she caught a glimpse of a bald man with tattoos covering his neck and head, but Rose didn't stop to introduce them.

Rose closed the door to a small office behind them. The light from the kitchen disappeared, and the windowless room became too dark to see. She took Sloane's face in both hands and kissed her with an intensity that made Sloane's knees buckle. Her arms steadied Sloane as they stumbled back against a low cabinet.

There was no talking, no savoring. Their tongues twined in a dance of possession that left Sloane molten inside. She slipped one hand under Rose's sweater, aching to feel her soft skin, while she felt along the table with her other hand, seeking a stable place to support their bodies. A few steps to the left, they fell against the office wall. Pressed together, Rose's hands slid up Sloane's sides and removed her T-shirt with ease.

Sloane had never allowed anyone to take her this way. A quick gasp of pleasure escaped her as Rose grasped her hips and nipped at her neck. Each bite flooded her core with blood, leaving her swollen and throbbing to be touched.

Rose lowered her hips, grinding her pelvis over Sloane's, rhythmically, over and over, only stopping to take Sloane's nipple into her mouth, sucking and flicking its erectness, holding her breast gently as she moved to the other one.

"Oh my fucking, God." Sloane's voice was more of an exhalation than words.

"Mmhm," Rose murmured and moved her mouth back to Sloane's, kissing her deeply, pulling their pelvises together again.

Sloane grabbed Rose's hips, positioning her, guiding her movements. Her breath was coming harder. She struggled to keep the sensations flooding her core from coming to focus too quickly. She wanted to feel the buildup longer, let it become stronger. But the sound of Rose releasing, her back arching, sent Sloane over the edge. Their bodies melted into each other after the last wave, and they held each other as their breathing eased.

"That was—"

Banging on the door interrupted Sloane, and Oscar shouted, "Absolutely not. Whatever's come over you, shake it. I'm not running the bar and the floor alone."

They listened to him stomp away and erupted into laughter.

Sloane held Rose close again and whispered, "Jesus, Keane, the way you make me feel."

Rose nestled her head against Sloane's neck. "The feeling's mutual." She tightened their embrace. "I have a gift for you, too. Upstairs. You could open it tonight if you stayed over."

"I would like that."

"Do I hear a but coming?"

"I want to spend the night with you, every night, but I can't tonight. Dorathea's expecting me for training, and I have to question Andrew Gildey in the morning."

"That sounds dangerous. Are you going alone?"

Sloane kissed her forehead in the dark and said, "Yes, but I'll be safe. Then I'm all yours tomorrow night."

CHAPTER EIGHT

The covenstead smelled of angelica, cinnamon, and sage. Sloane recognized the scent from childhood. Every day her mother would steep the root, bark, and herb in a small pot. Sloane now knew the brew was a protection spell. She also had a better idea of why Jane and she needed it. Her mother must have known about The Order before the magical world even gave the conspirators the name.

Dorathea, Elvina, and Jack waited for her in the sitting area near the large, stone inglenook fireplace. She could feel the roaring flames from across the room. The door closed behind Sloane, and she looked up. "Thanks, Alfred." A gentle breeze tussled her long black hair.

She sat in an armchair beside Jack. "Where's Elspeth?"

"The poor child is asleep upstairs." Elvina frowned. "I can't imagine what she's feeling. Her mother and father are gone. We haven't even told her about Calen."

"Why not? You didn't mind dropping a bombshell on the kid before," Sloane said, and Elvina wrinkled her nose and looked away.

"We'll tell her tomorrow, lovey. I used a considerable amount of energy to calm her," Jack said, his voice stolid, and Sloane thought he could use getting in touch with his sorrow.

Dorathea stood. "Let us begin your training while the child sleeps."

They followed Dorathea to a dark wooden lectern surrounded by three stools. With the wave of her hand, Dorathea opened a thick, leather-bound tome. It was the *Book of Hagorúnum*, the Wiċċan book of spells and curses. Its pages fluttered to a stop, and the High Priestess took her place behind the podium, placing her spectacles on the tip of her nose.

"The purpose of this training is to ensure you can detain and banish members of The Order—"

"Without killing them. Yeah, I know," Sloane said.

"Quite right." Dorathea peered at her through the round lenses and turned her attention to the book. "I have given our purpose much consideration. And believe I have figured out the best way to achieve it. You will learn three spells to detain and banish the magical members of The Order. But it will take the power of three to send the Half-Malevolents to the Abyss."

Sloane sat on a stool. "All right. I'm ready."

"We must teach you to summon our prison block from *Drusnirwd*. The four cells will be both real and transitory. You will learn to detain magical members within the cells. Once they are imprisoned, you will send them to our covenstead."

Sloane stared at her cousin. How the hell was she going to learn how to do all that in one night? She was still struggling to flick a light switch on and off. Now, Dorathea wanted her to summon a building, or part of one?

"Oh, how exciting," Elvina said, her voice purring. "I've been waiting for this day."

"Ooh, me too," Jack said. "Sloane learning to summon might just lift all our spirits."

Sloane shot a glare at them and turned back to Dorathea. "You said I wasn't ready for summoning."

"I did indeed. You are still unprepared. However, we have no more time to wait. We must capture and secure our enemies. As you said earlier, we must do so undetected, or they will go underground. Since we are unsure who we can trust in our Grand Coven, or the Weardas, and Drusnirwd guards, we must detain The Order members here in our covenstead."

"Here? Surely the prison would be a more proper location than our home," Jack said nervously.

Dorathea swept her arm through the air, and a hologram-like image formed in the library. The bored books, zigging from one shelf to another, settled quickly into open spaces, the constant sound of their movement quieting.

Sloane stared at the narrow concrete hall, separating four rooms made of thick stone blocks with iron-barred doors, two cells on each side. A section of Drusnirwd. "Jesus, Denham. How'd you do that?"

"I used a specific type of summoning spell. The one you will learn today."

"This isn't rational. How the hell am I going to make an entire room materialize?"

"We are beyond the reasonable. We must do what is necessary." Dorathea left the lectern and stood beside the stark prison cells. "Every Protector Coven has a section in their city's prison. These four cells belong to us. I have placed a *behydan* spell on them, concealing them at Drusnirwd. It forbids anyone from entering our prison block for five days unless I permit it. Even the Grand Coven will be unaware of whom we detain within these walls." She waved her hand, and the chambers disappeared.

"How? They weren't really here, right?" Sloane asked, confused.

"They were here in a state of transition. The spell to summon is *Čīeġ*, to call. It can be the root of many spells and curses. When we add *hwílwende*, which means transitory elements, whatever we summon will lend itself to us, but only for a limited time. In this case, the hwílwende will be our prison cells." Dorathea flicked her wrist and said, "Čīeġ hwílwende." The same type of image appeared, this time, Sloane's cottage living room.

"Whoa." Sloane got to her feet and walked through the image, making the Christmas tree, fireplace, and furniture ripple in the air. "This is real?"

Dorathea gestured and said, "You may sit in your beloved armchair."

Sloane touched the faint image of her chair. Solid. She sat. The chair held her weight. "Jesus Christ, this shit just keeps blowing me away."

Dorathea sighed. "Please refrain from the dramatics, pet. Your living room is here, but not here. It is in the cottage, but not. It is real in both places, but only temporarily so. It's a simple concept."

"Oh, yeah. So simple," Sloane said, sarcastically, and she had a thought. "So if I stay in the chair and you send it back to the cottage, I return there, too? Sounds like it would save me a walk home, or a teleport."

"We call it bestealce, dear."

Sloane looked at Elvina. "You know I know that, right?"

The former familiar lifted her chin. "It's still my job to remind you."

"You can travel in a hwílwende," Jack said to her as she returned to her stool. "But you have to be very careful. If you think it's bad to bestealce…" His body shivered. "Let's just say, if you mess up, you're left dead but not."

"He is right indeed. The incantation is quite dangerous. Whatever, or whoever, is within the hwílwende's borders will remain there, and if they are not properly returned, they will linger in a corporeal state forever. Nevertheless, it is the only way to hold our suspects."

"Jesus. I'd rather learn to čīeġ some whiskey," Sloane said, the words knotting her tongue.

"It's čīeġ, dear," Elvina said. "Chee-gah. Like *league*. Are you practicing your Old English pronunciations?"

"Yeah, I am."

"Clearly, not enough," Elvina said. "And hwílwende is wheel-wen-deh."

"Maybe my lack of progress has more to do with my teacher than my ability."

Jack elbowed Sloane's side and motioned with his head at Dorathea. Her cousin was scowling, her hands resting atop the Book of Hagorúnum.

"All right. This is serious. I'm ready," Sloane said with an apologetic smile. "What do you want me to do first?"

Dorathea snapped her fingers, and a rolled-up paper appeared in Sloane's lap. "Familiarize yourself with Drusnirwd. You must have an unobstructed view of our block of cells when you open your third eye."

"Wait. I have to open my third eye for this?"

"Oh, yes, lovey. You must visualize what you want to summon. It's harder than thinking or saying, 'Ooh, I'd like a glass of wine tonight,' and it magically appears."

Elvina cackled, and when her laughter stopped, she said, "That is why Jane's first summons flopped, and we had pasta and seafood to clean up for days. She wasn't ready to hold so many images in her third eye."

Sloane smiled. She remembered the story they told her about her mother. The idea that Jane had done something so spontaneous and risky seemed foreign to her. But she was beginning to understand her mother was forced to mask her true self after being driven into hiding.

"If you two are finished..." Dorathea said sternly. Then her face tempered. "Think of how you use your third eye when you bestealce. You open it and perceive yourself where you are and where you intend to be, holding the images there until you cast your spell. But when you use a čīeġ, you visualize the thing you wish to summon and where you want to place it."

"All right." Sloane unrolled the paper. It was a blueprint of Tagridore's prison and several photos of the West Coven's four cells with chiseled Ws above the barred doors. "I just visualize these in my third eye and say čīeġ? And they appear?"

"What? No. Could you imagine what would happen if the prison chambers appeared here *as they are*? My God, it would be a catastrophe. You can summon a bottle of wine after you've chosen a location for it to appear. But not the section of an entire building. We'd all die," Jack said with a panicked voice.

"Jesus, Jack. Don't pass out. I'm not going to kill us. I know I have to add whil-wenda."

"Wheel-wen-deh," Elvina corrected.

"Yeah. Yeah." Sloane looked at Jack again. Since they discovered Calen was missing, her cousin hadn't been his usual self, and now that they knew Calen was dead, he was barely holding it together. "Hey, are you okay?"

"I'm…I don't…Apparently not." His eyes filled with tears.

"It's all right, Jack," Sloane said, and gave Dorathea a look that said, *We're taking a break*. She wrapped her arm around his and walked him back to the sitting area. "You must be wrecked. You just lost Calen. And you haven't had time to process it. But you need to. The sadness isn't going away. When it surfaces, let it." Sloane waved her hand and extinguished the candles in the candelabras floating above them. She guided him into his armchair, sat on the chair's arm, and hugged him. "Stay here and cry until you have no more tears. Then do it again when they come back."

Jack nodded and buried his face in her side, sobbing. When his tears ebbed, he told her, "Calen almost fainted when he saw you in your office last week. He said it was like seeing your mother sitting there. I didn't tell you, but they went to school together. He was very fond of her. Everyone was." His voice trailed off, replaced with silent tears.

A few minutes later, Sloane returned to the lectern, and Elvina gently stroked her back. "That was very kind of you, dear. Calen's death seems to have dealt your cousin a heavy blow."

Sloane nodded, her gut telling her she needed to know the source of Jack's anguish.

She picked up the prison's blueprint again and studied the pictures of the West Coven's jail cells. After securing their image in her mind, she rolled the paper up and placed it on the lectern.

"Are you ready to begin?" Dorathea asked.

"Ready as I'll ever be." Sloane pulled her hair back in a low ponytail and pushed up the sleeves of her favorite navy cardigan, then stood at the library entrance.

"Very well. Jack was correct," Dorathea said, as she joined her. "When you summon items, they must fit within the area that you bring them. The ċīeġ hwílwende allows us to call forth items, temporarily, and fit them into the space we have at hand. That is why we can hold the cells here at the covenstead. And you can conjure them wherever you are. That is the first step. Repeat the incantation after me...Ċīeġ hwílwende."

"Chee-ga Wheel-windy," Sloane said.

"Ooh, okay. Better." Elvina said. "But it isn't *ga* though. Remember ċīeġ rhymes with league, like cheague. And it's not *windy*. It's *whehndeh*."

Sloane tried again. "Ċīeġ hwílwende." A shimmery movement glinted in the library. Enough to make the books scatter and reshelve themselves again.

Dorathea peered into the room. "I do believe you called forth our prison block, albeit briefly."

Elvina joined them and stood on Sloane's other side. "Oh, yes. I saw it too." Her dark-brown almond-shaped eyes grew round. "Your mother and I always knew you would be capable of greatness."

Sloane acted as if Elvina's comment didn't affect her, but it did. The damning messages of why she didn't save her mother played every time someone praised her. She had spent the summer in New York City seeing a therapist, working through her trust and anger issues. Her therapist had told her to acknowledge the negative messages she told herself, let them pass, then replace them with positive ones. But she didn't know what the hell was positive about losing most of her family and not being able to save them.

"Try again. These spells will require incredible concentration," Dorathea said, regaining Sloane's attention. You must connect more deeply than you ever have with your natural ability to protect. Whilst alone, facing a member of The Order, you must draw from this desire to defend *yourself*."

The emphasis in the High Priestess's voice on "yourself" made Sloane look away. She didn't try to be reckless. The behavior often preceded her thinking. She had no reason for rage to harbor in her marrow, but no matter how hard she tried to release it, it stayed.

"But if you're struggling, you can draw upon other desires, too. Such as safeguarding us, or Rose," Elvina said.

"Quite, right. But when the danger is imminent, you must first defend yourself. Hesitating to think about someone else could cost your life. You can save no one if you are dead." The softness in Dorathea's voice made Sloane think of Jane and the times her mother had had to soothe her anger when she was a child.

"Fine. I'll concentrate on protecting myself." Sloane closed her eyes, opened her third eye, and visualized the prison cells. But she only saw them briefly before her third eye filled with the images of The Order killing Jane, the runaway garbage truck smashing into the side of her mother's car. Her inability to stop Jane from being a victim overwhelmed her, and she shouted, "Ċīeġ hwílwende."

In a flash of brilliant white light, the cells appeared in the library.

She opened her eyes to find Dorathea and Elvina staring at the prison block. "What's wrong?" Sloane asked and walked over to a barred door. She grabbed one of the iron bars. "It's here. I did the spell. First try."

"You did indeed," Dorathea said. "May I ask how you tapped into your energy?"

Sloane's face warmed. "I focused on my desire to save my mother, not myself. I was pissed for not protecting her, for not even knowing she was in danger." Dorathea put her arm around Sloane's shoulders. It was uncommon for her cousin to show so much affection. Sloane hesitated. "You don't have to remind me not to cast a spell in anger. I know the rules."

"I believe you do. Let's move on," Dorathea said. "After you have summoned our prison block to wherever you are, you will detain the conspirators inside using the *bescufan* spell, which means to throw. Once you have captured them, you will cast the *efthweorfe* incantation, which means to return, and the prison block will reappear here."

Just then, Alfred sent a rush of air through the room, and the covenstead door opened. Elspeth entered and looked around. Her fearful gaze locked on Jack, and he waved her over. She climbed onto the sofa beside his armchair, and he snapped his fingers. A lavender container and a bottle of fizzy water appeared on the coffee table, and she gave him a slight smile.

"Looks like their common grief will keep them occupied," Elvina said.

"Yes, indeed. Grief does have a way of bringing us together when we are falling apart." Dorathea waved her hand, and the prison block disappeared, replaced by the cottage's living room again. "To learn the bescufan spell, you will choose an item in the covenstead and then throw it into the hwílwende."

"Why'd you switch back to my living room?" Sloane asked.

"Because we have to be able to check if you return the item in the hwílwende correctly," Elvina said. "We can't just drop into Drusnirwd whenever we want. Even if it is to look at our block of cells."

"Fine." Sloane looked around the room. "I'll send my tote."

"Oh, I would advise against that," Jack called to her. "Choose something you have no attachment to, especially your first time."

Elspeth raised her brow. "What is she doing?"

"An efthweorfe spell. It's our spell for returning things."

"Oh." She studied Sloane for a moment. "But she's old. Why doesn't she know how?"

Jack didn't respond right away. Then he cleared his throat and said, "No one taught her how when she was your age. And her mother and grandparents are not alive to teach her now. But she found us. And we are teaching her."

Elspeth listened to him, her frown deepening, and when he finished talking, she left the sofa and walked to Sloane. She didn't speak, only threw her tiny arms around Sloane's waist and silently cried. Sloane lifted the young girl into her arms and held her until Jack gathered her and carried her back to the sofa. Frustration swelled inside Sloane as she watched him use a calming spell on the child. The Order had caused so much pain, and a voice inside her head told her none of the traitors deserved to live.

"Are you ready?" Dorathea asked.

"Yeah." Sloane scrubbed her face with her hands and took a deep breath. "All right. I'll use a throw pillow."

"Good choice." Elvina snapped her fingers, and a pillow from the sofa appeared at their feet. "Mind your pronunciation. It's beh-shu-van. Bescufan."

"Got it." Sloane formed the words silently, one syllable at a time, and connected with a resolve to protect Elspeth from experiencing any more devastating loss. She cast the spell, and the pillow flew into the air. Then she flung her arm toward the hwílwende of her living room, hurling the dark-sapphire cushion against her favorite armchair.

"Hooray," Elspeth cheered, clapping her small hands.

"Very nice indeed," Dorathea said, smiling at the child. She looked at Sloane. "The last step is to send the prisoners back to the covenstead. This requires the efthweorfe incantation. We are unable to repair disordered matter, so it requires your utmost focus."

"Disordered matter? Jesus Christ, Denham. Don't you think there's less of a chance I'd kill them with my bare hands?"

"All the reason you need to practice the spell until you can cast it correctly on the first try," Dorathea said.

"It is pronounced, efth-weh-ohr-fe," Elvina said slowly. "Repeat it several times."

Sloane spoke the word inside her head several times, each articulation becoming less clear than the last. She threw her hands up. "Why the hell do our spells have to be in Old English? Can't we modernize them?"

"Calm yourself, dear," Elvina said. "Be patient and keep practicing. The word will come."

"Tell that to the pillow," Sloane replied. They were silent for a beat, and then laughter filled the room. It was a much-needed release of the tension that was building.

"You are so like your mother." Elvina lay her head on Sloane's shoulder.

When her former familiar straightened, Sloane looked up. "Sorry if I destroy your throw pillow, Alfred. I know you just redecorated. Which looks great by the way." She looked at the sapphire cushion on her armchair, closed her eyes, and visualized the return of her living room to the cottage. When she was confident, she said, "Efthweorfe."

The cottage's living room disappeared. But the outline of the throw pillow stayed.

"Oh, hell. That's not good." Sloane stared at the pixelated cushion.

"It's not, dear. The poor pillow will never be the same," Elvina said, without hiding her amusement, and Jack and Elspeth giggled uncontrollably.

"Summon a tea service," Dorathea called to Jack. "It's going to be a long night."

CHAPTER NINE

Last night's training at the hobbit house lasted until the early morning, and Sloane had only slept a few hours. Nothing a pot of Elvina's favorite Kona dark roast couldn't fix. She poured a third cup and sat at the breakfast table, staring into the garden through the bay window. Yesterday's cloud cover had moved out, and the trees and planting beds were becoming visible in the sun's first light.

When her phone's alarm dinged at eight a.m., she picked it up and made a call. "I need to see Andrew Gildey. Today. Preferably this morning," she told the man who answered. It wasn't a request for him to put her in Andrew's schedule. It was a demand.

"Mr. Gildey will not be in the office today. He is out for the holidays until after the New Year. You will need to make an appointment, and he is booked until January seventh. Would you like me to schedule you?"

Sloane ended the call without responding. Her best bet was to find Andrew at home. She tapped Alisdair's photo on the tabletop and sipped her coffee. She wanted to see the flash of recognition in the Gildey heir's eyes when she showed him the picture of himself and the two women, to catch his tell when he lied. That's all she needed. She didn't expect him to be forthcoming about his association with Ginerva Byrne or the other woman, and she also wasn't afraid he would hurt her. If either he or his mother, Isobel, wanted to kill her when she was alone without her coven, they would have done so by now.

She rinsed her coffee mug and placed it in the sink, donned her peacoat, and grabbed her tote. It was time to let the Gildeys know her coven suspected they weren't who they pretended to be.

A few minutes later, Sloane drove Pearl up the winding Mount Sutton Road. The Gildeys' mammoth home, an old-world stone castle looming on the side of the mountain, came into view. Why the hell did anyone need that much roof over their head? Even the cottage was more home than she needed. Bigger than anyone needed. Living there made her feel like a hypocrite, especially with Dorathea next door. She could sell the cottage and convince the coven to live together at the hobbit house. Yeah, she'd discuss the idea with Dorathea.

Sloane slowed Pearl as she approached the stone security building outside the Gildey mansion. The sizable iron gate that surrounded the estate was closed, and a man stepped from the guardhouse into the driveway. No one had met her there last week when she first visited the castle. Then again, Isobel had invited her to discuss a business proposal, which was strange in itself because, according to Rose, no other villagers had ever stepped inside the manor.

She studied the man and thought he must be the Gildey's greeting for uninvited guests. He had to be near seven feet tall, and he was built. Overengineered but not in a steroid way. He had a sloping forehead and shoulder-length hair surgically parted down the middle and tucked behind his ears. Sloane thought if the coven was right about the Gildeys being Magical, this man was an ogre or a giant or some creature, and the human form before her was masking his real identity.

She rolled down Pearl's window. "Hey, how are you?"

"State your business." The man's voice boomed through the car, and his eyes didn't quite meet hers, his gaze falling somewhere above her head.

"All right. No need to be rude." Sloane continued to stare at him and was startled when he finally looked at her. His eyes were dark as night and bore into her. "I'm here to see Andrew Gildey," she said, and quickly looked away.

He stepped back inside the guard booth. A moment later, his arm stuck out the door and waved at her to go ahead. The imposing gate crept open.

"Jesus Christ," she mumbled. If she had to detain that behemoth, he'd barely have room to stand up in the prison cell.

She stared at the intricately designed brick pavers of the Gildeys' front yard. The grassless, greenless space of bronze and marble statuary was missing something. Snow. The Gildeys were wealthy enough to heat the space, she thought. But that wouldn't make everything bone dry. Only a spell could do that.

She struck the iron knocker against the castle's massive ebony double doors and waited. A moment later, the same elderly man she had met before appeared. The top of his head was bald, and he wore a neatly trimmed, half-moon of silver hair below it. After shutting the doors behind them, he led her to the drawing room. His body bent slightly at the shoulders, and his steps so slow she had to avoid clipping his heels.

They entered the formal room, and he held out his arm. "Your coat and bag, Ms. West."

"No need. I won't be here that long. I just need a word with Mr. Gildey," she said, holding her tote close to her side.

He dropped his arm without responding and left Sloane beside a silver Christmas tree that rose to the height of the cathedral ceiling. They had decorated it in red and gold. Well not them—a professional probably had. Sloane glanced around the room. It resembled a picture out of a style magazine. Porcelain nativity scenes. Tall crystal vases filled with glittery ornaments. But there wasn't any garland, holly, or velvet ribbon to give the space a warm and cozy atmosphere. She guessed the rich liked it stark and expensive.

The last time she was in the grand foyer, the butler had quickly ushered her into Isobel's large study. She hadn't had time to check out the regal portraits of the family members that hung on the walls. They shared an uncanny family resemblance, the same dark hair and square jaws. The portraitists captured their likenesses in muted palettes of grays and browns, except for their eyes. Their eyes were painted with intense colors.

Sloane looked for Andrew's portrait, but the heir apparent didn't have one hanging with his ancestors. Maybe because each of the male descendants was displayed with a wife, and from what she remembered about Andrew, he hadn't married. Maybe he was gay. And she made a mental note to have Jack check him out.

"Ms. West. What a surprise," a sharp voice said, sending a shiver through Sloane. She quickly turned to face the Gildey matriarch. Isobel's silver-white hair fell perfectly along her chiseled jawline, and she wore a silver cashmere sweater with a scoop neck and a necklace with a multifaceted ruby the size of a quarter, the chandelier's light dancing off it.

"Yeah, I suppose you aren't used to drop-ins. I told James that I needed to speak to Andrew."

Isobel looked at her, confused. "Who is James?"

"Your butler, or whatever you call him."

"I assure you, we do not call him James. His name is Peter, and he's an important part of our family. He's been with us his entire life."

"Just not important enough to hang up on these walls."

Isobel's eyes narrowed. "Mr. Gildey is not here. You can give me your message. I'll be sure to pass it along."

A third set of doors off the foyer opened, and two young women in dark-gray uniforms entered. They carried a covered platter and a tea service. Sloane recognized one of them. Heddie. The young woman had served an afternoon tea when she last sat in Isobel's spacious meeting room. Sloane stared at the study's double doors. Isobel was entertaining someone, and that someone could be Andrew.

"Let's see if he's not here," Sloane said and walked toward the study.

"Stop right there," Isobel said, and the air in the room crackled like a live wire.

Sloane stopped and faced her. Isobel's stare felt as electric as the air did. No need for a detection spell, she thought. Isobel Gildey *was* a Magical—what kind didn't matter much at the moment.

"You will leave us now. I suggest making an appointment with Mr. Gildey's assistant if you need to speak with him. In the future, do not visit our home without an invitation. I will no longer grant you entry. You can be sure, Trevor, our guard, will honor my wishes."

For a moment, Sloane was unable to respond. A heavy dread clouded her thoughts. Was Isobel causing her confusion? Was she a Sensor? The corners of Isobel's mouth turned up. "I see you have nothing else to say, so if you'll excuse me. I do have a guest. In my humble opinion, one of the most visionary people in the world whom I shouldn't keep waiting."

Sloane's body fought against the confusion, the struggle frustrating her. Her growing anger cleared her head, and she opened her tote, retrieving Alisdair's photo. "They'll just have to wait, Isobel. I need to know what business the Gildeys have in Kirkcudbright, Scotland." She detected surprise and a flash of recognition on Isobel's face. "That's right. I know Andrew was there. And I know who he met." She thrust the snapshot at her. "What I want to know is why. Because I don't think the women he met there are in the salmon or real-estate development business." She braced herself for any number of violent reactions to her outburst. But Isobel only became more delighted with each word Sloane shouted.

"Are you finished?" Isobel smiled at her. "I can only assume by your aggressive tone that you think I keep tabs on Andrew's travels. I can assure you, I do not. The Gildeys have no business dealings in Kirkcudbright. As for why my son was there, that's his business." She looked at the photo. "Whoever those people are is also his business. I'm sure he'll tell you the same."

Sloane stared brazenly into Isobel's emerald-green eyes. "Oh, I think he'll talk to me. And trust me, I'm prepared for what he has to say."

CHAPTER TEN

Driving down Mount Sutton Road, Sloane slowed when she caught sight of a massive scar on the mountainside cut deep into the valley. This was the clear-cut that had upset the residents of Old Denwick for months. The Gildeys had secured permits to clear a large swath of old-growth forest for a housing development.

A major casualty of the Gildeys' war against the environment was the thousands of wintering animals forced to move. Sloane looked from side to side for blacktail deer and coyotes. Their deaths on the road were a daily conversation at the Spotted Owl pub, and she didn't want to add to the carnage. The Island had only been her permanent home for a short time, but her desire to defend it and all its inhabitants from senseless destruction was palpable.

She now had no doubt the Gildeys were evil Magicals. Since colonizing the area, they had displaced the Indigenous populations and stolen their coastlines and livelihoods to amass their fortune. But how did they escape detection by the West Coven? Water under the bridge, she told herself. They weren't going to escape their coven now.

Her cell phone buzzed. She looked at the screen and smiled. "Hey, Keane. What a nice surprise."

"Are you at home?" Rose asked. She sounded defensive.

"I'm headed there. Are you all right?"

"Have you talked to Andrew Gildey yet?" Rose whispered, but her vigilant tone remained.

"I tried, but he wasn't home. What's wrong?"

"I just opened the pub, and our first customer is drinking coffee at the bar. He's wearing a bespoke suit and dark glasses. He said he's waiting for you."

Sloane lifted her eyebrows. "Is that right?"

"What do you want me to do?"

"Absolutely nothing, Keane. He's dangerous."

"He might be. But I promise you, he should be more afraid of Oscar and me."

"I don't doubt it. But please don't do anything. Promise me." Sloane glanced at her wristwatch and pressed the gas. "I'll be there in fifteen minutes."

"Not even a wee bit of mind compulsion? I could make Andrew Gildey as docile as a puppy for you."

"As much as I want to see that, please don't expose yourself. The Gildeys are definitely Magicals. But we don't know what kind yet."

"Okay, fine. We'll be good."

Sloane tossed her phone on the passenger seat. Her thoughts raced as fast as Pearl sped through the valley toward the coast. Why the hell was Andrew waiting for her at the pub? It was only the second time the heir to the Gildey fortune had graced the Keanes' door. Did he know Rose...the Keanes...were Magical? Her hands gripped the steering wheel. It wasn't a coincidence, she thought. He was sending her a warning.

Sloane parked, hurried down the underground stairwell, two steps at a time, and entered the Spotted Owl. She saw Oscar first. He was seating three Nogicals at a table. They grinned at him, which most women did, as well as most men for that matter.

Rose's brother had high cheekbones, black, tightly curled hair, and dreamy, gold-brown eyes that matched his warm brown skin. He was nearly as stunning as his sister.

Andrew sat alone at the bar, and Rose stood at the other end from him, her hands on her hips, watching him like a grizzly bear protecting her cub. Sloane trusted that neither of the Daywalkers had messed with Andrew's mind. And by the look on Rose's face, he was lucky they hadn't. A shiver ran through her.

Sloane leaned against the bar beside him. "All right, Mr. Gildey. I'm here. Why don't we sit?" She spoke to him as if their meeting had been scheduled for days.

They moved to a table in the back corner of the dining room. Sloane studied him. His fancy clothes. Gold watch and cufflinks. Black, wavy hair with hints of gray at his temples. Hair too thick for a man in his fifties. His flawless pale skin. No wrinkles, except she couldn't see his eyes. His crow's feet, or the attempt to lift them away, would reveal his age. Maybe that's why he wore dark glasses. Vanity.

He extended his hand. "Hello, Sloane West. We haven't officially met. I'm Andrew Gildey."

She shook his hand and said, "I got the impression your mother doesn't care about any of your business or what you get up to. Seems strange she would immediately warn you that I was looking for you."

"What makes you think Isobel told me? You also called my PA."

"Fair enough. But I didn't give him my name." She caught a slight smile flicker on his face. "It makes me wonder how else you would have known. Unless you have some special ability the rest of us don't have." She stared into his glasses, but she only saw the black of his lenses and the reflection of the light above their table.

"Superpowers?" He chuckled. "Isobel did inform me of your visit. And I would be lying if I said your insistence didn't pique my interest. It's not every day someone shows up at the Gildey home uninvited and demands to see one of us."

"So I heard. But come on. Piqued your interest? She told you why I wanted to talk to you." She paused. "But we'll get to that. I have another question. What do you drive?"

His brow furrowed. "Why?"

"Call me curious about how the half-percent lives."

"Hmm. Our chauffeur uses a few different vehicles. I'm not sure what they are right now. Bentley, perhaps? I've been driving myself lately. I have a Maybach."

Sloane thought about the Rolls-Royce that had idled in front of the cottage just a few nights before and raced off when she drove up. She would have the car's plates run soon enough, and then she would know how forthright Andrew Gildey was. "I've never even been inside a Bentley or Maybach. I prefer Pearl. She's an MG I inherited from my grandparents. My mother drove it too. Jane West. Maybe you've seen Pearl before?"

The chiseled, lean muscles in Andrew's jaw flinched, but before he could respond, Oscar approached the table. "Would you like menus?" he asked, setting a coffee cup in front of Sloane, filling it, and refilling Andrew's.

"Not for me." The Gildey heir's voice was flat as if he had leveled any emotion their conversation had provoked.

"Coffee is good for me. Thanks."

After Oscar left, Andrew glanced at his watch. "I need to be on my way. What did you want to ask me about my business trip to Scotland?"

"You're leaving already? I thought your PA said you were on holiday. Can't you spare me a few more minutes? Now that Denwick's my home, I'm eager to learn about my grandparents and my mother's time here. From the locals." She sipped her coffee. "How old are you? Midfifties? You must have known my mom and her friends."

He set his cup down. "I did know of your mother and her friends, but I'm a couple of years older. I also attended private schools."

"So did my mother."

"That might be, but I didn't socialize with them. Not really."

"With the locals?" Sloane made sure to point out his classism.

"That's not what I meant. My schooling…my parents…they made it impossible to spend time in Denwick, except for the Main Street Commerce Committee meetings. And my great-aunt's house." He paused, and Sloane was sure his eyes had looked away into the past. "I think I knew your mom when we were children. Our parents were on the committee together. But I hardly remember those days. So I don't have any stories to share with you. Or insight into what she was like when she lived here."

Sloane stared into his dark glasses for a long moment, unsure if his eyes were on her or not. By the time he had finished talking, she was seething. Furious that she sat across from the reason Jane was dead, but was unable to exact justice, to feel better, at least not yet.

He glanced at his watch again. "I do have another appointment, Ms. West."

"All right. I'll get to the point. I'm working on a murder investigation. Three dead. Same family. Two of the bodies were discovered in Kirkcudbright, Scotland. Ever been?"

He hesitated. "I guess you know that I have, or you wouldn't be asking."

"Which means Isobel also told you about the photo," Sloane said. "So, when were you last there?"

"I'd have to check my schedule. But it was some time last month."

"Okay. And were you aware that a man's body was found underneath your family's mausoleum in the crypt? He was the third member of the family. You wouldn't happen to know anything about these murders, would you?"

"I wasn't even aware the RCMP found someone dead in the crypt." He looked surprised. "When did this happen?"

"Late Christmas Eve or sometime early Christmas Day."

His jaw tensed again. "I'm sorry I can't help you. And I'm not a murderer. As for my travels to Kirkcudbright, they were for business. I don't know any families there."

"Isobel said the Gildeys have no business there."

"I was there for personal business. To look at art. It's called the artist's town for a reason."

Sloane removed the photo from her coat pocket and handed it to him. "Were these women selling you art?"

He glanced at the photo and handed it back. "I have no idea who they are. You can clearly see I was only sitting behind them." He scooted back in his chair and stood, staring down at her. "If you have any more questions for me, ask away. I don't share every aspect of my life with Isobel. And I advise you to stay away from her. She's not as…charitable as I am." He pulled a business card from an inside suit pocket and dropped it into Sloane's tote bag.

His voice was even, unthreatening, but the words weren't, and they chilled her. She watched him disappear into the stairwell leading to the street above.

"How did that go?" Rose appeared beside Sloane, and she jumped.

"Jesus. I didn't hear you."

"Sorry," Rose said, massaging Sloane's shoulders. "It was that bad, huh?"

"He's claiming he has no idea about the murders or who the women in the photo are. Not that I expected him to admit anything."

"And you think he's lying?"

"Oh, yeah. He's involved." She laid her hand on Rose's and moved it from her shoulder to her mouth, kissing it softly. "Luckily, he gave me an open invitation to contact him if I have any other questions."

Rose whispered, "That makes me nervous. Like you said, we don't even know what he is, do we? Did you…you know…test him?"

"I'll detect him when it's safe to. Inside your pub isn't safe."

"Good point." She gave Sloane's shoulders one last squeeze and sat. "I spoke with my da while you and Andrew were talking. They haven't heard any rumors about our Assemblies being compromised. But they're asking around. He and my mam know several Defender families of other species that they trust. They'll find out what's happening with their governments."

"I don't like that idea. Anyone in those families could be in The Order."

"You can't keep us from joining the fight, especially defending our own," Rose told her. "My da and mam can take care of themselves. So all you need to say is, 'Okay, Rose,' and smile."

"Okay, Rose." But Sloane couldn't bring herself to smile.

Rose sat forward and stretched her upper body over the table. "If you won't smile, at least use those beautiful, pouty lips to kiss me."

Rose's lips were soft, and her breath tasted of coffee. "Mmm," Sloane whispered after they sat back. "We should agree to disagree more often."

"Disagreements are unnecessary." Rose held the jade pendant, rubbing it with her fingers. "You can have my lips and anything else. Just ask."

With everything happening in their worlds, Sloane felt a twinge of guilt over the heat unfurling in her body, the desire to hide from it all, take Rose upstairs, and lock the door behind them. She was about to suggest the idea when Oscar approached the table, in a mood.

"I'm the only one who can hear the two of you, but I'm not the only one who can see you." He frowned at Rose. "You have a business to run…and drink orders to fill." He angrily strode away, his gait still graceful, and Sloane laughed even though she knew he could hear her.

"I think he's forgiven me, don't you?" she asked.

"He isn't worried you'll leave and break my heart again. Now he's convinced you've charmed me with this necklace."

"Charmed you? Is that a bad idea?" she asked, and Rose laughed. "How about I come over about eight tonight?"

"I'd love that." Rose glanced at the bar. "I'd better go. Your coffee's on the house."

Sloane stood to leave, and Elvina's voice filled her head.

Sloane, dear. The Grand Coven has summoned us. Please return to the covenstead. We must leave at once.

CHAPTER ELEVEN

The hobbit house's front door opened as Sloane sprinted up the steps. Once inside, a stiff wind pushed her toward the covenstead.

"Take it easy, Alfred. I got here as fast as I could," she said to the house spirit and joined Dorathea, Jack, and Elvina at the lectern. "What's got him so uptight?"

"The Grand Coven sent a few Weardas here without our permission." Dorathea strode into the library. "He is quite upset, as I am. Their behavior is unconscionable. Unbecoming of our leaders. And disrespectful to our coven."

"We aren't the only ones they're harassing," Elvina said. "The Weardas are also surveilling my mother and the café."

Dorathea stood in front of an enormous Lavinia Fontana painting and replied dryly, "Yes, but unlike your mother, we have not lied to the Grand Coven or hidden anything from them."

Elvina flinched as if Dorathea's words had slapped her, and Sloane shot her cousin a side-eye. Her cousin's ease with lashing out and hurting Elvina disappointed her.

"Onpenne," Dorathea said to the women in the painting who controlled the passage through her portal. The art was a metaphor for silencing women, particularly women writers. The younger woman guarded a man at knifepoint while the older woman took possession of his writing desk. At Dorathea's command, the older woman got to her feet and opened a door at the back of the room.

Sloane nodded her appreciation to her and stepped through the canvas. It was the second time she had traveled by Dorathea's portal to Tagridore. Stepping into the canvas felt like passing through a doorway, providing a seamless connection between the two planes.

On the other side of the painting, they ended up on a cobblestone walkway beside Freya's café. Sloane was surprised Dorathea's portal still brought them to the charming, white-washed bakery with its lavender awning. Her cousin had refused to listen to Freya's explanation about why she helped Jane all those years ago. Since Elvina told her about it on Christmas Eve, Dorathea had shut Freya out.

"Quickly. Follow me." Dorathea walked toward the Héahreced.

"Wait? No pastries first? I'm not angry at Freya," Jack said, and Sloane elbowed him hard. "Ouch. What was that for?"

"Jesus, Jack. Just go, will you?" She shoved him toward the pedestrian street, and they caught up to Dorathea before she reached the steps to the city's headquarters. The building stood at the back of a wide, long grassy mall, and the outside reminded Sloane of New York City's Grand Central Station. But she remembered vividly that the inside was a mind bender with Escher-like, floating escalators and Goblins with bony fingers, pointy ears, and skin the color of dried sage, verifying appointments at several checkpoints.

They crossed a wide, marble landing and stepped through the warm, gel-like field that protected the Héahreced. Everyone passed through effortlessly, but when Elvina tried, the transparent shield shoved her back.

"Whoa. What the hell was that?" Sloane asked.

"I guess I'm not invited," Elvina said after steadying herself.

"This is entirely unacceptable," Dorathea said. "Another attempt to intimidate us that has only weakened my resolve to remain amiable."

Dorathea sounded angrier than Sloane had ever heard her. She could understand her cousin's frustration, but now was not the time for their High Priestess to lose her usually perfect composure. "I can't believe I'm the one to say this, but we need to keep our cool. Stay focused," Sloane said. "The GC has demanded we appear, but they don't know we suspect one or more of them is in The Order. We have the advantage. We can ask questions that will catch them off guard."

"Ooh, yes. We'll use clever subterfuge. I love it," Jack said.

"You are right. Now is not the time to share my displeasure." Dorathea looked at Elvina. "Wait for us here, dear." Then she set her jaw and, with a swish of her cloak, disappeared inside the building.

A few minutes later, they entered the Grand Coven's chambers. Sloane studied the three Wiċċan on the stage. They had achieved the most authoritative positions in the Northwest Quadrant, but according to Elvina, they were not the most powerful Wiċċan. Those titles belonged to Dorathea as well as Freya, their coven's past Attendant.

The governing Wiċċan sat in high-back chairs at a long wooden table. Polydora Nenge, the Telekinetic, sat in the middle. Her long salt-and-pepper hair was loosely braided and draped over her shoulder, and the angular bones in her face looked even harsher under the auditorium lights. She had her arms crossed on the tabletop and watched the Wests with a penetrating stare, the same look Sloane would give suspects sitting on the other side of an interview table.

She avoided Polydora's gaze and looked at Cenric Verner, the Wyrtdrenc—a potions expert, as Sloane recalled—sitting to Polydora's right. The wiċċa had a scrunched face, his eyes, nose, and mouth pinched together. He sat back against the chair with his hands resting on his middle. His cheeks were already ruddy red as if someone had embarrassed him, even though no one had spoken yet.

Holding her necklace, Millicent Panas sat to Polydora's left. She watched them sympathetically with soft eyes the color of lapis lazuli, a deep blue with flecks of brilliant green and gold. It was a look Sloane knew well, a look Sensors had when they thought they needed to calm a situation.

A rostrum appeared at the end of their aisle in the dark wood-paneled auditorium. Dorathea stepped up to it and clasped its sides. "*Ealdormenn*, why have you convened this meeting? And why have you excluded Elvina?" She tried to hide her frustration, but it edged her voice, and the Grand Coven stared at her, surprised.

"Isn't it obvious?" Cenric said. He sat forward with a grunt. "We want to ask you about the assault on the Gòrdan Coven. As for Elvina, your coven's Attendants will appear before us when we are ready for them."

"You could have avoided this assembly if you had allowed the Weardas entry," Polydora said. "We only wanted information."

"Seeking information is no excuse for sending them to enter our covenstead without permission," Dorathea snapped, and Polydora narrowed her eyes.

"We did no such thing," Cenric said. His face contorted, and the wattle under his chin jiggled.

"And what if we had?" Polydora asked, talking over Cenric. "Given the current state of our worlds, would you blame us for wanting to gather information about The Order quickly?"

Dorathea stiffened. "How would searching our covenstead provide such information?" She held Polydora's gaze, and the tension in the room went from a reasonable undercurrent to a breaking-the-dam flood. "Our rules are in place for a reason, Ealdormenn. You erode our trust with such blatant disregard."

"Please, please. Let's take a breath," Millicent said. "This is all my fault, I assure you. Cenric asked me to contact Dorathea, and regrettably, I forgot to inform her." She shot a glare of disapproval at Polydora and an apologetic look at Cenric. "I certainly meant nothing by the oversight. You have my sincere apologies, Dorathea. And I can assure you, my only intention for agreeing to send the Weardas to your covenstead was to make sure you were okay."

"Nevertheless, your hasty dismissal of our guards would lead anyone to question if you're hiding something," Polydora said, and Millicent's shoulders rose as she took a deep breath while Cenric stared at his folded hands. She avoided their gestures of disapproval and demanded, "Tell us, why your coven was at the Gòrdan covenstead?"

"As I told the Uachdaran, Alisdair invited us to spend time with them on Christmas," Dorathea said to Polydora without missing a beat.

The *Ealdormann* raised an eyebrow ever so slightly. "That surprises me. I've never known you to celebrate Christmas in another's home, let alone in a different quadrant. Not since you were young."

"You have known little about me since then, Polydora. What you did know in the past, you have clearly forgotten."

Sloane could hear history and accusation in her cousin's voice. She could feel the tenuous connection that faded memories kept between the two. Were her cousin and Polydora close at one time? Were they lovers before she was with Freya?

"I can understand why Alisdair reached out to your coven," Millicent said, breaking the awkward silence. "Your coven has experienced unspeakable loss this year. And of course, the joy of finding Sloane. It was kind of him to invite you and share in your grief and celebration."

Polydora's expression hardened as Millicent spoke, and when the other wiċċe finished, she leaned forward. "You also told the Uachdaran you arrived after the attack and found Lachlan and Bella dead and Alisdair near death. But Calen and Elspeth were missing, presumably in danger. So why didn't you alert the Northeast Quadrant's Grand Coven when you discovered what had happened? Why wouldn't you want the Uachdaran to search for Calen and Elspeth immediately?" She lifted her chin, looking down her pointy nose at Dorathea. "Then again, we know now it was too late for Calen. But maybe not for the child."

"Polydora," Millicent said curtly. "We have no evidence to suggest our Protector Coven is lying to us. This situation is critical, and we must work together to find the child." She looked at Dorathea. "Do you know where Elspeth is? If Alisdair sent her somewhere? We need to find her so the Uachdaran can guard her."

"I think because Calen was killed in Denwick at your Tree of Life, Elspeth is also here." Polydora pressed the palms of her hands together, tapping her index fingers. "Do you have the child? Is that why Alfred and you refused the Weardas entry into your covenstead?"

"We don't know how Calen died or why he was in the crypt," said Sloane. "But I would guess the owners of the building had something to do with it." She knew the Grand Coven frowned upon speaking out of turn, but the way Polydora said "your Tree of Life" pissed her off. Dorathea reached back and squeezed her arm.

"I'll tell you how he died," Polydora continued. "Like Lachlan and Bella, his murder was at the hands of a Sensor, an influential one. Like you, Jack, or Freya. Only one such as yourselves could have melted his brain so completely."

The news made Jack stumble back, and Sloane felt an instant need to protect him. She anchored him and lashed out. "Or like Millicent."

Cenric gasped and pointed a stubby finger at her but uttered no words from his gaping mouth.

"Are you accusing your Grand Coven of conspiring with The Order?" Polydora's voice dripped with contempt.

"Enough," Millicent shouted and eyed the other Grand Coven members. "Polydora, you have distrusted Jane West for the entirety of your appointment on this coven. When she became a victim of The Order, you continued to persecute her. Her child. Her coven. Even though you have no proof to back your accusations. I say it's gone on long enough. We cannot allow The Order to plant seeds of distrust and destroy our world. We must work together to fight them."

Dorathea released Sloane's arm. "Thank you for your support, Millicent, but I have no problem answering the Ealdormann's questions." She looked at Polydora. "We arrived after The Order killed and gravely injured our friends and had no need to contact their Grand Coven because the Freiceadan appeared only minutes after we did. Which we found odd." She grasped the sides of the rostrum and glared at the Ealdormenn. "The Order left no one able to call for help. How did the Freiceadan know what had happened?"

Silence spread through the room.

"Maybe Mòrag alerted them?" Cenric said.

"She did not." Dorathea's voice was crisp.

"Well, I'm sure we have no idea who alerted them," Polydora said. "Maybe Elspeth Gòrdan did. We are still waiting for you to tell us if you know where she is."

"And I would tell you if I could," Dorathea said.

Her cousin was skillful at hiding the truth in truth, Sloane thought. She studied the Grand Coven as they considered Dorathea's response.

Millicent was the first to react. "Really, Polydora. Cenric and I have grown weary of your constant suspicion. Your continued abuse of prominent Magicals will crumble our authority."

Cenric straightened and grunted in agreement.

Polydora ignored the other two and locked eyes with Dorathea. "As this quadrant's leaders, we are compelled to find those conspiring with The Order. Prominent Magicals are as likely to be traitors as any others."

"That goes without saying." Millicent eyed Polydora suspiciously. "Still, unfounded accusations against our Protector Coven only make you look like the one with something to hide."

Sloane felt the pressure in the room drop, and Dorathea spread out her arms like a mother protecting her children in the front seat of a braking car. She moved them back several steps, her gaze never leaving Polydora's face.

Cenric stammered, "Well…Millicent only means…your… your insinuations seem like deflection. Not…not that we're accusing you of anything. We would never do that."

"Your coven is dismissed," Polydora told Dorathea. "Inform us immediately if you discover information about the attack or the child's whereabouts." Then she looked at Millicent and Cenric, and a contemptuous smile spread across her face. "Ealdormenn, I prefer we discuss your opinions of me in private."

CHAPTER TWELVE

Elvina rested against a wall lining one side of the Héahreced's grassy mall, her face tilted back, soaking up the sun. When they approached, she opened her eyes. "Well, what did the Grand Coven want?"

"Hard to say." Sloane put her fists on her hips. "Either they think we're guilty of attacking the Gòrdans, or we at least know something we refuse to tell them. They didn't allow us to ask any questions. And by the end of their interrogation, they were fighting amongst themselves."

"How interesting. I would have loved to have seen that," Elvina said.

"We didn't get to stay for the best part. Polydora dismissed us so they could continue their row in private," Jack said.

"Ooh, to be a cat in the corner of that room," Elvina said, and Sloane couldn't help but chuckle at her ex-familiar's delight.

"They're also keen on finding Elspeth. We have to consider if they want to locate her to protect her or kill her." Sloane's comment hung in the air. "They're either genuinely worried about her or acting. One thing's for sure, they seem nervous. Nervous people make mistakes."

"Absolutely they're nervous." Jack held up his hand with his thumb and index finger almost touching. "The Order is this close to taking over the Northeast Quadrant, not to mention the Nogicals who live there. Alisdair and Elspeth are the only ones standing in their way."

"Do you think they're all acting?" Elvina asked Sloane.

"Not sure. For now, we need to treat each of them as suspects."

Dorathea sighed. "I would have once considered that question and your answer heresy. My naiveté embarrasses and upsets me."

Elvina gently took hold of Dorathea's arm. "My mother has something to tell us, dear. She's asked that we come to the café."

Hurt replaced irritation on Dorathea's face. She tightly wrapped her emerald-green cloak around her lanky body. "I am returning to the covenstead. You can bring me your mother's news later."

Sloane knew Dorathea's brusque response only masked her heartbreak. Last March, Sloane had arrived in Denwick, angry and confused at what she saw as her mother's betrayal. Dorathea told her then that living in anger was too dangerous for a wiċċe like her, that she needed to forgive Jane's lies, that her mother's reasons for hiding the truth about them being Magical had to have been important. Her cousin never forced her to forgive Jane, but in the end, she did. Now she needed to encourage Dorathea to do the same. To forgive Freya.

"Denham, I know what it feels like for someone you love to keep you in the dark for years. To withhold the truth from you, even if for good reason. Finding out what Jane did to me altered my life, and I'll never forget what happened." Sloane glanced across the street at Freya's café. "But it didn't negate the wonderful life I did have with my mother. And I wish I could have her back."

"Listen to her, dear. You have every right to be upset." Elvina tightened her grip on Dorathea's arm. "But please don't freeze my mother out of your life. Allow her to explain herself when you're ready. Until then, we need her."

Dorathea lowered her head, shaking it faintly. Her body slumped as if her usual erect posture could not withstand the gravity of her emotions. "Fine," she finally said. "I'll listen to her news, and that is all."

A soft tinkle of bells sounded when they entered Freya's cafe. Sloane breathed in the familiar ambrosial scent of rising dough. The Magicals seated at intimate tables for two and cozy suites of armchairs for four were fairies and goblins, werewolves and vampires, and a few wicce and wicca who sent strong vibrations through Sloane's body. What they all had in common, she thought, was a polished look. Freya never struck her as a snob, but the proprietors' guests were the more refined creatures of the magical world. She couldn't imagine any of them sitting in Stella's, the dive bar she had frequented back in NYC.

After they had taken seats in a grouping of chairs, Freya entered the room from the kitchen. She looked as though she hadn't slept the last two nights since telling Elvina her secrets. She moved slowly toward them, her eyes locked on Dorathea. "Hello, my love," she said. "I was unsure you would come."

"I am not here to see you," Dorathea said, and looked away. "You have information. We need it, and then I will leave."

Freya looked at the floor, shuttering her eyes, and said softly, "I knew helping Jane would hurt you." Then, in a strength-mustering exhalation, Dorathea's lover of over thirty years, demanded, "Look at me, please. I wanted to be the one to tell you the truth. To explain why I chose to help our dear Jane. But circumstances intervened."

Dorathea shook her head. "I am not ready to hear why you chose to betray me and my family. You robbed us of a lifetime of emotions with my cousin and her child. And if you had told us the truth, my family might not be dead now."

Freya's olive skin paled. "Very well. I will be here when you are ready."

Sloane's heart ached for her at her crushing sorrow. She wanted to ease the tension and give Freya a reason to move past Dorathea's horrible remarks. "I don't know about anyone else, but

I'd love one of your cardamom scones and some bergamot and yuzu tea, Freya."

"Oh, yes, please. I'm starving," Jack said, sounding pleased with the change of topic. "I'd never pass up a chance to indulge in your delicious food, deary. I'll have a meat tart and make that two cups of tea."

"I'll have a meat tart and tea, too. Thank you, Mother. I appreciate everything you do for all of us," Elvina said.

Everyone but Freya looked at Dorathea. The High Priestess stared into the room. "Nothing for me. I am not here for your hospitality. Only the news you have for us."

Freya's shoulders slumped as if the weight in her chest had become too heavy to bear.

After she left, Sloane snapped at her cousin, "Jesus, Denham, you're being a bit harsh. I mean, the news about Freya and my mom stung for all of us, but it's not like she didn't have her reasons for helping Jane. Just like Jane had reasons for hiding her and me."

"I will not discuss the matter here. Or with you." Dorathea did little to temper the displeasure in her voice.

They sat together in the quaint café without speaking until Freya returned. She placed their food and drink on the table and stood behind her daughter. "On Christmas Eve, Polydora visited the café and questioned me. She asked why we weren't together, and I refused to tell her. Then she demanded to know where you and the coven were. I assured her you were at the covenstead. But she's suspicious of me and threatened to detain me for further questioning. I think the only reason she didn't is that a telepathic communication distracted her, and she left. This happened only minutes before The Order's violent attack on the Gòrdans." She finally looked at Dorathea. "I fear she will take me into custody."

"You've done nothing wrong, Mother," Elvina said.

"That's right. Her suspicions are unfounded," Jack added.

"You are both mistaken." Dorathea stood and pushed her chair back under the table. "Polydora is seeking the truth. Freya has hidden the truth by lying to the Grand Coven and to us. She did aid in Jane's disappearance. Her deception is why they distrust her." She turned her back on Freya and said, "As do I."

Freya gasped at her words as if they were a curse of fire thrown at her, and she disappeared.

Sloane opened her mouth to shout at her cousin, but the energy around them pressed on her chest like an anxiety attack. She couldn't expel enough breath to sound the words. A moment later, Dorathea and the pressure vanished.

"I need to see my mother," Elvina said, rising to her feet.

"Yes, we'll stay here," Jack said. After she left, he shook his head. "Our cousin is entirely unreasonable. Treating Freya like that. Without the decency of listening to her explanation. I can only imagine how dreadful the circumstances must have been for her to keep Jane's secret. I mean, what would compel both of them to lie for thirty years?"

"Must have been?" Sloane poured more tea into her cup. "It's been almost a year since The Order killed my mother. Something or someone is still forcing Freya to stay silent."

"This mystery is beyond my abilities to solve," he said and bit into a meat tart.

"I couldn't agree more." Sloane grinned at Jack's faux-injured look.

"Really, though. What could it be?" he asked.

"That's what Freya is going to tell me. She owes me answers, and now is the time to give them to me."

"Well, not now, now. She's hardly in a place to endure your interrogation." Jack sipped his tea. "Mmm. I like this bergamot and yuzu combination."

"It was Jane's favorite." Sloane turned her teacup in circles on its saucer, staring into it. "Sometimes I feel like I've woken up in one of the fantasy worlds my mother would create for me at bedtime. Being in Denwick and Tagridore. Knowing she sat in this café, where she learned that this tea was her favorite. She had this whole other life she couldn't share with me." She stopped fidgeting. "And I'm going to find out why."

"You will. If anyone can find the truth, you can." Jack placed his teacup in its saucer and looked past her shoulder.

Sloane could feel Elvina and Freya approach before she could see them. At one time, she thought the ability might mean she was also a telepathic like her mother. But Elvina told her Wiċċan have a physical and emotional connection with their familiars, some stronger than others. Hers and Elvina's was powerful.

Sloane pulled out a chair for Freya. "Please, sit with us. I hope you don't think I'm upset with you. I'm not. You have your reasons for keeping my mother's confidence." She poured Freya a tea. "And don't worry. Dorathea will come around when she hears what they are."

Freya smiled at her and lovingly stroked the side of Sloane's face with her hand, tucking strands of her long black hair behind her ear. "You're so beautiful, dear one. So strong and clever, just like your mother. I promised her I'd protect you as long as I'm alive. And that is what I am going to do."

"No one doubts you," Elvina said, and she held her mother's free hand.

"Thank you, *Graymalkin*. It's time for you all to go." Freya got to her feet and kissed the top of their heads. "I need to stay busy, distract myself. I will send dinner to the cottage at five p.m. I can't imagine Elspeth has an appetite, though, so please encourage her to eat."

CHAPTER THIRTEEN

Sloane stood under a steamy shower for a considerable time, imagining Rose's and her evening and every way she planned to satisfy her. But before her date with Rose, she had to have dinner with the coven and discuss their meeting with the GC. They needed to figure out if one of the three members was trying to kill them. Or if it was all of them.

At five o'clock sharp, Freya's dinner appeared on the breakfast table, and Sloane opened each lavender box, breathing in the meaty, earthy scents in some boxes, and the buttery, sweet scents in others. Freya had made Elspeth comfort food from home: haggis with neeps and tatties, and several containers of cranachan for dessert.

Sloane spoke to Elvina in her mind. *Freya's dinner is here. Would you thank her for us? It smells incredible.*

Of course, dear.

Are you at Dorathea's?

Yes. We are waiting for you.

All right. I'll be right over.

Sloane decided not to risk taking dinner to the hobbit house by teleporting and losing the food, along with suffering a headache, so she packed the meal in two shopping bags, grabbed her overnight bag, and carried them next door, hurrying through the cold air.

Inside Dorathea's foyer, a mini wind funnel swirled around her as Alfred breathed in the food's aromas. After she descended the stairs to the covenstead, she looked up. "Sorry you can't eat any of it. Hate that for you."

He sent her stumbling into the room with a strong gust and shut the door behind her.

"Jesus, I was kidding," she mumbled. "Sort of."

"Wonderful, you're here with dinner," Jack said, patting the seat of an armchair beside his. He waved his hand, and five dinnerware settings appeared on the coffee table.

"Where's Elspeth?" Sloane asked, setting the bags down.

"I have asked Alfred to bring her." Dorathea snapped her fingers, and a fifth velvet armchair appeared in front of a mellow fire burning in the fireplace.

Moments later, the young girl entered. It had been less than two days since she had bravely escaped The Order through the Morisot sketch in Sloane's cottage, but the heavy hand of grief had etched her face.

"Come sit with us, dear. We have evening tea for you." Dorathea smiled and motioned to the fifth chair. She snapped her fingers, and the gentle flames in the fireplace roared, enveloping the sitting area in a warm embrace.

Elspeth curled up in the chair, hugging a velvety scarlet throw. Sloane felt a tug in her chest for the child. She knew what it was like to lose a parent, to have them suddenly and violently taken away. Sometimes, she would sink into the grief, but she was an adult and could pull herself out of the darkness. Elspeth was a child. How was she supposed to process this kind of pain?

"You might not be hungry, Elspeth. But you must eat," Dorathea said.

"You will like dinner, dear. My mother made haggis with neeps and tatties for you," Elvina said. "She also made cranachan."

Elspeth glanced at her and looked at the blanket again.

It was a start, Sloane thought, and filled a small plate for the wee girl. Then she scooped a double serving of cranachan into a clear glass bowl and handed it to Elspeth. "If I were you, I'd start with dessert."

The corners of Elspeth's mouth lifted, and her small hands clasped the dish.

"Well, I would never have guessed you'd possess such instinctive qualities," Jack said, grinning at her, and Sloane glared back, filling a plate for herself.

A few moments of silence passed among them, and then their young guest took her first bite. After the first, she didn't stop until she had finished her dessert and dinner.

"Elspeth, we have news to share with you," Dorathea said, when the dishes were cleared from the coffee table. "Your grandfather is home now, and he would like you to return to him tonight." She smiled at the child, but Elspeth shook her head slowly and covered herself up to her chin with the throw.

Sloane knew the thought of returning to the place that had irrevocably changed her life petrified the child. "When did this happen?" she asked Dorathea.

"Alisdair returned home after we left him in the hospital. He is satisfied with our protection spells and believes Elspeth will be safe at home with him now."

Elspeth's eyes widened as she listened to Dorathea. "He's okay?" she asked, in a voice no louder than a whisper.

"Yes, your grandfather has recovered and is excited to see you," Dorathea said.

"I'm scared." The child squeezed her eyes shut.

"Hey, I get it, but we're going to keep you safe," Sloane said gently. "I promise."

"Quite right. Many powerful spells safeguard your home now. And two fierce Magicals will stay with you until you and your grandfather are no longer in danger," Dorathea added. "Elvina and I will return with you. Then—" She abruptly stopped talking and stared at the covenstead's door. "Alfred has informed me that

Millicent and Cenric are requesting permission to enter." She looked at Elvina. "You must take Elspeth home at once."

"Now?" the young girl asked, opening her eyes wide.

"Why can't she wait upstairs?" Sloane asked.

"Millicent will sense her presence. She must leave at once. And I need a moment to clear her energy."

Elvina gathered Elspeth in her arms, and they disappeared as Dorathea waved her arms in a counterclockwise motion. After several passes, she flicked her wrist, and the fifth chair disappeared. With no signs that the child had ever been there, she instructed Alfred to grant the Grand Coven members admittance. An instant later, the portly man and bone-thin woman stood before them.

Millicent stood at the threshold of the sitting area, looking around the expansive room. "My goodness, Dorathea. I love what you've done with the place. Such a rich sapphire color. So regal. It's my favorite, you know. Picks up the deep blue in my eyes."

"Thank you, but Alfred deserves the compliment. He remodeled for us a few weeks ago." She waved her hand, and two armchairs appeared. "Do sit down, won't you?"

"Delighted to, but we won't take up too much of your valuable time. I know your coven must be overwhelmed with...well...I guess we should call it a battle now. After another horrific assault on a Protector Coven."

"It's awful," Cenric said. He sat with a grunt.

"Yes, and we want you to know all of our resources are available to you. The Weardas. Anyone at the Héahreced you think could be helpful. The days of our Protector Covens being able to guard the entire nogical world are gone, I'm afraid. The Order has become a Goliath, as the Nogicals would say. We must employ everyone to find them before the unthinkable happens."

"Really?" Sloane asked irreverently. She never could stay quiet while someone purposefully ramped up the drama. "Do you speak for everyone? Where's Polydora?"

"I speak for Cenric and myself. But I promise, Polydora agrees. She was unable to be here tonight," Millicent said, and she unconsciously grasped her necklace. This time, Sloane saw the pendant, a striking green emerald, the size of a quarter, before it disappeared in Millicent's clutches.

"All right. Besides offering your resources, what are you doing to stop The Order?" Sloane asked. Millicent and Cenric reminded her of every politician she had ever known in the nogical world. They all had empty talking points about problematic issues when they were more often than not openly or secretly the cause of the problem.

"Everything we can, I assure you," Cenric said.

"I agree. Cenric and I feel our meeting earlier did not convey that the Grand Coven unreservedly supports you. You are our visionaries, our protectors. Without you, our world and the nogical world could fall to The Order, ending our lives as we know them. We will assist you in whatever you need to destroy them," Millicent added.

"And do you speak for Polydora? She's not here to agree. Do you even know where she is?" Sloane asked, pushing them in hopes they would reveal something about the missing Ealdormann.

Millicent raised an eyebrow. "I did not ask, nor would I expect Polydora to tell me why she declined."

"Doesn't it make you curious?" Sloane asked, but Millicent and Cenric only stared at her, refusing to answer.

"I am grateful to you and Cenric for taking the time to assure us," Dorathea said, and Sloane sensed her cousin wasn't a fan of her interrogation. "I have a question for you as well. You disagreed with us about The Order infiltrating the most highly ranked magical positions. It is no secret that those with power and influence can secure their innocence even when they are not. Are you willing to authorize the Weardas to investigate anyone we suspect if we need their help?"

"You have our word," Millicent said, as she rose.

"Yes, yes. Our word. Be safe, West Coven," Cenric said, lumbering to his feet.

After they disappeared, Jack let out a deep breath. "It doesn't matter how carefully I follow rules, talking to the GC makes me feel like I'm one step away from Drusnirwd."

"No shit. I was a cop back in NYC, and my heart still races whenever a squad car pulls up behind me. It beats double time with those three."

Dorathea frowned at them and stood. "I must join Elvina at Alisdair's."

"Wait. You and Elvina are protecting them?" Sloane asked. "How long will you be gone?"

"Of course we are not. Our coven must stay together. Elvina and I will be back shortly. We must train to banish a Half-Malevolent in the morning. It will not be an easy feat." Dorathea's cheek twitched. "Ken and Rose Keane will protect what is left of the Gòrdan Coven until we capture those responsible."

Sloane shot to her feet. "What? Are you serious? Are they there now?"

"They are indeed, pet. Our spells will keep out Magicals, but if a Half-Malevolent has forged a path inside, we need the Keanes' help," her cousin said.

"No way. It's too dangerous," she shouted, her heart pounding. "Jesus Christ, Denham, The Order killed half the Gòrdan Coven. What do you think they'll do to two Daywalkers?"

"Your girlfriend and her father are more dangerous to a Half-Malevolent than we are, lovey. We can use magic to trap and send them back to the Abyss…but Dhampyres have a psychic shield that Malevolents and their offspring cannot penetrate. That's how the Malevolents kill. They destroy the life source…and well…" Jack's voice trailed off, and Sloane didn't push it. She guessed his comments had brought him too close to thinking about Calen's death.

"You have nothing to worry about. They are well-suited for this assignment," Dorathea said. "Besides, we cannot trust anyone else now. Can we?"

Her question sounded more like a frustrated mother trying to persuade a stubborn toddler, and Sloane fought the urge to shout at them again. After her anger passed, she questioned her intense reaction to Rose's help. *You have no say in the choices Rose makes.* She didn't think Rose was weak, but she didn't want her to risk her life for them either. "What about other Protector Covens? Why can't they help?" she asked Dorathea.

"The Gòrdans and the Baptistes in the Southwest Quadrant have suffered great losses, and they cannot risk their remaining members' lives. The Protector Coven in the Southeast Quadrant has avoided The Order thus far. I dare say, we have to wonder why."

"All right. Fine." Sloane stood and grabbed the overnight bag she had intended to take to Rose's apartment. "But that doesn't mean I'm not pissed about it."

CHAPTER FOURTEEN

A lamp on a side table dimly lit Sloane's living room, once aglow with Christmas lights inside and out. She had turned off the decorations after Elspeth appeared, no longer wanting to pretend for the Nogicals.

With the snap of her fingers, flames erupted in her living room fireplace. She tossed the overnight bag on the floor and dropped into her armchair, feeling forlorn. Her only plan had been to be with Rose. Now Rose was in Kirkcudbright. To make things worse, she hadn't felt her phone buzz with a text or call. Rose hadn't even told her she was leaving and that their date was off.

The fire quickly heated the room, and she stripped off her cardigan. She had learned to start a fire instantly but had no idea how to control it. Her cousin's house and the covenstead were always the perfect temperature. She figured it was Alfred's doing and wondered if the Wests' house spirit would ever consider returning to Mallow Cottage. And then she thought of Pearl. Would her mother's car spirit ever return? She understood why they both left. They lost their people. But she would welcome them back. They could have a family again, like she had found with her coven, like she wanted with Rose.

She opened her third eye, picturing a bottle of Fulsmécte and a tumbler behind the misty veil. "Ċīeġ," she whispered. They appeared on her side table. She would have taken pleasure in the successful spell, but she could only think about the tightness in her chest. She downed two fingers of whiskey and decided to call Rose. The other line rang once.

"Hey, you. I was hoping you'd call." Rose sounded pleased, which made Sloane's chest constrict even more.

She poured another measure, wondering why Rose didn't sound upset. "How's the jet lag," she replied, her disappointment seeping out.

Rose sighed, and Sloane could hear her shifting her body. "You're upset. I'm sorry. I didn't want to tell you we had to postpone tonight in a text or voice message. You were the first person I tried to talk to after I found out my da and I would be helping the Gòrdans. You'll see a missed call from me." She paused, but Sloane wasn't ready to respond. "And you know I don't have jet lag. You're not the only cool kid in town. I came through my tartan portal just like you use your Degas. Except I don't have to convince three snooty ballerinas to let me pass."

"Hmm." Sloane struggled not to smile at the playfulness in Rose's voice, and the tightness in her chest began to ease. "I'm just upset. Tonight was important to me."

"It was to me, too. I will say, though, I'm pleased to hear the disappointment and worry in your voice. It makes me believe you must really like me."

"You don't even know how much. So much so, I'm sitting alone in the dark, pouting. Because I wanted to show you."

"Are we talking about flowers and chocolate or something a little more hands-on?"

"Not *or*. I'm a firm believer in using all the senses."

"Ooh, me too. I look forward to using each one on you many, many times," Rose said, and her breathy voice sent a tingle through Sloane. "For now, though, don't worry about me. Dorathea and Alisdair made sure no Magicals would breach Mòrag's boundaries

again. And if a Half-Malevolent has created a path back inside…"
Her voice faded.

"You and Ken are strong enough to handle it," Sloane said.
"That's what everyone keeps telling me."

"Yeah. We can. We're strong. Our strength isn't what makes
us capable of protecting others from evil supernaturals and their
offspring. We can because we're part of the undead. It makes us
resistant to their attacks, at least more than other Magicals. I can't
imagine how that sounds to you. Undead. You probably haven't
learned much about my kind. I hope it doesn't upset you." Her
words were tumbling out.

"Keane, slow down. Who you are could never upset me.
Dhampyres were the first Magicals I wanted to learn about, to
know everything about you and your history, where you come
from."

"Thank you for saying that." Rose sounded more comfortable.
"Do you have a book on Magicals? I'm curious what the Wiċċan
have to say about us."

"Jane's old schoolbook. I'll let you read it anytime."

"Okay. Can I suggest you use the library in Tagridore to find
some books written by the Blodaeters?"

"Jesus. Sorry, I know better than that," Sloane said, her cheeks
warming. "I will."

"Apology accepted. But since you've done some research, albeit
questionable, if you want first-hand knowledge of Dhampyres,
you can ask me anything."

"And you can ask me anything, as soon as we know exactly
what I am. All Wiċċan. Half Wiċċan. Half Nogical. Who the hell
knows?"

"We'll take a trip to the library together when you figure
it out. Truth is, I haven't read enough about the Wiċċan," Rose
said, and Sloane could hear her body shift again. "Have you heard
anything about your father?"

"Jack has a list of possible men. They're mostly Nogicals, but
I think the man who fathered me was Magical." She didn't want
to tell Rose that she suspected he was a bent Magical. Why else
would her mother have hidden them? If he wasn't a part of The

Order, wouldn't he have revealed himself to her by now? She changed the subject. "Right now, I need you to assure me you won't get hurt. You're not immortal like Fiona, right?"

"Not exactly. We're more like you than her. Daywalkers live longer than humans and other Magicals because we are Half-Blodaeters, the undead, like my mam. It's unusual for a Blodaeter and a Daywalker, like my da, to have children. When it happens, their offspring…Oscar and me…are required to live in the nogical world as Defenders of our kind. The same as you being a Protector."

Sloane closed her eyes tightly and rubbed her forehead. "Jesus, I don't like you being there without me."

"What's stopping you from joining me? There's plenty of room. The bed I'm in is king-sized," Rose teased.

"I knew you'd be in bed." Sloane groaned. She pictured Rose's tight auburn curls falling around her face. Her long body. "You're killing me. Dorathea scheduled a training session in the morning. If I come over now, I won't leave." She resisted the urge to skip her cousin's lesson and teleport to the Gòrdans right then, but it wasn't easy. "How about after my training? It'll be eight or nine p.m. your time. We could have a late dinner."

"Sounds wonderful," Rose said, and she was silent for a beat. "This might be a good time to talk about our sleepover."

"Talk? Does this conversation include physical participation?" Sloane rested her head on the cushion.

"Hmm. No phone sex this time. I need to talk about being with you." The sultry sound of Rose's voice became hesitant.

"Hey, are you upset? If I'm pushing you too fast, please tell me."

"It's not that." She paused. "I've only been with partners while pretending to be Nogical. I've hidden parts of myself for so long. Desires I have…things Nogicals wouldn't understand. Being with you will be the first time…I could be myself…But sex with me can be a lot different from sex with a Nogical. If you're okay with that. It doesn't have to be. I can keep…" Her voice trailed off.

"Rose?"

"I'm here," she whispered.

"I always want you to be yourself. Fully. And I don't mean just sex. I want to be the person you feel safest with, the one you share your deepest fears and insecurities with for the rest of your life." Rose caught her breath, and Sloane thought she had turned the conversation too serious, even though it was how she felt, and she wouldn't lie, not anymore. But for Rose's sake, she lightened the mood. "Just promise not to be too rough with all your power and whatnot. I'm delicate in bed."

Rose burst out laughing. "I promise pain is not what you'll be feeling. Unless you want a little."

"All right. Now I'm nervous I won't measure up. Maybe I should ask Elvina to teach me some spells to spice up my moves."

Rose's laughter subsided, and she whispered, "You make me very happy."

"Then I have everything I need. I hope I make you very happy, too," Sloane said, and Rose agreed in a soft moan.

Sloane swallowed the rest of her drink. The intimate conversation had left her satiated and ready to drift off to sleep. "Good night, Keane. I'll see you tomorrow."

"Good night, West. Sweet dreams."

CHAPTER FIFTEEN

The next morning, Sloane awoke to the aroma of coffee. She lay for a moment, thinking about Rose before wrapping herself in a thick robe and heading to the kitchen.

Elvina sat at the breakfast table, staring out the bay windows. She turned and watched Sloane pour a cup. "How was your sleep, dear?"

"Not too bad. How about you?"

"I always sleep well, one of the benefits of living as a cat in my former nine lives."

Sloane carried the coffee carafe to the table. "Must be nice. Do you miss sleeping all day?" She sat and joined Elvina, staring into the dark garden.

"I didn't sleep all day. You kept me busy. You weren't the easiest to watch over." She smirked and sipped her coffee.

"I suppose not." Sloane blew into her mug, breathing in the steamy aroma.

"If you're having trouble sleeping, dear, we can teach you how to prepare a *slæpan* wryneck. Slæpan means to sleep."

"Yeah. I got that." Sloane shook her head. "Some of the Old English words we use make perfect sense, and some are just gibberish to me. I still think we ought to modernize the Book of Hagorúnum."

"I suppose you have every right to try to change things. Although I'm not sure how far you would get in your crusade with our current Grand Coven."

"That's the truth." She yawned and shook her head. "Maybe I will take you up on that potion."

After a few cups of black coffee, Sloane showered and donned a pair of jeans, a white T-shirt, and her favorite cardigan. When she returned to the kitchen, Elvina waited, holding Sloane's tote bag. "Ready to go?"

"Yeah, I'll meet you over there." She put on her heavy peacoat and slung the tote's strap over her neck.

"There's no need to go out in this weather." Elvina sucked her teeth and grabbed Sloane's arm, and the floor disappeared. They fell into a void, reemerging in a flash of white light that left Sloane's head feeling like she had awakened from a two-day bender.

"Jesus, Elvina. You can't bestealce with me whenever you want. That's abduction. I prefer to walk across the yard so I don't feel like my head wants to explode.

"What did you say about your head? I have never heard of a headache being a side effect of bestealcedon." Dorathea's voice came from the sitting area.

Sloane looked at her cousin. "Well, it is. The first few times it just made me dizzy, but now it hurts, and the pain is getting worse."

"We must find out why indeed," Dorathea said, staring at Sloane, concerned.

Elvina sat beside Dorathea and snapped her fingers. A lavender box appeared, and Jack said, "Fabulous, deary. I'm starving." He leaned forward and stacked three scones on a plate.

"When aren't you?" Sloane took a bite of a cardamom scone and sat in the armchair beside him.

"I'm very active, day and night. I need my calories," Jack said, and Elvina simpered, while Dorathea tsked at him.

"All right. I'm learning to vanquish Demons and Cambions today. Can't even explain how much it freaks me out to say that. But here we are. So let's get started." She didn't want to be the first to stand, to look too eager, but she was determined to keep her date with Rose.

"While I appreciate your enthusiasm, pet, I would like to finish my tea," Dorathea said, shaking her head instead of correcting Sloane on her nogical choice of names.

After an hour of conversation, Dorathea finally stood, and they moved to the lectern. Sloane glanced at her watch and growled inside. It was already seven p.m. in Scotland, and they hadn't even started training. Her cousin flicked two fingers at the Book of Hagorúnum, opening its cover.

"We won't accidentally summon The Order to our covenstead or create a path for them to break in, will we?" Sloane asked, and the crackling fire shot up the chimney. She looked at the ceiling. "Calm down, Alfred. I have complete faith you'd never let that happen. Some of us like to prepare for the worst. It makes us feel safer." The flames subsided, and a gentle breeze blew back the long black strands that had escaped from Sloane's ponytail.

"The *deofol* incantation is safe, but it is a complicated process to send a Malevolent or Half-Malevolent to the Abyss." Dorathea peered down her sharp nose at the book. "The 'devil' incantation has three parts. First, we must capture it with a *gefon* spell. Second, we use our power of three to open a portal to the Abyss. Finally, we cast the curse that returns it there, *Asellan*."

"Why only the 'power of three'?" Sloane asked. "Why can't Elvina and the others help?"

"Only a Protector Coven can open a path to the Nether realm." Elvina stood beside Sloane. "Your blood doesn't flow through my veins. But I will be here to help detain and return whomever we capture."

"It's a magnificent sight when our collective energy breaks through to the Abyss," said Jack.

"What would you know about it?" Sloane asked, mocking his enthusiasm.

"There's no need to be rude," he said, pouting.

"I'm just saying. We're both new. Have you even seen this forcefield?"

"Well, at least the Grand Coven trained me," he said.

"Is that supposed to make me jealous?"

"Enough bickering." Dorathea breathed deeply, unable to contain her irritation.

Jack gave her an amiable smile. "My apologies for upsetting you, cousin. We really are just teasing each other."

"Like children do," Elvina added, the corners of her mouth curling up.

"Children indeed. Shall we continue?" Dorathea's eyes bore into them until they nodded in compliance.

Sloane climbed onto a stool beside the lectern. "We need to consider we're probably dealing with more than one Half-Malevolent." She chose the magical name instead of Cambion to appease her cousin.

"Why?" Jack asked, sitting on the stool next to hers.

"We know one of the women in Alisdair's photo is Ginerva Byrne, a Sensor, and we suspect Andrew is also a Magical, so we could reasonably consider that the other woman is a Magical or Half-Malevolent." Sloane waited for signs they were following her logic.

Elvina pinched her brows together. "Why would that suggest more than one, dear?"

"I don't see it either," Jack added.

"Very clever," Dorathea said to Sloane. "Malevolents and their spawn are bound to their ancestral lands. The second woman could be the evil supernatural strength behind The Order in the Northeast Quadrant. It also clears up another issue. Our West ancestors and the Gòrdans' banished the Malevolents tied to the lands we protect. We are therefore dealing with their progeny. Which means they learned to elude us, until now."

"My God. There could be thousands of them," Jack said, shifting on his stool uncomfortably. "Wait, what do you mean now?"

"Your cousin has felt the presence of evil since arriving on the Island," Dorathea told him.

"My mother has sensed it too," Elvina said.

"I suspect Freya only perceives those the Half-Malevolent has possessed," Dorathea said, brusquely.

"Not the point, Denham. We are feeling them. That's what matters. And Andrew and Ginerva together in the photo could prove that Magicals in the quadrants are working together, helping the Malevolents bound to our quadrants."

"Half-Malevolents, dear," Elvina corrected.

Dorathea pulled her round spectacles to the tip of her nose. "I agree. Which is why your training must ensure you can capture both. Two Malevolents still exist in the nogical world after all." She silently read the open pages, while the others stared at her nervously. After she finished, she raised her arms like a conductor, and the floating candelabras flickered throughout the covenstead. The air became colder, causing goose bumps on Sloane's skin. "We will train the deofol using another undead being."

The books shelved themselves in a clumsy scramble for open spots as a shadow grew darker and longer in the middle of the library. A moment later, the frigid air thinned. Became so rarefied, Sloane gasped. Fear began to seize her, and she looked at her cousin.

Dorathea held out one hand, palm forward with fingers spread. She bent a finger toward her palm. Sloane glanced at the library. The shadow had the distinct form of a dark, flowing robe. She turned back to her cousin. She had bent another finger down. Sloane wheezed, her lungs on fire. A third finger against her palm. Sloane's head became dizzy. Now, only one finger left, and Dorathea raised her other hand, sending pulsing waves through the air that surrounded the floating phantom.

Instantly, the air in the covenstead became denser, and the goose bumps that had taken over Sloane's body subsided. "What the hell is it, Denham?" She stared at the fully formed presence behind the translucent cage.

"A Wraith, the supernatural closest to a Malevolent in our universe. However, they haven't a Malevolent's strength and pure wickedness. This poor dear escaped the watery realm where Wraiths exist, and I caught it misbehaving in Tagridore. Now we must return it."

Jack walked around the suspended specter. "I've never seen one up close. Not that I'm sad about that fact."

"From its entrance, I can tell this one is quite impetuous." Elvina walked around the shadowy cloak in the opposite direction from Jack.

"He is indeed. I've been looking for him for a few weeks now." They stared at Dorathea. "Why do you look surprised? I don't like boredom. Sometimes, hunting a misguided spirit distracts me."

"So the energy thingy protects us from whatever was happening to us, right?" Sloane asked, still concerned about the inability to breathe in the Wraith's presence.

"What was happening was the Wraith rendering us unconscious so it could feed on our life force," Dorathea said.

"Which is a nice way of saying suck you dry until you're a shell of yourself," Elvina said.

"Oh, yes. Elvina's words are much more accurate." Jack bent his head back and looked at the black void that filled the robe's hood. The Wraith crashed against Dorathea's energy field, and he leaped back, losing his footing and falling hard. He got back to his feet and brushed himself off. "That was unnecessary," Jack said, wagging a finger at the figure.

"Let us continue with the lesson, please." Dorathea looked at Sloane. "I captured the Wraith alone in the *energy thingy*, which is the forcefield the incantation gefon creates. To secure Malevolents and their spawn, we must cast the spell together."

"Gefon means to capture," Elvina said to Sloane. "G-E-F-O-N. You pronounce it ye-von. Ye-von. Practice it slowly. We will wait."

"Yevon," Sloane said easily, and Elvina clapped. "Oh, how we wish they were all so easy."

Dorathea frowned at her and continued, "After we cast the spell together and the Half-Malevolent is trapped, we must encircle it and open a passage to the Abyss." She turned the Book of Hagorúnum around and held it up. "To do so, we visualize with our third eye a space so deep and boundless that light and life are incapable of penetrating it."

"Jesus, that's unsettling," Sloane said as the pulsating blackness on the pages made her shiver.

"The Nether plane is a place of eternal void. It would be unkind to send this specter to the depths of hell." Dorathea waved her hand, and the book's pages quickly skipped ahead and settled on two more. "This is where Wraiths live, another plane in our vast universe."

Sloane stared at the image of crashing ocean waves in shades of dark blues and grays against black, rocky cliffs. Each pounding wave against the jagged rock sent white spray up from the book. Drab dark-brown phantoms floated above the waves and cliffs.

Dorathea set the tome back on the book stand. "We will visualize this realm in our third eye. Then we will chant *geweald of þrī*. G-E-W-E-A-L-D of Þ-R-Ī

"The power of three," Elvina clarified. "Ya-wheeld of three."

Sloane practiced the phrase several times in her head, then said it aloud. Yeh-wheeld."

"Ya, like *a*..apple, dear," Elvina corrected.

"YA-wheeld."

"Much better. And when we open a passage to the Abyss, we will cast together, Asellan, which means to banish. Ah-sel-lun. Take a moment to practice," Elvina said.

"Ah-sel-lun. It's as easy as yevon," Sloane said.

"Very good. We will wait for you to practice your pronunciation. Let us know when you are ready to return my capture to its plane," Dorathea said.

After a few minutes, Sloane climbed off her stool, the coven surrounded the Wraith, and Elvina stood just outside their triangle. It threw itself at them, and the three remained unflinching, holding hands and tightening their formation around it.

When they started chanting, the shadowy phantom screeched, a pitch so shrill that Sloane broke the coven's connection to cover her ears. "Jesus Christ, make it stop."

"You must focus. It's best to learn casting under challenging circumstances. I believe this counts as one," Elvina shouted.

"She's right. A Half-Malevolent will do much worse," Jack yelled.

"What the hell could be worse than this?" Sloane shot back.

"Excruciating images of your loved ones dying...their cries... implanted into your mind forever." Jack grimaced.

"You must manage your surroundings and keep hold of our hands no matter what the Half-Malevolents try to do to us," Dorathea said to her, and Sloane nodded, holding their hands. "We must begin our chant again."

Sloane imagined the Wraith plane, the crashing waves, and jagged cliffs. The coven called out the power of three in unison, the words growing louder and more intense. After several recitations, the covenstead's ceiling turned into a swirling darkness, like a hurricane moves around its eye.

"Prepare to cast the curse," Elvina said. "After two more chants..."

"Asellan," they called out, and a burst of icy white light surged into the eye of the storm, like a fiery flash of lightning, and the floating dark brown robe was gone.

"Oh, my," Elvina said, her voice like a purr.

"That was something. I've never seen such an explosive expulsion," Jack said.

Dorathea looked at him. "It was quite intense indeed." She turned her troubled gaze to Sloane. "We are more powerful than I imagined. Nevertheless, a Malevolent and its spawn are far more complicated to banish than a Wraith. We must continue to practice. I will find another participant for the morning."

"Are we done for now?" Sloane asked.

"What's the hurry?" Jack folded his arms. "I was going to invite you to a late lunch at the pub, but you obviously have somewhere better to be. Do share."

Sloane grinned. "Much better, believe me."

"You're visiting Rose. How wonderful. Do say hello for me," Elvina said.

"We are finished, but you must promise to practice. Our deofol incantation has to be precise." Dorathea returned to the sitting area. "Do not keep dear Rose awake all night. She needs to be sharp."

"I won't. I promise."

"Oh, please," Jack said, chuckling.

Sloane's cell phone buzzed in her back pocket, and she looked at the screen. It was Sharma. She picked up her tote and answered, "Sharma, what's up?"

"Glad I caught you," Sharma whispered, and Sloane figured the lieutenant wasn't alone and was taking a risk just to call her. "I've got some forensics you need to know about. Are you home? Can we meet?"

Sloane closed her eyes slowly. The last thing she wanted was to miss another chance to be with Rose, but Sharma sounded worried. "I'm a little busy. Can it wait until tomorrow?"

"I really need to speak with you today. I can stop by the cottage."

"All right. Can you be here in five?"

"Yeah, see you in a minute."

Sloane glanced at the time. It was already after ten p.m. in Scotland. She was only a few hours late, but if she showed up after talking with Veena, Rose wouldn't get much sleep. Reluctantly, she texted her. *I'm sorry training took so long. Now Sharma needs to meet. Let's try again tomorrow.* She waited for a response, but nothing came.

CHAPTER SIXTEEN

Sloane waited for Veena at the cottage's front windows, wondering about what forensic evidence the lieutenant had to justify an impromptu visit. Was it another memory of the crimes in the crypt that the Weardas failed to remove?

Veena's unmarked car pulled into the circular drive, and Sloane opened the front door. The lieutenant waved as she got out of her vehicle. Her thick, dark hair was pulled back in a low ponytail, and the basic tan pantsuit she wore fit her perfectly like a couture piece.

"Hi, Sharma. Come in."

"Thanks. Damn, it got cold. Supposed to snow by dinnertime."

"Has the Island ever had this much snow?" Sloane asked.

"Not since I've been alive."

Sloane led her friend to the kitchen. "What can I get you to drink?"

"Water's good." Veena sat on a barstool at the long marble island. "Listen, Inspector Nichol is riding me hard on this one. It's gotten complicated."

"All right. If you need my help, you have it, and my discretion." She handed her a glass of water and retrieved a can of diet soda for herself.

"Thanks," Veena said and sipped the water. Then she cleared her throat. "We've been in communication with the Scottish Police. They informed us that Calen Gòrdan's family in Kirkcudbright was attacked on Christmas Day. His father survived. But his sister and brother-in-law didn't make it. And his niece is missing."

"Shit, Sharma. The two incidents have to be related." Sloane kept her face neutral, but she berated herself for lying to her friend.

"Yeah. We agree. Their police have also shared some evidence with us." She shifted her weight on the stool. "They've also asked for our cooperation in their case. Which is another reason Nichol is riding my ass." She averted her eyes and took another sip of water. Her fidgeting was clearly an act of stalling, and Sloane braced herself for the lieutenant's information because whatever it was, it was bad enough that her friend was mentally preparing to share it.

"I'm only disclosing this to you because I trust you," Veena said. "And I know you can help us. They have closed-circuit television of Calen meeting a man several times over the last few months in Kirkcudbright. Their last encounter was the day of the attack. The other man was Jack." She fell silent, looking at Sloane, waiting for a reaction.

"Oh, Jesus. The gallery," Sloane said. "I knew I'd seen the victim before. I thought he looked familiar when you showed me his ID, but I couldn't place him. Now that you put him together with Jack, I'm sure it was the same guy I saw at my office last week. He came upstairs to ask if the gallery was opening. I figured he just wanted to look at some art. I had no idea Jack knew him, but it makes sense. Jack's been securing paintings from Scotland for an exhibition."

"Okay. I also wanted to tell you the ME's preliminary cause of death for Calen is traumatic brain injury. It's the same for his deceased family members in Scotland. Minor wounds in appearance, but massive internal damage."

"That's really strange." Sloane leaned her hip against the island. "You'll let me know what the official cause of death is?"

"Yeah, sure." Veena paused. "I have to interview Jack. We need to establish Calen's movements in the area leading up to the time of his murder. And Jack's a potential witness."

"Do you want to do it now? He's at home. I could ask him to come over."

Veena glanced at her wristwatch. "I can walk next door."

"Nah, let him walk in the cold. Besides, if he has to go outside, it'll ensure he's dressed. He hangs out in nothing but a robe by this time of day if he's not at work."

Veena laughed. "Okay. But I need to talk to him alone."

"I'll stay in my room until you're done. Promise." Sloane removed her cell phone from her back pocket and tapped Jack's number.

"Hello, lovey. I was just getting comfortable. Are you done with the gorgeous lieutenant? Do you want some company?"

"Hi, Jack. Lieutenant Sharma is here. She was hoping you could answer a few questions for her about Calen." Sloane kept her voice neutral.

"Well, I'm impressed. The RCMP only needed two days to link us, huh?" He chuckled, but Sloane remained silent. "Ooh. It's serious, then?"

"Yeah. So put some clothes on, and we'll see you in a few. And, Jack, please use the back door." Sloane ended their call. "He'll be right over."

Less than five minutes later, Jack breezed through the French doors in the breakfast room and held Veena's hand in his in a mock gesture of kissing it. "Lieutenant Sharma. You look smashing."

"Try not to be completely inappropriate, Jack." Sloane picked up her soda can. "I'll be in my bedroom if you need me." Her room was down the hall from the kitchen. The same guest room she used when she'd first arrived in March. She didn't want to use any of the bedrooms on the second floor, leaving her grandparents' and mother's just as she had found them.

She paced behind her closed door. Not because she feared the RCMP would arrest her cousin. But because she knew what the

Weardas would do to Veena if she tried. Then again, would they if they were a part of The Order?

She sat on her bed and thought about the photo of Andrew, Ginerva, and the unidentified woman. Was she right about Ginerva and Andrew being Magical and the other woman being a Half-Malevolent? She retrieved the business card Andrew Gildey had given her. And her blood ran cold at the thought that she could be wrong. He—the Gildeys—could be the descendants of the Malevolent that her ancestors banished to the Abyss.

After she considered the possibility that the Gildeys were the source of evil in Denwick, she decided there was only one way to find out. She entered his number into her cell phone and pressed the call button.

"Andrew Gildey speaking."

He had answered quickly, and Sloane felt like a spotlight had been shone on her. "Mr. Gildey. It's Sloane West. Do you have time to meet with me today? I have a few more questions for you."

"I have meetings for the rest of the afternoon, Miss West. But you could come to my office after business hours. Seven p.m.?"

"All right. See you then." She ended the call and blew out a long breath. It was risky to meet with him alone, but she wanted to detect him.

There was a soft rapping at the door, and Sloane dropped his card back into her tote. "It's open."

Veena peeked her head inside. "We're done. I had to advise Jack not to leave the area. Sorry. It's for the best."

"I understand. Just hope he was helpful."

"He was. And flirty. And over the top. I can't wait to tell my girlfriend she has competition."

"Sorry about that."

"Well, he's consistent," Veena said.

Sloane laughed. "Come on. I'll walk you out." At the front door, she stopped. "Hey, one more thing. Will you run a plate for me?"

"I can. But do I want to?"

"It's nothing to do with a case. Someone's been following me. I found them parked outside the cottage a few nights ago. I don't think it's the first time they've been here."

"Are you serious? Yeah, I'll run it for you. Text it to me. You need to come down to the department and file a complaint. You know that."

"I will. Don't worry about me. I can take care of myself. Well, except for accessing vehicle registrations."

"You kill me." Veena shook her head as she walked away.

"I'll call you tomorrow," Sloane shouted and shut the door. She hurried back to the kitchen to talk to Jack, nervous that he had made the lieutenant suspicious. But he was gone. She pulled out her cell phone to call him when Elvina's voice sounded in her head.

Sloane, dear, you must come to the covenstead. We are waiting. Bestealce dear. There's no time to waste.

Fine. I'm coming. Sloane sighed and closed her eyes, dreading the pain she was about to feel.

When she emerged from the brain-shattering light, she found the rest of her coven in the sitting area, waiting for her. A fire burned in the stone fireplace, and classical piano played quietly in the background. It was Dorathea's favorite album, *Chopin's Nocturnes.* She played her favorite recording of the nocturnes when something troubled her.

"What's happening?" Sloane asked, bracing for their next problem.

"Another headache?" Dorathea asked. "Do describe what you are experiencing."

Sloane joined them, pinching the bridge of her nose, and sat in her armchair. "Don't you all see a light?"

"Not bright enough to jolt our brain," Jack said.

"Fine. It's like a million icy white Christmas lights flashing all at once."

Dorathea considered Sloane's answer for a long moment. "I have investigated what is causing this discomfort for you and found nothing yet. I will focus on the light."

"Great. Thanks. So why am I here?" She glared at Elvina. "You made it sound like an emergency."

"We need to discuss Jack's interview with Lieutenant Sharma," Dorathea said as she refilled her cup of tea.

"I just didn't want you out in the cold," Elvina said.

"Jesus, Elvina."

"At least I didn't come over and abduct you."

Sloane shook her head in disbelief. "Veena told me you need to stay in town, which means they have more questions about your involvement," she told Jack.

"Oh, I know they do. First, she wanted to know how I knew Calen, how we met. When and where. I told her part of the truth. We both dealt with fine art. Of course, I didn't tell her we are Wiccan." Jack downed what remained of his drink.

"Sounds like standard questions," Sloane said.

"Oh, yes, routine," Elvina said, sneering. "Then Veena asked her next question."

"She asked if I could explain how I was in Kirkcudbright and Denwick, only hours apart," Jack said.

"Oh, shit. What did you say?"

He looked at her worriedly. "The only thing I could say. She had to be mistaken."

Sloane groaned. "If the police ask something that specific, you have to know they have the proof. Sharma was gauging how you'd react. And you lied."

"Well, if you knew they had recordings of me, you could have warned me."

"How? I don't know how to speak telepathically."

"Of course you do," Elvina said. "It's how we communicate with each other."

"Because you created some kind of pathway for us," Sloane said, irritated.

"True. But it's still telepathy. And please watch your tone." Elvina stuck her nose in the air, looking away like an annoyed feline.

Sloane turned her attention back to Jack. "Sharma showed me pictures of you and Calen in Kirkcudbright on Christmas Eve. But I didn't know she had pictures of you here."

"Well, she did. I was walking along Old Main. Unmistakably, my handsome self."

Dorathea sighed. "If the Weardas fail to remove the evidence from her mind, I fear we will have trouble with her, pet. She also asked if he knew why Calen was in the crypt. She made a point to mention how strange it was that the two murders in Denwick this past year both took place there." She looked at Jack. "Tell us again what you thought Veena was insinuating."

Jack held his whiskey up to Sloane. "Your industrious detective friend implied that something ritualistic, occult, might be taking place in the crypt. She wants me to answer more questions tomorrow. I fear she'll have a few for you, too."

"Fucking hell. This is why we need to tell Sharma the truth. She remembers details she's not supposed to have in her head. She's smart. We can't fool her," Sloane said, her voice pitching to anger.

"I hear how upset you are. And I am sorry. Nevertheless, we cannot expose ourselves to the nogical world." Dorathea's voice softened. "It is not our place to out other magical creatures, especially those who live in great fear for their lives. We must protect them. That is our purpose here."

"I get that," Sloane said. She matched the calmness of her cousin's voice even though she wanted to shout in protest. "But that's only your opinion. I've lived my entire life with Nogicals. Some are intolerant. Cruel. Violent. Many aren't, and even more are allies for those who are different, in minorities. Sharma is one of those. She could help us, and we can help the RCMP. We might drive out and imprison The Order members we know about. But there are others in all the quadrants. They'll go underground until it's safe to return. When they do, we can trust Sharma to help us. She's loyal, and she won't say anything we don't want her to say."

Dorathea listened patiently and waited for Sloane to stop talking. "It is simply not the time. The Weardas will have to erase the CCTV images from the Nogicals' minds and change the image of Jack."

"This discussion isn't over. The perfect time to make a change never comes." Sloane pointed at Jack's glass. "I'll take one of those."

Jack nodded and snapped his fingers. Another highball glass appeared. He filled it and handed it to her.

"Since we're together," Sloane continued. "We need to talk about Alisdair's photograph and our assumptions about Andrew Gildey." She sipped the fulsmécte, the earthy smell and taste warmed her throat on its way down. "The Half-Malevolent bound to our quadrant could be him." The others stared at her in disbelief, and she added, "When I arrived in Denwick, I felt Denham. A vibration so strong, I knew she was lurking behind the rosebushes."

Dorathea tutted. "I was hardly lurking."

"Sure you weren't. The point is, there have been times since arriving in Denwick that I've also felt a biting chill, bone-deep. I've thought about each time. In Tagridore, when I saw the man in the shadows. Outside the cottage, when we were decorating for Christmas. At the pub. And at the Gildey mansion." She paused, and the rest of the coven stared at her, brows furrowed. "Sharma is running the plates on the Rolls-Royce parked outside the cottage last week. But I'm guessing it belongs to the Gildeys."

"What are you saying, dear?"

Sloane looked at Elvina. "I think Andrew and Isobel are the descendants of the Malevolent our ancestors sent back to the Abyss. The Gildeys are the source of the evil that has been spread throughout the quadrant for nearly two centuries."

Jack's face twisted in confusion. "You've met with them several times. They haven't tried to hurt you, have they?"

"That doesn't mean anything," Sloane said. "They could be waiting to attack us together."

Dorathea shook her head in disagreement. "Jack is quite right. If they are Half-Malevolents, it makes no sense for them to have you in attendance and not strike you down. You are the strongest of our coven, the natural-born Protector."

"Maybe they don't know what I am."

"If the Gildeys are who you think they are, they certainly know who you are, and our coven. If they lead The Order in our quadrant, they were behind your mother's and grandparents' murders."

Dorathea's comment felt like a punch to her sternum. Sloane breathed in sharply and downed her whiskey. "And I have a plan to find out if that's true. And if it is, they will pay."

CHAPTER SEVENTEEN

Elvina had spent the rest of the day chattering in Sloane's head about how displeased they were with her decision to confront Andrew Gildey, which was an understatement. They were pissed, and rightly so. Sloane had no way of fighting a Cambion, but she wasn't afraid. She had been in Isobel's and his presence before, and they didn't try to kill her. She figured they needed something from her, something in her possession at the cottage or the gallery. Something worth keeping her alive until they got it.

At seven p.m. sharp, she pulled into the Gildey Corporation's parking lot with no intention of entering the building alone. She'd wait outside for Andrew and keep enough space around her to fight or escape if she needed to. During the day, she had seen hundreds of cars fill this surface lot, but this evening, there were only a few. She recognized Andrew's, even before she saw the "Reserved for Vice President" sign at the head of the stall. It wasn't hard to miss the sleek, black Maybach. To her, when a person needed to make such a show of wealth, it always indicated they were compensating for something.

She drove past his car to the far end of the treeless, shrubless car park. It was all concrete. The office tower was a severe 1950s brutalist building. They also spent little on lighting the lot. She pulled her tote bag's strap over her head and walked to Andrew's car equipped with her cell phone's flashlight to combat the darkness. The luxury sedan's windows were tinted, but Sloane could still see bucket seats in the front and back that looked more comfortable than her chairs at home. She straightened and walked to the front of the car, leaning against the bumper's cold metal, and waited.

Snow began to fall just like Veena said it would. Sloane glanced at her wristwatch. She had been waiting for half an hour in the cold with the idea that Andrew wouldn't wait for her if she were late, and he would leave his office. But she was wrong, and her peacoat and leather gloves weren't cutting it. She decided if he didn't appear in the next five minutes, she'd turn up at Gildey castle again, unannounced. Might as well find out if Isobel can go through with a threat. Just as the thought bubbled up, the uncomfortable tremor she felt around evil shot through her, and she looked toward the building.

A figure in a hat and an open, long wool coat slowly walked toward the parking lot. It was too dark to make out who it was at first, but as the figure grew closer, she could distinguish that it was the Gildey heir. He wore a black suit, his dark hair pulled back in a short ponytail, and his felt hat pulled low on his brow. He wasn't wearing his dark glasses, but he held his head at just the right angle to mask most of his face. She lifted off the bumper, her hands jammed deep in her coat pockets.

"Ms. West, why are you waiting for me in the cold?"

"I thought it best we talk out here."

He glanced around the empty lot, his gaze stopping on the antique MGA Deluxe roadster. "You could have waited in your car with the heater on."

"Pearl's heater doesn't work so well."

"You should have texted and told me where you wanted to meet. I would have been right down."

"No problem. You're here now."

"Well, I'm not standing in the cold. If you wish to speak with me, it'll have to be in my car." He pressed a button on the fob in his hand, and the sedan's handles deployed. "You said you've never been inside a Maybach."

For a split second, Sloane stood flat-footed. What the hell was she doing? Why would she trap herself in a car with Andrew Gildey if she wouldn't risk being in an office building with him? But the driver's side door closed softly, and she thought, to hell with it. She wanted the truth, so she yanked the passenger's door open and slipped into the leather seat.

"At least you have some common sense." He pressed the car's ignition button and turned up the heater. The air warmed quickly, a hundred times faster than Pearl's heater could manage. "It's never wise to wait outside at night. Especially alone in the middle of nowhere with no one around."

"Are you scolding me or saying I shouldn't trust you and your employees?" Sloane asked and turned in the seat to face him.

"I'm saying it's not smart to be alone in a dark parking lot at night. That's all." His voice was calm, but it held a warning.

"I'll take that under advisement." Sloane looked at the dashboard, aglow with laptop screen-sized control panels, and ran her fingers over its hand-sewn leather and herringbone rows of natural-grain wood. "At least I get to see how much car two-fifty K buys." She couldn't help the sarcastic tone.

"You don't approve." He tapped an arrow on the center screen, and the hot air flow lessened. "Isobel bought this car. She expects me to drive it. Truthfully, I don't even like to drive."

"Why would you when you have a chauffeur driving you around in...what did you say you had? A fleet of Bentleys?"

"I didn't hire him or buy those cars. The Gildey family... Isobel Gildey...has an image to uphold. One she expects me to share."

Sloane stifled a laugh. "Let me guess. You only drive around in luxury cars to keep your mother happy."

"Would you believe me if I said I wish I didn't have to?"

"Not a chance. You don't act like a man unhappy with his wealth." Sloane caught the corners of his mouth turning up. "What?"

"You're not the first to accuse me of that." He lowered his head. "How is your murder investigation progressing? I heard the RCMP confirmed the victim in the crypt was from Kirkcudbright. I presume you are here to ask more questions about my dealings there?"

"That's right." She tried to catch his gaze, but he held his head just so that his eyes stayed in the brim's shadow. "The last time we talked, you said you hadn't been there for a month."

He thought for a moment. "Right, although I didn't verify that with my schedule, so I could be mistaken."

Sloane pulled out a brown envelope from her tote. "You also said you were there to buy art. Who's your art dealer?"

His fingers drummed on the slick, black console separating them. "I don't fault you for doing your job. But you're wasting your time questioning me. I had nothing to do with this poor man's murder. Why would I?"

Sloane took Alisdair's photo out of the envelope and handed it to Andrew. "I want to ask you about this picture again. Do you remember when this was taken?"

The muscles in his chiseled jaw twitched as he studied the image. "I have no idea."

"I do." She turned it around and showed him on the back where Alisdair had jotted the date he had taken the picture. "You were there with these women a week ago." She waited for him to respond, but he stayed silent. "I also know who this woman is." She pointed to Ginerva. Can you tell me the other woman's name? Is one of them your *art dealer*?"

"As I said before, I was only sitting behind them."

"Oh, come the hell on. We both know that isn't true. You can tell me, or I'll find out on my own. It won't be hard. You know I can."

"Listen to me." His voice was taut, and he lowered it, taking a breath. "I apologize. It's just that Isobel and I have been very forgiving of your meddling in our lives. That is bound to change.

It's in your best interest to stop trying to connect me to this murder." He became agitated again, and up until now, she had been unafraid. "The women in the picture are important. They're very important. And they won't tolerate being harassed either. Do you understand me? You must leave them alone." Heat emanated from Andrew, and he gripped the steering wheel.

She wanted to grab his hand and cast a detection spell, but the rising temperature in the car clouded her mind. She struggled to move and form words. "You can threaten me...all you want... I'll...find out...who they are...and you..." She heard her voice falter as her consciousness slowly slipped away.

When Sloane woke, she was sitting behind Pearl's steering wheel. The motor was running, and the air was warm. She looked in the direction of Andrew's Maybach. It was gone.

Pretty sure that went as well as it could have. The voice startled Sloane. It wasn't in her head, and it didn't sound like Elvina. She fumbled with the door handle to get out. *Geez, relax. You're fine.* The locks engaged as if someone pressed both at the same time. They were not electric. *I'm Pearl.*

Sloane sat stunned for a minute. "Pearl? You've come back?"

Obviously. I am to watch over you. And this time, I believe you need me.

"What do you mean, this time?"

You really are just like your mother. Questions. Questions. Someone who cares for you asked me. Now, I need to take you home. Be a good passenger and buckle up. Oh, and hold the wheel. We don't want any Nogicals witnessing an old MG as a driverless car. Even they wouldn't believe that.

Pearl backed out of the parking stall, and Sloane quickly clutched the wheel. Her thoughts raced. What did Pearl's return mean? Would the spirit tell her about Jane? And why was such a young voice named Pearl?

* * *

After the car spirit drove her home, Sloane called the coven to the cottage and explained what had happened with Andrew Gildey.

"He did what?" Dorathea was enraged.

"I don't know how to explain it any better," Sloane said. "I showed him the photo. Pushed for answers. Next thing I know, it's hotter than hell in his car. I wake up inside Pearl, completely disoriented. The car is running and warm inside, which is unusual. And Pearl is back."

"I am astonished she's returned. I figured after Jane left her without saying goodbye, she'd never come back," Elvina said.

"Oh, it's her. Why is she so young? And why's her name Pearl?"

Elvina smiled. "Because your mother wanted a young spirit friend. And she named her Pearl because the spirit was a gift from the Denhams for her sixteenth birthday, instead of a string of pearls."

Dorathea looked at Sloane. "Which was customary. Your mother was not." She smiled affectionately. "It is unusual Pearl has returned. We will speak with her later. For now, we must focus on Andrew Gildey. Controlling temperature. Reality warping. Those are Malevolent and Half-Malevolent abilities indeed."

"That's what I read." Sloane rested her head against the back of her armchair. "I wouldn't have survived if he didn't want me to. I think the Gildeys need something from me."

"Or they realize they need to kill us together," Jack said. "One at a time hasn't worked so far. And we still have two more cousins in the bloodline. Mildred and Baxter. Twins. They're bureaucratic sloths in licensing at the Héahreced. Not the friendliest, believe me. And they could use some vitamin D. Or just a trip outdoors once in a while." Jack shivered. "If The Order kills only one of us, the GC can train either of them as replacements."

"How would they know we have two more cousins?" Sloane asked, and he shrugged.

"Their behavior is curious, and we will investigate the reasons behind it, but right now, tell us what precipitated Andrew's reaction?" Dorathea asked.

"I caught him in a lie. He said he hadn't been to Kirkcudbright since last month. So I showed him Alisdair's photo and the date it was taken. I told him I knew who Ginerva was and would find out who the other woman in the picture was. And that triggered the reaction." She searched for her memory of the incident. "I also asked him what he was."

"For goodness' sake. Your reckless interrogation could have cost you your life." Dorathea stood and motioned to Jack. "We will all stay at the hobbit house tonight. It will be safer. And Alisdair has asked for our assistance this morning. Their morning. Which is only three hours from now."

"You go on. I'm safe here. Besides, Andrew isn't in a hurry to take us out. If he were, I'd be dead."

Jack frowned. "Please don't say things like that, lovey."

"All right. But it's true."

Dorathea wrapped her cloak around her tall frame. "Very well. We leave for the Gòrdans' covenstead at eleven. Don't be late."

After Dorathea and Jack disappeared, Elvina kissed the top of Sloane's head. "Try to rest, dear. And don't be angry with me if you find me by your side."

CHAPTER EIGHTEEN

Alisdair Gòrdan lifted himself from a brown leather chair. He wore a white linen tunic, the length of which grazed the floor, with only his bare toes exposed when he stepped toward them. "Come, sit," he said.

"Thank you, dear." Dorathea glided across the dark hardwood, but Sloane closed her eyes tightly, the discomfort of teleporting growing stronger. She dug inside her tote for the small glass vial that would dull the pain. She took a swig of the elixir and joined the others.

"You deserve the thanks. Foregoing a decent night's sleep to help me," Alisdair said. "I'll summon breakfast before we begin." He waved a trembling hand, and a platter stacked high with butter tarts and a teapot appeared.

"Oh, wonderful. I don't mind if I do," Jack said, piling three tarts and a large helping of preserves on a small plate. He sat in the armchair beside Elspeth, smoothing the sleeping girl's golden hair from her face. Then he rested his hand on her forehead and closed his eyes. After a few seconds, he looked at her grandfather.

"She has calmed considerably. If you'd like, I could help her further along."

Alisdair shook his head. "Elspeth is strong enough for grief's journey. And I will accompany her for as long as the universe allows."

"She is fortunate to have you indeed." Dorathea patted his hand and looked at the others. "Mòrag and Alisdair have been unable to reverse the gestillan curse that binds him. We are here to assist them."

Elvina glared at Dorathea, her usually full black pupils now only slits. "You are mighty, dear, one of the most powerful wiċċe in our world. But breaking curses and spells is my mother's specialty."

"Quite, right. If we are unsuccessful, you can inform her that we need her help."

Elvina stuck her nose in the air. "I refuse to be your go-between, Dorathea."

Sloane stared at her roommate. Since she had been in their presence, Elvina had never called the High Priestess anything other than "dear," and always in an affectionate tone. She felt guilty for the tension between them. When would she stop being a living reminder of how Jane's secret had cast a long shadow that still reached into their present, affecting them. She stood. "All right. You two work out your issues and help Alisdair. Jack and I will find out who the woman with Andrew and Ginerva is."

"We will?" Jack asked, rising to his feet. "How?"

"The photo. Come on, we're leaving." Sloane pulled her tote over her shoulder, and Jack stared at his plate, sighing loudly.

"You're leaving so soon?" Rose asked from across the room.

Sloane turned toward the grand staircase. At the sound of Rose's voice, excitement coursed through her. "Hey, Keane." She looked at the robust man beside Rose. "Ken, you're looking well."

"Aye, can't complain. Not when I have my wee lass here for a bit. She makes everything better."

Ken's accent was stronger, a natural consequence of retiring from The Spotted Owl Inn and Pub the past summer and returning to Scotland. Sloane could tell the thick brogue was no longer for show to entertain his regulars. She hugged him first and then took Rose's hand. "I need a minute," she said to Jack.

"I figured as much, but don't worry about me. I'm always at your beck and call. I'll just be over here finishing my breakfast," Jack mumbled and sat down again, smiling at the plate of butter tarts.

Sloane led Rose behind a wall of books in the Gòrdans' library. The low lighting came from the soft glow of floating candelabras. She pulled Rose close, leaving no space between them. "Holding you is so much better than talking on the phone," she whispered, and buried her face in Rose's hair.

Rose tilted her head back, her jade eyes skimming Sloane's face. "Kissing me will be even better." She brushed her soft lips across Sloane's, kissing her, gently at first until the soft caresses of her tongue became deep explorations, and she pressed her against the books, kissing her so thoroughly that every inch of Sloane's body melted into her. Then she pulled back.

Sloane opened her eyes. "Are you okay?"

"More than okay." She trailed a finger down the side of Sloane's face, slowing on her neck. "Sometimes when my emotions overwhelm me, I want…to hunt. Usually it's when I'm angry." Her fingers stroked the pendant Sloane had given her. "But now I get the desire when I'm thoroughly content."

"I want to know more about your urges." Sloane held Rose close again. She had read about Dhampyres' needs. They could subsist on food but had strong cravings for blood. "Jack and I are searching for the second woman in the photo. Why don't you come with us? You'll have to put up with him, but at least we can spend the afternoon together."

"God I want to, but my dad and I have to stay here." She glanced at the library's entry. "The last members of two Protector Covens are out there. If ever you needed our help, it's now, here." She lightly kissed and bit Sloane's lower lip, sighing into her mouth.

"You are destroying me," Sloane whispered. "Why don't we spread out a nice dinner on that king-size bed upstairs when I get back?"

"Sounds perfect."

A few minutes later, Mòrag led Sloane and Jack to the front door and closed it behind them. They stood on the wide stone-tiled porch of a large Georgian townhouse with similarly sized homes on both sides of the street. An ornate metal estate fence and gate separated the house from the road. Sloane pulled the picture out of her tote.

"What's the plan?" Jack asked, peeking over her shoulder at the photo. "You have one, I presume?"

"We don't need a plan. The picture is all the information we need to find the woman. Look, we know they're sitting on a patio in front of a yellow building. How many yellow cafés can Kirkcudbright have? I've made a list of the ones in town and a few on the A711 heading south. We'll check each one. If the woman is a Cambion, she's passing as a Nogical, and someone will know her." She opened the gate. "Let's start with The Alleyway Bistro."

He shook his head and cleared his throat. "I've been there. Calen took me. It's not where they are. The bistro is in a whitewashed building at the end of Bramble Close. A very charming atmosphere. But no outdoor seating."

"All right. We've already eliminated one." Sloane walked down the snow-covered path in the Gòrdans' front garden and turned back to the house, taking a picture of it on her phone.

"Worried we'll get lost?" Jack chuckled.

"Shut up, Jack." She closed the heavy gate behind them, descended the steps to the sidewalk, and started walking.

"Where are you going? You mean for us to tread in the snow?" he asked.

"Seriously? The first café is only ten minutes away. I'm sure that fancy wool coat will keep you warm. Come on, keep up." Sloane tossed the photo into her tote.

"Ha. If only you were as funny as you are peculiar. I cannot for the life of me understand why you continue to hold on to nogical ways."

After a couple of hours walking around Kirkcudbright in dreary weather, they arrived at The Painter's Tearoom, a pale-yellow building of rough stone with a bright-orange door. There were four tables and two heat lamps on the patio. "This is it," Sloane said.

"Of course it is. It had to be at the bottom of your list," Jack complained, standing under a heat lamp, rubbing his hands together.

Sloane opened the windowless wood door, and the aroma of cinnamon, the sharpness of yeast, and the warmth of vanilla instantly comforted her.

A handful of customers filled the few tables in the cramped space. A stout man with a head and chin full of fiery red hair and fair skin stood behind a long, glass case with a butcher-block top. He eyed them as they entered and motioned to a teenage boy.

The teen was gangly but handsome, with delicate features and sandy-brown hair. He stopped loading used dishware into a bucket and greeted them. "Guid mornin. Wylcome to The Painter's Tearoom," he said, his voice soft and pitched like a choir boy.

The other patrons stared at Jack and Sloane, but their curiosity wasn't surprising. Living in a small town, you know a stranger when you see one. Sloane glanced at several curious faces as she made her way to the counter and slid Alisdair's photograph across the butcher block to the red-headed man. "Hi, we're hoping you can help us. We're looking for her." She tapped the face of the unidentified woman. "This picture was taken at your café about a week ago. Do you know who she is?"

He squeezed his bushy ginger eyebrows together and snorted at her, pushing the photo back. "We don't share information about our customers."

His accent was so thick that Sloane had to confirm. "No? You don't know them?"

He shook his head, but his eyes had clearly shown he knew at least one person in the picture. Why was he denying it?

"Do you mean you don't share information about customers with strangers, or everyone? Because I'm asking on behalf of Alisdair Gòrdan. His family has suffered an unspeakable tragedy, and he wanted this woman to know." She tapped the unidentified woman's face.

Conversation in the small dining room fell silent at the sound of Alisdair's name, and the man's face became red. "As I said, don't bother asking me personal information about my guests." He turned away and disappeared through a swinging door.

"Isn't he the bright spot we all need today?" Jack said. "I suppose this means he isn't serving us either. After all that walking, I could devour a scone and cuppa."

"We don't need him. Someone here will recognize her."

The teen boy approached them, standing between Sloane and a table of customers. He glanced furtively at the swinging door and whispered, "I can take a look at it."

"Thanks. What's your name?" Sloane asked.

"I'm Ewan. That's my da. He's usually not such a crabbit. Sorry."

"No worries, Ewan. Nice to meet you." Sloane handed him the picture. "We're trying to find this woman for our friend."

"Oh, that's why," he said in a low voice and glanced at the door again. "It's Dowager Baroness MacCain. My da would never want her to know he was talking about her. I don't know the other two, but everybody knows her." He handed the photo back to Sloane as if it were the hot sides of a teacup.

"Thanks, Ewan. We appreciate your help. You'd better go. We don't want to get you in trouble." Sloane shoved the evidence into her tote and turned.

When they were outside, she searched for the Dowager Baroness on her cell phone and scrolled through the results.

"Well, that went splendidly, don't you think?" Jack asked. He blew out breath and watched its condensation spread through the frigid air.

"Mmhmm." She continued to scroll and stopped on an article, reading for several minutes. "Interesting. Catriona Dunaid MacCain, The Dowager Baroness of Kirkcudbright, is a highly regarded philanthropist and donates to local artists...including the Gòrdans' rare books store."

"Really?" Jack asked, and she continued to scroll.

"Yeah, and it looks like the Dowager likes the better things in life. Just like the Gildeys, wouldn't you agree?" She held her phone out to Jack and showed him a picture of the MacCains' estate.

Jack whistled. "Oh, lovey. I'd say so."

Sloane searched for a cab company and tapped the number of the first result, putting the call on speaker. After a few rings, a woman answered. "Langlands Taxi. How can I help you?"

"I need to hire a car to Ingle Manor. Pick up at The Painter's Tearoom," Sloane said.

A slight hesitation followed. "Ingle Manor. Will that be a round trip?" the operator asked, and Jack shook his head, pantomiming that they should teleport. "Ma'am?"

Sloane mouthed *fine* at him and said, "Round trip won't be necessary."

"Okay. One way to Ingle Manor. We have a driver a few minutes away from your location."

"Great, thanks." Sloane ended the call and looked at Jack, annoyed. "What's wrong with you?"

"Nothing. I don't think we should make some poor Nogical wait for us when we aren't sure what the Dowager is capable of. And now that I think about it, we shouldn't even be visiting a possible Half-Malevolent, certainly not without the others."

"You can go back to the Gòrdans. But I'm asking the Baroness Catriona MacCain some questions."

Jack sighed. "Oh, fine. I can't let you go alone. Please don't make me regret this."

CHAPTER NINETEEN

The taxi passed through an elaborate stone archway with what looked to be the MacCain family coat of arms, a red-and-gold shield with two intertwined black vipers rising out of a green hill, sculpted on each side. The driver pulled around the expansive motor court and dropped them off in front of an enormous Georgian mansion's grand portico. They stood for a moment in the cold. The only sounds were the whistling winds off rolling hills and the shrill caws of crows. Sloane looked around the estate. The house was surrounded by undulating countryside, dotted with mature bare trees.

Jack leaned closer and whispered, "Have you alerted Elvina? We may need them."

"We don't even have to enter the manor. I'll know if the Baroness is evil when she's near me. You'll sense her and make sure she's not a possessed Magical, and we'll teleport the hell out of there."

They ascended the stairs, and a man with thick salt-and-pepper hair, dressed in a red-and-gold kilt and a traditional black Prince Charlie jacket and vest, opened the front door.

Jack looked at him from head to toe and whispered, "Ooh, I feel better already."

"Not the time, Jack," she grunted back at him.

"Sorry. I say whatever pops into my head when I'm nervous."

The man met them on the landing. "May I help you?" he asked.

"I'm Sloane West, and this is Jack Denham. We have news to share with the Baroness, and it's not what one gives over the telephone."

His expression remained unaffected. "Follow me, please."

He left them in a small room to the left of the entry hall. Jack exhaled a long breath when the door closed behind him. "My God, he's locked us in the coat closet."

Sloane turned the doorknob. "Door's unlocked. Jesus, relax, Jack."

"Have you had any...you know, shivers?" he asked anxiously.

"It doesn't happen until the evil is near me."

Jack nodded and began to pace. A few minutes later, the man returned. "The Dowager Baroness of Kirkcudbright will see you now. Follow me, please." They walked down a corridor extravagantly decorated with antique tables, porcelain vases, and family portraits on both sides. Men, women, children, and even dogs and horses. Generations of the MacCains. At the end of the hall, he opened a set of double doors and announced in a deep voice, "Ms. Sloane West and Mr. Jack Denham." Then he backed out of the room and shut the doors.

"Please excuse Carson. He is so formal," the Baroness said in a slight Scottish accent, and Sloane was surprised by how much more severe the woman standing before them looked than the image of her in their photo. Her white hair was wrapped so tightly in a top knot that the strands pulled the freckled skin of her face upwards, and her mouth looked like she had disapproved of life for many years. "Sloane West and Jack Denham. Tell me, why have you presented yourselves at my home without invitation?

I'm sure you can understand my curiosity is piqued as to why Americans—"

"Oh, no. I'm Canadian." Jack pointed to himself. "She's American."

The Dowager lifted an eyebrow and gave them a slow once-over. "You are quite the handsome couple." She looked at Jack. "Such a charming smile. And you…" She held Sloane's gaze. "Extraordinary gray eyes. Like diamonds."

"We're not a couple," Sloane replied.

"But thanks for the compliments," Jack added.

"As I was saying, I am curious to know why you want to speak with me." The Baroness crossed her arms, and her gray-tweed suit cuffs lifted, revealing several amethyst and diamond bracelets.

"We're just here to relay some information. It won't take long," Sloane said curtly. She tilted her head back and regarded the gilded ornamentation on the dark scarlet walls and vaulted ceiling. "This room is impressive."

"Yes, it is." The Baroness turned away and walked toward the center of the foyer.

Sloane took the opportunity and leaned close to Jack, whispering, "I feel her evil. You'll have to sense her."

A look of terror crossed his face. Sloane squeezed his arm reassuringly, and they joined the Baroness. She stood beside a round, claw-foot table, the circumference of which was the size of a baby swimming pool. Bronzes of animals and human nudes were scattered about its inlaid mahogany surface, in the center of which was an ancient-looking bonsai tree.

The MacCain coat of arms drew Sloane's gaze to the back wall. It hung prominently above another set of double doors, and two life-sized portraits flanked each side. She studied their subjects' faces.

"Exceptional, aren't they?" the Baroness said to her. "My husband and me in our youth. He is deceased now. Regretfully, we never had children, so the Barony of Kirkcudbright is dormant. But eventually I'll pass the estate on to an heir."

Sloane held the Dowager's gaze. The woman's eyes were the same intense amethyst color as the representation of them in her portrait. "Lucky guy. I'm guessing it's a man…male primogeniture is still the law, right?"

"Only for those born before 2011. The laws have changed." She looked at Jack, picked up a pair of pruning shears, and began trimming leaves from the bonsai. "He is from Canada, actually. If the heir had to come from outside the UK, I'm pleased he's from a Commonwealth country. But I'm sure you aren't here to ask about our dormant Barony and future heirs."

"We're not. We came to inform you that the Gòrdan family was attacked on Christmas Day. The only survivor is Alisdair."

She held up the shears. "My God, you must be mistaken. I would have heard of such a tragedy."

"I'm afraid it's true, and since you were a faithful patron of their rare books store, we thought you might want to know. We also hoped you would use your position to keep their murders the police's top priority."

"Poor Alisdair. He must be inconsolable. How could such a tragedy happen? Everyone else is dead? Even the child?" She sighed and lowered her head as if in prayer. After a long moment, she looked up again and asked, "How do you know the Gòrdans. Are you related?"

"Just family friends. Jack was close to Calen, but I only met them recently." Sloane unbuttoned her peacoat and wiped the sweat forming on the back of her neck with her hand.

"Yes, Calen and I go way back. Of course, his sister and I were also friends. And Alisdair…well, who wouldn't have wanted him for a father?" Jack said, his voice straining. He tugged at his shirt collar, and beads of perspiration were slicking the hair around his temples. Sloane saw him catch himself from falling forward.

"Are you alright, Mr. Denham?" the Baroness asked. "You don't look well."

Her words sounded distorted and faraway, and Sloane attempted to stand beside Jack, to steady him, but her step trudged as if she were walking upstream in a raging river. "Oh, my. You don't seem to be feeling well either, Ms. West."

Sloane stripped off her coat, and it dropped to the floor. The room smelled like a blazing fire, and the air stung her lungs and her bare arms. She looked at Jack. He was swaying back and forth, and the room began to spin. She reached out to him. "Jack, we need to tel—"

"Such confidence, Ms. West. I'm impressed you think you can?" The Dowager burst into uncontrolled laughter, and Jack collapsed.

Sloane called to him, but no words sounded. The air was fiercely licking at her skin now. She needed to get Jack out of there. She tried to open her third eye, but it was shrouded by smoke. She steadied herself against the table with both hands.

The tabletop began to move under her palms. It swirled quicker and quicker, becoming a funnel of flames. She yanked her hands back and watched as some of the figures crawled up the branches of the bonsai to safety while others fell into the vortex of fire. The sounds of their shrieking filled the room.

The Dowager's laughter grew more maniacal, and Sloane looked up just as the Baroness's likeness from the hanging portrait flew out of its canvas, stopping within an inch of Sloane's face, and screamed, "You dared to face me with only an inferior wiċċa by your side, Sloane West. Now you both will die." The image flew through the Dowager's body and back into its gilded frame.

"Is that all you have? Parlor tricks?" Sloane shouted, rage pulsing through her. She looked at Jack. Sweat had turned his crisp lavender button-down shirt purple under his arms and around his neck. She concentrated on his chest, making sure it was rising and falling. It was, but barely. She wasn't letting him die. Not as long as she had breath.

"Your impertinence has taken all the sport out of killing your coven. We were hoping for at least an entertaining fight." The Dowager's face was red with fury, and her voice strained.

Sloane sank to her knees, and her head lolled toward Jack. Blood trickled from her cousin's nose. She tried to clear the smoke from her third eye, but it was thicker now. No longer able to hold herself upright, she fell back in a heap against the scalding stone floor, her hand landing on Jack's shoulder.

"Goodbye, West Coven." The Baroness's cackling sounded like the whistle of a passing train. Before it faded into oblivion, an icy tremor ripped through Sloane, and her world went black.

* * *

Sloane could hear frantic voices around her. She struggled to clear her mind, to hear what they were saying. Consciousness brought feeling to her body, and she realized her backside was soaked and freezing, and the air she breathed stung from her nostrils to her lungs.

"Can you hear me, pet?" Dorathea asked, and Sloane could feel her cousin's hands on her head before she could understand her words.

"What's happened to them?" Rose asked, and her terrified voice penetrated Sloane's muddled thoughts. She wanted to reach out and hold Rose's hand, but the command was lost in pain.

"We must continue to cool their bodies. But faster," Elvina said, and suddenly, Sloane lifted into the air, suspended, tethered only to her former familiar's hand on her chest. Her arms fell toward the snowy ground, and her legs bent at her knees.

She struggled to open her heavy lids, to remember why she was there…what had happened…She thought of Jack, and her heart quickened. "Where's Jack?" she mumbled.

"He's right here. You're both here," Rose said.

In a flash of light, they appeared inside the covenstead. Over the next hour, Dorathea circled Sloane as she lay on a long metal table. She hummed a low, melodious incantation that sounded more like a Gregorian monk's chanting. She could make out three words she didn't understand, Old English for something. Slowly, her thoughts became clearer until she could open her eyes and sit up. Without saying a word, Dorathea stepped away and joined Elvina and Alisdair, already working on Jack.

"There you are. I was so worried," Rose said and kissed Sloane's forehead. She wrapped her arms around her shoulders.

"I'm sorry. I didn't mean to worry you." Sloane's throat felt hoarse, and her voice rasped. Rose released her, and she looked at the table beside hers. Jack lay there, motionless, and Dorathea, Elvina, and Alisdair circled him, chanting. As their voices grew louder, she saw a violet light rising from his body. "Is he going to be okay?"

Rose stroked her back. "Dorathea said he will." She cupped Sloane's face and turned it back to hers. "She also said it was a brilliant idea of yours to teleport you both into the snow to cool you off as fast as possible. And I agree. It doesn't snow like this here, not very often. We were so lucky."

Sloane didn't feel lucky. She was confused and mad at herself. Getting attacked was her fault. She hadn't expected Catriona to overpower them without warning. The Baroness had to have cast a curse from the moment they entered. For the first time in her life, Sloane had been rendered helpless, unable to tap into her anger in time to use it.

"I don't know what happened." Sloane closed her eyes and tried to recall the moment before they appeared in the Gòrdans' garden, trembling when she saw herself fall to the stone floor, reaching out for Jack. But that was all she could remember. She didn't know if she or Jack teleported, but she didn't think they did. So how the hell did they end up there?

"Oh, thank goodness, dear. You are back with us," Dorathea said, standing over Jack.

"He's okay?" Sloane asked.

"I've been better." His voice was weak. He sat up with Alisdair and Elvina's help and looked at Sloane. "I thought we were dead. I owe you my life."

"I didn't do anything…Catriona's curse immobilized me. We were under her control the minute we set foot in Ingle Manor. She was toying with us. I didn't realize it until it was too late." Everyone stared at Sloane, and Rose held her tighter.

"Who is Catriona?" Dorathea asked, and Alisdair threw his arms out and grasped his head.

"She's the second woman in Alisdair's photo," Sloane said. "The Dowager Baroness of Kirkcudbright, Catriona MacCain."

"You went there without telling us?" Elvina asked, visibly upset.

"Yeah. And I don't know how the hell we got out. I lost consciousness and woke up outside." She locked eyes with Dorathea. "Someone is protecting me, and we need to find out who."

Rose glared at Elvina. "Why didn't you know they were in danger? I thought you were supposed to know when she needs you."

Elvina smoothed her hand over Sloane's arm. "We had no connection open. Or I would have been," she said, and Rose pulled Sloane closer to her, away from Elvina's hand.

"Only a Malevolent or its spawn could have gained entry into your body and brain and tortured you in this manner. You have survived a maleficium curse," Dorathea said. "You are right about this woman."

"Sloane sensed her evil," Jack said and looked down at his hands, palm up in his lap. "I intended to detect her. We see how well that went."

"Is this true?" Dorathea asked Sloane.

"Yeah." Sloane let herself down from the table. "The sensation was strongest right before I lost consciousness."

Rose gripped Sloane's hand tightly and glared at the others, her jade-green eyes burning with fury. "Who the hell thought it was a good idea to send just the two of them to a Half-Malevolent's lair?" She spoke slowly, enunciating each word more loudly than the last. The energy around her drew everyone as if they were being spirited to her. "If you refuse to keep her safe, then she will stay with me, and I will."

"Rose," Ken shouted from the top of the double staircase.

Rose looked at him with the expression of a scolded child. The room snapped back to normal, and a red flush crept up her long neck.

Sloane had seen Rose become furious with Oscar in the pub, felt the charged energy between them, but those moments were nothing like what just happened. This was protective. Primal.

"I'm so sorry. I don't know what came over me." She let go of Sloane's hand and rushed toward the stairs, disappearing straightaway into the house with her father.

Sloane tried to go after her, but Rose moved like a sped-up film, and Sloane had only taken a step before the door at the top of the staircase closed.

"Leave her. She needs to be with Ken," Dorathea said, and she exchanged a troubled look with Elvina.

"What was that look? Why don't you want me to go after her?"

"It appears Rose might have bound herself to you," Elvina said. "But it isn't normally how Blodaeters or Dhampyres claim a mate."

"What the hell is that supposed to mean?" Sloane asked.

"I thought you would've read everything about Rose's kind in your mother's schoolbook." Jack grinned, but Sloane's fierce glare choked his amusement. "Seriously, though, it means for her, you're as good as married."

CHAPTER TWENTY

The next morning, Sloane awoke before sunrise and brewed a pot of coffee. Ken thought it was best if she returned to the cottage. His daughter needed space, he said. His request stung because Sloane figured he was relaying Rose's wishes.

She listened to her messages while the kitchen filled with the nutty, earthy aroma of Elvina's favorite coffee beans. The first message was from Rose.

Hi, it's me. I am so sorry for losing my temper. If my da hadn't stopped me…it wouldn't have been good. I'm even sorrier you didn't stay over. But I think my da was right. I needed time to figure out what happened. And I'm pretty sure I have. Could we find some time to talk? Call me when you can.

How Rose stressed the word "talk" might have sent Sloane's thoughts spiraling in the past, but now, hearing Rose's voice only calmed her, drawing her in like an ocean tide slowly pulls sand safely into its depths.

She saved Rose's message and listened to the next one. Veena had called just after midnight and asked Sloane to meet her at the crypt at eight a.m. The lieutenant said she needed her help with some evidence, but her voice sounded strained, as if she were hiding her real emotions. The message created a knot in Sloane's stomach. She replayed it a few more times and combed through her memory of the crime scene on Christmas Day. Did Sharma want to discuss new evidence or Jack's interview? He would be meeting the lieutenant later that afternoon at the RCMP headquarters.

"Thank you for making our morning coffee, dear." Elvina had silently appeared in the kitchen on the other side of the island from her. "Were you able to sleep?"

"I got a few hours. How about you?" She filled two mugs and handed one to her roommate.

"Same as you. I'm surprised you were able to sleep at all. Yesterday was stressful. The attack. And Rose."

"Yeah. It was a shit show. Except for Rose. Before you start, I'm not talking about her." She gave her old familiar a stern look and sipped her coffee. It was hard not to share her feelings with Elvina. When she knew her as Bear, her cat, she told her everything.

"I understand, dear. But you must have many questions about her bonding with you. When you're ready to talk about it, I'll be here." Elvina waved her hand, and a lavender box appeared. She opened the lid and slid the box toward Sloane. "Scone?"

Sloane shook her head. "I'm not hungry. And I'm on my way out. Veena left a message last night to meet her at the crypt." Sloane finished the last gulp of coffee, rinsed her cup out, and put it in the sink. "She knows something's not right with Calen's murder. And I don't like lying to her, not that she doesn't see right through it when I do." She wrapped a couple of scones in a napkin. "I'll take these to go."

"Please be careful. And let me know at once if you need me. I may no longer be your familiar, but I will still protect you with my life."

"Don't get all soft on me. I'll be fine."

Sloane pressed the garage door opener, and when the door was halfway up, Pearl's engine started, and her reverse lights came on. "Jesus, how'd I forget?" she said, startled. Her mother's car spirit had returned, but it had slipped her mind. She climbed behind the wheel. "Good morning. Did you assume I needed to go somewhere?"

Duh. No one visits the garage in winter unless it's to drive.

Sloane grinned at Pearl's crabby teenager voice. She wanted to correct her as they would be boxing up Christmas decorations and spending a day or two in the garage, but her therapist's voice sounded in her head. Pearl was looking for validation, not a debate. "I suppose that's true. Do you get lonely?"

Nah. Onyx and Alfred used to hang out with me. We've been friends for ages. They know I'm back, and we've already played some poker. Pearl slowly backed out.

"Poker?" She chuckled, trying to imagine a house and two car spirits playing cards. "I've met Onyx. She's nice enough." She remembered riding in Dorathea's small, black Fiat, but the spirit had hidden from her that day. She had met her since, a more mature voice. Alfred and Onyx must be like parents for Pearl.

She's great. Bad at poker, though. Pearl laughed.

"If you want to drive, I'm headed for the cemetery."

Of course I'm driving. Geez. It's my purpose. Pearl pulled onto Mallow Drive in the direction of the Old Denwick Church. The car spirit sounded like an impatient teen but also reminded her of Gary, her quirky upstairs neighbor in New York. He was tough, sometimes abrasive, but he had a heart bigger than the City. The thought made her smile.

A few minutes down the road, Sloane asked, "Were you and my mother close?"

Oh, Slo…you don't mind if I call you Slo, do you? she asked, and Sloane shook her head and waited with anticipation for any new stories about her mother, any insights into what she was like before she had hidden in New York City.

*Jane and I were the best of friends. We went all over this Island together. I was her confidant. Especially when Elvina was driving her crazy. She told me her secrets. We laughed. Cried. She was so wonderful. So kind to me…*Pearl's voice trailed off.

"I'm sorry your best friend left. But I can tell you she didn't want to leave you. She was forced to. And I'm going to find out who made her leave everyone she loved," Sloane said, and Pearl slowly pulled into the cemetery parking lot. "Maybe you can help me. Did my mother ever talk about collecting research on Magicals before she left?"

Nah. She was busy dating some guy from the mainland. I'd take her to the ferry for their dates. But she didn't even let me meet him. Not once. I think he was a Nogical. Pearl parked beside Veena's unmarked vehicle. *Here you are. Please be careful. I haven't spoken with Elvina or Dorathea yet, and I don't want them to be mad at me for bringing you here when I do.*

"I'll be fine. Wait here. I won't be long."

Sunrise had started, and a cacophony of winter birds made their presence known in the cemetery. The piercing whistles and caws of grackles and crows were far from the melodic dawn chorus of spring. Sloane looked up the hill. The mausoleum lights glowed a soft amber, fading into the sun's presence.

The white, opulent building still had crime scene tape across its entry, even though she hadn't seen RCMP Ident in the parking lot. She ducked under and walked to the stairwell in the back.

"West, is that you?" Veena's voice sounded from below.

"Yeah, be right down."

Only Veena was inside the crypt. Ident had finished processing the scene a few days ago, but their floodlights still illuminated the musty, dirt-floored tomb. She paced in front of the back wall, stopping when Sloane entered. The lieutenant had tossed her light-gray blazer over one of the sarcophagi, and her dress shirt sleeves were rolled up to her elbows. The look on her face made Sloane pause.

"Hi, what's going on?" Sloane asked.

"I was hoping you could tell me." Veena crossed her arms over her chest. "We've helped each other on several cases now. Two murders. Trafficking. And we work well together. Because I trust you. And I consider you a friend."

"I feel the same. Why do I hear a but coming?"

"No but. I'm making more of a preface." She paused. "Forensics came back on the footprints, and the ME concluded Calen's cause of death."

"All right. That's good, isn't it?"

"It should be. If his body hadn't been tampered with." There was a finality in Veena's voice, the kind of assuredness that Sloane knew she couldn't undermine.

"What? Tampered?" Sloane's surprise was genuine. The responding Weardas had to be bent. Not only did Veena remember details of Calen's death, but she also knew evidence was changed. The only thing the lieutenant hadn't figured out was by whom.

"Hear me out," Veena said. "Forensics matched two sets of footprints found on the stairs to Sam, the caretaker, and Calen. A third set of prints is unknown. But when I first arrived at the scene, there was just *one* set on the stairs, and I took pictures of the evidence and wrote notes. I showed you. Remember? But my pics and notes are gone. Disappeared. It doesn't matter, though, because I remember the only shoe print was a men's size ten, and Calen was size twelve. The caretaker is size ten. So how did Calen's and the third set's prints get there? And more importantly, how the hell did he and his murderer get down here? Because they didn't use the stairs."

Sloane put her fists on her hips and shrugged.

"That's not all. The medical examiner says Calen died from a brain bleed caused by blunt force trauma to the side of his head. But when I inspected Calen's body, he had no visible injuries, only a minor abrasion on his forehead. You saw the pictures I took. Tell me you remember the side of his head wasn't bashed in."

Sloane was silent for a beat.

"Son of a bitch. Not you, too?" Veena's arms gestured wildly.

"No. Wait. I had to think about your question, that's all. I seem to recall a conversation about the staircase, but I can't say for sure." She watched her friend struggle to accept what she was hearing. "I was shocked, Sharma. Triggered by the whole thing. Another dead body in the crypt." She hated herself. The suspicion and hurt on Sharma's face crushed her. A long silence passed between them, and she finally asked, "What do you mean, me too?"

The lieutenant shook her head. "This is just like last March. Ident and the officers working on the case don't remember the scene the way I do. The evidence at the station is not what I saw them collect." She narrowed her eyes. "Something's wrong in this crypt and with these murders."

"Sharma—"

"Don't lie to me again, West. In all of our cases, you are always one step ahead of us. You're an ex-cop. You don't forget conversations or evidence. Which means you're deciding to keep whatever's happening from me."

Sloane didn't want to continue hurting her friend. Veena deserved better. Regardless of what the Grand Coven and the other species' governments believed, they could trust some Nogicals, even accept their help, and Sharma was one of them. "Okay. I'll try to recall. For what it's worth, I believe you."

Veena didn't respond. She stared at Sloane as if she wanted to trust her but couldn't bring herself to. She turned away and said, "Come look at this."

Sloane followed her to the back wall. The pendant under her T-shirt pulsed with the desire to open the West's portal to Tagridore.

"This wall." Veena ran her fingers over several veins in the stone and took a few steps back. "Can you see it?"

"See what?" Sloane forced herself to say the words, and Veena frowned, moving closer and taking hold of the chain around Sloane's neck. The muscles in the lieutenant's forearm twitched, and she lifted the Tree of Life pendant into the air.

"Are you going to stand there and tell me these two things don't look alike?" Veena asked, looking from the pendant to the Tree of Life now visible in the granite's veins. She dropped Sloane's necklace and retrieved two baggies from her pocket. "Do you want me to believe it's a coincidence these necklaces were found at both murders, and that they're identical to yours?"

Sloane didn't respond, deciding that if she couldn't tell Veena the truth, she wouldn't say anything at all. The crystal beads in the center of both pendants the lieutenant held gleamed in the floodlights, and Sloane could hear all three portal keys pulse with purpose. Behind Veena, the indentations in the Tree of Life in which each key fit glowed faintly, revealing themselves.

"Okay. Don't answer. You probably think I'm losing my mind. Or maybe you want me to think I am. But you're wrong. And I'm not going to." Veena scrubbed her hands over her face and stared at the magical barrier between the nogical and magical worlds. "I know what's happening here isn't normal. I don't understand how. But I know it's not."

"Sharma, you're my best friend. I'd have to have a damn good reason to lie to you," Sloane said. It wasn't as clever an obfuscation as her cousin could create, but Veena nodded.

"I know, which is why I need you to believe me." Veena leaned against the wall. "My Nani, my mother's mother, died when I was six. The times she came to visit from India, she brought me small blankets in these jewel-toned colors. They had mirrored charms sewn on them. She told me that when I was born, she performed a ritual to ward off *nazar*, the evil eye." Veena held out her arm. "She had tied a red thread, like this one, around my wrist to protect me from evil spirits. She taught me they exist in this world. And I can feel them here, in Denwick."

Sloane concealed her surprise at how close Sharma was to knowing exactly what was happening in the crypt, in Denwick, and the nogical world.

Veena continued, "At bedtime, Nani told me stories about supernatural beings. She told me they weren't make-believe. She insisted I must honor my third eye, keep it open to ward off evil spirits and their plans to harm me." She rubbed the back of her neck and used her shirt to fan her chest.

"That's good advice. Your Nani sounds like she had acute intuition."

"Is that all you have to say? Intuition?" Beads of perspiration formed at Veena's hairline, and she wiped them with the back of her forearm. "I think you know what's happening here. And you're hiding it from me."

Sloane noticed Veena's labored breathing. "Are you okay?" Her friend dropped to her knees, and Sloane recognized the look on Veena's face, the confusion and pain brought on by burning from the inside out. "Where the hell are you?" she yelled, looking around frantically. She felt the icy tremor before she saw the shadow pass over them, disappearing the floodlights like a black hole swallowing stars.

She reached for Veena, and as soon as her arms grasped her friend's arm, green-and-white light exploded around them. She opened her third eye, quickly looking past the veil, and the floor dropped away.

CHAPTER TWENTY-ONE

Sloane and Veena appeared in a heap on the floor of the West Covenstead's library. Alfred had removed his barrier, allowing Sloane to bring Veena there, where no other Nogical had ever been. The library books above their heads scuttled onto their shelves, hiding themselves from the rare intrusion.

Before Sloane could speak, Jack lifted her onto her feet, and she saw Dorathea holding her hands over Veena's unconscious body. "It was a Half-Malevolent. I know because I felt it in my bones, and Sharma had the same look on her face that Jack did when Catriona tried to kill us."

Jack scooped Veena into his arms. "The poor lieutenant. I wouldn't wish that pain on my worst enemy."

"We must act quickly." Dorathea waved her hand, and every candle, pestle and mortar, and burning Bunsen disappeared from the first table outside the library.

As soon as Jack laid Veena on the table, Elvina, Dorathea, and he began to move around her clockwise, hands inches above her body, chanting the same dulcet phrase they had at the Gòrdans' covenstead.

Sloane watched Sharma for a sign that the incantation was working, but her face remained motionless. No movement behind her eyelids, no muscles twitching. Why did she agree to meet Veena in the crypt? The Gildeys and Catriona wanted her dead. What the hell was she thinking? She held her head in her hands. She had done this to Sharma. "This is all my fault. Jesus, I led them right to her. Please don't let her die." Her coven continued to move around Veena's body without acknowledging Sloane, and she made fists, slamming them against her sides. "You should have taught me the healing spell. I could have started it right away."

Calm yourself. You tore the Nogical from an evil supernatural's clutches. I have not seen such power since your great-great-grandfather, the Sycyldend, our Great Protector. Even he would have been unable to carry out such a feat.

The voice in Sloane's head was calm and soothing, resonant like the narrators on the nature documentaries she watched as a kid. *Who is this?* She was surprised to find she could speak to the voice telepathically. The way she did with Elvina. *How did you know my great-great-grandfather?*

I'm Alfred. I've inhabited your great-great aunt's covenstead since she arrived in the village with the Sycyldend.

Sloane looked up. *Alfred? I didn't expect you to ever speak with me...or sound like that.* She glanced at the others, healing Veena. *Thank you for letting me bring my friend here.*

It is my pleasure to assist you now and throughout your reign.

Before Sloane could ask Alfred what he meant by her "reign," the others stopped moving. Their mantra grew louder, and with each iteration, they drew a green light from Veena's body. At the climax of their voices, the light tore away and vanished. Sloane stood beside Jack. "Is she going to be all right?"

"She will be, thanks to your quick action, lovey."

"Jack is correct. You saved Lieutenant Sharma's life." Dorathea laid her hand on Veena's forehead. "She'll wake in a few minutes. Tell us everything that happened before she does."

"I didn't save her. I caused her injury." Sloane raked her hands through her long black hair.

"We have no time for misplaced guilt, dear. You must tell us what the lieutenant knows," Elvina chided, and they stared impatiently at Sloane.

"She knows the recent murders and assaults in Denwick are connected. I'm not saying she's Magical, but she is incredibly intuitive and believes in the supernatural. Which probably makes her more receptive to our world. Maybe that's why the Weardas haven't been able to wipe her mind completely. She remembers evidence that her colleagues no longer do and doesn't think she's losing her mind. She accepts there's a preternatural reason for it. We could use her help, Denham. We need to tell her the truth about the magical world and The Order."

Dorathea frowned at Sloane and stared into the room, engaging in a discussion with Alfred. After a few minutes, she said, "It would seem Alfred agrees with you and has no regrets about allowing Lieutenant Sharma into our covenstead. But if what you say is true, we will be unable to erase the image of our sacred space from the lieutenant's mind. I fear neither of you nor Alfred can grasp the peril you have put us in."

A gust of wind pushed them forward, and Sloane could sense Alfred had stormed out of the covenstead. After he left, Veena groaned, her head rolling from side to side on the table. "You're wrong about her. She would never put us in danger. Sharma would respect and value us for who and what we are."

Jack scoffed. "What makes you think at this point in human history, Nogicals are more open-minded than they were in the past when they hanged, stoned, burnt, and drowned us? If anything, they've regressed. Don't you watch their news?"

"Jesus, Jack. They don't all behave the same way. Even if they did, hiding from them isn't the answer."

Elvina gently rubbed Sloane's back. "I agree with you. But we must be wise about how we make the change we seek. For me, the best path is small acts in my immediate circle. This includes Lieutenant Sharma. And telling her the truth." She looked at

Dorathea. "We have never experienced a force like The Order. It's possible the old laws will not serve us in our fight against them."

Veena sat up and gasped for air. After a few deep breaths, she patted her abdomen and chest and looked at Sloane with wide eyes, the lines across her forehead deepening. "What just happened? And don't tell me I passed out and you drove me here. I know we didn't drive. So tell me the truth." Her voice faded as she looked around the room.

"Everything's all right, Sharma. You're okay."

She looked at Sloane. "Where the hell am I?"

"I brought you to Dorathea's. We're in the hobbit house's basement..." Sloane glanced at Dorathea. "Our covenstead."

"Covenstead...I knew it," Veena said, and even though her voice was weak, it had a strong sound of satisfaction. She slowly moved her legs to the side of the table and stood, wobbling on her feet.

"Careful, dear," Elvina said, steadying her.

"Why did you lie to me?" Veena asked Sloane. "I asked you if you knew what was going on. I told you the supernatural didn't scare me. And you let me believe I was imagining things."

"Sloane did not have the authority to tell you about our world," Dorathea said. "That belongs solely to me, and I disallowed it. Come, let us calmly discuss what you are seeing here."

"You're witches. That's what I'm seeing."

"We prefer Wiċċan, dear," Dorathea said, sharply.

Veena frowned at them and looked around the room. Her gaze stopped on the various liquids bubbling and hardening, the shelves full of herbs and bones, and jars full of animal parts floating in clear liquids. "My grandmother practiced a type of magic and told me a natural race of witches...Wiċċan...existed. But they left our world long ago."

"Well, cat's out of the bag," Jack said, elbowing Elvina.

"I'm a transitioned being, dear. Not a wiċċe," Elvina said.

Veena stared at her, unable to react. Sloane grabbed the lieutenant's arm and led her to the armchair Jack usually occupied. "It's true. I couldn't tell you about our world. Even if I disobeyed my cousin, our Weardas...they're the police in our quadrant...

would remove whatever I shared from your memory. Except they haven't been successful in erasing everything from your mind."

A look of validation crossed Veena's face. "Your Weardas messed with our cases. That's why everyone believes the murders are isolated events. And the ME says the cause of death was brain injury without any trauma to the victims' heads. That's why I remember the evidence, and no one else does."

"Yeah, I'm sorry. You deserved the truth—"

"Then tell me what's going on right now, like you should have last March when this shit first started. You know, I could arrest you for obstruction, except you'd just have the Weardas clean that up, right?" Veena said with a hard edge to her voice, and Sloane's heart sank at the look of betrayal in her friend's eyes.

"Sloane has done nothing to you maliciously, Lieutenant Sharma," Dorathea said. "She has always wanted you to know her truth. Now that you do, you must understand we take a great risk disclosing the magical world to you. You must keep our existence to yourself. No one else can know."

"At least for now," Sloane added.

Dorathea sighed and withdrew into a conversation with Alfred again. The candles in the floating candelabras flickered, and she turned her attention back to the others. "Alfred will shield the hobbit house's exterior." She moved her arm in an arc above their heads, and a pulse of energy, like a giant iridescent bubble catching the wind, surrounded them. "We may speak freely now."

"Oh, wow. That was incredible." Veena watched the rippling force field and then looked at Sloane. "Who's Alfred?"

"The house spirit."

Veena raised her eyebrows. "Seriously? Like a ghost?" She looked at them with a childlike wonder, and Sloane felt a profound sense of relief that her friend was excited about their world, rather than fearful.

"Sharma, your grandma…who I'm sure was very wise… probably didn't know a fraction of what you're about to learn about the universe."

"She is correct," Elvina said. "Our world is as ancient and filled with as many different beings as yours. Well, it was. We had to protect ourselves and all the creatures still living among us from humankind. For obvious reasons."

"I get it. You've been hunted, exterminated. But humans aren't a monolith. Some would probably freak out and act violently toward supernatural beings. But some of us know magical beings are more than myths and fairy tales. We would welcome the chance to learn about your world."

"It is not a risk we can take right now," said Dorathea. "And if you remain cognizant of our world, you must know, not unlike your world, we are in the throes of battle."

"I've wanted to tell you about The Order," Sloane said. "It's a group of subversives. Magicals conspiring with what you may know as Demons or Cambions to take control of the magical world and yours as well."

"And they're not your red, horned, spiked-tail devils, dear. Those are make-believe," Elvina said. "They are Malevolents, from the Nether world, and Half-Malevolents, their children with Nogicals."

"Nogicals?" Veena asked.

"You and your kind, deary. Non-magicals," Jack said.

Veena's face fell blank, but her eyes moved with the thoughts racing in her head. "So the murders in Denwick are part of a coup. Perpetrated by evil supernatural beings," she said finally.

"Yes, but there have been more murders than those you're aware of," Sloane continued. "They killed my mother and grandparents, too. Calen Gòrdan and his family. The Gòrdans in Scotland are like us, a Protector Coven."

"Okay, so why is The Order fixated on your Protector Covens?"

"We are an ancient line of Wiċċan," Dorathea said. "Our purpose is to defend against evil. We are the only beings in both our worlds capable of banishing Malevolents and their offspring to the Abyss. We also capture other magical creatures that have broken our Interspecies Laws."

Veena sat back, sinking into the dark-sapphire cushion. She looked at Sloane. "So when you said you were busy earlier, you meant saving the world?"

"Something like that." Sloane leaned toward the lieutenant. "The Order is just like any other organized crime syndicate. The power runs vertically from the top to bottom. And here in the Northern Hemisphere, we've figured out who at least one of The Order's leaders is. We suspect we know the other one. Now we have to stop them."

"So they want to kill you because you can banish them?" Veena asked.

"It's more than saving themselves," Jack said. "If they destroy our Protector Covens, they release every Malevolent and Half-Malevolent we've ever sent to the bowels of hell. That's a lot of evil released into both our worlds. They'll use it to gain total control and wield absolute power."

Veena searched their faces. "Is this for real?"

"I'm afraid so, dear," Elvina said.

"We were hoping you could help us stop the members we've identified," Sloane said.

"Me? How am I supposed to help you capture supernatural beings?"

"Maybe you can't arrest them like nogical criminals, but you're one of the best detectives I've ever known," Sloane said. "Some of The Order have spent their lives in your world. They'll have IDs, financial trails, and backgrounds you can investigate. You can help us find them."

The lieutenant stared at the others for a long moment. "Yeah, okay. I'll do whatever I can. You have my word."

"We are deeply appreciative," Dorathea said. "And on our word, we will protect you."

Sloane added, "When you have a case that involves the magical world, I'm here to help you."

"Okay. This is a lot to digest, and the incense in here's too strong." She stood, and a gust of wind blew through her long ponytail. "Sorry...Alfred? No offense intended."

"He's sensitive," Sloane said as she got to her feet. "I'll walk with you back to the church. I need to pick up Pearl."

Veena shook her head at Sloane. "I appreciate the offer. But I need to be alone. Clear my head."

"In case you are worried. You will be safe. The Half-Malevolent's focus was Sloane, not you," Dorathea said.

A few minutes later, Sloane returned from walking Veena to the front door. From her favorite armchair, she watched the flames dance in the massive fireplace, thinking about the incident in the crypt. After a while, she looked at Dorothea, "Why didn't the Half-Malevolent affect me the way it did at Ingle Manor?"

For the first time since Sloane met her second cousin twice removed, the polished High Priestess was unable to look her in the eyes. "I do not know, pet. But perhaps Freya does."

CHAPTER TWENTY-TWO

Freya rose from a round, marble table, never losing eye contact with Dorathea. "My apologies, everyone. I must close the café," she announced and twirled her index finger. The OPEN sign in the picture window flipped to CLOSED. Within seconds, a majority of the patrons vanished from the dining room, and the few remaining looked questioningly at the West Coven and Elvina as they left through the front door.

"The Weardas are watching me and the café, my love. If you speak with me here, we will need protection," Freya told Dorathea.

"Very well," the High Priestess replied without the same emotional resonance, and the dejection on Freya's face could have melted the cruelest heart.

"Maybe the three of us should go into the back and give you some privacy," Jack said.

"That won't be necessary. You wait here. Have your afternoon tea. Freya and I have much to discuss. We may be a while." Dorathea held out her hand, and the Sensor clasped it timidly.

Sloane watched the swinging door to the back room settle. At least the long-time partners agreed to talk, a positive step in breaking down the wall of silence Freya's secret had erected. It was a good sign, she hoped. She needed it to be.

"Well, that's progress," Jack said. "Let's hope they come to an understanding. I can't take any more of our cousin's miserable mood. She's been impossible to live with, and I can handle just about anyone."

"The love of her life let her believe a part of her family was missing. Or worse, dead, Jack." Sloane sat at a gathering of chairs closest to the cozy fire burning in a simple brick fireplace. "My grandparents and Dorathea had to fear the worst and convince themselves to believe the best. Every day. For years. Never knowing. None of us could begin to understand that kind of pain. So excuse me if I don't sympathize with your discomfort. And cut her some slack. She deserves to sit with her feelings for as long as it takes. Jesus, it's only been a few days since she found out Freya lied."

Jack nodded and folded his hands on the table, looking like his knuckles had just been rapped.

"I'll summon lunch," Elvina said. The former familiar sounded conflicted, unable to meet Sloane's eyes. She snapped her fingers, and a hand-painted teapot with pink and lavender peonies appeared along with a platter of baked pastries just out of the oven.

Jack ate his first meat tart in two bites and said with his mouth still full, "Your mother's baking is the finest. I haven't eaten a better tart in all my travels."

"Thank you, dear," Elvina said. "Let's swallow our food before we speak, though, shall we?"

The food and Earl Grey tea settled the tension in the room. Sloane watched her cousin reach for a third tart. His appetite for the finer things in abundance spread to all parts of his life: romance, food, drink, and clothing. But she knew he was compensating for the hole in his heart. The loss of his husband, Nathan. A story he hadn't given her in great detail, but she knew the basics. Nathan was a Weardas, and during an investigation into infants disappearing, he found a Changeling mother was feeding off them in the Deep South, in Louisiana. Nathan and his colleagues lost their lives to her and her children. The love of Jack's life had died horrifically. She understood his desire to self-medicate. She thought about his relationship with Calen. Then she remembered that Jack was supposed to be at the RCMP headquarters, providing a statement.

"What is it, lovey? Why are you staring at me like that?"

"Aren't you supposed to be with Sharma right now? Did she cancel your interview?"

"Rescheduled for later this week."

"Not surprising after this morning." Sloane grinned at him. "The good news is you can answer my questions instead."

"Oh, joy," he muttered.

"What were you and Calen working on? And don't tell me you were obtaining art."

"Well, I won't then. Calen was a friend. I'm not saying any more."

"Come on, Jack. Don't you understand your relationship might be pertinent to our investigation?"

"Yes, she's right about our case," Elvina said. "But I also want to know because your secrecy is very suspicious. Why won't you tell us?"

"We may be a coven, but our loyalty to each other doesn't mean you deserve to know everything about me. When I say I don't want to discuss it, let me be." He had lost his usual jocund disposition.

"All right. I hear you," Sloane said. She wouldn't push or make him more uncomfortable. He'd talk when he was ready. Witnesses usually knew things about an event, details they didn't consider relevant but were often of considerable importance, and if you were patient, they'd offer them eventually.

"You don't believe me, do you?" He closed his eyes and took a deep breath. "I assure you, my friendship with him had nothing to do with the attack on their coven or the damn traitors who did it."

"All right. Good to know." The added comment suggested Jack wanted to talk, so Sloane asked, "Did your friendship have to do with why Calen was inside the crypt, trying to enter Tagridore?"

He nodded, reluctantly, his eyes filling with grief. Sloane was about to ask him another question when Dorathea and Freya returned arm in arm.

"You're already done talking?" Elvina asked and looked at her mother.

Freya gave her daughter a slight nod and a smaller smile.

"We are indeed," Dorathea said. Her voice had softened. "Your mother has information to share with us regarding our Grand Coven."

Freya looked at Sloane. "I swear upon my love for Dora, I have not informed the Grand Coven that Jane came to me the night she left the coven, nor will I. Doing so would only heighten their suspicion of her…and you. Nevertheless, they continue to watch me and the café. They want to know with whom she was romantically involved. And if she knew about The Order or of anyone in the insurrection. But what they seek the most is the name of your father."

"And interestingly, each member of our Grand Coven has personally summoned Freya, to talk with her apart from the others," Dorathea added.

Sloane considered the information. "All right. Their actions show they don't trust each other. And the questions they've asked you reveal a few things. They think my father is or was in The Order, and I know who he is or will lead them to him."

"We've already contemplated both notions," Elvina said as she pulled another chair into the grouping for her mother.

"Right. We haven't considered that if he's in The Order, they will know him. Which means the bent GC knows him. Maybe not as my father. But they're clearly trying to connect my mother and me with someone."

"You make a good point," said Jack. "We ought to think that a conspirator in the Grand Coven already knows who your father is. And they're allowing the others to waste time trying to find him. They could also be encouraging the other Ealdormenn to watch us in case he reaches out to you. To warn you. Or help you. Maybe they don't trust that he will kill you when they command him to." Jack tipped his teacup at Freya. "And they continue to question you in case he comes to you for help like Jane did."

Sloane listened carefully. Usually, her cousin didn't contribute substantially to the conversation. He added comic relief or a flippant observation, but this time, what he said made perfect sense. "Because you don't easily entrust your life to someone who betrays and kills freely, right?" Sloane looked at Freya. "Could your contacts in the Weardas find out the names of anyone the GC is having surveilled?"

"I will reach out to them right away," Freya said.

An idea occurred to Sloane. "Jack, tell me the truth. Did you spend time with Calen to figure out if he was my father?"

Jack blinked in surprise. "Of course not, lovey. I would never keep something so important from you. I did wonder, but I didn't ask."

"You deserve answers, dear one." Freya reached for Sloane's hand and held it. "I regret not having them for you. Your mother only told me two things about your father. He was capable of creating a potent protection spell for you both, and his family would never accept her or their baby. She said his family would kill her and all of us if they found out who we were. I couldn't say no when it was clear she had put all our lives in danger."

"Kill? Why? Not because we're Magicals. Evidently my father was too." Sloane tried to make sense of it. She thought about the list of names Jack had compiled. There were five Magical families sent to the Island to defend against a Malevolent in the 1850s. Two of them succumbed to the evil, joining what she figured was the beginning of The Order. When her ancestors sent the Malevolent back to the Nether, they also banished those two families to Drusnirwd. She learned last March, they had escaped the prison and hidden in the nogical world, waiting for their revenge against the coven. Could her father be from one of these families of bent Magicals? Had her father fallen in love with Jane and disavowed his family's mission?

Freya released Sloane's hand. "I said I would add to the protection spell if Jane allowed Elvina to join her." Her eyes glistened with unshed tears. "Your mother agreed, and it was the last time I saw her."

"I'm not angry with you, Freya. Your help saved me. And gave my family thirty more years of life." Sloane looked at Dorathea. "What I can't figure out is why my father turned his back on us and joined The Order. Why protect my mother and me for thirty years but hunt us now?"

"We don't know that he did, dear. You have always said not to assume. To verify," Elvina said.

"Elvina's right," said Dorathea. "The Order's latest attack on you has given us many questions to answer. Freya will investigate how you escaped Catriona and why you were able to fend off the Half-Malevolent in the crypt and bestealce with Lieutenant Sharma."

"All right." Sloane looked at Jack. "When all this is done. We'll examine your list of potential fathers."

"You have my word, lovey," Jack said.

Sloane looked at Freya. "One more thing. Could you find out from your contacts if any of the Northeast Quadrant's GC have visited the Gildeys or our GC recently?"

"Of course," Freya said, and everyone stood. She walked them to the door and held Dorathea back by the arm. Drawing her close, she whispered, "Please return tonight, my love. The loneliness in our bed is swallowing me."

Sloane heard Freya's request but had stepped outside the café before hearing her cousin's answer, and when Dorathea joined her on the cobblestone sidewalk, she held their confidence behind an impassive face. Her cousin's rigidity was making it easier to absolve Jane and herself for Dorathea and Freya's problems. But the yearning in Freya's voice still made her chest ache.

CHAPTER TWENTY-THREE

I am pleased you have returned safely.

Alfred's voice spoke in Sloane's head, and she instinctively looked at the ceiling. *Yeah, thanks. Me, too.* The dim light in the covenstead brightened, and the logs in the inglenook fireplace burst into flames. *So where are you? Do I talk to the ceiling or a wall?* Sloane asked as she followed Dorathea, Jack, and Elvina to the sitting area.

Alfred chuckled. *I am everywhere. You don't have to look up or down or at anything. But I've been highly entertained watching you do so. Now tell me, did they reconcile?*

Ah, you like gossip, huh? Sloane tried to laugh, but she only made a breathy noise, and the others stared at her. "What? I thought of something funny," she told them, and quickly averted her eyes. *Laughing telepathically is harder than I thought it would be.* Alfred chuckled. *I think they came to some understanding. If Dorathea leaves tonight, they're good. If not, she may need more time.*

Hmm. Sounds like a positive development. I've only seen our High Priestess this broken-hearted when her mother died.

"Are you okay, dear?" Elvina asked Sloane. "You look a thousand miles away."

"Yeah, sorry, I'm okay. I'm talking to Alfred."

"Alfred?" Jack pouted. "I've known him my entire life, and he never established communication with me." He looked at Dorathea. "What did I do to make your house spirit hate me?"

"For goodness' sake. Alfred does not hate you. He has very discerning taste, but he means no offense," she said, and Elvina cackled, drawing a stern look from the High Priestess. "Is it any wonder neither of you has made his acquaintance?"

Alfred's laughter rang in Sloane's head, and then he stopped.

Dorathea had fallen silent. "Alfred has just informed me that Polydora demands entry. I have asked if he senses more than one being at our threshold. He does not. She is alone."

"Then let her in," Sloane said. "We've wanted to question her, and now she's made herself available." Sloane tossed her tote against an armchair and sat.

Dorathea snapped her fingers, and a fifth armchair appeared.

"Why not leave the chair this time, deary. Our covenstead has been as busy as a Scottish pub on Sunday," Jack said.

His cousin frowned. "Do keep your humor to yourself in the Ealdormann's presence."

"Yes, I find your lightheartedness strange at this perilous time," Polydora said, her hard facial features set as chiseled marble. She stood before the heavy wooden covenstead door, and Alfred slammed it shut behind her. "Why have you and Alfred forced me to wait an unacceptable time to enter? I am your Ealdormann."

"Yes, indeed. I know who you are. You seldom let anyone forget it," Dorathea said. "The delay was not personal. Surely you understand, our coven must be vigilant at this time."

"Yes, vigilant. Alfred made Cenric and Millicent wait even longer to enter, if I recall," Jack said, his voice lulling.

"Are you trying to calm me?" Polydora laughed at him. "Do you honestly believe your feeble abilities could ever measure up to mine?" Her admonishment made Jack sit deeper in his chair.

"Please take a seat. Or is your visit to be brief?" Dorathea asked, and the Grand Coven wicce gathered her cloak in front of her, pulling it a few inches off the floor, and sat.

"Are you offering me tea?"

"We have no time. Alisdair expects us."

Sloane hid her surprise at Dorathea's lie, but Polydora wasn't as skilled at hiding her frustration.

"I see. It isn't the time for niceties, is it? Very well, right to business. When did the other members of our Grand Coven appear here?"

"Two days ago. Surely you knew of their visit?" Dorathea asked, and Polydora gave a slight nod.

Sloane recognized the Ealdormann's body language. Polydora had no idea the other GC members had come to their covenstead. She also seemed suspicious that they had. Now was the time to ask her questions. She carefully retrieved her cell phone from her back pocket, accessed its video, tapped record, and placed it beside her on the seat cushion.

"Of course, she knew about their visit, Denham," Sloane said. "Millicent and Cenric said she was unable to join them, remember?" She looked at Polydora. "They didn't tell us why you were absent. But they assured us the Grand Coven supports our efforts and will assist us in any way we need to dismantle The Order. You don't feel differently, do you?"

"Why would I refuse to help our quadrant's Protector Coven? You are the only ones who can defeat them." She turned her suspicious eyes to Dorathea. "Have you not explained to your *Leornestre* the gravity of this situation?"

"For goodness' sake, Polly. You know I have, and you do not need to call her a student any longer. Her training is anything but the experience our students have."

Polly? Her cousin abhorred nicknames. So why did she have one for the Ealdormann? Sloane felt the same surprise she saw from the rest of the coven. When she looked at Polydora again, she saw the nickname had softened the GC wičče's expression.

"Very well." Polydora looked at Sloane. "Then you know everyone and everything conspiring with a Malevolent or its spawn can only be rid of their power when we banish them to the Abyss."

"Or if we kill them," Sloane said in contradiction. "I've seen that first hand."

Polydora seemed to consider Sloane's comment. Her eyes narrowed. "Yes, you have. The two Order members and the magical creature you killed may have died. But the evil that possessed them was released as a consequence." The Ealdormann turned her attention to Dorathea. "I am here to ask what your coven was doing at Freya's café this evening."

"Are you spying on us?" Dorathea asked, affronted.

"Do I have a reason to be?" Polydora matched the edge in Dorathea's voice. "A dissatisfied customer mentioned that Freya asked everyone to leave her establishment when the four of you arrived. The Weardas also detected a concealment spell inside the café. I'm curious what matter of discussion required such privacy?"

"We are under no obligation to share our conversation with you," Dorathea said. "However, I will because the West Coven has nothing to hide. We were discussing the Gòrdan assault. Our coven needs Freya's assistance. She has always offered her superior sensing abilities to our family."

"Yes, she has been such a devoted friend to your coven and you, Dora. I wonder what lengths she'd go to for you. Perhaps I will detain her for questioning and find out."

"Do not threaten my mother," Elvina hissed.

Polydora looked at her, amused. "You poor thing. I would think you'd be wary of challenging those more powerful than you, having lost your familiar life at so young an age. I'd hate to see your last form end before you have the chance to bear your own little familiar."

Elvina leaped at her, but Jack caught her by the waist before she could reach the Ealdormann. Polydora grinned in satisfaction, and Sloane grasped the arms of her chair. Her disdain for the woman urged her to beat the smug look right off the GC wiċċe's face.

"Ealdormann, you will refrain from disrespecting members of my coven in our sacred space. You are a guest here."

"A guest?" Polydora laughed at Dorathea. Then the look of amusement on her face faded. "I continue to be dissatisfied with your answers to the Grand Coven's questions, High Priestess. Detaining you without clear evidence would be unprecedented, but I will if you continue lying to me." She looked at Sloane. "I want to know the truth. Why did The Order begin their campaign to end the Protector Covens at the same time you became known to our world?"

"How the hell should I—"

"I did not ask you to speak," Polydora said, cutting Sloane off. She looked at Dorathea, her tawny face reddened. "You will answer my questions. Why has your Leornestre killed every Order member she has captured before we could question them? Why didn't Alisdair reach out for help sooner during the attack? Had he done so, Lachlan and Bella might be alive. And where is Elspeth?"

She changed her focus to Jack. "How well did you know Calen Gòrdan? Why was he murdered in your family's crypt beside your Tree of Life?" She took a deep breath and looked at each of them. "You can't deny how connected your coven seems to be to The Order's actions."

They refused to respond to the accusations posed as questions.

"Very well. I expect more cooperation the next time we speak. If you continue to be unforthcoming, I will send you to Drusnirwd until you change your minds."

Dorathea stood. "And I expected more from you, Ealdormann. You have always had a judicious mind. It seems to have failed you here. You are free to do as you wish. But carefully consider what is at stake if you choose to detain us without cause. It is not a loss either one of us wants."

"And I expect you will come to your senses." Polydora got to her feet.

"You forfeited the right to expect anything from me a very long time ago," Dorathea said.

Polydora's gaze fixed on Dorathea, and Sloane could see an emotional storm in her eyes. "Let me be clear, you will leave the Grand Covens to deal with The Order's recent crimes. You are especially forbidden to meddle in the Northeast Quadrant's inquiry." She lifted her chin, but the defiant gesture didn't mask the hurt on her face. "You are Protectors, and the dead do not need protecting."

After she disappeared, Jack laughed nervously. "She's the breath of fresh air everyone needs in a time like this."

"She makes my blood boil," Elvina said, glaring at Polydora's empty chair. "I will take great pleasure exiling her to Drusnirwd."

Sloane looked at Dorathea. "They're not all dead. She can't prevent us from helping Alisdair and Elspeth, can she?"

"Of course not. She is just lashing out." Dorathea sighed.

"What was *Polly* all about?" Jack asked her. "I thought you loathed nicknames."

"I do indeed. We grew up together and have known each other for far longer than you have been alive. Those were our school-age names we had for each other." She sat. "I still find it hard to believe Polydora Nenge would betray our world. At least not the woman I knew. But I agree, she is acting peculiarly."

"We don't have to believe one way or the other." Sloane held up her cell phone. "I recorded the entire conversation."

"Listening to it again won't help us figure out if she's in The Order," Elvina said.

"I didn't record it for us. Elspeth says she heard two women before Alisdair helped her escape. She can tell us if one of them was Polydora." Sloane stood, pulled on her coat, and grabbed her tote. She retrieved Elvina's elixir and dosed herself against the impending headache. "Would you ask Mòrag to let me enter their covenstead?"

"Yes, pet." After a moment of silence, she said, "Mòrag has granted you entry."

"Now?" Jack asked. "I mean, the lead is good and all but isn't it four in the morning there. Don't you think you should wait a few hours?"

"I don't plan on waking anyone, Jack. I'll stay in the covenstead until they get up."

Elvina grinned at Sloane. "Not even Rose?"

CHAPTER TWENTY-FOUR

Alisdair sat beside a warm fire with a crocheted blanket across his lap. He looked frail, sitting there absentmindedly smoothing his hand over the cover. His long, gray hair was tousled and cascading over his shoulders. "My Bella made this for me," he said, as Sloane approached, his Scottish accent thick and his voice full of sorrow. "So much grief lives inside this house now. For my daughter and son. For a mother and father." He sighed. "Mòrag fills the house with cypress and frankincense, but it doesn't help the emptiness."

"I'm so sorry." Sloane laid her tote against a coffee table leg and sat across from him. "I'm sorry we didn't arrive in time."

He looked up at her with watery eyes. "Your coven is not to blame—" His voice abruptly stopped, and his sadness turned to frustration. He wanted to say more, but the curse suppressed his words.

"No worries, Alisdair. I know you want to help. Not being able to must be so hard for you." Sloane held out her cell phone. "Even though you can't tell us about the attackers, Elspeth can.

She heard their voices. And I think this recording will prove the identity of one of them. I'd like her to listen to it."

His grip on the quilt slackened. "My poor child is finally asleep, hopefully until sunrise. We gave her a calming elixir. I'm afraid neither of us is sleeping well."

"I'll wait if it's okay with you?" she asked, and he nodded.

The covenstead door opened, and Sloane knew before looking that it was Rose. A warmth spread through her body, calming her agitation. It wasn't like her mother's spells, not against her will. The comfort came from inside her. She watched Rose descend the curved double staircase. She had read that Dhampyres were wondrously beautiful, a kind of beauty far beyond mere attractiveness. It was true. When Rose entered the room, the atmosphere altered, as if everyone turned into daisies tracking the sun.

"I sensed you were here. Has something happened?" Rose said, kissing Sloane's cheek. She tightened the tie on her robe and sat beside Sloane.

"Polydora just demanded entry into our covenstead and questioned us about being at Freya's. Which means she's surveilling the café. She accused us of being involved with The Order. But I think she's trying to deflect from her own involvement. I think she may be one of the women Elspeth heard." She held up her cell phone. "I recorded her. I'm hoping Elspeth recognizes her voice."

Alisdair sighed. "I've known Polydora Nenge since our years at the academy. We were in the same class as Dorathea. And we were all friendly, especially your cousin and her. If I remember correctly, they were inseparable, even spending holidays together. Those days were a lifetime ago. But people don't really change that much in one lifetime, do they?"

"I'm not sure." Sloane stared at him, unable to unpack his idea so quickly. "I could tell my cousin and Polydora had history. What happened between them?"

"Ah, hurt feelings, I suppose. Dorathea fell in love with Freya. I imagine Polydora considered the intrusion on their friendship a betrayal. It's only hearsay, but supposedly the Ealdormann suffered a broken heart and turned her back on your cousin."

"Even though they weren't romantically involved?" Rose asked. She tucked her legs under her, completely engrossed in the conversation.

"Aye. I suppose ending a lifetime friendship, especially if it is one of unrequited love, is grieved like any other loss, painfully and completely."

"Oh, that is so sad," Rose said. She reached over and grasped Sloane's hand. Then her head jerked up and her grip tightened. "Someone's here."

Alisdair held up a finger as he listened. "We have guests. Mòrag has announced the world's preeminent Sensor and her lovely child have arrived."

Freya and Elvina appeared in front of the fireplace with arms locked around each other's waists. "Hello, Alisdair," Freya said, warmly. "It's been far too long since we've seen each other. I'm terribly sorry for your loss, my friend."

He acknowledged Freya's condolences with a mournful sound, not much more than a clearing of his throat. "Please sit. Thank you for coming."

"Why are you here?" Sloane asked.

"Dorathea asked me to reverse the gestillan curse on Alisdair."

"Finally," Elvina added, still annoyed.

Sloane caught the accusation in her ex-familiar's voice. Sure Freya's help a few days ago might have bolstered the case. But all that mattered now was that Freya was there, which meant Dorathea had forgiven her enough to trust her. God, she hoped so, and not to assuage her own guilt, but because she wanted her cousin and Freya to work out, to prove that in this messed-up world, maybe she could have a love that lasts a lifetime, too.

Just as the thought sprang to Sloane's mind, Rose squeezed her hand and released it. "I hear Elspeth waking. Let me check on her. If she's calm, I'll bring her to the covenstead. If not, come find me upstairs before you leave."

Sloane nodded and watched Rose slowly ascend the stairs, remembering yesterday when Rose moved up the staircase and out the door in a rapid blur, so fast she barely saw it happen, and the words Rose shouted at the coven had been so raw and protective.

She had a sinking feeling in her stomach, remembering Rose's message. *We need to talk.* Is that why she wanted her to find her upstairs?

"Sloane, dear," Elvina said, breaking into her thoughts. "Would you like coffee?"

"I'm good. Thanks." Sloane returned her attention to the group to find Freya sensing Alisdair in the unnerving and intimate way the Sensor had once detected her. Freya moved her face a breath away from his skin, breathing up and down his body. After a few minutes of exploration, she stepped back.

"Well?" Alisdair asked.

"It is ancient and strong, infused with what I feel is dark magic, but I can't tell for sure. The spell gives confusing energy." Freya spoke matter-of-factly. "Breaking it will take me longer than I thought."

"Not if I can prove Polydora cast it," Sloane said. "If she did, we need to find something of hers to help you break it, right?"

"You're correct," Freya said, but her expression didn't look any more hopeful. "I have known the Ealdormann for as long as Dorathea has. And I find it hard to believe she could have taken part in these killings."

"How can you say she's innocent, mother?" Elvina asked, frustrated. "It was bad enough when she was ordering the Weardas to spy on you and your customers. Now she's directed them to detain you for questioning. Why are you defending her?"

"She did what?" Sloane asked.

"There's no need for the anger I hear in your voices," Freya told them. "Polydora's actions are appropriate for her position. We cannot blame her. I will stay here until the Gòrdans are safe." Her face softened. "When they are, it is time for me to leave Tagridore and my beloved café for a greater love."

Elvina clasped her hands. "Oh, this is such exciting news. I'm so happy you'll be together at the hobbit house. Now we'll be next door to each other, mother. Ooh, and you could open a café in Denwick. On Old Main Street. There are a few empty stores. Isn't that right, dear?" She looked at Sloane.

"Yeah, and if we can send the Gildeys back to the Abyss, there'll be a few more available," Sloane said, and her attention shifted to the covenstead door at the top of the staircase. Rose and Elspeth entered. This time, knowing Rose was there before seeing her, surprised her. Once might have been a fluke but twice constituted more than chance. If sensing Rose was a new ability, she needed to know why she had it.

When the golden-haired child looked down and saw the gathering in the sitting area, she hid behind Rose. "Ellie, you must be nervous, huh?" Rose spoke in a soft, Scottish accent as she lowered onto her knees, eye to eye with the child. "You remember Sloane and Elvina. The other person with your *seanair* is Freya. She's Elvina's mother. They're friends just like me and my da are."

Elspeth crawled into Rose's arms, and she carried her down the stairs to Alisdair. "Are you feeling better, *stobag*?" he asked, as Rose gently placed the child onto his lap. "You're trembling. Are you cold?"

She gave a faint nod and settled her head against his shoulder as he wrapped the ends of her mother's quilt around her. He smoothed the child's hair off her ashen face. "Stobag, Sloane would like to play a recording for you. We think it might be—" His words turned to breath sounds, and Elspeth jerked her head back to look at his face.

"Seanair?" she said, fearfully.

"He's okay, Ellie. The Order took his ability to speak about what happened, remember?" Rose said and pointed to Freya. "Freya is here to make him better. Okay? But first, Sloane needs your help. Can you listen to a recording and tell us if the voice you hear is one of the women you heard break into your covenstead?" She held the child's eyes with such gentleness that Sloane thought she'd never seen anything more compassionate in her life.

Elspeth stared at her grandfather, and her bottom lip trembled. He was unable to respond to the conversation. His face remained unnaturally blank.

"It's okay to say no," Sloane said to her.

"No one's left. Seanair only has me," she said in a small voice. "I'll listen."

The way Elspeth looked at her grandfather left a lump in Sloane's throat, and she wanted nothing else at that moment than to go back and arrive at the Gòrdan covenstead in time to save the child's parents. But that was a feat even the magic world hadn't achieved. She placed her cell phone on the coffee table. "I think you are brave to help your grandfather. But if hearing the woman upsets you, I'll turn the recording off right away," Sloane said, and Elspeth nodded. "Okay, here it goes."

Sloane tapped the phone's screen, and Polydora's sharp voice entered the room like an unwelcome guest. Elspeth nervously sat forward, her expression slowly changing from fear to confusion. She wriggled out of her grandfather's lap and moved closer. After a few seconds, she picked up the phone, holding it closer to her ear, listening. When the Ealdormann gave her last threat, and the recording ended, Elspeth shook her head and handed the cell phone to Sloane.

"She wasn't one of the voices you heard? Are you sure?" Sloane asked.

Elspeth stared at her, frightened, and ran back to Alisdair.

"Why don't you listen again?" Sloane held out the cell phone and tapped the play button, oblivious to the tears rolling down the child's face.

"She's heard enough." Rose lowered Sloane's hand and knelt beside Alisdair and his granddaughter, wiping the tears from the girl's cheeks with her thumbs. "You have been so brave helping us, Ellie. We are grateful to you."

"The wee lass needs a break. I'll be back in a bit." He stood with his granddaughter in his arms and disappeared.

Sloane's emotions raced, a mixture of sorrow for Elspeth, shame for putting her through more trauma, and frustration about being wrong. Her exasperation won out, and she growled, "What the hell? Do you think she couldn't remember?" She hoped the others would say yes, because if Elspeth was right, then she had been wrong about Polydora all along.

"I sensed Elspeth as she listened," Freya said. "She was hearing Polydora Nenge's voice for the first time. As I said before, this outcome does not surprise me."

Sloane bent her head back and slammed her fists on the chair's arms. "We're back to where we started with no fucking clue who the woman is."

"We're hardly back at the start," Elvina chided. "You have discovered essential information. We know The Order has infiltrated the Northeast Quadrant's Grand Coven because Alisdair's picture shows Ginerva with Catriona, who we now know is a Half-Malevolent. And we suspect the Gildeys are too. That's hardly the start, dear. We just need to refocus. The other woman with Catriona could have been Millicent or another higher up at our quadrant's Héahreced. Only a handful of Sensor wiċċe are capable of breaking through Mòrag's defenses and killing Lachlan and Bella."

"She's right. And we'll find her," Freya said and snapped her fingers. A coffee carafe, teapot, and platter of pastries appeared on the coffee table. "If you intend to start over, you must nourish yourself."

"All right." Sloane poured herself a mug of black coffee. She walked the hours back in her head. It was after ten p.m. in Denwick, but she had no intention of sleeping. Alisdair and Jane had uncovered enough evidence that the Grand Covens and The Order had noticed. They had collected the answers. She just had to find them.

When Alisdair returned, he collapsed onto the love seat, defeated. "She's asleep again. My poor stobag. I'm unable to help her."

"You are a great comfort to her, even if you can't talk about the attack," Rose said sympathetically. "And she has us. We will all help her."

The wall sconces in the covenstead's library became brighter, illuminating the dark room, and a loud bang sounded as the door to the cupboard with the hidden compartment flew open and slammed against the shelves. Alisdair pointed at it with a surprised look on his face. His mouth mimed a rush of words.

"Your books? Mòrag showed us the hidden compartment before the Freiceadan could find them. I have them at home," Sloane said, and Alisdair closed his eyes.

"The books you collected were similar to those my mother had. Business history, and nogical and magical genealogies. I think you both were looking for those original members of The Order, weren't you?" She was talking to herself now, deep in thought, trying to make connections. "I think Jane found the traitors in our quadrant. And she ran from the danger. I don't think you've found them yet. Maybe you still need the right book. But The Order found you before you could secure it." The flames in the fireplace shot up the chimney.

"We can find genealogy books at Miadarbaile's library. They also have history books on nogical businesses. I'll take you there." Rose got to her feet. "Alisdair, where's your portal to the city?"

"The family tartan hanging between the stairs," he said, and a fierce gust tore through the room. Everyone braced themselves against it until the fury passed.

Freya stood. "Mòrag has opened communication with me. You must be careful. She believes Alisdair's search for the book brought about the attack."

CHAPTER TWENTY-FIVE

"Where's the forest the quadrant's headquarters is located in? It was amazing," Sloane said as she looked over the tops of a row of white-harled businesses with red tile roofs. The Gòrdans' portal had brought them to the rear entrance of the family's rare books store.

"The Caledonian forest is enchanting," replied Rose. "We can't see it from here. It forms Miadarbaile's perimeter. And we're in the heart of the city. We only travel through the forest to attend our Prìomh-oifis. For good reason, the magical creatures who live in the ancient forest dislike intruders." Rose led them to a cobblestone path. "We don't blame them, though. Humans destroyed half the forest and thousands of its inhabitants. The Wiccan shielded what remained, and it is a part of our world now." Rose paused. "Has your family told you how our quadrants and cities came to be?"

"They've said Magicals returned to a different plane of existence because of human violence. And guardians like us stayed behind to protect Magicals when they came to the Nogicals' world."

"That's a sanitized version but correct. Before we left the human dimension, they killed over three-quarters of our population. Many of our species ended."

"Jesus," Sloane whispered.

They turned right and headed down another path toward a park with large red sandstone buildings on three sides. It reminded Sloane of Central Park, and she hoped they would walk through it.

"I don't understand how humans were able to overcome so many Magicals?" Sloane asked, unable to let the tragic history go.

"There were too few of us to fight both Malevolents and the Nogicals." Rose stopped at the outskirts of the heavily treed park and breathed deeply. "I miss this place."

The scent in the air struck Sloane right away. "Mmm. The park smells like you."

"Because it has the only grove of citrus bergamot in the quadrant." She put her arm around Sloane's waist. "We can thank the Wiccan for that, too. A bergamot grove this size could normally never survive outside the Southeast Quadrant."

"How will you be thanking me?" She grinned and pulled Rose into a gentle kiss.

After their lips parted, Rose whispered against Sloane's neck, "With a lot more of those, for starters." Her warm breath felt safe and comforting against Sloane's skin, and she could think of nothing better than holding Rose in that moment in the quiet morning, under an evergreen canopy dappled with snow, as she melted into every inch of her.

"Do you want to see the grove?" Rose said, finally, and Sloane nodded, unwilling or maybe unable to risk letting words end the deep serenity she felt.

They released each other and walked holding hands through the park. As they approached an opening in the pines, the spicy, woodsy, citrus aroma grew stronger. Rose pointed ahead. "The grove grows behind those Scots pine." When they exited the trees, Rose stopped and lay her head on Sloane's shoulder. "I told you the Wiċċan made it possible."

"It's amazing," Sloane whispered, as if in the presence of such beauty they should be reverent. She didn't know what to expect, but it wasn't this. In the middle of the snow-covered park, a large stand of trees with deep, glossy green leaves, full of white, star-shaped blossoms, thrived under a protective dome of captured sunlight.

"It's one of my favorite places in Miadarbaile. Let's warm up," Rose said and led Sloane by the hand through the translucent shield. The luminescent rays warmed their bodies as they walked through the bergamot grove. Before they left on the other side, they picked a few fragrant blooms from the trees.

"My second favorite place is the library." Rose slipped her arm around Sloane's. "One summer, I spent every day from sunrise to sunset in the basement tracing my family lines. My da's was extensive. His paternal line went back seventeen generations to a paternal Blodaeter from the House of Ó Céin and a Gaelic woman. Nogicals think human mothers can't survive our births. But that's just a myth. She was turned by his blood and lived in Miadarbaile after the Magicals left the nogical world. Our name changed from Ó Céin to Keane about twelve generations ago. My mam's lineage was another matter," Rose said.

"Why? Because she's from Jamaica? Was it hard to find research?"

"Not really. I was able to request books from the Southwest quadrant. It's because the undead have a different heredity." She paused, and Sloane held her arm tighter, encouraging her to continue. "Nogicals think the undead are reanimated corpses. But they're not. They're just immortal. Full Blodaeters like my mam come from one sire and are turned by passing on his blood. Which makes them pure bloods."

"I read that in my mom's book."

"I'm glad the Wiċċan had it right." Rose smiled. "Fiona's lineage goes back to Anou, my ancestor who created the House of Anou. Their clan is small. Like most other pure bloods. Not many full Blodaeters have been created in centuries. Most chose to mate with Nogicals or Daywalkers. My mam's clan is different. She's the only one to have children with a Daywalker. The rest think it's beneath them."

"Whoa," Sloane said. "Have you met them?"

"Not one." Rose rested her head against Sloane's shoulder. Throughout the walk, Sloane had listened carefully, wanting to learn everything she could about Rose, to catch every nuance in her voice. She realized she had been so eager to hear about Rose's life that she hadn't disclosed any stories of her own. But there would be time for that. They had countless strolls in their future.

Rose stopped at the edge of a brick road and lifted her chin toward a massive, red-stoned building with turrets and crow-stepped gables. "Our *leabharlann*."

"Jesus. That's an impressive building. And it's open this early?"

"It doesn't close." Rose grinned and almost ran to the library's entrance, dragging Sloane along. "Wait until you see the inside, but I need to warn you about something first." Her voice was serious. "The *Sgàthan* is responsible for preserving all forms of magical communication. The first additions of anything ever created in each quadrant are stored in their libraries. And they take their job seriously."

"Never heard of them. Who are they?"

"An ancient race of the Tuatha Dé Danann."

"Oh, faes, like the Daoine Sìth? Jack told me about them."

"Yeah, no. They are nothing like them." Rose hesitated. "They are descendants of the goddess Danu, but they are more benevolent than the Sìths. And we can't see their faces."

"Are they masked?"

"In a way. It's hard to explain. Where their faces should be, we see what we love mirrored back to us. They become infuriated because we don't see their beauty. They think we're selfish and only want to use them when we try to make eye contact. So you can't stare at them. Okay? I mean it."

"Seriously?" Sloane stopped, and Rose tilted her head, nodding. "Okay. I'll try not to look, but now I'm curious. How do you know they're beautiful if you can't see them?"

"Because their artists have painted portraits. And there are no words for their beauty. Trust me."

"Can we see one of them?"

Rose nodded. "There are a few paintings inside. You can look at the art version of the Sgàthan all you want. But not the real ones. If you upset them, they'll toss you into the middle of Caledonian, and no creature will cross them to help you find your way back."

"Now you've made me nervous."

"Sorry. But I have to prepare you." Rose opened the library's large, intricately carved wooden door. "Just *don't* stare."

"You first, then. If I mess up and make eye contact, I'll hide behind you."

The enormous lobby's tile floor was a triskele mosaic, and its dark wood and picture paneling walls soared two stories. Portraits of Magicals hung in each panel up to the vaulted ceiling. Sloane bent her head back and whispered, "Who are they?"

Rose smiled as if she were seeing old friends again. "They're famous authors, philosophers, musicians, and artists from the Northeast Quadrant. There are more paintings in the other lobby areas. I remember wishing I'd be famous enough one day to hang on these walls." She laughed at herself. "I was such a strange kid."

"Strange? Are you kidding? Sounds like you were just as fabulous back then as you are now." Sloane laid her hand gently on the curve of Rose's back and followed her through a modest set of doors. The ceiling was lower in this room, but the space was quadruple the size of the lobby. Floor-to-ceiling bookcases covered three walls, breaking only for hanging tapestries of vibrant forest scenes and creatures that, until this year, Sloane had spent her life thinking were mythological. The doors from the lobby were between the two sides of a double staircase with marble risers and elaborate banisters.

"The books we need are in the basement. Follow me." Rose hurried toward an opening under the right side of the grand staircase. But a voice called out before they could descend the steps.

"Rose Keane?"

Rose froze on the first step and whispered, "Ready? Only glance, then look away. And don't gasp."

Sloane's stomach clenched, and she turned with Rose toward the ethereal voice. The faerie floated a few inches off the hardwood floor, her light-blue gown rippling and her auburn hair flowing in a phantom breeze. The Sgàthan was upon them in less than a second. Sloane found the courage to lift her eyes and glance at the faerie's face, and then quickly stared at the back of Rose's head, confused. The faerie hadn't mirrored anything to her.

"You have not visited me for nearly a year, my scholar. What has kept you away from your books?" She moved her long, slender arm toward Rose's neck and lifted the jade pendant. "Or should I say who?"

"I'm sorry it's been so long, Sadhbh," Rose said. "I've taken over the family business in the Northwest Quadrant. I'm in Miadarbaile for a quick visit, and I couldn't leave without visiting the library. The necklace is a gift from someone special."

"It's beautiful. The stone matches your eyes perfectly."

"Thank you." Rose touched Sloane's arm. "This is my friend Sloane West."

"Lovely to meet you, Sloane." Sadhbh released the necklace and floated even closer to Rose's face. "Would you like something from me? A look into my face to see if the one who gave it to you is your true love, perhaps?"

From the top of her vision, Sloane could see that Rose still had her head lowered. Even with an invitation, she wasn't budging. "That's a generous offer, but I have too much respect for your time. We're here to look at some history books. We'll be on our way."

The faerie sighed. "Very well. Let me know if you need my assistance."

When Sadhbh turned away, a light breeze blew over their skin. Sloane looked up in time to see the faerie drifting across the room. Her graceful back, the outline of her hips and legs, were splendid.

"Come on," Rose said, pulling on Sloane's arm. "She can still sense you staring even with her back turned."

Sloane followed Rose down the stairs to the basement. "Her name's Sigh-ve? How long have you known her?"

"Since I was a child."

"She's intense for a kid. Did she scare the hell out of you?"

"They're nicer to children." Rose stopped on the landing and looked behind them. "Hopefully she won't bother us anymore."

"You didn't look at her even though she gave you permission?"

"Especially because she did. The outcome's the same whether they give us permission or not. They only mirror back to us what we love most, and it makes them angry."

Sloane hesitated. "When I glanced at her face, it was muddled like a bad impressionist painting. It never became a clear image of..." She couldn't finish her thought because Sadhbh hadn't mirrored Rose back to her.

"Hey," Rose said, gently nudging her. "We can't look long enough to see what they reveal. That's the game. They seduce many people to risk it only to suffer their retribution. Which is a form of face blindness in which you can no longer see your love."

"Jesus. That's harsh."

"Luckily, some of us trust we have found our true love without the aid of magic." Rose lightly kissed Sloane's lips and opened the doors into the basement room, walking inside and leaving Sloane embarrassed and elated, her desire now pulsing in her ears.

She caught up and wrapped her arms around Rose. "I don't need to see anything reflected on her face," she whispered and kissed her long and deep. Sloane wanted to make love to her right there on a reading lounger, but they weren't alone. A loud clearing of the throat warned them how public the space was, and they stepped apart, stifling their laughter.

Sloane glanced around the room as she followed Rose. This level of the library resembled an old covenstead without the Wiccan accoutrements. It was a resplendent space filled with loungers, sofas, and chairs in dark leathers and velvets with built-in dark-paneled alcoves lining each wall. Between some of the reading nooks, ornate brass sconces lit portraits.

"She's a Sgàthan?" Sloane drew closer to one of the paintings. The woman had sublime, symmetrical features and raven black hair cascading over her olive skin. The image captured the woman from the waist up in a sheer wrap, revealing the curve of her waist and her round, full breasts.

"They don't all look the same. But, yeah, they all share perfect features in some way or another."

Sloane shrugged and turned her attention to Rose. "You're so much hotter than her."

"Oh, please. You can do better than flattery." She stopped in front of another alcove. "Who do you want to start researching?"

"I think we need to search for any business dealings between the MacCains and Gildeys or anyone else on Vancouver Island. As far back as we can go."

"Okay. Those books are over here."

Sloane followed her to a larger alcove on the other side of the room. She looked up and read aloud the words carved in the archway and adorned with gold leaf. "Kirkcudbright's Malairt: Aon."

"Not too bad," Rose said. "It means Kirkcudbright's economy in the first years."

Sloane chuckled. "I think the Old English helped." She ducked into the alcove. "All right. Here we go. Financial surveys from the eighteenth century through the nineteenth century." Sloane traced her fingers along the leather-bound book spines. Since the Island was colonized in the 1840s, let's look at those years until the end of the century."

They removed several tomes from the shelves and dropped their stacks on the square table in the center of the niche, causing dust particles to rise into the air. Rose sneezed and waved her hand to clear the particulate matter away. They sat in high-backed wooden chairs on opposite sides of the table and opened their first books.

Sloane breathed in the pages, overcome with a charming sense of vellichor. She loved antique bookstores and had a few favorites in midtown Manhattan, but they were nothing like this. The Barony of Kirkcudbright's financial interests were easy to find. The MacCain family owned most of the land in Galloway and had amassed a respectable fortune in agriculture and government positions. However, after searching the 1840s, 1850s, and 1860s, she could see no connection between the MacCains and any business on the Island.

"Found anything?" she asked Rose.

"Nothing. But this is interesting, the eleventh Lord of Kirkcudbright had almost lost everything."

"Well, something turned it around for them. Catriona's estate is not hurting." Sloane sat back. She thought about the portraits at Ingle Manor. There were so many descendants with different features. The Gildeys' portraits were different. Strikingly similar features. No children. No pets. And the MacCains portraits hung in the hallway, except for the last Baron and his wife, Catriona. Their likenesses were grand. Hanging in the Grand Foyer, like the Gildeys. She leaned forward, excited. "Catriona's the Half-Malevolent. Not the MacCains. What was her maiden name?" Sloane was talking to herself now. She retrieved her phone and found her search results. "That's it. Dunaid. We need to look for the Dunaid family."

With renewed energy, they dived back into the volumes. After a few minutes, Sloane found the first mention of a Ruairí Dunaid, the family patriarch in the early 1820s. The family owned thousands of acres and dominated the trade routes out of Scotland's southwest shore.

"Hey, look at this," Rose said, and turned her book around to face Sloane. "These are the Dunaids' business records up to the 1890s. See here, their shipping routes have doubled. And their wealth." She tapped a map. "Look where their newest routes were. British North America. Vancouver Island."

"Is this the first mention of the Island?" Sloane asked, scanning the page.

"It's the first time it appears on their sailing schedules."

"Yes," Sloane whispered and ran her finger down the pages, quickly turning them. "From 1849 to 1887, the Dunaids did business with a William Tindall on the Island, but he doesn't appear on their shipping schedule after 1908."

"Tindall? Why does that name sound familiar?"

"Because they were one of the founding families of Denwick. Their ashes are in the crypt." Sloane straightened. "The Grand Coven said the Tindalls were Nogical, and when our coven searched for them, we couldn't find any information on a living descendant."

"Okay. A nogical family on the Island, the Tindalls, and the Half-Malevolent here in the Northeast Quadrant, presumably the Dunaids, did business with each other." Rose thought for a moment. "How does their relationship help us figure out the identity of the second woman Elspeth heard during the attack?"

"I'm not sure yet. But it's not a coincidence." She closed the record book. "I have a hunch I'm basing on Alisdair's photo evidence. If the Gildeys are Cambions...Half-Malevolents, then Catriona has her Northwest Quadrant counterpart in Andrew. Which means Ginerva will also have one. I don't think they would recruit any Sensor. A less risky target would be someone with family relations. And if there are business connections, I'm guessing there are family ones too."

Rose got to her feet. "Come with me. We have all of Miadarbaile's family histories." Rose dashed out of the nook, and Sloane hurried to keep up with her. When they were only a few feet from a wall of alcoves in the back of the expansive room, they hit an invisible wall that knocked them to the floor.

"What the hell was that?" Sloane rubbed her back, slowly getting to her feet. Then she helped Rose up.

"I don't know," Rose said. They both reached out, touching the barrier, looking like a pantomime. "I'll call for Sadhbh."

"Do you think that's a good idea?"

"I think you can control yourself." Rose grinned and shouted, "Sadhbh."

The faerie floated from the wall beside them, startling Sloane. "Your friend is easily excited, isn't she?" she said to Rose. "I've never seen her before, and I've laid eyes on everyone who has ever walked through our doors." The faerie looked her over, but Sloane kept her gaze on the floor. "Surely you would have visited the library if you were from here. But you're not, are you?"

It felt rude not to acknowledge Sadhbh with eye contact, but Sloane resisted and said, "I'm from the Northwest Quadrant."

"Aye, Tagridore. A beautiful city and an excellent library. You must know the Sgàthan there. Which makes me wonder why you are nervous around me."

"I don't want to offend you."

"I'm not easily upset." She hovered closer to Sloane. "I noticed you have the most striking gray eyes. Like ice, aren't they? Why don't you let me have another look? And you could share what you notice about me."

"We need access to the genealogy books," Rose said, pulling Sloane away from the faerie. "It's crucial, and we don't have a lot of time."

Sadhbh jerked back, and the gentle breeze surrounding her turned into a tempest. "The rooms are restricted." Her delicate voice was dark and thunderous. "A thief has stolen a genealogy book from us. Until it is returned, no one will ever enter these rooms again!"

CHAPTER TWENTY-SIX

In a flash of blinding light, Sloane and Rose appeared in the Gòrdan covenstead beside the door to the potions room. "Oh, my God. I've never teleported like that. It's amazing." Rose's voice was full of excitement.

Sloane pressed her palms against her head, unable to respond. Her legs felt ready to buckle.

"Are you okay?" Rose asked. She helped Sloane to a chair, and Freya rushed to them.

"What is happening? Let me see your face." Freya's gentle hands lifted Sloane's head. "When did this reaction begin?"

"Not long after I started teleporting," Sloane said, flinching as she spoke. "Elvina made me an elixir for the headache. It's in my tote."

"I'll get it," Rose said, rushing to the bag propped against a coffee table leg. She retrieved the vial. "Is this it?"

"Yeah. Thanks." Sloane shot the dose in one gulp as if it were neat whiskey, and Rose held her hand. The warmth and softness of her skin helped ease the discomfort. After a few minutes, she opened her eyes and looked around the Gòrdans' sitting area. "Where's Elvina?"

"She has returned to the hobbit house to assist Dorathea." Freya studied Sloane, concerned, and asked, "Does Dorathea know about your headaches?"

"She's looking into it."

"Very well," Freya said, sitting in her chair again.

"Is my da watching the perimeter?" Rose asked, and Alisdair nodded. "Okay. We can fill him in later. We found something important at the library." She paused and looked at Sloane.

"You tell them, Keane," Sloane whispered. They sat on a love seat, and she closed her eyes again, waiting for the elixir to start working.

"Okay," Rose said with the same enthusiasm in her voice as in the library. "We searched economic data for Kirkcudbright and found that the MacCain family weren't involved in business with anyone on the Island. So we searched for Catriona's maiden name, Dunaid. Her Dunaid ancestors had shipping routes to Vancouver Island, not long after our governments sent us there. But what's more interesting is that the name Tindall appears on their shipping schedule. The Tindalls were one of Denwick's original families. One of their descendants might connect The Order members in our quadrants."

"The Tindalls left Denwick before my time," Freya said, her voice skeptical. "We didn't find any living successors when we searched for banished Magicals last March. And our Grand Coven confirmed the family was Nogical."

Sloane opened her eyes. "True, but the Grand Coven could have lied. Rose and I think family connections might help uncover Catriona's or Ginerva's counterparts in the Northwest Quadrant."

"We couldn't verify our suspicions because someone stole a genealogy book and the Sgàthan have shut down the archives." Rose flinched. "They're pissed, to put it mildly."

"What foolishness," Freya said. "Who would challenge the Sgàthan's commitment to their calling?"

Sloane looked at Alisdair. His face was empty, and his mouth opened to speak words that wouldn't come. "Jesus. You stole the book, didn't you? Is it one of the books I took back to Denwick?"

He was unable to answer her questions, but Mòrag made the cupboards in the enormous room open and slam shut at once.

"You did. Because you suspected a connection between the Dunaids and someone in our quadrant, didn't you?" Mòrag caused the candles to flicker. "All right. Now that we have the genealogy book from Miadarbaile and the one from Tagridore that Jane had, we'll find the link." Sloane held Alisdair's eyes. "You know, the gestillan curse seems more of an inconvenience than a sound way to hide information."

Alisdair pointed a finger at her and chuckled. "Aye. And it helps to have a wickedly smart house spirit."

Sloane rested her head against the cushion. Until that moment, she had been unaware of how exhausted she was. The time in Scotland was almost noon, but for her it was almost four in the morning.

"Our search can wait until tomorrow. Sloane and I have yet to sleep," Freya said.

Sloane opened her eyes. "I'm fine. I'll sleep after we look through the books."

"It's your decision. But I do advise you to rest." Freya stood. "Alisdair, if Mòrag could show me to my room, dear."

"No need. I'll take you." He slowly got to his feet.

Freya turned her gaze to Rose. "Perhaps you can convince her to rest."

After the door closed behind Alisdair and Freya, a quiet stillness settled over the covenstead. Sloane could once again feel the hum flowing through her body as freely as her blood. Did the gentle vibration have something to do with what Elvina and Jack had said about Rose? That she had claimed her?

"Hey, I agree with Freya. If you don't want a full night's rest, how about a nap? You can take one in my room."

Sloane scooted over in her chair and patted the seat cushion. "Come sit with me."

Rose cuddled beside her with her legs over Sloane's lap and nestled her head into the crook of Sloane's neck. "I like being right here," she whispered, her breath raising goose bumps over Sloane's body. "But lying down for a nap on my bed might feel better."

"If you joined me, we would not be sleeping." She could feel the warmth of Rose's smile deep in the marrow of her bones. Was that part of the bond? She wanted to ask, but like Alisdair, she couldn't form the words. Except her inability wasn't a curse. She was simply afraid of what the answer might be.

"Big talker. You're exhausted, and trust me, you want to have all your energy when we spend a sleepless night together."

Sloane chuckled. "Point taken."

Rose lifted her head. "Good. Now take a nap with me. I want to give you a gift."

"Are you trying to hurt my feelings?"

Rose swung her legs off Sloane's lap and stood. "Aw, never purposefully. Come with me, I promise you won't be disappointed."

Alisdair had provided Rose with a large but surprisingly comfy guest room. The king-sized bed Rose had mentioned earlier only took a fraction of the floor space. The rest of the room was furnished with antique bureaus and dressers, a desk and chair, bookshelves, and a sitting suite with two armchairs. Heavy drapes were swept to the sides of a large, mullioned window, and tapestries with woodland scenes adorned the walls.

"Wow. This is beautiful."

"I know, right?" Rose shut the door behind them and dragged the velvet drapes closed. The room darkened. "I love my apartment in Denwick, but I'm not missing it."

Sloane stood at the bed's footboard. "I want you to know I'm not avoiding your voice message. Do you want to talk now? You said we needed to." She surprised herself with the words tumbling out of her mouth. They came out of nowhere.

"You don't need to worry about it." Rose cupped her face. "You sleep first. Then we'll talk." She tugged Sloane's T-shirt from her jeans and slipped it and her sports bra over her head with ease. She slid her hands up Sloane's bare back, and heat seared through

Sloane, sending a sudden rush of blood between her legs. "I find napping in the nude very comforting."

"For one or both of us?" Sloane unbuttoned the top button on Rose's shirt.

"Uh-uh." Rose stopped her hand, placing it on her covered breast. "My present is only for you." She smiled at Sloane's look of disappointment. "But we'll both be comfortable. Trust me."

Rose continued to undress her, slowly, methodically, narrating every move with a husky voice until Sloane thought a glancing touch of Rose's hand across her skin would send an orgasm tearing through her.

"Remember when I told you how I can please you in ways only a Daywalker can?" Rose led her to the bed and pulled back the corner of a thick duvet. "You have to be lying down before I can share one of those ways with you."

Sloane slipped under the covers and watched Rose undress. She took her time, playfully holding out each piece of clothing before tossing it on their growing pile. It was the first time she had seen Rose naked, and her breath caught. The Dhampyre's physical beauty extended further than her facial perfection. Her breasts, perfectly round and perky, reminded Sloane of Greek goddess sculptures. She wanted to trace her tongue down every inch of the golden skin from Rose's belly button to the damp curls of dark hair between her legs.

"Turn over. I have to hold you in my arms from behind," Rose said as she slid into bed and pressed the full length of her body against Sloane's. She wrapped her arm around Sloane's waist, and Sloane moaned when Rose's taut breasts pressed against her back.

"I'm not sure what you were planning. But I'm too turned on to sleep."

"Lucky for you, a blissful, deep sleep is my gift," Rose whispered. "I have several abilities. Mostly cognitive. If you trust me and are willing, with a little bite from me, you'll only wake when your mind and body are refreshed."

"I trust you." Sloane tightened Rose's arm around her. "Does this gift come with pleasure or pain?"

"A little bit of both. Are you okay with some pain?"

"Yes, please." Her voice nearly failed her.

"Okay, close your eyes." Rose removed her arms from Sloane's waist and lifted herself onto one elbow. She kissed Sloane's neck lightly while gently cupping each of her breasts. She increased the pressure of her mouth and tongue on Sloane's neck and trailed her fingers down her abdomen. Her fingers slowly spread through the slick hairs on Sloane's mons.

Sloane's breathing became rapid, and she struggled not to turn around and face Rose. She needed to touch her, taste her, feel her wetness. "Please," she begged, aching for Rose to spread her and give her the release she needed.

"Trust me," Rose moaned, and just as waves of rapture swept through Sloane's body, Rose's fangs pierced Sloane's neck, sharing blood and releasing her beloved into pleasurable sleep.

CHAPTER TWENTY-SEVEN

Sloane awoke in a dimly lit room. She felt Rose against her back, and the ecstasy she had felt earlier with Rose flooded her body. This woman was everything, she thought as she turned to face her. Rose was still nude, and she quietly watched her soft breathing, overwhelmed with the desire to do anything for her.

The clock on the side table read eleven p.m. For a moment, she was confused. It was noon Scottish time when they had lain down for a nap. Had she been asleep for over ten hours? She sat up quietly. Jesus, she felt great. Rose had promised her the best sleep of her life, and it was. Her hand moved to her neck, feeling the spot Rose had bitten, but found only smooth skin. No puncture wounds. No soreness. She was unclear about the consequences of giving Rose her blood, and she didn't care.

When her eyes adjusted, she scanned the room. Rose had been up. A silk robe lay across the foot of the bed on her side. She figured Rose had left her to sleep and had only returned to bed an hour or so ago when the rest of the house retired for the night.

She had left her clothes folded at the foot of the bed, and her tote bag was on the floor leaning against the side table.

Leaving their bed felt like a punishment, but the coven would be waiting for her, and they had much to discuss. She dressed and kissed Rose goodbye softly on her head, careful not to awaken her.

Standing in the middle of the room, Sloane shook her head. Why hadn't she asked Alisdair which painting was the portal to her cottage? *Damn it.* She dug the elixir from her bag and took a swig. Preventative medicine, she thought, and vanished.

She appeared behind her armchair in their covenstead.

"How was your sleep?" Dorathea asked her.

"Best I've ever had." Sloane's cheeks warmed, and she didn't bother asking her cousin how she knew. Most likely, Mòrag told Alfred, and he relayed the information to her cousin. She didn't want to think about how much gossip they might have shared.

The whirling, bubbling, and zigzagging noises that were always prominent in their sacred space were missing. The books were shelved, the flames under Bunsen burners were turned low, and Alfred had not spoken to her. She settled into her favorite armchair and asked, "Why's everything so quiet?"

"We had a late night, and the house is taking an afternoon nap." Jack poured a measure of Fulsmécte into two glasses and handed one to her. He gave her a salute with his drink, and she returned the gesture.

"Where's Elvina. Freya said she came back to help you with something."

"She did indeed," Dorathea said. "We researched why you have pain when you bestealcedon, among other things. We have yet to find an answer. As for Elvina's whereabouts, she left for the cottage a few hours ago. I believe she wants to adjust to Scottish time." The teapot on the coffee table floated to her cup, filling it. "I understand it was not Polydora's voice Elspeth heard."

"Yeah, I was wrong."

"I was so sure we were right, lovey," Jack said, pointing his glass at Sloane. "No worries, though. We'll figure out who it is."

"Rose and I made progress today. She took me to Miadarbaile's library, and we discovered some valuable information. Did Mòrag and Alfred already tell you about it?" Both her cousins shook their heads no. "All right. It's not the MacCain family who are Malevolent descendants, it's Catriona's. The Dunaids. We found a business connection between the Baroness's Dunaid ancestors and the Tindall family here in Denwick from about the 1850 to the 1900." Sloane waited for her cousin's reaction. Dorathea's face registered surprise instantly. "Yeah. Too much of a coincidence, right? We wanted to look at the family history books, but Alisdair took one—"

Jack choked on his whiskey, coughing and clearing his throat until he was able to speak again. "My God, he removed a book from the library? What was he thinking? The Sgàthan are not to be crossed. Believe me, I know. I dated one. Let me tell you how tricky dating him was—"

"Not interested," Sloane said abruptly. "I have the genealogy book he stole at the cottage with the books Jane collected from Denwick and Tagridore. The information we need is in those books. I know it. I also think stealing books from the libraries is why The Order knew what Jane and Alisdair were doing. The Sgàthan alerted the Grand Coven about the thefts, and because The Order has infiltrated both GCs, they were found out."

"My God. It makes perfect sense," Jack said, and then he thought for a minute. "But if Jane knew about The Order over thirty years ago, why have they waited until now to destroy our covens? Their absence has never made sense to me."

"I don't know." Sloane sipped her drink. "Maybe they were busy putting other pieces in play before attacking us. Maybe something forced them to stay underground."

"Or someone," Jack added.

"I do know, we have to keep them from hiding again. Being isolated helped them become strong. If every Defender species could live openly, stop hiding and isolating ourselves from each other, we could work together to find them. Keep them in the open."

"Our laws are not to punish difference, pet. They are to protect," Dorathea said, but Sloane thought her cousin sounded unconvinced by her own words.

"Yeah, right. How's that working out for us?" Sloane finished her drink and held it out for Jack to pour her another. They remained silent for a while, and she stared at the flames dancing in the fireplace. "I'm glad you and Freya are talking," she said finally, and Dorathea placed her cup on its saucer. "She told us that Polydora issued a notice for her to be detained. And she doesn't think she can live in Tagridore any longer."

"Yes indeed. I am very disappointed in our Ealdormann. She is letting her unfounded suspicions obscure her ability to see the truth."

"At least Freya can stay here now. You can be together." Sloane looked at Jack. "Does that mean you're getting kicked out?"

Dorathea chuckled. "The hobbit house has plenty of room."

"It's not like we need another bedroom for her, do we?" Jack said, his usual teasing replaced by a cutting tone.

Sloane raised an eyebrow at him and looked at Dorathea. "Well, I'm very happy for you both."

Jack scoffed at Sloane and turned a sour gaze to Dorathea, "Ah, yes, deary. Here's to true, long-lasting love, and all that."

"Jesus, Jack. How much have you had to drink?" Sloane asked. "I understand the sarcasm. You've had a lot to deal with. Your husband. Family. Friends. And now Calen." She tried to hold his gaze, but he stared into his whiskey glass with tears pooling in his eyes. "I know how bleak it feels to experience so much loss, but don't begrudge others their happiness. They've spent thirty years waiting for this chance to be under one roof. To be together."

His eyes gave way to streaming tears. He dried them with a handkerchief and blew his nose. "I was lashing out. A completely selfish behavior. I apologize. It was wrong of me."

"Apology accepted, dear, and I do understand your sorrow."

"I'd be a shitty detective if I didn't recognize that Calen's death has hit you hard," Sloane said to him. "Maybe talking about it would help?"

"Seeing a therapist doesn't make you one." He shook his head. "I'm sorry. There I go again." His voice sounded as tortured as his expression.

"You carry so much grief, dear," Dorathea said. "I am so sorry I have not encouraged you to unburden yourself to me. I always cared deeply for Nathan. I knew you suffered greatly when he was killed, but I was not truly there for you."

"It wouldn't have mattered. I wasn't ready to talk about his death." Jack sighed mournfully, and tears collected in his eyes again. "Calen was helping me. He was a close friend. Years ago, he spent many summer weekends with us. And he was there for me when Nathan was killed."

"Calen's murder must have felt like losing your husband all over again," Sloane said, and Jack gave a slight nod. "It won't bring them back, but we'll find those responsible for killing them. I promise."

He scrubbed his face with his hands. "That's what Calen promised me. To find Nathan's killer. We'd spent years searching for that Changeling bitch." He pressed the heels of his hands against his eyes. "I thought she was responsible for Calen's death too. Just like Nathan. I almost couldn't stand the guilt." He was crying now, body-shaking sobs, and Sloane wanted to hold him, show him he wasn't alone. But he needed to release his grief, and she didn't want her touch to distract him.

After his tears began to wane, Dorathea said, "A Changeling mother did not kill Calen, dear."

"I know that now," he whispered.

"But you thought she did," Sloane said. "Does that mean you and Calen found her? Do you think she followed you here?"

"I don't know. We heard people had disappeared off the streets in Florida, the Miami area. Never seen again. Their bodies never discovered. It was the same in Louisiana. We believed it was her and her children. It was. We found her lair. But they were gone."

"I thought Changeling mothers stole human babies and replaced them with illusions. Or something like that," Sloane said, unsure.

"An abominable excuse Nogicals created to justify infanticide if their children appeared or acted differently than others," Dorathea said, angrily. "Changelings are malevolent supernatural creatures from the Abyss, and humans are their preferred nourishment.

When they escape the Nether, the only way to rid our worlds of them is to banish them."

"Or burning them alive in their dens can kill them. Once a Changeling mother dies, all her offspring die," Jack added. "The Nogicals had that right."

"Is that what you and Calen had been trying to do? Find her den and set fire to it?" she asked him, and he nodded. "Then I'll help you. We'll banish the Changeling that killed Nathan."

"Your help would mean the world to me. Thank you. I'm so grateful you're a part of my life." He stood and kissed the top of Sloane's head. "I'll see you later. I need to go lie down." He disappeared before Sloane could tell him she would always have his back.

"I am pleased to see you and your cousin growing closer," Dorathea said with a hint of pride in her voice. "We will train detaining and banishing spells in the morning. I suggest you have a good night's rest."

"I just got ten hours of sleep, Denham." Sloane got to her feet. "And I don't plan on sleeping tonight. Not when we're close to discovering who is at the top of The Order."

CHAPTER TWENTY-EIGHT

Sloane saved herself another splitting headache and returned to the cottage on foot. The sun had set, and biting, frigid air sank from the clear night sky.

She unlocked the front door. The lights inside were off, and she figured Elvina had returned to the Gòrdan covenstead in an attempt to adjust to Scottish time. She stood in the foyer and listened to the house, hearing only the electrical buzz of kitchen appliances, an intermittent creaking as the walls contracted in the cold, and the tick-tock of her grandparents' mantle clock.

Satisfied no one else was in the house, she made her way to the kitchen, grabbed a diet soda from the refrigerator, popped the top, and took a long drink. She flipped on the light switch for the breakfast room and jumped. "Jesus Christ, Elvina." Her former familiar sat at the table with a full glass of wine, her eyes fixed on the bay windows. "You scared the shit out of me. Why are you sitting in the dark?"

"My apologies," she said without averting her gaze. "I see perfectly well in the dark, remember? Please turn the light off before you sit. More crows than usual have gathered in the Garry oaks. The ones that live here are never keen to share their territory. So who is this larger flock they've allowed to stay?"

"Want me to turn the garden lights on and scare them off?"

"Let's keep the lights off for now. In the darkness, I see them better than they see us, and if they are Shifters, I might see one of them reveal itself."

"That's great and all, but I plan to look through Jane's and Alisdair's books." She picked up a box of books from the kitchen island. "Rose and I found a lead at the Miadarbaile library."

"You'll need light then." Elvina sighed. "I'll let the impostors go. This time." She snapped her fingers, and the breakfast room chandelier and the garden floodlights pushed out the darkness.

"Whoa. What's this all about?" Sloane asked as she set the box on one side of the table. Tarot cards were spread in front of Elvina on the other side.

"Divination, dear."

"Yeah, I get that. Anything coming up in my future I should know about?" Sloane tried to lighten the mood, but Elvina only gathered the cards slowly and returned the deck to its black velvet drawstring bag. "All right," said Sloane. "Guess you don't divine and tell."

Elvina looked at her without responding to Sloane's attempt at humor and asked, "What are we looking for? I can help you."

"No need. Dorathea said you were trying to adjust to Scottish time. It's already two in the morning there. You should go to bed. Give your eyes a rest. They're red and tired from sitting in the dark."

"Sleep has eluded me, so I prefer to stay busy," Elvina replied, her voice somber, and Sloane wondered what was bothering her roommate. Her mother and Dorathea were no longer estranged, so it wasn't that.

"All right," she said, deciding not to pursue the reason for Elvina's mood. "Do you have the list of Sensors?"

Elvina flicked her wrist, and a piece of paper appeared on the table. "Dorathea and I narrowed possible suspects to these wiċċe."

Sloane scanned the list. "Great. This is helpful." She set it aside and separated the books into two piles, the nogical records and the magical records. "I think the books will tell us two things. The identity of the woman with Catriona when she attacked the Gòrdans, and if the Gildeys are Half-Malevolents."

"Well, isn't that chilling. Coffee?" Elvina waved her hand, and the coffee maker on the kitchen counter sputtered to life.

"Sure. So, we know a powerful Sensor caused Lachlan's and Bella's injuries. You look through the records Alisdair stole from Miadarbaile's leabharlann. Search Ginerva Byrne's family tree for any of the Sensors on your list." She handed Elvina a volume with an embossed title in silver on its cover, *The Northeast Quadrant Generations, 1790-1890*. "I'll search for any familial ties between the Sensors and the Byrnes in the genealogy book Jane took from Tagridore. I'll need to know all the surnames in Ginerva's family, if you'd jot them down."

"Of course." Elvina waved her hand, and a pen appeared.

They silently read marriage, birth, and death entries for several hours. With a thud, Sloane closed the tome Alisdair had taken from the Sgàthan in Miadarbaile. She hadn't found any connections between Millicent or the other four Sensors on the list and any members of Ginerva Byrne's family. On the chance that the Tindalls were banished Magicals, she searched for any mention of their surname but came up empty again. She sat back and stretched her arms over her head, releasing a loud groan. "Maybe this isn't the right line of inquiry."

Elvina looked at Sloane sympathetically. "I haven't had any success either, dear. But I have a few more generations to read through. Shall we have another pot of coffee?"

"Coffee would be great. How about some food, too? Can you still summon from Freya's café?"

Elvina lowered her eyes. "My mother has freezers full of her pastries." She snapped her fingers. "As soon as the oven preheats, your favorite scones will bake."

"Thanks. I'm sorry about what's happening to her. She doesn't deserve to be forced from her life in Tagridore. If she wants, I'll make Polydora apologize to her after we prove who in The Order is hunting us."

"I believe if anyone could avenge my mother's name, you could, dear." Elvina sat quietly for a moment, blinking back tears. "Polydora is also the reason Dorathea and my mother couldn't live together. When your cousin passed up her Grand Coven seat to Polydora, she chose to spend her life continuing the tradition of being your family's High Priestess, here, in the nogical world. And only Defenders can live here. My mother gave up her role as your family's Attendant long before."

"So if Freya resumes that role, can she stay?" Sloane asked, and Elvina nodded.

"My mother is not upset with the Ealdormann. She and Dorathea have lived in separate worlds far too long. She's happy the issue has finally forced them to settle in one. So am I."

"Yeah, me too. It'll be amazing with your mom next door. Maybe Denham will lighten up a bit."

"One can always hope." Elvina returned to the book in front of her. "I'll finish the last two generations in Tagridore. What will we look for next?"

"We'll search the nogical records…" Sloane stopped talking when a grin spread across Elvina's face. "What?"

"You said nogical, unprovoked, and I'm just very proud. You seem to be struggling with other terms."

"I misspoke. Don't get used to it," Sloane said firmly, but she was pleased inside that her friend had finally smiled. "Rose and I figured out the MacCains have nothing to do with the evil in Kirkcudbright. Catriona's family is the Malevolent's descendants. We found shipping records of trade between her Dunaid ancestors and the Tindalls, one of the original colonizers on the Island. So we know the Dunaids had a business connection with Nogicals in our Northwest Quadrant. And we have a picture proving Andrew and Catriona know each other. We know she's a Half-Malevolent, so connecting them through business ties or family lines could help us prove the Gildeys are too."

"Oh, that does sound promising."

Sloane slid a book Jane had taken from the Old Denwick Church to Elvina's side of the table. Then she gently opened the yellow, brittle pages of a genealogy book Alisdair had from Kirkcudbright, the *St. Andrews Old Parish Records*.

"Our history tells us Malevolents and their offspring have hidden in the nogical world, passing as regular people," Sloane said. "Let's start by searching the Gildey and Dunaid family trees for any ties with each other."

Soon the aroma of cardamom wafted through the room. Elvina flicked her wrist, and freshly baked scones appeared on the table. They pored over the books into the early morning hours.

Sloane stifled a yawn and refilled her coffee mug. "I'm not finding anything," she said, frustrated.

"It's been a long night, dear." Elvina closed her book. "We need a break."

"I'm good." Sloane placed two more pastries on her plate.

"Well, my eyes are tired. I'm going to rest them and watch the garden. Have you noticed the outside lights did not scare off the crows? In fact, they've drawn closer. It's very peculiar." Elvina's pupils became slits.

Sloane looked out the window. "I can't see them," she said, and Elvina snapped her fingers, the inside lights turned off, and the crows became visible in the garden, flying low, then hopping on the ground toward the porch. "Yeah, their movements are strange." She dragged the volume Elvina had been reading to her side. "You watch them while I finish searching the Denwick records. How far did you get?"

Elvina turned the lights back on. "I looked at the entries for the Gildeys' first generation."

Sloane turned to their family title page. "They only have five generations here and hardly any entries."

"I told you. My eyes are tired."

"Fine. Watch the birdies." Sloane scanned the Gildeys' first generation on the Island. The patriarch of the family then, Edward Gildey, had a son, Joseph, with Fortune Walker in 1858. She turned to Joseph's entry and stopped. "I found another connection. Joseph Gildey married Ruth Tindall. They had a daughter in 1908, Zelda."

"Well, there weren't many choices for brides in Denwick at the time. I don't see how Joseph marrying a Tindall tells us anything," Elvina said, her gaze still fixed on the crows.

Sloane continued to read. "Interesting, Joseph married again two years later to Anna Harlow and had a son, Henry." She flipped the pages to Henry and Zelda's generation and scanned. "Zelda never married. Her half-brother, Henry, married Prudent Tremblay. They had a son, Sean, Andrew's father. So Andrew's great-aunt Zelda was a Tindall." She paged to Sean's generation. "He married Isobel Tulach, and they had a son, Andrew." She paused. "That's weird for the time period, right?"

"What is?" Elvina asked, looking at her this time.

"Each Gildey generation had just one child. Except for Joseph."

"Yes, but the others had sons first. He had a daughter. Back then, you needed a male heir, dear."

Sloane turned the pages to the Gildeys' death records. After a few minutes, she whispered, "What the hell?" She closed her eyes and cast, "Ċīeġ." Her mother's magical creatures book appeared on the tabletop.

Elvina looked at it with pride. "Splendid. And on your first try."

"Don't get too excited. It's a book from down the hall. It's not a cage to capture corrupt Magicals." She scanned the table of contents and flipped through the pages, tapping on the image of a Malevolent. "Jesus, it says a nogical woman can't survive the birth of a malevolent child."

"Very true. And your point is?"

"All the Gildey wives—Fortune, Ruth, Anna, and Prudent—died in childbirth."

"Oh, my." Elvina gave Sloane her undivided attention. "Which suggests their children were Half-Malevolents. You were right."

"But what about Isobel?"

"What about her?" Elvina asked, and then she answered her own question. "Isobel did not die."

"Right." Sloane opened *St. Andrew's Old Parish Records*, riffled through the fragile pages. "Because she's not a Nogical. She has to be the connection."

Sloane found the Dunaid family history in the Old Parish Records. Four generations were recorded during the same period, from the Gildeys' arrival on the Island until now. She scanned the generation in the 1850s. One son, Wallace. Dead mother at childbirth. In the second generation, the Half-Malevolent Wallace Dunaid had a daughter, Una, with his first wife, and a son, Horas, with his second. Both mothers died in childbirth. Sloane's skin broke out in goose bumps at the eerily similar family histories.

She flipped through the pages to Una Dunaid's entry. The female Half-Malevolent married Andrew Tulach and had one child, *Isobel Tulach*. Her heart pounded even faster as she leafed through the pages and stopped on Una's brother's entry. Horas Dunaid married once and had a daughter: Catriona. Like all the others, his wife lost her life giving birth to the Half-Malevolent's child.

Sloane sat back abruptly. It was the link both her mother and Alisdair must have known existed, but they each had only one side of the story. Thirty years later, she had finally made the connection.

"Jesus, we found it," Sloane whispered.

"Do tell," Elvina said excitedly.

"Not here." Sloane closed both volumes and quickly rose. She turned off the inside lights and peered out the bay window. The crows had settled on the back deck's railing, tilting their heads down and to each side, as if they were listening. She banged on the glass and shouted, but the birds remained. "You're right. We're being watched."

Retrieving her cell phone from her tote, she called Dorathea.

After one ring, her cousin picked up. "Why are you calling when it would take you a split second to see me in person?"

"You sound like a millennial, Denham." Sloane lowered her voice. "Listen, we need to know if the GC sent crows to watch us again. They're on the back porch and very interested in what Elvina and I have been doing since last night."

"Have you found something?" Dorathea asked.

"Yeah, but I don't want to say anything or move the books if we're in danger."

"Quite, right." Dorathea was silent for a moment, and Sloane could hear her cousin moving and a door opening. "The Grand Coven would be foolish to surveil us again," she said, and a bright light blasted through the yard. The crows shrieked and scattered, rising high into the air and flying out of sight. A door closed. "Yes, indeed, pet, they were spies."

"Yeah, we thought so. We'll be right over." Sloane ended the call and shoved the two genealogy books into her tote. "You'll need to make more of that elixir for me. It doesn't look like I'll be avoiding the need to bestealcedon."

"Of course, dear." Elvina wrapped her arm around Sloane's waist, and in an instant, they appeared inside the covenstead.

Dorathea greeted them and pointed at the library. The books in Sloane's tote flew into the air. "Conceal yourselves," she ordered, and the two volumes floated about, finding new spots on the floor-to-ceiling bookcases, their covers changing with every reshelving. "We must hide these books. Whatever it is you've found has piqued The Order's interest."

"The crows?" Sloane asked, and her cousin nodded. "What makes you think it was them and not our GC?"

"Because the Ealdormenn would have demanded I explain why I blew their Shifters out of the yard." She sat in her armchair.

"Jesus, all of those Shifters were in The Order?"

"Oh, no. Those weren't Magicals. They were crows doing the Half-Malevolent's bidding," Elvina said, sitting in her chair across from Jack. "Am I right?"

Dorathea nodded. "Tell us what you have found," she said to Sloane, eagerly.

Jack leaned forward "Yes, lovey, out with it. I can't stand the suspense."

Sloane sat beside him. "Alisdair and my mother's research proves the Gildeys are Half-Malevolents. And so is Isobel. She and Baroness Catriona MacCain are half-first cousins. Wallace Dunaid was their grandfather. He had two children, Una and

Horas, by two Nogical women, who, of course, died in childbirth. Una Dunaid is Isobel's mother, and Horas Dunaid is Catriona's father."

"My God, lovey. Sean…Isobel…" His eyes were wide. "Andrew is the child of two Half-Malevolents," he said, shocked. He looked at Dorathea. "What does that mean?"

Sloane looked at Dorathea, waiting for her cousin to respond. She had never seen the High Priestess so stunned. "I have no idea," Dorathea said finally. "I do know, however, the truth has always been available to us. How did we not see it before?"

"To be fair, half the truth," Sloane said. "And it's been hidden from you in the floorboards of my mother's room. Even when I found her research, we still needed the connection to Kirkcudbright and Alisdair's records."

Dorathea sighed. "Why did Jane keep what she had found from us? Not confide in us with what she suspected? We would have helped her. Stopped The Order in its early days."

"I don't know," Sloane said. She hated hearing the hurt in her cousin's voice. "But we'll find out. The Gildeys and Catriona know the answer. And I plan to confront Isobel about her denial that she knows Catriona. If I agitate her enough, she might—"

"Absolutely not," Dorathea said. "Now that we know Isobel and Andrew are Half-Malevolents, you must never be in their presence without the power of three."

"I hear you," Sloane said. "But if we all show up, they'll assume it's to banish them. And they'll fight. We also don't want to send them to the Abyss until we uncover all the members of The Order. I'm sure Isobel and Catriona are the founders, at least in the northern quadrants." She waited for her cousin's response, but Dorathea only set her jaw. "Listen, Isobel and Andrew have had several opportunities to kill me, and they haven't." She stood and slung her tote's strap over her head. "I need a few hours of sleep. Then I'm paying Isobel and Andrew a visit. I promise to keep communication open with Elvina."

"You can be quite impossible indeed," Dorathea said.

"Ah, but you love me." Sloane grinned. "I'll be safe, Denham. Besides, my gut tells me Jane had something of theirs, and they want it back. And they're keeping me alive so I can lead them to it."

Jack visibly trembled. "Well, lovey, let's hope they never find it."

CHAPTER TWENTY-NINE

Sloane waited until eight a.m., a proper time to pay a visit to a wealthy Half-Malevolent. She downed a shot of Elvina's elixir to minimize the aftereffects of her teleport. She wouldn't have chosen the Wiccan mode of travel, but she remembered Isobel's threat and the size of Trevor at the front gate. Showing up undetected would be as important as being unannounced.

She appeared on the mansion's porch, and after she slammed the large iron knocker against the wood a few times too many, the Gildeys' butler allowed her in. He escorted Sloane to the formal foyer without speaking. "Thanks, Peter," she said, and smiled. She figured he didn't receive many of those during the day.

Peter entered the double doors that led to Isobel's study, the large, impeccably designed room into which Sloane had been invited just a week ago, and where the matriarch conducted business like some New York don. When the door closed, she studied the portraits on the antechamber's walls again. Now she could put names to their faces. Every Gildey she had found in the

Old Denwick records, all five generations, had a likeness hanging there, except for Andrew.

After a few minutes, she felt a chill stab through her skin to the bone and heard the clicking of high heels on the marble floor.

"Ms. West," Isobel said, and Sloane turned around. "I'm not an unforgiving woman, but I do have my limits. I made myself clear not to visit my home uninvited."

Standing in Isobel's presence, Sloane no longer doubted the origin of the evil she'd felt since arriving in Denwick. It was time to poke her, hard. But she wouldn't be able to contain Isobel on her own. So she opened her third eye to teleport quickly if the Half-Malevolent began assaulting her, if she hadn't started already.

"Don't just stand there. Answer me." Isobel's voice was full of scorn, and Sloane glared at her, returning the sentiment.

"Did you ask me a question?"

Isobel's jaw clenched. "We do not entertain drop-ins at Gildey Manor. I am speaking with an important guest this morning. A dignitary. Your interruption has caused me a great deal of embarrassment."

"I don't care how you feel or about your high-ranking guest. She can wait."

Isobel raised an eyebrow. "You really are confident. Or maybe you're just arrogant enough to speak to me that way." She folded her arms. "I didn't say my guest was a woman."

"You didn't deny it either." Sloane grinned. "Let's just say I have a good *sense* of who your guest is."

Isobel moved into Sloane's personal space, close enough she could see her green eyes darken, and the air around them became heavy. "You have one minute to state your business, and not a minute longer, or you will regret the foolish decision you made this morning."

"I don't even need a minute." As an NYPD cop, Sloane had faced more than her share of hard asses who used physical intimidation to make a point, and she had never backed down. Isobel's move didn't impress her either. She checked her third eye. Still clear of smoke.

She removed the snapshot of Andrew, Catriona, and Ginerva from her tote and thrust it at Isobel's face. Recognition crinkled the corners of the matriarch's eyes. "Yeah, this photo again," said Sloane. "Last time you said you didn't know anyone in it besides Andrew. But you lied. I know all about the Dowager Baroness and Ginerva Byrne. What I'd like to know now is why Andrew would kill three innocent people with these women?"

"How dare you accuse my son of murder?" Isobel hissed, and the door to her study creaked open behind them. "Go back inside, love. I can handle Ms. West."

The door closed before Sloane could see who had opened it. *Love?* If Andrew wasn't in there, who the hell was? She looked at Isobel again. "Or did *you* kill them? We know one of you did it for The Order."

The photo burst into flames in Sloane's hand, burning her fingertips. She dropped it. "The pyro show's a nice touch." Her next breath stung. "We know who the Gildeys and the Dunaids are. You can't hide from us any longer." She struggled for air. The photo erupting into flames had distracted her, and Isobel had begun her attack. Catriona had done the same thing. Distracting them. A silent assault. She needed to get out of there, to call for Dorathea and Jack, but her thoughts started to drift away, and she couldn't keep them tethered.

"I did believe you would be worth more to me alive than dead, but clearly I was mistaken." Isobel spread her arms wide, a pulse of green light arced between her hands, and her eyes turned the same glowing color.

Fear, profound and unfamiliar, gripped Sloane. For the first time, she felt an overwhelming desire to protect herself, to live for her coven, for Rose, but her third eye was lost behind the opacity of smoke, and she had no other way to contact Elvina. She struggled for breath. The air was on fire. Transparent flames ripped over her, and she fell to her knees.

"Isobel, not yet. We need them together." The voice came from the study. It was distorted, tinny, and drawn out, seeping into Sloane's slipping consciousness.

The sensation of pain began to disappear, an emptiness replacing it, inch by inch, disconnecting her from her body, and she thought, this is dying. The realization was neither frightening nor pleasant. It just was.

Then a shadow covered the room, and Sloane could feel another presence. She strained to stay awake, to see who it was. In her last moment of awareness, a blackness without form or sound enveloped her.

Sloane woke in her bed a few hours later. The encounter with Isobel rushed back into her mind. The Gildey matriarch was a Half-Malevolent, and she had tried to kill her.

Sloane lifted herself and rested against the headboard. *Son of a bitch.* Her head throbbed, and the pain made her nauseous. She tried to recall what had happened, how she got away. Who had been there with them? Did that person save her again? Could it be her father? A glass vial with a clear liquid sat on her bedside table. She had no memory of Dorathea or Eliva caring for her, and Jack wouldn't have brewed an elixir. She contemplated taking the potion. It could be poison. Then another wave of nausea hit her, and she uncapped the vial, downing the clear liquid. It burned her throat on the way down, and after a few seconds, it spread heat through her body.

In the time it took to walk to the kitchen, she felt physically better than she had in years. Emotionally, though, she was all over the place. Who the hell was her father? If it was her father protecting her, why was he risking his life for her after all these years? Why hadn't he tried to be a part of her life when he could have been? Why now? She decided if it was her father, he had no real interest in her. He probably had another family but felt obligated to protect her. She was his flesh and blood after all. It was apparent he knew about The Order, but she was convinced now he wasn't a part of the insurgency, not if he was hell-bent on keeping her alive.

She filled a glass with cold tap water, taking small sips to soothe her throat. She sat at the breakfast table and opened communication with Elvina. *I'm at the cottage. Things did not go well at the Gildeys. But I'm okay now.* Her comment garnered only silence.

An instant later, Dorathea, Jack, and Elvina appeared in the breakfast room. "What do you mean, didn't go well?" Elvina asked, pulling Sloane to her feet and inspecting every inch of her.

"You can let go of me. I'm fine," Sloane said, wrestling herself free. She looked at the others. "Whoever rescued me left a potion. I haven't felt this good since I was a kid. I don't even feel my all-nighter going through the old records with Elvina."

"Hmm. Are you sure someone left it, or was it something you bought for yourself…a little pick-me-up?" Jack grinned.

"Jesus, Jack. I don't do drugs."

Dorathea raised her arms to the ceiling and gracefully spun around once, releasing a surge of energy that surrounded them. "Tell us exactly what took place at the Gildey manor, pet."

Sloane looked at the shimmering dome under which they all stood. "Why the extra spell? I thought the cottage was impenetrable."

"Don't complain, lovey. Extra precautions are a good thing," Jack said.

"That's true. I think I'm going to need all I can get. Maybe I should have a house spirit. Do you get them from Tagridore?"

"You don't buy house spirits, dear," Elvina simpered. "You have to invite the one already inhabiting your home to return. Which would be difficult. Brita has taken the loss of your mother and grandparents extremely hard. But Dorathea can ask Alfred to talk with her."

"I can ask Alfred," Sloane said.

"Don't be a braggard," Jack replied, pouting.

"For goodness' sake, focus, we have more pressing issues. We need to know what happened," Dorathea said and exhaled loudly.

"Don't get frustrated, Denham. It's a lot to unpack, and it's going to take a minute." Sloane waited for the others to sit at the table. Isobel's attack had been the first time she had truly feared for her life, and it wasn't going to be easy to admit. "When I arrived, Isobel was pissed. She said she had a guest, and I interrupted them. She said the person was a dignitary. We can easily search if any nogical bigwigs were on the Island today, but Isobel called the person *love*."

"Oh, plot twist," Jack said, and shifted in his chair like he was settling in for a story.

Dorathea tsked at him, and Sloane continued, "I can't be sure, but it might have been Andrew. Point is, I made her angry, and she got in my face. I told her I didn't care if she was busy and shoved Alisdair's photo at her. I asked why she and Andrew killed three innocent people. She didn't like my accusation." She hesitated. "Then I told her we knew what the Gildeys and Dunaids are. She lost it. Alisdair's photo burst into flames in my hands, distracting me. And she used that opportunity to strike me. Then the person in the study told her, 'Not yet, we need all of them together,' or something like that. But she didn't stop."

"My God, you must have been terrified," Jack said.

"Yeah. I won't lie. I thought I was dead." Sloane replayed the confrontation in her mind. It had happened so fast, and the details were sketchy. "Then I sensed the same presence again. A shadow came over us, and I woke up here. I know it doesn't make sense, but I think it's my father. Who else would keep rescuing me?"

Dorathea considered Sloane's words for a long moment. "Perhaps it is. What we do know is a Magical with great abilities has just saved your life."

Sloane nodded. "Whoever it is could be a strong ally. They also saved Jack and me from a Half-Malevolent," Sloane said. "Who can do that? Who can teleport and brew potions to reverse the effects of a maleficium curse? And who would know Isobel's and my identity?"

"Sounds like a Wiċċan to me," Jack said.

"He's right. They must be," Elvina added.

Dorathea tapped her fingers on the tabletop. "The list of possibilities is short. A Wiċċan makes the most sense."

Sloane nodded and thought about their next move. "We need to know if any of our GC members have met with Ginerva or Catriona. Did Freya hear back from her Weardas source?" she asked Elvina.

"I'm afraid not. Polydora's order to detain my mother has dried up her access to the Weardas."

Sloane frowned. "And the curse on Alisdair? Is Freya close to reversing it?"

"Apparently, an ancient energy binds it in place," Elvina said. "One she might not be able to reverse."

Sloane stared at her. She had heard those words before. "That's how your mother described the protection spell around me when she sensed it. The one the Grand Coven was so interested in. Does the GC have access to that kind of energy?" she asked, and they stared at her.

"There are several primeval wells of magic, and our Grand Coven does have access to a few." Dorathea looked at Sloane, concerned. "You may have taken a strong healing elixir. But your eyes tell me it is wearing off. We will pursue these inquiries after you have rested."

"I agree," Jack said. "You look dreadful. Very pale. Circles under your eyes as dark as your hair. All-nighters are harder to pull off at your age."

"Shut up, Jack."

Dorathea stood. "We will train later this evening. Sleep now. You will need your full strength when The Order attacks. And now that you have exposed the Gildeys and Catriona, I fear they will again soon."

CHAPTER THIRTY

An unrelenting ringing awakened Sloane. Someone was being aggressive with the cottage's doorbell. She groaned and crawled out of bed in the dark room and glanced at her watch. It was after five p.m. Rose was the only person she wanted to see on the other side of her front door, and the possibility that she was made her run-walk toward the foyer. After only a few rushed steps down the hallway, she froze. The icy shiver that overtook her meant it wouldn't be Rose standing on her porch.

She sucked in a deep breath at the image on the security monitor. Andrew Gildey. She hid behind the arched entrance to the living room. Her chest tightened, and she opened her third eye to teleport to the covenstead.

"I know you're in there," Andrew called through the door. "I mean you no harm. Don't disappear. I need to speak with you."

His voice was calm and soothing, and Sloane thought either he was being frank with her, or he was a damn good liar. Yeah, a Cambion is a good liar. *Dumbass*. A nervous laugh escaped her, and she said, "I don't think that's a good idea, Mr. Gildey. We both know why."

"Yes, we do. You know what I am. But you don't know everything about me. We are not all like Isobel and Catriona. Some of us chose not to be evil. I promise you need not fear me. I am on your side. If it makes you more comfortable, please tell your coven I'm here."

Sloane pressed against the wall, considering her next move. She needed to alert the others, to get the hell out of there. But she thought, something in his voice rang true, and what would it hurt to hear him out? The coven was only a split second away if she needed help.

"All right. I told them you're here," she lied and pushed off the wall. "Don't misstep, or they'll be here in an instant, and you don't want them here. We're ready to send you to the Abyss." She opened the door and stepped aside. Andrew entered, his head lowered, and she glanced at the circular drive. "Where's your Rolls-Royce?"

"You knew?" he asked, and she cocked her head slightly. "I'm sorry if I frightened you. But I needed to make sure you were okay."

Sloane didn't respond. It was hard to read him, or Catriona and Isobel, for that matter. They could be in a conversation one minute, and the next, they were trying to melt her from the inside, and she had no clue until it was too late.

"I didn't drive here because I couldn't risk Isobel knowing where I am. And I don't need a car to travel."

"Good to know. Neither do I." Sloane led them into the living room and waved her hand. The logs in the fireplace burst into flames. "Have a seat."

He removed his heavy, dark-wool coat and sat on the sofa. "That was impressive."

"I've learned a few spells since moving here."

"I'm sure your High Priestess is an outstanding teacher." He sat silently looking in her direction, although for all she knew, he could have been studying the house. He wore those damn dark glasses, and it pissed her off. The eyes could reveal more than words, and when she spoke with people, she wanted to see theirs.

"What's so important you'd risk upsetting Isobel to speak with me? And why should I believe you're different than her?"

"I can only give you my word."

Sloane scoffed. "How the hell is your word supposed to carry any weight?"

He frowned, and although she couldn't see what his eyes were saying, she felt his demeanor change. "I have caused you so much pain," he said. "The loss of your mother…the grandparents you never had the chance to meet. Your grief is all my fault."

His emotional admission confused her. "What do you mean, all your fault? I thought you were the non-evil kind of Cambion, or were you lying?"

He winced when she said Cambion. "It's my fault because I failed to protect your family from the ones you call The Order."

"Do you expect me to believe you're not a part of them?"

"I'm not. My father and I kept Isobel and the other Half-Malevolents contained the best we could for over forty years. They recruited and possessed your kind as well as human beings, but we ensured their uprising was weak. But then Isobel…" He hesitated.

Sloane remembered a weeping Lore Reed telling her about all the deaths in Denwick in the months before her mother died. Andrew's father, Sean, had supposedly died of Alzheimer's. Obviously that was a lie. And it struck her. "She killed your father, didn't she?" It made sense. The West Coven hadn't known Sean had descended from the original Malevolent in their quadrant. They hadn't exiled him. "Your kind can send each other to the pit of hell?"

Andrew nodded. "To the Abyss. We can kill each other in a viler way too. We can consume each other's souls."

"Jesus," Sloane whispered.

"How much have you learned about our kind?" he asked.

"That you live in the Nether. Which must be one hell of a place. I know your kind aren't supposed to be anywhere else. And that seven Malevolents escaped. They pretended to be Nogicals in this world and exacerbated the pain and suffering that destroys so many lives to this day. Then my kind sent five of them back to the Abyss. But not before they bred and created Half-Malevolents, like you, killing nogical women in the process. Now the nogical world has just two Malevolents, and who knows how many spawn, driving the Nogicals into ruin."

"Well you know more than I thought you would. Although, to be clear, human beings are capable of moral atrocities on their own." He stared into the flames dancing in the fireplace. "We aren't the Demons and Cambions they have codified in their religions. What they call Satan, Lilith, Cambions, or Half-Demons, or Half-Fiends, or my least favorite, Demon Spawn, are myths to explain their human failings. I am Half-Malevolent. I am both a human and Malevolent."

"All right. I sense I've offended you. Just so you know, I was raised as a Nogical, so I'm learning the correct terminology. It's a journey," she said, and could swear she saw him stop himself from frowning.

"I understand." He looked at her. "As you said, the Protector Covens sent five of the Malevolent spirits back to the Abyss. But that happened millennia ago. Since then, Protector Covens have banished Half-Malevolents, like me."

Sloane considered him for a moment. *Millennia?* "Jesus, how many of you are there?"

"Your covens have exiled most Half-Malevolents to the Nether, regardless of whether we were evil, neutral, or benevolent. We numbered thirteen during my lifetime, but four of us died recently. Killed for working against the movement."

"We call it The Order."

Andrew nodded. "I've heard the term. My father, Sean, and Zelda, my great-aunt, were two of the four killed. Isobel found out we were betraying The Order and murdered them. She would have destroyed me with no regrets if she had known I was also involved in the fight against them. But she only suspected my father and great-aunt. The other two that fought with us lost their lives in what Magicals call the Southwest Quadrant. For forty years, we have saved many Nogicals and Magicals from death at

The Order's hands. We've ensured they didn't recruit masses into their movement." He paused. "My father forbade me from telling her I was a resister and made me promise to keep our fight going."

Sloane sensed in his voice that the imposing man sitting across the coffee table from her was struggling to control his emotions. She felt his battle was with sorrow, but she needed to see his eyes to be sure. They would mirror the truth. But he kept them hidden, making her unsure she could trust him.

"You're telling me nine Half-Malevolents live in the nogical world now?" she asked. "I know Isobel and Catriona are hell-bent on killing. Do you and the other six make up this resistance?"

"Unfortunately the numbers go the other way. Only two of us are benevolent."

"Those are shitty odds." Sloane frowned. "Am I right that Isobel and Catriona founded The Order?"

He nodded. "Along with two Half-Malevolents in South America and three in Asia. They want to control the nogical and magical worlds. But they need to increase their numbers."

"Yeah. We figured as much. They need to kill the Protector Covens to release the Malevolents and Half-Malevolents we've banished."

"Yes. And we cannot let that happen."

Sloane would have considered Andrew's story unbelievable less than a year ago. Today, she accepted what he was saying to her, as mind-blowing as it all was, but she wasn't convinced about *why* he was telling her. She stared into his dark glasses. "So are you here because you and your friend need my coven's help fighting the other Half-Malevolents?"

"In a sense." He stared at his lap for a silent minute and sighed. "I want to fight The Order with you. I failed to keep the love of my life safe from Isobel. Once my mother destroyed my father, we lost the full strength of the protection we had placed on her and our child. I have mourned the agonizing day since. Unable to bear the light of day. I am not strong enough to banish Isobel on my own, but I will die before she ends the last person I love on this earth."

He reached up and pulled off his dark glasses, and Sloane locked eyes with him for the first time. His eyes were bloodshot, full of sorrow's tears, and *ice gray*. Her stomach dropped.

"No, no, no," she said, barely above a whisper, shaking her head violently. She leapt out of the chair, fumbling her way behind it, putting it between her and Andrew. "You can't be. Your eyes… this is some kind of trick." She was shouting now. "You're trying to distract me. Make me call the others. Yeah, that's what this is about. Is Isobel here?"

"Please, calm down. This must be so hard to understand. I don't want to upset you any more than I have already. But you need to know the truth. When Isobel finds out you are my daughter, if she hasn't already, she will not allow you to live." He was pleading with her, but she couldn't hear him over her heartbeat pounding in her ears. "ZeeZee, please."

She froze, recognizing the name, and mumbled, "Oh my God, this isn't happening."

"It is, and I can prove you are my child. My biggest regret was altering your reality so I could be a part of your life." He held her gaze, and images flooded her mind. Vibrant. Real. Memories of him playing board games with her after school, when none of the other kids would come to the strange lady's house to play with her daughter. Him tucking her in bed, reading her stories. Him holding her hand as they walked through Central Park. Him calling her ZeeZee. She gasped, and her eyes burned with tears.

She was unsure how long Andrew regarded her in silence, but as he did, she felt more fully aware of his presence in every part of her life. And she knew, he was the shadow that swept over her when she was in trouble. "I don't understand." Her tears ran, and she sank to the floor.

Looking tortured, Andrew knelt on his knees beside her. "I am so sorry. Your mother and I thought hiding you in New York City was our best chance at shielding your family from The Order. My heart has broken every day because you only knew me in your dreams. Then last year, even though my father's protective spell was gone, your mother wanted to come home. She convinced me you were strong, and we could tell the coven about you and fight

The Order. I was scared but so happy we could be together." His voice cracked. "But they killed her before she could bring you home."

Andrew's words were landing somewhere in her mind, but she had stopped hearing them. Her thoughts raced through memories, clues she might have missed, and the truth came together into a terrifying realization. "Fucking hell, I'm…I'm one of you?"

He leaned closer, and she shrank away as if he were a venomous snake. "When you arrived, I wanted to tell you who I was…who you were. But I had to keep you safe from Isobel." He reached out to her in contrition. "ZeeZee, please, I made a mistake. I know that now. You have always deserved to know who you are."

Her face burned hot, and she pushed his hands away.

"Please," he said, gently holding her arms. "You have nothing to fear. We choose whether or not we submit to the evil inside us. It doesn't control you any more than your Wiccan heritage does. You are still the same good and loving person you've always been."

He wrapped his arms around her, and she resisted until her fight, her anger from decades of lies and broken trust felt unnecessary to carry anymore. She surrendered to the embrace, letting the rage flow out of her in heaving sobs.

Andrew held her steadfastly, and when her tears ended, she wiped her hands over her face. There were so many things she needed to know. Questions she wanted answers to. But she felt like a rag doll without the strength to endure any more revelations.

"I will tell you anything you want to know when you're ready," he said. "And I'm not reading your mind. I can see the need for answers in your eyes." He smiled. "I knew how much you loathed it when your mother read your mind. But she only did so to calm you because she wanted to ensure you could handle the evil inside you as you grew older." He helped her back to her chair. "Can I make you tea? Coffee?"

Sloane shook her head in disbelief, not at the question. She had thought this man was an arrogant asshole. Then she had thought he was an evil supernatural responsible for her family's murders. He was none of those things. He was gentle and kind, and he was her father. *Her father.* "Jesus, no," she finally replied. "I need a drink."

She focused her third eye, moving past the veil, and visualized the bottle of Fulsmécte on the kitchen counter and two rocks glasses in a cupboard. Then she pictured them on the coffee table and said, "Čīeġ."

"Now I'm really impressed," her father said, picking up the whiskey bottle. Your mother told me the funniest stories about summoning. If I remember correctly, it took her several semesters at her Academy to land things where she wanted them." He gave her a smile that was genuine but had a world of pain behind it, and she returned the same.

"Make mine a double," she said, as he poured their drinks. "I'm sorry, but this has been more than I can process in one sitting." She downed the amber liquid. "I need to exit memory lane. That doesn't mean I don't want to talk about the past or the future. I just need some time."

He lifted his glass to her. "I hear you. Let me know when you are ready to talk more. We have forever before us."

Forever? Did he mean forever literally? She had barely accepted the fact that Wiċċan had longer lifespans than Nogicals. Immortality was incomprehensible. She pushed the thought away. "Sure. We'll have time. But only if we stop The Order."

"And we will. What does the coven need from me?"

She appreciated how effortlessly her father changed subjects for her sake. "I'm sure you know Catriona attacked the Gòrdan Coven with another woman, a wiċċe," said Sloane. "But it wasn't Ginerva Brynes because she was at the Prìomh-oifis. We believe the other woman came from our quadrant. We need to know who she is. More specifically, is she in our Grand Coven or any other magical governing bodies?"

"Your mother was sure someone in her upper government was a part of The Order," said Andrew. "She told me she had been close to finding the proof before we had to move you. But if Isobel turned a wiċċe in your government, she's kept her identity from me."

"Why keep it from you? Do you think she suspects you?"

He shook his head. "I've been careful. She's directed me to meet with Catriona and Ginerva many times. But never anyone from our area."

"Did you know about their plans for the Gòrdans?"

"Not until it was too late," he said sadly. "I could only save Alisdair."

"So they kept their plans from you."

Her father knitted his brows. "They did."

"Still think they don't suspect you?"

"I suppose they might."

"Which means you're in as much danger as I am."

Andrew looked concerned. "I can still try to coax the name out of Isobel."

"She doesn't strike me as the type who lets anyone wheedle her." Sloane held out her glass. "One more splash, please."

He poured her a measure.

"Can your friend…the other benevolent one…can he try to get the information?" Andrew opened his mouth, then closed it, and Sloane knew by the look in his eyes. "Jesus, you were talking about me."

He nodded. "What about Alisdair. Can't he identify the wiċċe?"

She took a deep breath, exhaled, and focused. "The Order silenced him with a binding spell. He can't talk about anything related to the assault. It's reinforced with some type of ancient energy. Our best Sensor can't undo it. Could it be from a Cambion…I'm sorry, a Half-Malevolent? Like the spell you and your father placed on my mother and me?"

"It could be. If Isobel or Catriona placed a maleficium spell, I can break it."

Sloane rose to her feet as if the emotional turmoil she had just experienced hadn't affected her at all. "Then that's our next move."

Andrew stood slowly with more hesitation. "I'm not sure your coven would welcome my help as easily as you have. We may need time to prepare them."

"We don't have time to ease them into accepting you. Besides the last time you used the wait-and-see strategy, it didn't work out so well for us, did it?" She averted her eyes from her father's regretful expression and opened a communication path with Elvina.

We can't train tonight. Have Dorathea ask Mòrag to wake everyone at the Gòrdans and meet me there. I have a way to break Alisdair's curse.

Of course, dear, Elvina replied at once.

Sloane rested the Morisot sketch Jack had given her for Christmas against the wall. "Calen Gòrdan enchanted this painting. It's a portal to their coven. This is how their youngest, Elspeth, escaped."

"Thank God he had the forethought to do so. But I will have to meet you there. The woman in the painting will not allow me through."

"Ah, crap. I forgot you have to be part of the coven." She bent her head back, releasing a long sigh. "We can teleport. I know how, but it hurts."

He looked concerned. "What do you mean by 'hurts'?"

"My head. Every time I do, an explosion of bright light damn near drops me."

He thought for a minute. "You received the ability to travel in the light from your mother. But you also inherited the power to shadow-walk from me. Perhaps you are to use the darkness." He disappeared and then walked out of a shadow in the dimly lit foyer.

"I don't want to have anything to do with my dark abilities," Sloane said.

"There is nothing to fear. The lack of light is only a state. Neither good nor evil. Our choices make it so. I find the total darkness soothing. A place of deep contemplation. Void of the distractions the light of day brings. Let me teach you how to shadow-walk."

Sloane shook her head no. "I can't think about learning anything new right now. Just take us to the Gòrdan Covenstead. And we'll see how your shadow stuff affects me."

CHAPTER THIRTY-ONE

Sloane and Andrew emerged from a shadow in the Gòrdans' library to a chorus of gasps. She stood in place, astonished. Shadow-walking felt like a combination of moving through a portal and Wiċċan teleporting without the blinding light and debilitating headache.

"What's happening?" Rose asked and moved across the room in a blur, standing in front of Andrew, the air around her electrified, her voice threatening. "Why are you here?"

"Please don't fear me, Ms. Keane. I mean no one harm," he said, and his eyes lowered. He stared at the necklace around her neck and then at her eyes. "I will never allow anyone to hurt you. Love binds us to the same person."

Rose followed his gaze to the jade pendant.

"You don't need to worry about my *nighean*," Ken said, his brogue so thick Sloane could hardly recognize his words. The fierce Dhampyre instantly appeared beside his daughter, hands on his hips, the thick muscles in his arms tense. "Why are you here, Andrew?"

Alisdair took two shaky steps toward them with his fist held high, but Dorathea caught him by the arm. "How did you get inside my covenstead?"

"You are in no shape for confrontation, dear," the High Priestess said.

"I brought him here to help us," Sloane told them. "Everyone calm down, and I'll explain."

"I will not have his kind in my home," Alisdair shouted, and a burst of air pushed him backwards, dropping him into his armchair. He stared into the room, and his face reddened. Sloane knew he was having a heated conversation with Mòrag. After a tense moment, he looked at Andrew and grumbled, "Say your piece, quickly, Gildey, and be on your way."

"Andrew is on our side," Sloane said reproachfully. "He's agreed to undo the spell fortifying the curse that binds you."

Freya's eyes narrowed, and she stared at Andrew. "Now I understand. The ancient source comes not from the light." She looked meaningfully at Dorathea. "She is born of the dark."

"You're right. But Andrew didn't strengthen the curse. He's been fighting The Order, just like us, but for much longer." She looked at her father. "For at least forty years. So let him help."

"My mother isn't speaking of the curse, dear," Elvina said, her head tilted, studying Sloane.

Andrew placed his hand on Sloane's back. "It's okay, ZeeZee. You don't have to defend me. I've nothing to answer for."

"Crivvens." Ken's breath caught, and he looked back and forth between Sloane and Andrew. "We were right, lass."

"Indeed," Dorathea whispered.

"I should have known," Freya said.

"What?" Jack asked. "Will someone please tell me what's going on?"

"Zelda Gildey was Andrew's great-auntie," Elvina told him, and she looked at Andrew. "You loved her very much. I remember you spent most of your time in the apartment above her office on Old Main. And you called her ZeeZee."

Andrew smiled and removed his dark glasses. "She was like a mother to me."

"And you had her eyes," Dorathea said.

Jack looked from Sloane to Andrew, and his body shuddered. "Oh my God. Andrew's your…but that means you're—"

"A West. Just like she's always been," Rose snapped.

"And a Gildey as well," Sloane added. "But Andrew and I are nothing like Isobel and Catriona. If you believe I'm not evil, you can believe he isn't either."

They sat in an uneasy silence—at least Sloane thought it felt awkward. This wasn't how she wanted to tell her family about Andrew. Hell, he wasn't the father she imagined introducing. The entire situation unnerved her, but at the same time made complete sense. He had given her the missing pieces of her jigsaw life.

She looked at everyone. They could never understand that her childhood dreams had been real. That his man had always been in her life, loving her. They would only see him as a Half-Malevolent. Evil and untrustworthy. Would they now see her in the same light?

"I understand your silence and your skepticism." Andrew's voice brought her attention back to the room. "I promise you, I only want to protect my daughter and end The Order. Please allow me to join your fight."

"I believe you, and so does my father," Rose said.

"Aye, that I do," said Ken.

"Because you loved Jane, and she loved you deeply, I will fight with you," Freya said.

Dorathea considered him for another long moment. "You will be invaluable to our cause indeed."

Sloane looked at Jack, and he shrugged. "We need all the help we can get."

"And you can start by breaking the maleficium energy placed on Alisdair," Dorathea said.

"Right away." Andrew stood behind the High Priest's chair. "I need to place my hands on your shoulders. Are you ready?" he asked, and Alisdair sighed, his scowl deepening. When Andrew made contact, a pulse of brilliant white light energy surrounded the High Priest like an aura. Within a few minutes, the glow began to extract a faint lavender color from his body. Andrew drew it out slowly, but then his body started to shake, and his face winced.

"What's wrong?" Sloane asked her father, but he was unable to answer. She turned to Dorathea. "Can you help him?"

"He does not need *my* assistance, pet."

Sloane understood her cousin and ran to the two men, kneeling before Alisdair. She laid her hands on his knees and focused on her desire to protect them. The luminous white light intensified. Everyone else in the room shielded their eyes. Suddenly, a surge threw Andrew's hands off Alisdair's shoulders, but Sloane's remained in place. She tightened her grip until an explosive flash of deep purple and white knocked her on her back.

Andrew ran around the chair and lifted her in what seemed like one motion.

"I'm all right," she said, staring at her hands, and then at him. "Did it work?"

Her father nodded. "You forced Catriona's dark energy from Alisdair's body."

"Our energy matches our eye color?" she asked, and he nodded. "I knew it. I saw Isobel's emerald-green release from two Magicals who conspired with her, and a magical creature…"

Dorathea moved to Sloane's side and cupped her face. "I am so proud of you. You are truly the Sycyldend of our time."

When Sloane was free from her cousin's embrace, Andrew held her troubled gaze. "The darkness has always been inside you, and you've never used it maliciously. You've used it to help people." His face softened. "Your mother and I knew this day would come. And when it did, we trusted you would use the power I gave you to enhance the natural gifts from your mother. Perhaps it's time I taught you how."

Sloane stared at Andrew, unable to speak. How could she even begin to understand what had just happened, what he was saying to her? Everyone looked back and forth between them, waiting for her response.

"I know that look on your face. You are overwhelmed." Andrew paused. "We can talk about all of your powers later. Isobel expects me at the manor. I'll try to learn the name of the wicce who helped Catriona. I can stay if you want me to," he said, and Sloane shook her head no. "Okay, I'll call you tonight." He gave everyone a quick nod, and a shadow of darkness descended. He stepped into it and departed.

Alisdair awoke, gasping as if the air in the room met his lungs for the first time. Everyone turned their attention to him, and Sloane knelt by his side. "Can you tell us who did this to you?" she asked, and the High Priest opened his mouth, but he uttered no words.

He slammed his fists on his legs, and Freya glided to him, laying her hand against his cheek. "Patience, Alisdair. Now that Andrew has removed Catriona's spell, I will be able to reverse the gestillan in a few hours."

The tension in Alisdair's face diminished with Freya's calming. When his voice returned, he sounded despondent. "Our Coven is as good as ended. Calen was our last of age. We have only one more cousin we could train, but she is younger than Elspeth." He closed his eyes. "Lachlan and my Bella will bear no more children. Calen will never either. A decade will pass before our power of three can battle The Order." He opened his eyes and looked at Dorathea. "If only the obligation of one's eldest sister had continued."

"Do not blame the sisters, Alisdair," Dorathea said. "It was a selfish tradition to force the eldest daughter to join her Protector brother's coven. We must all have free will. I am the last for the West Coven. But they will survive without my line. And so will yours. We will keep you safe until you have the power of three again."

While Dorathea was talking, a soft voice with a Scottish accent and tinged with sadness broke into Sloane's thoughts.

Latha math, Sycyldend. I'm Mòrag. Thank you for respectfully seeking my permission to bring your father to our home. I am pleased to have you. And I want you to know that your father did more than release the High Priest from the evil one's dark magic. He saved Alisdair's life. I saw him cover Alisdair where he lay, under the heavy shelves, with a shadow. It saved his body from being crushed. No matter what Alisdair says or does out of anguish, you and your father will always be welcome here. I have no doubt Andrew wishes he could have done more. I can feel the pain he carries.

Sloane looked into the room, stunned and grateful for the house spirit's kindness. *Thank you for telling me this, Mòrag. And I am deeply sorry for your loss.*

The house spirit didn't respond, and Sloane turned her attention back to the group in time to see Dorathea gesture for Jack and her to stand. "In addition to Andrew Gildey, we need one more person's help to fight The Order. But to earn that assistance, I must make amends, and you will accompany me."

CHAPTER THIRTY-TWO

The West Coven appeared on the front porch of a large contemporary concrete home. It had sharp, angular lines and a two-story plate-glass front, through which you could only see opaque light.

Sloane downed the last of the elixir Elvina had made her. This would be the last time she'd teleport like Wiċċan. From now on, she'd shadow-walk, and the coven would have to accept it.

Dorathea rang the doorbell a few times, and Sloane checked out the quiet neighborhood. She couldn't be sure, but she figured they were in Tagridore. "Maybe they're not home, Denham? Some people have lives and aren't in bed by ten p.m."

The lock on the door clicked, and the door swung open. Polydora Nenge was clad in a gray *samue*, her long, salt-and-pepper hair loosely braided and hanging over her shoulder.

Jack chuckled at the timing, and Dorathea gave him a look that made him visibly swallow.

"What are you doing here?" the Ealdormann asked in a leery voice. A ball of glowing amber was revolving above her open palm.

Dorathea cliqued her tongue at her. "Put away your defenses. You know I could never hurt you. We have appeared at your door for goodness' sake. If we meant you harm, I could have easily convinced Nyx to let us inside." She breathed deeply. "We want to share new information about The Order with you and only you."

The Ealdormann read their faces in a stretch of silence that left them standing in the bitter night air. Then she closed her palm into a fist, and the ball disappeared. "Very well. Follow me."

They sat in a minimalist living room on sleek sofas and chairs with chrome frames and thin, black leather cushions. Bold abstract paintings in primary colors hung on the concrete walls, and equally impressive rugs lay on the glossy, stained concrete floor. Sloane liked the simplicity of Polydora's home, but it was the only thing she liked about the woman.

"Are you sure we're safe here?" Sloane asked Dorathea.

Polydora scoffed. "I assure you, Nyx makes my home the safest in Tagridore."

"Her house spirit," Jack whispered to Sloane.

"Yeah, got it. I'm not an idiot."

Polydora frowned at them and turned her attention to Dorathea. "Are you unsafe? Is someone following you?"

"I believe we are alone at the moment. However, I fear The Order may know we are here if they are surveilling you."

"Me? The Weardas would know if they were watching me." She smirked. "I find your sudden fear for my safety dubious. Now, if you are finished trying to gain my trust, do you have information for me, or was that a ruse to enter my home and question me again?"

Dorathea sighed. "We have spent far too long at odds, Polly. For that, I apologize. I want to make amends for turning my back on our friendship. For hurting you. I fondly remember the time we were inseparable. The holidays we spent together, visiting the four quadrants. Those will always be among the best years of my life. I was afraid to make room for you when I fell in love with Freya. To figure out how you could fit. The love you and I felt for each other was complicated for me. And I walked away from my feelings instead of dealing with them. But I would like to develop a friendship with you now, if you'll have me."

After a long pause, Polydora said, "You flatter yourself, High Priestess. Our issues have never been about a past friendship." She responded contemptuously, but Sloane noted her tawny cheeks had reddened while listening to Dorathea's apology, the type of embarrassment that surfaces when someone exposes your hidden feelings.

"I understand, and I will respect how you feel. However, I want you to know that I have missed our friendship. Furthermore, we must set our differences aside and work together now," Dorathea said, and the two powerful wiċċe locked eyes, neither speaking.

Sloane tensed. She couldn't believe age-old, hurt feelings were derailing their purpose for being there. She finally broke the silence. "Luckily, you don't need to be friends to fight The Order together."

"Bravo. Brave move," Jack whispered to her.

"For once, your cousin says something I agree with." Polydora glanced at a massive gas fireplace the length of the back wall. Blue-white flames, tipped with orange, erupted out of a bed of crystals. "Get on with why you are here, Dorathea. It's a chilly night. And I had already retired to my sleeping quarters."

"Very well. We have discovered that the Gildeys of Denwick are Half-Malevolents. Moreover, Isobel Gildey is also a Half-Malevolent and the leader of The Order in our quadrant."

"That's impossible." Polydora tilted her head at Dorathea as she considered the revelation. "If it is true, I find it interesting you've only now discovered evil at your doorstep? Am I to believe your coven has been oblivious of them for over a century?"

"Why the hell is that hard to believe?" Sloane said sharply. She bit her lip before she added what an arrogant bitch Polydora was.

"Because your ancestors banished the Malevolent who would have created them. Your great-great-grandfather and Dorathea's great-grandmother would have known of his progeny."

Sloane glared at her. "You don't know what you're talking about. Trust me. You think our Protector Covens sent the escaped

Malevolents back to the Nether less than two hundred years ago. But they didn't. The ancients exiled them over a thousand years ago. Protector Covens have been banishing their human offspring."

"How would you know such things about them?" Polydora narrowed her eyes. "Unless, as I've said all along, you have been assisting The Order."

"Oh, I know a lot more," Sloane said, and Dorathea flashed her a look that pleaded for her to remain calm, but she had barreled past that feeling. "I know that two Malevolents and nine Half-Malevolents still live in the nogical world. And like I've said every time you've asked me, I have nothing to do with The Order, and neither did my mother. I'm learning about Malevolents and their half-blood offspring because Andrew Gildey is my father."

Jack grimaced and muttered, "Oh, nice. Not sure we should have gone nuclear, lovey."

Polydora's acerbic grin faded. "You are Andrew Gildey's child?" She thrust out her hands, and orbs of spinning energy grew larger above her palms. "I was right to suspect you all along. You've been conspiring with your father for thirty years to overthrow our worlds. Did your mother find out that a Half-Malevolent seduced her? Is that why she ran away and hid? But Andrew found you and corrupted you." She was shouting, and Sloane battled against her growing rage from bursting forth. "Together you killed her and your grandparents. Now you've tricked Dorathea into accepting you into the West Coven's sacred space." She pulled her arms back, preparing to hurl the fiery energy.

"Polly, wait," Dorathea said, sternly. "Listen to us before you do something you will regret, I assure you."

"I've heard enough, Dora. I'm doing this for you."

"You haven't heard anything," Sloane yelled. "You're making assumptions, and you're wrong. My mother knew Andrew was descended from a Malevolent. She also knew an uprising was forming. She had even suspected they had infiltrated the upper levels of magical governments, even the Grand Coven. You summoned her to stand before you because of the books she had taken to research her suspicions. You questioned her and accused her, so no, she didn't trust you with what she had discovered. She also discovered Sean Gildey, his aunt Zelda, and Andrew were waging a battle against The Order, trying to keep them from becoming too powerful. But Isobel killed Andrew's father and great-aunt."

"It is all true. I give you my word," Dorathea said, and she carefully stepped toward Polydora. "Andrew Gildey is *benevolent*, as were his father and great-aunt. Andrew fears for his life, but even so, continues to defend our covens from The Order's attacks."

"Defend? The Order has struck three Protector Covens, almost ending two of you."

"My father can't do it alone. Isobel is working with another of her kind in the Northeast Quadrant, Baroness Catriona MacCain. He tried to prevent the Gòrdan assault but was only able to save Alisdair…" Sloane hesitated and glanced at Dorathea. "And Elspeth was able to escape."

"The young child is alive?" Polydora's hands closed, extinguishing the menacing light. "You've seen her?"

"Yes indeed," Dorathea said. "We cared for her until Alisdair returned home from the hospital. He sent her to us because he didn't trust his Grand Coven or ours. He had figured out that Catriona and Ginerva Byrne are in The Order."

"Ginerva?" Polydora whispered in disbelief.

"Yes, indeed. We believe Alisdair and Jane were close to identifying who in our government was collaborating with them. We also believe the person they suspected helped Catriona kill Lachlan and Bella."

"That's a preposterous accusation," the Ealdormann said as she sat down again. "The Wiċċan leaders are devoted, especially Cenric and Millicent."

"Are you sure, Polly? A powerful Sensor wiċċe attacked the Gòrdans. At the time, Ginerva was holding council with the other Grand Coven Ealdormenn. So we know it wasn't her."

Polydora tapped her long, slender finger on the arm of her chair. "Why hasn't Alisdair identified the assailants?"

"The Order cast a gestillan curse on him, one fortified with an ancient dark magic," Dorathea said, and the Ealdormann raised an eyebrow.

"But my father and I broke it. And Freya will have the curse reversed soon."

Polydora sat back and looked at Sloane. "Then we will wait until the High Priest tells us who it is."

"We didn't come here to wait," Sloane said. "We came here to get your help. We need to stop Isobel and Catriona now before they finish destroying the Gòrdan Coven and ours. I have a plan. But we'll need Andrew's help, too. I can call him to join us."

Polydora laughed dismissively. "You would bring a Half-Malevolent to Tagridore? To my home? And what do we do if he has deceived you? If Isobel and he appear? Are you prepared to send him back to the Nether?"

"Absolutely," Sloane answered.

Polydora looked at Dorathea, and her old friend nodded. "Fine. I will hear what you and he have to say."

Sloane retrieved her cell phone from her tote and tapped Andrew's number. She had no fear in bringing him to Tagridore and no doubt he was telling her the truth. The number rang a few times before he answered. "Hi, I need you to come to Tagridore. It's important. We're at Polydora Nenge's home. Do you have a way to enter the city, or should I come get you?"

"I can pass through the Tree of Life. And I know exactly where Polydora lives. I'll be right there." He ended their call.

Sloane dropped her phone in her bag. "He'll be here in a few."

Polydora's head tilted as she looked at Sloane. "How does a Demon Spawn have access to Tagridore?"

Sloane shrugged. "You'll have to ask him. And I don't appreciate you calling him…us…derogatory names. The Nogicals created them to control each other. We're supernaturals from the Nether. Most of us are evil, but some of us aren't. You can call us by our names, Malevolent and Half-Malevolent."

They stared at her, unable to speak, so they sat in silence, except for the sound of Jack's foot tapping against the floor.

A few minutes later, a knock sounded at Polydora's front door. "I've asked Nyx to see our visitor in. We need to be prepared for anything," the Ealdormann said, rising to her feet and conjuring her defensive energy.

Polydora was the only one standing when Andrew entered, and Sloane swelled with pride for her coven's support. Her father no longer wore his dark glasses, and she realized for the first time his presence, rather than his name, naturally demanded attention. He was statuesque with alluring facial features, and his movements were confident. But he didn't demand all eyes on him, and he humbly asked, "May I sit?"

"I have only now learned of your family, Mr. Gildey," Polydora said. "What you are. And who you are to Sloane West. The news makes me outraged for many reasons." She didn't invite him to take a seat, and the spheres swirling above her hands had turned from the warm color of amber to fiery red. "How did you enter Tagridore?"

Andrew glanced at Dorathea and Sloane. Then he retrieved a Tree of Life pendant from under his black sweater. "Jane gifted me a key."

Polydora scowled. "Untold numbers of Nogicals and Magicals have died at your hands. The West Coven says you have worked against The Order, and that might be the truth. But if you and Jane had told us what was happening thirty years ago, we could have saved many of those lives, if not all of them. But you chose to hide and work with only your father and great-aunt against powers far greater than you."

"I respectfully disagree," Andrew said. "We had no way of knowing who in your government was conspiring with Isobel and her cousin. It would have cost the West Coven their lives if we had told the wrong person."

"And yet they did perish," Polydora said, her voice getting angrier.

Her words seemed to strike Andrew, and he lowered his head. "Yes. I failed them."

"You were one fighting against all of them," Sloane said to her father. Then she glared at Polydora. "The Order has murdered many. But Andrew, his father, and great-aunt have stopped more atrocities than you will ever know. Deaths that the Grand Covens and their guards had no way of preventing. For years, they've kept The Order from recruiting more Magicals into their force."

The Ealdormann considered them for a long moment, and the defensive energy she wielded dissipated along with the tension in the room. "I will hear what you have to say. It seems your daughter has a plan."

"Yeah, it's simple," Sloane said after her father sat beside her. "We send Isobel and Catriona to the Abyss."

"Oh, is that all?" Jack crossed his legs, holding his unwieldy foot.

"We've trained to exile them, Jack, and now we have my father's help and hopefully, hers." She looked at Polydora, and the Ealdormann pursed her lips. "Here's my plan. First, Andrew confesses to Isobel about me. Tells her that I betrayed him tonight. That our coven ambushed him and tried to banish him. He apologizes for doubting her and says he understands why our coven has to die. Then he tells her that I'm hiding in Tagridore, and he's found a passage to the city in the crypt. He convinces her to meet him at the mausoleum, where we'll be waiting. Polydora and my father can help us capture her, and with our power of three, we can banish her."

"You make it sound so easy. We've never successfully done either of those spells on a real evil supernatural," Jack said.

"I believe with the power in this room, you will be successful," Andrew said.

"So do I," Dorathea added.

Polydora narrowed her eyes at Andrew. "Why should we believe you would banish your own mother to help us and stop The Order?"

"I hold no loyalty to Isobel Gildey. She is evil, not a mother. She chose hate long before I was born. She has never loved me, and her one desire is to possess humanity absolutely."

"Well, I believe his reason," Jack mumbled. "I would have banished my mother. And she was only half as bad as his." Sloane backhanded him on the arm. "Ouch. I'm just saying it wouldn't be out of the question."

Andrew met Sloane's eyes. "I must send her to the Abyss. Isobel murdered my father and great aunt. She took your mother, the love of my life, away from us…and your grandparents. Jane was so excited for you to meet them." He hesitated, clearing the grief from his throat. "Isobel didn't try to kill you earlier, Zee. If she had intended to, you'd be dead. She was testing me, forcing me to reveal the truth about you. And now I will. I'll return to the manor and confess where I've been tonight, and as you planned, tell her your coven attacked me." Andrew stood. "We must be ready, though. After I affirm you are my daughter, she will want us both dead."

CHAPTER THIRTY-THREE

After sunrise, Andrew shadow-walked Sloane to the Gildey mausoleum, where Dorathea, Jack, and Polydora waited for them in the crypt. He stayed above to meet Isobel, and Sloane joined her coven.

When she stepped into the tomb, she stopped abruptly. Dense air crawled over her, pricking her skin, enveloping her.

"What is it, pet?" Dorathea asked, holding Sloane's arms.

"Do you see something in your third eye?" Polydora spun Sloane around to face her. "You must tell us what you see."

"I don't see anything. The air is just really oppressive. Isn't it for you all?" Confused, Sloane searched their faces.

Jack shook his head. "Oh, no. Please tell me we aren't being cooked from the inside again."

"Of course, we are not," Dorathea told him and looked at Sloane. "Do you feel Isobel's presence?"

Sloane shook her head, and Jack looked at her, holding himself tightly. "Well maybe she can feel a family member from the Abyss."

"Sensing them is a possibility," Polydora said, shifting her gaze to Sloane. "You descend from two Malevolents. I have no way of knowing which ones. But they could force communication with you."

"Jesus Christ," Sloane mumbled, not having considered that, like her father, her lineage included not one but two evil supernaturals.

"You make me appreciate my family, more and more, lovey."

"Shut up, Jack." She scowled at him and glanced at her watch. "We need to get into position before Isobel shows."

The coven and Ealdormann hid in the crypt's stairwell. The thick stone kept the temperature just above freezing. They could have seen their breath if the shaft hadn't been pitch dark. Sloane rehearsed the spells they would soon be casting, mentally walking through each step. Just as she mouthed the power-of-three chant, a freezing sensation seized her, and she whispered, "Isobel's here."

They listened to the Gildey matriarch's high heels stride across the mausoleum's marble floor and heard her greet Andrew. Sloane held her breath, her chest tightening. It was almost time. Andrew would cajole Isobel, weaken her defenses, and when she agreed to travel with him through the portal to find Sloane, they would capture her at the top of the stairwell.

"Where is this entry to their magical city?" Isobel asked sharply.

"It's in the crypt."

"Well go on then. Let's finish off your bastard child." Her voice was full of contempt, and Andrew was silent for a moment.

"We haven't been in the vault together since Father's interment. We can at least say our respects. I didn't realize how much I missed him. Don't you?"

"Why would you ask me such a question?"

"What do you mean? I asked you if you missed your husband. My father. He's only been gone a year." Andrew sounded like he was losing control, and the tension in Sloane's chest arrested her whole body. He wasn't sticking to the script, and they hadn't prepared for alternative scenarios. "If I didn't know better, I'd think you were pleased he was banished."

"Oh, Andrew. You are such a disappointment. And quite frankly worse than your father at manipulation. You know very well I destroyed Sean. But I didn't vanquish him and his dear Aunt Zelda. I absorbed their energy. Not that they had much to give. They were weak. Just like your grandfather and his father. Inadequate because they diluted our dark energy with human blood. I was sent to strengthen your line, and with you, I did. You were to do the same." She paused. "I'd dare say, those of us who walk this plane are becoming as strong as our wicked ancestors. Except of course for you and your daughter. Such a waste. I failed to rid you of such meaningless emotions as empathy and love."

Sloane fought the urge to burst through the door, and Jack reached out, clasping her hand as if he knew what was raging inside her. She appreciated his ability to understand her, and his touch cooled the lava in her veins.

"You're right. I did know you killed my father and Zelda. And many others," Andrew told her. "But you're not as clever as you think. I know you've never intended for Sloane to join us. Your plan has always been to kill her and me. But you will only have me. I won't take you through the portal now."

"Weak and stupid. You are truly an embarrassment to our line. Why don't you invite Ms. West to join us? It must be cold and cramped in the crypt." She paused, and Sloane jerked her hand free from Jack's. "Don't look so surprised, Andrew. Of course I can feel the presence of her evil. What were the two of you planning? To bring me here and ambush me? For what? To reason with me? I'll admit your daughter could be an asset to our kind. So full of anger. But the evil she inherited would be better used by me. So be a good boy and call her to join us. We'll have a family reunion. Then I'll reunite you with your father and great auntie. Oh, and I'll take your key to Tagridore."

"No, stop," Andrew shouted, and Sloane could hear a struggle. "I'll return to the Nether before I let you kill her."

Sloane threw open the door just in time to see Isobel pin her father against the niches of their forebears with streaks of emerald-green light. Isobel turned her attention to Sloane and thrust a bolt at her.

"*Ábýge*," Sloane yelled, and the light deflected, hitting the marble wall in an explosive fireball, spreading shards of stone throughout the tomb.

Polydora and the rest of the West Coven were right behind Sloane and formed a semicircle. "Did you think Andrew and his daughter would meet with you alone?" Dorathea shouted.

Isobel's eyes grew wide, and she released her son. He dropped like dead weight, his body hitting the floor with a thud. Sloane ran to her father, turning him over. He regained consciousness and slowly got to his feet. "Don't let her walk," he managed to whisper.

Sloane looked at Isobel and saw a shadow speck forming above her head. "Take her now," she shouted to the others.

"Gefon!" The Wiċċan collectively cast the spell, and translucent energy began to cage Isobel, blocking her from the shadow, while Dorathea, Jack, and Sloane centered her in their triangular formation.

"Did you think my love would be alone?" a voice boomed, and Sloane recognized it immediately. Millicent. She had appeared at the entrance with several Weardas.

"Do not break your concentration. We must finish," Dorathea instructed. "Polydora. Andrew. Take care of our uninvited guests."

Together, Polydora and Sloane's father engaged in a fight as volatile as a fireworks stand set ablaze. Millicent screeched curses, one after another, and Polydora deflected them, sending deadly flashes around the room, scarring the walls and floor. Andrew slammed the Weardas against the ceiling, holding them with a blanket of blazing white light.

"I should have known you were the *lǣwend*, you bitch," Polydora shouted at Millicent, her voice repulsed. "What did Isobel promise you for your betrayal? Money? Power? You already have those. Did you need more?"

"You would never understand," Millicent replied, taunting Polydora. "I have always had nothing but pity for you. Suffering. Spending your life alone."

"Oh, you pathetic woman. Love? From an evil being. Did you believe she could give you such a thing?"

"Millicent, help me," Isobel yelled as the power of three surrounded her.

The emerald pendant on Millicent's necklace glowed, and Andrew snatched it from her neck with a flash of energy. The pendant flew into his hand. The Weardas he had suspended against the ceiling plunged to the floor. "No one's left to help you, Isobel," he said. "You will never steal another living soul." He crushed the gemstone in his hand and blew its dust from his palm.

The Protector Coven began to chant.

"Millicent," Isobel shrieked, but her lover was unable to help her. She was failing to save herself against the onslaught of Polydora's magic.

As a dark smoke twined up Isobel's legs, her voice became wheedling. "Andrew, son, don't do this. Stop them. They will kill you next. They can't deny their purpose. Please, my child, save us." She reached out to him, but he made no response, and she became enraged. "Do as I say, you fool. Or our kind will perish. You will be the one to end our reign."

"And I will be honored to bear that title," Andrew shouted back as the power-of-three chant grew louder.

"Geweald of þrī. Geweald of þrī. Geweald of þrī."

The darkness continued climbing up Isobel's chest, snaking around her neck, as she bent her head back, clinging to the world she had terrorized for so long, trying to remain for one more instant.

Then she was gone.

"No. Isobel," Millicent screamed. She sent a flurry of curses at the coven, and the Weardas had regained consciousness, joining in her assault.

Sloane shouted, "Ċīeġ hwílwende." Their coven's holding cells from Drusnirwd appeared in the back of the mausoleum. She held her hands up to cast a throwing spell to imprison Millicent and her bent guards when Elvina spoke to her.

Sloane, dear. We need you. Catriona and Ginerva have broken into the covenstead. Elvina's voice was frantic, a tone Sloane had never heard from her. *We are trying to hold them off, but we need the coven's help.*

Panic seized Sloane. Her first thought was of Rose, and the bottom dropped out of her stomach. *I'll be right there.* She shouted to her coven, "Catriona and Ginerva have broken into the Gòrdans. They need our help."

"Go, now," Dorathea called to her. "We will imprison the traitors and join you."

Andrew grabbed Sloane's hand and pulled her into the blackness puddling at his feet.

CHAPTER THIRTY-FOUR

Sloane and Andrew emerged from the shadows. She quickly scanned the Gòrdan covenstead for Rose. Ken and she stood eerily motionless at the bottom of the imperial staircase, facing off with Catriona. The Daywalkers' eyes glowed red, and with open hands, they outstretched their arms toward the Half-Malevolent, holding her power at a pale-lavender aura surrounding only her. The blacks of Catriona's eyes had swallowed their violet color.

Near the suite of sofas and chairs, Elvina, Freya, and Alisdair cast spells and curses at Ginerva and several of her corrupt Freiceadan. Their deflected magic scorched the soft leather upholstery, set the rugs and other cloth material ablaze, and the room filled with smoke and the stench of burning hide. Mòrag quickly made it rain wherever fire broke out. The battle consumed everyone so completely that they hadn't noticed they were soaked or that Sloane and her father had arrived.

Sloane ran into the fray, shouting at Andrew, "I'll help the Wiċċan. You help the Keanes hold Catriona until my coven gets here." Then she opened communication with Mòrag. *Where's Elspeth?*

She is hidden in my chambers with the portal to your cottage. If Alisdair perishes, I will send her through. Now go, Sycyldend. End this.

Sloane ran to Elvina's side. Dangerous magic raged around them. Powerful. Heavy. "Deflect their casts, dear. My mother will handle Ginerva's attempts to control our minds."

Sloane recognized them at once, the seven Freiceadan guards who had appeared in the Gòrdan covenstead right after The Order assailed them. The traitors sent deadly curses, one after another, but none at her. No one had taken the risk to change targets. Even so, she had the defensive spell *ábýge* at the ready. Unlike a shootout on the streets with bullets flying and bodies hiding behind walls and car doors, the Magicals faced each other in a standoff, sending and deflecting shots to the detriment of the surrounding room. The entire scene was tantamount to a deadly game of concentration. The first one to blink, died.

Before a barrage of curses was hurled at her, Sloane needed to summon the coven's prison cells from Drusnirwd. She was unsure if she could cast the spell without closing her eyes and speaking the incantation aloud. But if she didn't cast it silently, Ginerva and the Freiceadan would know what was happening and flee.

She pictured the dark side of the library and opened her third eye, drawing from her intense desire to protect her friends and Rose. *Čieġ hwílwende.* She cast the spell and glanced behind her. The four cells appeared, one of them already holding a few of the bent Weardas from the crypt. Which meant Dorathea, Jack, and Polydora were still fighting Millicent and the remaining guards. She turned back to the battle before her.

A Freiceadan subtly shifted his position, and Sloane predicted that his next move would be launching a curse at her, and that wasn't happening. She raised her hands and shouted, "*Ascylfan.*" A burst of brilliant white blew through the fireworks of curses, flipping the guard into the air. Her spell held him suspended, upside down, until she flung his body into a cell.

"West, look out!" Rose shouted, and Sloane turned back in time to deflect another guard's death curse.

Catriona shrieked in anger at the Freiceadan, "She's mine. Her power will now be my power. Touch her and you die." She also seized Rose's momentary lapse in focus like a hyena snatches a lion's kill and struck the Dhampyre with a raw, wild flare of dark energy, sending Rose crashing into the wall behind her.

"Rose," Ken and Sloane cried out together. He ran to her crumpled body.

"Let him tend to her," Freya shouted. "You'll not help her if we all perish."

Sloane threw another guard into the cells and called to Ken, "Is she okay?"

Ken collapsed against the wall and pulled his daughter into his wide chest, holding her. "She's alive. But unconscious."

Relief washed over Sloane, and she glanced at her father, left alone with Catriona. Without the Daywalkers' help, he struggled against her energy. Her black eyes glowed dark purple, and she snarled at him. "How dare you raise your hand against me? We share blood. The same purpose. You and your child cannot turn your backs on your nature."

"Leave us and help your father," Freya said, and Sloane looked at her, conflicted. Elvina and Freya were formidable, but even with Alisdair, they were outnumbered and at a disadvantage. And suddenly, a crack boomed through the covenstead, and everyone ducked. The sound left Sloane's ears ringing, and she turned to the source. Catriona's violet energy had nearly consumed all her father's power and was inches from devouring him.

"The only use you and your daughter have for us is the evil in your souls," Catriona yelled at him. "Surrender. You have no more strength to fight me."

"Help him, dear one. We will be okay," Freya said, her voice insistent, and Sloane ran to Andrew.

She stood behind her father and laid her hands on his shoulders. As soon as she touched him, the same arcane sources of power from the Nether they shared caused their eyes to blaze frost-white. But from her mother, Sloane inherited the strength to protect, forged in the ancient sources of creation—air, fire, water, and earth. Combined, the energy she sent through her father straightened his collapsing body. Its hungry crawl subsumed Catriona's dark energy like an ice flow shoved onto a lake shore. The Half-Malevolent struggled against it, her arms buckling.

"Ginerva, tell Isobel we need her," she hissed.

"It's too late for that, unless she knows how to contact the Nether. Isobel Gildey is no more," Andrew said, and Catriona screamed in fury. What little strength she had flared from her entire body, but it disappeared in their blazing white light.

"Don't worry, though. You'll be seeing her soon." Sloane grew enraged thinking about Isobel and Catriona's victims: her mother, her grandparents, as well as Sean and Zelda, and the Magicals and unsuspecting Nogicals who found themselves drawn into their plans. She wanted nothing more than to banish the evil woman right there and now. Her desire opened her third eye, bringing her behind the hazy veil where she stood at the mouth of a chasm and stared into the never-endingness, the pain and suffering, in its damning infinity.

Outside the veil, Sloane heard Catriona's faint cries and felt her lashing out furiously, but she remained focused on the bottomless pit. The sound of the evil supernatural's thrashing and chaos slowly diminished, and just inside the darkness, clouds of dark-green flies glowed at the entry of the deep gorge, forming an image. Was it their Malevolent ancestor? Had Catriona somehow summoned it to help her? Sloane swallowed her fear and concentrated on banishing the Baroness as the flies amassed, one swarm upon another until the figure was complete, and they melted into a human form. Bracing, she inhaled deeply. She had pulled Catriona into this bottomless chasm in her third eye. Was it the Abyss?

"Elvina!" Freya's terrified voice yanked Sloane from the veil.

She opened her eyes to find black smoke claiming the last visible part of Catriona's head and Freya kneeling over Elvina's body, frantically touching her daughter for signs of life. "Elvina," Sloane cried. The fight instinct barreled through her as she ran toward them.

Ginerva cackled, "Such are the hazards of having a child. The parasites leave you weak and vulnerable." She raised both hands, and Freya threw her body over Elvina's, shielding her from Ginerva's death curse.

"No!" Sloane shouted, as the curse struck Freya's back. She extended her hands, releasing a shock wave of energy that cracked the air before it slammed Ginerva and the remaining Freiceadans into the wall behind them. She ran to Freya and Elvina, oblivious that Millicent and the last Weardas had appeared in the prison cells. Unaware that Dorathea, Jack, and Polydora had also arrived at the covenstead.

"Move away, pet." Her cousin's voice was full of terror. She pushed Sloane out of her way. "My love? I'm here now." She rolled Freya onto her back, laid her hands on her chest, and closed her eyes. Her lips moved furiously, forming silent words. Jack and Polydora knelt and held their hands above Freya's head. With each passing second, the lines in Dorathea's brow deepened, and her hands trembled.

After several more minutes of silent healing spells, Dorathea fell forward, burying her face in Freya's cloak, clenching handfuls of material.

Sloane's stomach clenched. "What's happening?"

Jack stood and shook his head. His eyes welled with tears as he watched his cousin lie across Freya's body.

"No, Jack. Do something," Sloane said, her voice shaky, but he only stood there, stunned. She looked at Polydora. "You can't stop." The Ealdormann didn't respond, unable to avert her gaze from Dorathea.

With only one desire, Sloane looked for Ginerva and the Freiceadan, but the wicce and her guards were gone, no longer on the floor unconscious where she had put them.

Alisdair met her eyes. "I've sent them to your prison cells. They will be held accountable…for all this misery."

She glanced at the hwílwende. The Order members were there, and the desire to kill them began to consume her until Andrew put his arm around her shoulder and held her steady. "They will be punished," he whispered, "but not by you."

Sloane turned her attention to Freya again, her eyes stinging with tears. Elvina lay unconscious beside her mother's body, and Dorathea remained lying on her, still and silent.

The High Priestess shed no tears and made no protestations to change reality. There was only a shift in the air around her that wasn't Mòrag's doing. When Dorathea finally got to her feet, the dense air began to spin around her with an intensity that made her dark-sapphire cloak spread like wings.

Sloane could feel the wrath in the wind's eddy, and Andrew stood between her cousin and her. She looked for Rose. Ken was shielding her with his body from the growing tempest. And Alisdair and Jack were hiding behind two large, wooden columns. No one dared to move as Dorathea faced the prisoners in the hwílwende and lifted her arms.

"You don't want to do this, Dorathea," Andrew said, stepping toward her. "Revenge won't bring Freya back. And it will cost you dearly."

"Listen to him, please," Sloane said. "You're too powerful to act out of anger. Our justice will be seeing them perish inside our prisons while we destroy the rest of The Order."

"My vengeance today will be an eye for an eye," Dorathea roared, and the Wiċċan in the cells began to plead for their lives. Every word they uttered caused the orbs of fiery energy in her palms to enlarge. Without warning, she thrust her hands forward, and the curse she had been intensifying struck the prison cells. Pieces of stone and human flesh sprayed across the covenstead.

When the fallout settled and silence ensued, Sloane opened her eyes and raised her head. She understood her cousin's actions and prepared herself for the destruction, the chaos in the universe, they had created. Mostly, she braced for Dorathea's despair, which would surely follow her cousin's outburst of anger.

But Dorathea was gone.

CHAPTER THIRTY-FIVE

Sloane sipped a black coffee at the breakfast table. The only light in the room emanated from Elvina's arcana. The cards shimmered, desiring to be touched, but she had no interest in divinatory arts. For her, reconciling the past and living in the present was hard enough. Why would she add knowing the future? She thought about when she'd last seen Elvina at the table with her cards. Had they revealed to her all that was going to happen in the Gildey mausoleum and the Gòrdan covenstead just a week ago? Did she know her mother would die? If she did, why the hell didn't Elvina tell her? She could have saved Freya.

"Ruminating only prolongs the grief process." Andrew had appeared and sat beside her. "You must let the what-ifs go. Or they will consume you."

She frowned at him. "Are you reading my thoughts?"

"I wouldn't need to. Not much else takes place at a kitchen table before the sun rises." He covered her hand with his. "Freya was a kind friend to your mother and me."

Sloane fought back the sting of tears, summoned him a cup, and pushed a silver carafe of coffee toward him.

"Have you heard from Dorathea?" he asked.

"Not a word. I guess you haven't found her?"

"I will not stop looking. I know she's important to you. She is family, and we denied you the gift of her presence in your life for too long."

"Yeah. I need her back." Sloane stared into the dark garden. "What did you mean when you told her revenge would cost her?"

He sighed as he filled his mug. "It's the same for any creature with empathy. When the anger and grief wane, she will struggle to reconcile that she killed. The weight of her new reality could drive her away from those she loves and shut her down emotionally."

Jesus. What the hell would she do if Dorathea never returned? She needed her cousin, especially now. She feared her own anger—rage from her dark side—would only grow, and Dorathea would know how to help her. She sipped her coffee, her gaze returning to the garden. She couldn't see the imposter crows as Elvina could. But she could feel them if they were lurking about the trees and patio. They had been gone since Dorathea cast them off, and she figured it was a sign that The Order had gone underground.

"Is there anything else distressing you?" Andrew asked after a long pause.

The answer was yes. But she wasn't sure she was ready to talk about it. She breathed deeply, gathering the courage to speak, and asked, "When I accessed my evil to send Catriona to the Abyss..." Her voice faltered. "Did I send her there...or did I kill her and absorb her energy?"

"Oh, ZeeZee," he replied affectionately. "You've been holding that fear inside all week? Of course you sent her to the Abyss. One must choose to consume another's life force." He frowned even though relief spread across his daughter's face. "The choice to help people and the world, not hurt them, will always be up to you."

Sloane nodded, her mind still racing with questions. "And do we...our kind...experience other people's deaths differently?"

"We do, but I have no idea why. We don't all have the same relationship with the loss of life, though. For me, the smells and energy of natural deaths are much different than inflicted deaths. One is serene and the other chaotic."

"Yeah, same here," she said. "That's all I can bear to learn about myself right now." She topped off her coffee. "Wait, I do have one more question. Why the hell did you name me after Dorathea's dog?"

He chuckled, and a look of nostalgia spread across his face. "Your mother loved that Lab. I think she wanted a name for you that reminded her of home and unconditional love."

She listened to him, the grief still etching his voice. The sorrow filled her with longing to see her mother again, to hear her, and smell her. But the desire was only a part of the chaos death left behind, always in her subconscious, ready to bleed into her thoughts. She forced a smile. "That's touching."

"I thought so too," he replied. "How are the patients today?"

"They're doing better. Polydora and a Mender wiċċe from Tagridore worked on Rose's back, but it'll take time to heal. Something to do with Catriona's dark energy. They also couldn't counter the emotional damage she caused Rose."

"No, they wouldn't be able to. That will be up to Rose." He poured himself more coffee. "For many years, I have watched you have less-than-satisfying love relationships in your life. I'm happy you have found your soulmate. She is absolutely wonderful. When did you bond?"

"I don't know. She said she wants to talk. I guess she'll explain it to me."

"*She'll* explain?" He frowned. "You wouldn't know. Because we hid it from you. For our kind, when you find your soulmate, you are drawn to a stone or gem, a gift forged in the earth's power, and you ask them to receive it."

She had bound them? Sloane stared into her coffee mug, thinking about Rose's and Ken's reaction to her gift, their overprotectiveness of her, and Rose wanting to talk. Had they figured out who she was from the necklace? Then a horrifying thought came to her, and she asked him, "Did Rose have a choice?"

"Of course she did. Rose is a powerful Dhampyre with senses beyond our abilities. She would have felt the bond your gift created as soon as it touched her skin." His piercing eyes softened. "Forcing her would be something done out of evil. Your gift was out of love. And Rose accepted it. Our bond is not an inescapable union. You both have free will to leave on your own terms."

She stared into the back garden, turning over all the information. She thought about the diamond necklace her mother always wore. After The Order killed Jane in broad daylight on the streets of New York City, the police returned the necklace along with her other effects. She looked at her father. "Did you give my mother the diamond pendant?"

"On the day she left Denwick," he said, and they sat silently for several minutes. "What about Elvina? Is she sleeping yet?"

"Since yesterday. She finally exhausted herself crying. I figure sleeping is the only state of being she can bear right now. She hasn't eaten since…" Her words faded.

"Victims of evil suffer the most unimaginable pain. Keep trying to feed her. Cook her favorites for when she wakes up. Hopefully, she'll choose to eat…to live. It is a struggle, as you well know."

Sloane peered at the garden again, clearing the lump from her throat. The night sky had turned deep indigo as the blue hour approached. She had no desire to talk about the hurt settling in every facet of her consciousness, and she appreciated that Andrew didn't expect her to share or push her to let him into her life at a pace with which she wasn't comfortable. She looked at him and changed the subject. "How did you explain Isobel's death to the RCMP?"

"Your Grand Coven relocated her body to the manor house and made her death appear as a heart attack. I called the police the next morning and told them I found her in her bed." He hesitated. "I also told the papers there'd be no funeral. We'll intern her ashes in the crypt in a private ceremony."

"For real? Do the Gildeys have ashes at the mausoleum?"

"Yes. Every urn. Our spirits return to the Nether…or they're consumed…but our bodies from our human ancestry remain."

"Makes sense. Apparently, when Magicals like me get too old, or we die in the nogical world, we either return to the magical plane, or our guards take our bodies back. Cremations. Funerals. They're all a show for the Nogicals. There are no West ashes in the crypt."

"I had no idea the urns were empty until your mother told me." He smiled, but his expression slowly turned serious. "I want to be done with everything connected to Isobel, if you agree."

"What do you mean?"

"I want to give the mausoleum back to the Church. They can create something for the people of Old Denwick. Perhaps restore it to a simple chapel. When our ancestors turned the original one into a vault and built the new church, they wanted to parade their wealth and make others envious. All the Gildey ashes can go back to the crypt. And I'd like to return the Gildey manor, land, and business to the Coast Shalish people. I have no interest in continuing a legacy of theft and genocide."

"Whoa. I'm speechless. And so fucking on board with all of it."

"Are you sure? It is your inheritance I'm giving away."

"Inheritance? It's a curse of ill-gotten means, and we're both better off without it."

"I'm so glad you agree."

Sloane glanced out the bay window. The sky above the soaring fir trees had a hint of vermilion. Morning was breaking, and her father's plans filled her with hope. "Do you want to stay for breakfast?"

"I must decline. Our lawyer is meeting me at the manor to draft the reparation paperwork this morning."

"Where are you going to live when you give the castle away?"

He smiled. "When I am ready to leave the nogical world, Polydora has offered me a home in Tagridore. And I couldn't be happier." He laid his hand over his chest in a gesture of gratitude, but Sloane knew it was more. She saw his fingers caress Jane's gift, the Tree of Life necklace he'd worn for over thirty years, the key to Jane's life.

She stood. "That's great. It'll be nice to spend time with you there."

"And me with you." He got to his feet and hugged her. "I'll be back this evening to check on everyone." He released her, stepped into a shadow, and vanished.

Soft morning light filled the kitchen. Sloane placed two mugs of coffee and two vials on a tray. She had spent the last week caring for Rose and Elvina, and she would continue doing so for as long as they needed. She carried the tray to Elvina's bedroom first.

Her former familiar was asleep. She set the coffee mug on the side table and sat beside her bed. She didn't want to wake Elvina. She just wanted her friend to know she was there, would always be there. She held her roommate's hand, and after a few minutes, Elvina opened her eyes briefly and gently squeezed Sloane's hand.

"Good morning, beautiful," Sloane said softly. "I brought you some coffee. Your favorite, Kona."

Elvina pulled her hand away. "I'm not thirsty." Her voice was barely above a whisper.

"Yeah, I understand. I felt the same way after my mother died. Thankfully you and Gary stayed with me, supported me, until I managed to get food and drink down. You helped me even though you were grieving the loss of your best friend, too."

Tears spilled from Elvina's closed eyes. "Leave it. I'll drink it. I promise."

"And the medicine. You only have three more doses. And you might want to sit up in a few minutes. I'm making your favorite breakfast, cinnamon pancakes."

Elvina opened her eyes and asked, "Is Dorathea home?"

"Not yet." She stood and kissed Elvina's forehead. "I'll be back in a few minutes."

Outside Elvina's door, she leaned against the wall and released the tears she'd been holding back. Her heart ached over Freya's murder, but it shattered knowing her best friend's life was forever changed. After a few minutes, she wiped her face dry and gained her composure before entering Rose's room.

"Aw, here's the best sight to start the day," Rose said, and Sloane put the tray on a dresser.

"Seeing you awake and not grimacing in pain is the best thing I've seen all year."

"I am feeling better. Maybe we could move me into your room today." Rose grinned.

Sloane put the coffee mug and vial on the bedside table and sat in a chair she had placed next to Rose. "You're so flirty, and I haven't even given you this pain elixir yet." She held Rose's hand. "It kills me to say this, but we need to wait a bit longer before we move you."

"My worrier," Rose said playfully, and then her voice turned serious. "How are you feeling this morning? Did Dorathea come home last night?"

"No. But my father and Polydora are looking for her." She kissed Rose's hand. "I'm feeling better. Your and Elvina's recovery is helping. My father answering all my questions helps too."

"I'm so happy you found him. You deserved to know where you come from, and bonus, he's a good man."

Sloane rested her forehead against Rose's. "Thank you for not turning your back on me when you learned who I am."

"I could never do that. I love you. And not because you chose me and this beautiful jade binds us." Rose held the pendant in her hand. "I've loved you since we lay under that Garry oak, and you let me eat our entire picnic without so much as one comment."

Sloane recalled the spring day they went to Rose's favorite spot in the foothills of Mount Sutton, and she chuckled. "I think that's when I fell for you, too." She leaned over the bed and kissed her gently.

Rose groaned when Sloane sat back and ended their moment of intimacy. "Did Polydora say how long it'll take to be good enough to return to my normal life, where you aren't kissing me like I'm a wilting peony?" She lifted herself higher against the headboard. "And I'm sure Oscar is ready to walk out of the pub by now."

"I would say, more like an orchid. But I'll try for peony later." Sloane grinned. "The Spotted Owl is fine. Oscar still has his distillery closed to the public. And Jack's helping him in the pub."

"Oh, tell me the latest. How's he doing?" Rose laughed, sat forward like she was readying herself for juicy gossip, and clutched at her lower back. "Ouch, damn it. I hate being laid up in bed."

"I'm sorry. We'll do some stretches today." Sloane adjusted her pillow and eased Rose back. "The next time you spend too much time in bed, I'll make sure you stay limber."

"Who's being flirty now? Promises, promises."

"I keep my promises." Sloane smiled and handed Rose the small glass vial. "Take your elixir."

"Yes, ma'am."

"Thank you." Sloane got to her feet. "I'm making breakfast. It'll be ready in a few minutes. Text me if you need anything."

She returned to the kitchen and gathered the ingredients for cinnamon pancakes. Her cottage felt so different now. Everything was different. She knew death was more than a lack for the living. It forever changed them, and she had to fight the desire to fix it for Elvina and Rose, to make them happy, to take away Elvina's grief and Rose's pain. But she knew that wouldn't help them. They only needed her to be present. Her support. Her love. She also couldn't distract herself from her own grief. This time, she would allow it space. Let it come over her in waves until it receded.

"Are you cooking, lovey?" Jack asked, appearing beside the kitchen island, and Sloane startled, throwing a mixing spoon at him.

"Jesus, Jack. You promised not to appear out of nowhere anymore."

"Ooh, sorry. I forgot." He climbed onto a barstool. "I smell Elvina's favorite pancakes. Do you think she'll eat this morning?"

"That's the plan." She picked up the spoon off the floor and rinsed it in the sink. "What are you doing here? Aren't you working at the pub this morning?"

"I was until that young thing showed up. You know. His rude, albeit dishy, assistant from the distillery.

"Michael's waiting tables again?"

Jack pulled a face. "Yes. He's back. Apparently, Oscar doesn't want to abuse my generosity."

Sloane chuckled. "He fired you."

"Without even a kiss goodbye." He grinned and summoned the coffee carafe from the breakfast table, poured a mug, and heated it with the twirl of his finger. "I was in Tagridore last night.

Freya's funeral will be on Saturday. You don't think our cousin would dare miss it, do you? Polydora hasn't called for any charges against her. She's free to come home." He looked at Sloane as if she would tell him it was all going to be okay.

"I don't know, Jack." She mixed her wet ingredients with the dry in a glass bowl. She wasn't sure how much longer she could let her father and Polydora look for Dorathea alone. A strong desire to protect the High Priestess had come over her in the last few days.

"My heart breaks for our cousin. Just when she and Freya told the Grand Coven to be damned and decided to live together..." He blinked his eyes rapidly, but not fast enough to contain his tears. "I loved my white-picket-fence life with Nathan. And I'd happily do it all over again if I could."

"This must be so hard for you, Jack."

"Not any harder than it is for you." He sipped his coffee and watched her sprinkle water on the griddle. It sizzled. "Polydora has made all the arrangements for Freya's funeral. But she left her headstone for Elvina to design when she is able. She and Cenric are meeting with the Interspecies Council at a summit to discuss how to expose The Order members who have gone underground. When they return, there's the business of choosing the next Grand Coven member."

Sloane nodded and spooned batter onto the griddle. The cakes started to bubble, and she met Jack's eyes. "What happens if Denham doesn't return?"

He looked shocked by her question. "She will. Right? My God, she has to. I'd sooner live with a troll than either of our remaining cousins." He shivered. "And you and I aren't adding to the family tree."

"Probably not, but you never know." Sloane flipped the cakes whose bubbles had burst. Her cell phone rang. It was in her tote, which hung on a chair at the breakfast table. She summoned it successfully and answered the call while Jack gave her a golf clap.

"Hi, Sharma. What's up?"

"Hi, yourself. How's everyone this morning?"

"Doing well so far. Had any luck tracing Dorathea?"

"Nothing. No credit card use. No bank withdrawals. She must be using magic."

"All right. Thanks. That info helps."

"Listen, I have a couple of things I'd like to run by you. Well, one of them is just information. It's too late to matter. But you were right. The Rolls-Royce outside your home was registered to the Gildey corporation."

"No worries. Thanks for running the plates," Sloane said as she stacked the first batch of pancakes on two plates with ramekins of whipped butter and warmed maple syrup.

"No need to thank me. I hoped we could discuss the other issues in private. I understand you're busy. But can you make time to meet?"

"Do you like cinnamon pancakes? I'm starting a second batch in a minute. Why don't you come over now?"

"I'd love some. I'll be there in ten."

Sloane ended their call and turned down the heat on the griddle. "Would you put three plates on the table for us and bring the coffee to Elvina and Rose for refills?" she asked Jack. Then she left to deliver the first batch of hotcakes to her patients.

They returned to the kitchen several minutes later, relieved they had coaxed Elvina to eat. Sloane was spooning a second batch onto a sizzling hot griddle when the doorbell rang. "Jack, let Sharma in, will you?"

"It smells delicious in here," Veena said when she climbed onto a barstool at the island.

"Wait until you taste them." Sloane flipped each cake carefully. "Jack, get Sharma a coffee and put the butter and syrup on the table."

"How about a please? I feel like I'm at the Spotted Owl again." He looked at Veena and grinned. "I suppose the Nogical way of setting a table isn't necessary any longer." He snapped his fingers, and the items vanished from the kitchen counter and reappeared on the table.

"Absolutely not. I'm never getting tired of seeing magic," Veena said.

Sloane piled the steaming pancakes onto a platter. "Can we talk in front of Jack? It's as good as being alone."

"Ouch, that almost hurt, lovey," Jack said.

Veena laughed. Then her expression became serious, and she looked at Sloane. "Yeah, Jack's good. Over the past month, three people have gone missing on the Island. Their last known whereabouts were in the Lake Shawnigan area. I've been to each scene. We have nothing. No witnesses. No evidence. It's like they vanished."

Sloane and Jack exchanged a glance.

"I saw that," Veena said. "I thought this could be a paranormal case. That's why I'm here. If it is, will you help me with it?"

"Of course I will," Sloane said.

"You should change your office sign to Sloane West, Wiccan Detective and RCMP consultant," Jack said, pouring maple syrup over a giant stack.

"Please don't do that," Veena said uneasily. "Inspector Nichol would…I actually don't know what he'd do. Lose it for sure."

Sloane glared at Jack. "I'm not about to advertise my magic or my relationship with Sharma." She looked at Veena again. "I'll take a look at their last known locations and help you until Rose and Elvina are back on their feet. Then Jack can help you. I have something to do out of town."

"Wait. Where are you going?" Jack asked, swallowing hard.

Sloane glanced around the room. She didn't know when during the last year this house had become her home, but it had. She wasn't exactly sure when the people in her home had become her family, but they were. And one of them was missing.

She looked at Jack and cocked her head. "I need to find Denham and bring her home."

Bella Books
Happy Endings Live Here
P.O. Box 10543
Tallahassee, FL 32302
Phone: (800) 729-4992
BellaBooks.com

More Titles from Bella Books

Jones – Gerri Hill
978-1-64247-598-2 | 260 pages | Mystery
One weekend getaway, six friends, and a deadly secret that will wash away everything they thought they knew.

Merry Weihnachten – E. J. Noyes
978-1-64247-610-1 | 292 pages | Romance
Christmas traditions aren't the only things getting mixed up when these two hearts collide beneath the mistletoe.

Sweet Home Alabarden Park – TJ O'Shea
978-1-64247-570-8 | 362 pages | Romance
She came to restore a royal estate—she never expected to rebuild her heart.

Dr. Margaret Morgan – Christy Hadfield
978-1-64247-628-6 | 286 pages | Romance
Facing the professor on campus everyone hates is terrifying—but falling for her might be even worse.

Overtime – Tracey Richardson
978-1-64247-630-9 | 278 pages | Romance
A charming romance about second chances, found family, and scoring the goal that matters most.

The Big Guilt – Renée J. Lukas
978-1-64247-657-6 | 206 pages | Romance
What if the one who got away became the one you can't have?